Avalon

Lee Souleles

Music is my muse.
For your listening pleasure, go to leesouleles.com and download my Avalon
playlist. It's free through Spotify.

CHAPTER ONE

Morning Sun

Sol de la Mañana
   Sunday, August 16, 1981

They drove into town before sunrise. He parked the stolen van along the empty avenue and waited while the boss went to make a pass by the bitch's house. Looking into the rear-view mirror, he opened his mouth and stuck out his chalky, swollen tongue. He took a sip of his Big Gulp and sneered. Thank heaven for 7-Eleven.

The girl, her face hidden behind sunglasses and a full head of black hair, turned the new red Corvette onto the freeway, just like the boss said she did most Sunday mornings. It didn't matter that she was early. He considered himself a professional, and part of being a professional was expecting the unexpected.

He put the black van into gear and followed, driving east at an unnoticeable distance. Hot and twitchy, he dialed up the air and was hit with a burst of choking heat. He rolled down the window. Outside, the sun stoked the furnace. It didn't matter; the van would be dumped in Kagel Canyon before noon.

Crank, not coke, made his body sing, and he'd been howling for over twenty-four hours. Lately he'd been scoring his speed from the Angels in the desert, but he liked mixing business with his own pleasures and often thought about trading favors with somebody who was a front-line source.

The 118 was almost empty. Agitated and itching to climb the bumper of the Corvette, he blew past a junky, white station wagon trudging in the slow lane.

Once there, he backed off some to admire the sleek profile of the blood red car. It didn't matter to him the Corvette had been bought with bills stolen by the bitch's old man. Too bad the boss said to leave the car on the side of the road. The ride would be a kick-ass bonus, even if he could only drive it for a few hours. And judging by the closed windows, the air worked too.

But right now, the girl was at his fingertips and the next best thing to her husband. It would send the message: You can't hide forever.

The freeway dipped into the Valley. Beyond, the slash of De Soto Avenue divided neighborhoods. He smiled, tripping on the morning sun that already began to sear the concrete. As stage director of this production, the bright backlighting was an extra, unexpected touch.

He watched her change lanes. She must think he wanted to pass.

Instead, he pulled alongside and spent more time staring at her than the road. This was the girl he'd waited for, a tiny beaner with long, curly hair.

Confusion marked her pretty face as she motioned for him to go ahead.

The little bitch wasn't going to direct this scene. He took his foot off the gas and slid behind the Corvette. The tremors melted away, his brain became a guided machine, focused, as he moved to center stage.

Speeding up, she returned to the fast lane. He followed. The van rattled but kept pace, going strong. When he was almost on her, he glanced down at the speedometer. They were doing ninety-five. Pulling the van into the median, he pushed the Corvette to the right until she had no choice but to change lanes.

Their business was off the freeway. So he came alongside the girl again, and was pissed the windows of the van were tinted. He wanted her to see him, watching her.

She wouldn't turn to look at him, but he read her lips—*Idiot!*

The girl was the idiot. She should have been more careful about who she fucked, he thought, watching the Corvette shoot forward.

In seconds, he was close behind, coaxing the van to its limits. His pulse throbbed through his body, coursing up his legs. When they were head-to-head, he edged her over another lane.

Frozen lines marked her terrified face, and he smiled.

Soon.

Her sunglasses were fixed on the road, as her hands gripped the steering wheel.

A flash of paranoia urged him to look for cops, and he checked the rear-view mirror. Except for the junker slogging far behind, the freeway was empty. But the boss said he might come by to watch.

When the off ramp was less than a mile away, he bulldozed the pedal. The van shuddered forward, crowding the Corvette over another lane.

Trapped, the girl slowed.

Easing into position, he nudged the bumper just to freak her out.

She bolted up in the seat.

He smiled, knowing the ramp was coming up fast. Needing to move her soon, he tapped the ass of the Corvette again.

Stepping on the gas, the bitch suddenly veered onto the exit, doing the work for him.

He gunned the engine and rode up the edge of the asphalt. Swerving around, he gave her no choice but to slam on the brakes. They didn't make it to the top of the off ramp. The Corvette screamed to a halt, sprawled across the road, inches from his van.

❦

Sofie scrambled to find the lock and ducked against the steering wheel, her heart pumping wildly inside her chest. Her mind struggled to understand and blanked. Nothing made sense.

No sound came from outside. Inside, the Eagles resonated through the stereo system. Cool air blew against her skin. The Corvette rumbled beneath her as if it wasn't ready to end the chase. She was unable to stop shaking, and afraid her foot would slip off the brake at any moment, sending the car lurching into the van. Fumbling for the gear shift, she put it in park, and turned off the engine.

Gulping air, she worked to even her breathing. Finally, she was able to peek up over the windshield, praying her stalker had tired of his game and left.

The van was still there. Her heart sank.

Two loud thwacks hit the driver's window and Sofie jumped, bumping against the headliner of the Corvette.

Sofie's brain clicked into gear. *Apologize.* For what, she didn't know—but she was willing to say anything to get out of this horrific situation.

Her tormentor bent down and stared into the Corvette. Even teeth gleamed within his delighted grin. Surprisingly, he didn't seem angry. Nevertheless, something monstrous raged behind his volatile eyes.

A faded Iron Maiden T-shirt swallowed his tall, thin frame. Age hadn't weathered his face, but a full, scruffy beard made him appear older than he probably was. Sunglasses rested on the crest of his long, blond hair. Greasy

3

strands escaped a haphazard ponytail, tied with a strip of leather.

The pupils of his glassy, gray eyes were constricted into tiny, black beads. She decided he was quite possibly high, likely insane, maybe both.

"Roll down your window," he mouthed.

Hoping to somehow reason with this crazy freak, she gathered the shreds of her composure and managed half a smile. She hit the wrong button, and both windows descended. An explosion of heated air shot through the Corvette's interior.

"I'm sorry…" Sofie offered, bewildered.

He placed his right arm on top of the door, leaning in. With his other hand, he lifted a gun and casually centered it on the middle of her face.

Icy panic sluiced through her. She'd never seen a real gun before. A nervous laugh flew past her lips. This square-edged, ebony-colored nightmare resembled a toy.

Instinct told her better, and she cringed. The edges of her life began to close in as she faced the reality of her imminent death.

Raising her arms in defense, she begged, "Oh God… I'm sorry, I don't… Please. I didn't…"

"Put your arms down."

Sofie had no choice. She thought about her dad—she wouldn't ever see him again. And Tía Sofía—how would she survive another loss? And her mom—*I'm not ready*. Sobs rushed up her throat as Sofie struggled to maintain control. She didn't want to die. Her life was just beginning to click and slip into place.

He pushed the gun closer. Without breaking his smile, he used the barrel to knock her sunglasses to the floorboard.

"You have green eyes."

Confused and terrified, she could only stare.

"I didn't expect that," he said, placing the cool edge of the barrel against her lip. He moved it up, scraping the skin along her nose, settling on her forehead.

She heard a click and squeezed her eyes shut. The tears spilled anyway, rivers running down her cheeks while she prayed. Waiting.

A deep, foreign voice called through the passenger window. "She's not the one."

Sofie blinked. The rest of her body was frozen, transfixed by hard, cold steel.

Not the one?

Time seemed to stop. Finally, as if a long-awaited pleasure had been snatched from his grasp, his smile twisted into a cruel smirk. The lucidity in his milky gray eyes melted into disdain. "Today's your lucky day, bitch."

Slowly, he ran the gun back down her nose, hesitating at her mouth. He slid it across her lips in a grotesque kiss before stuffing it into the waistband of his dirty jeans.

Turning, he walked toward the van.

Sofie groaned a searing sob of relief.

Who was the other man?

Whoever he was, he was gone.

The van made a left and crossed the freeway.

Seconds, maybe minutes, passed. She couldn't tell. Fear and heat bonded together, fusing her cerulean, silk blouse to her skin. Unable to swallow the giant wad of sandpaper that seemed to swell in her throat, Sofie shuddered.

Opening the visor, she looked into the mirror. Having been up all night, she expected the black smudges of mascara beneath her eyes and the mass of messy hair. But the long, crimson scratch left by the gun was a repulsive surprise.

She touched her nose.

It had really happened.

Burying her head against the steering wheel, she sobbed.

❧

"Señorita?"

Sofie yelped.

A middle-aged man with wide, frightened eyes put his hand on the door and leaned into the open window.

"Are you okay?" he asked in Spanish.

The man had the gentle face of her Uncle Ricardo. His fingernails were traced with dirt. He might work in landscaping or, like Tío, just be an avid gardener. She pushed her hair away and wiped at sweat and tears with trembling hands. Glancing between him and the rear-view mirror, she saw the white station wagon she'd passed earlier parked along the edge of the off ramp.

"Oh, thank God." She clutched his arm. "Can you help me?"

"We saw the whole thing," he explained. Turning, he pointed to a woman and a cluster of kids in the car. "Me and my family. He cut you off, pushed you up here."

"Did you get the license number of the van?" The moment Sofie asked, she realized it was pointless. Earlier she'd looked for it herself. The plates were missing. "Did you see the other car? Did you get that license plate?"

"What other car? I saw only a black van. We had to come around again to find you."

Still shaking, more sobs gathered and began to rise in her throat.

The man put his hand on her shoulder. "He scratched your face. He hurt you."

She felt the sting along her nose for the first time. "I'm okay. Thank God you saw the van. They're looking for somebody. I'd hate for him to find the girl he was looking for. Will you come with me to the police station to help me make a report? It's right down the street."

"Yes," he said, glancing toward the station wagon. "But first I need to get my family to Mass."

"I was going to Mass this morning too. With my tía." Sofie suspected he might be illegal. If so, he probably wouldn't show up, afraid he'd be deported. She put her hand on his arm. "You remind me so much of my Tío Ricardo," she said, in a voice she hardly recognized. "You're my angel. I know you were here for a reason. Please, *please*. Meet me at the police station."

❧

The man, Sofie's guardian angel, did eventually show up at the Devonshire Division to corroborate her story. Afterwards, Detective Anderson escorted her to his cubicle for a more detailed statement.

He pointed to a chair on the opposite side of his desk, and gave her a box of Kleenex, just in case. Sofie grabbed a few sheets, crumpling them into her palm.

Behind his shoulder, a photo of Detective Anderson and his young family sat on a shelf. A broken air conditioner hummed in the background, pumping hot, stale air into the room.

Earlier, she'd found the restroom and splashed water onto her face. She'd wiped herself down with stiff, brown paper towels that did little but smear around mascara, sweat, and the salt of dried tears. It had been impossible to do anything with her perpetually rebellious hair.

Gripping the arms of the chair, she fought the impulse to leave the cubicle, get back into the Corvette and head to Ben's place. While Sofie wanted to stay and make the report; she was also desperate to get to Ben's, so she could shower and wash away the morning. She needed him now, more than ever.

Also, Tía Sofia was expecting to meet for Mass. Sofie had to call her aunt soon with an excuse. Tía would suspect something awful had happened. Sofie was a terrible liar. This was going to freak her aunt and uncle out. But she needed to talk to Ceci before she told Tía any details.

Detective Anderson's dark mustache, sprinkled with a few gray hairs, moved when he spoke, "Full name?"

"Sofia Morgan Mendoza Davis."

He smiled and raised his eyebrows. "That's a mouthful."

"Call me Sofie. My mom was born in Mexico. Mendoza is her family name. My dad is American. And my middle name, well, it's a long story."

"Address?"

"I live on campus at UCLA." She gave him the address of her dorm.

"So you're a student? Do you work or have a part-time job?"

"I'm a full-time student. I'm not working at the moment."

He looked up from the form. Apparently, he wanted an explanation.

"My family helps me with school. My dad pays for my tuition and board. My cousin in Mexico helps out with the rest of my living expenses."

Detective Anderson watched her carefully. "Are you involved in any illegal activities?"

She realized how disheveled she looked. Nevertheless, she answered his question with one of her own. "Why would you ask that?"

He didn't speak.

Defensively, she crossed her arms. "Of course not."

The firm reply seemed to satisfy him. Returning to the form, he moved to the particulars of what had happened on the freeway.

Unlike when she'd first arrived at the station, she was able to relay the story without tears. But still, she struggled, taking deep breaths and forcing herself to speak carefully. Instead of spewing the story out in a frantic jumble like she had before, she let him lead the questions, answering each one as clearly as possible. He put the incident in chronological order, culminating with the assault along the off ramp. "The assault" had been the detective's apt words.

Flashing on the scene, Sofie's chest constricted and she gasped. The gunman's lucid gray eyes. His smile. The greasy blond hair. She was in the Corvette again, her body quaking with terror as he pushed the gun into her face. Shivering, she remembered the sensual way he played with the gun, hideously stroking it against her skin. Then, when the other, foreign man spoke, she'd opened her eyes to see the gunman's features shift. A warring internal debate, deciding whether or not to shoot anyway. The shroud that lowered over his features and lifted, instantly moving his glassy, lethal eyes to disdain.

"It's hard to forget the look on the gunman's face… He wasn't angry at first, he was… happy, excited. Like it turned him on."

Detective Anderson scribbled on the paper. "We've talked about the guy with the gun. What about the other man. Describe him."

"I can't. I only heard his voice."

"Was there anything distinctive about it? Take your time. Think."

It would be awful, *horrible*, if the gunman and his partner found whomever they were looking for. Sofie took a deep breath. "It was foreign. I'm not sure from where. He wasn't a Mexican, I know that. But he might be from somewhere in South America, or possibly even Spain. I couldn't tell."

"You're driving a high-performance sports car. Why didn't you try to outrun him?"

"I did at first, but we were going really fast and I was afraid of losing control. It isn't my car."

The detective lifted his pen from the paper, his intense blue eyes suddenly curious. "Whose car is it?"

"It's Cecilia's. She's my cousin."

"Why were you driving it?"

The interview had just become a minefield.

"There was a BBQ and pool party at Ceci's… my cousin Cecilia's house. I got there early yesterday evening… Her boyfriend, Eric, bought a new house in Simi…"

Actually, the party had started on Friday night, soon after Ceci called and invited Sofie to a Saturday house warming with a "few friends." When Sofie arrived, she was lucky to snag a spot in the driveway. People had clogged the property and the party was already twenty-four hours old.

"We played cards."

This was only partly true. A few people, including Sofie, and Ceci's little brother, Rich, sat around the dining room table playing gin rummy and drinking wine. After midnight, they switched to soda. Other guests mingled between the back yard and living room, regularly stopping by Ceci and Eric's bedroom to snort lines from an ample supply of coke. By dawn, the cocaine was gone and most of Ceci's friends—the ones who hadn't left to find their dealer—were crashed around the house.

"We stayed up all night. I told Ceci's mom, my Aunt Sofia, we'd meet and I'd go with her to Mass this morning. That's where I was headed."

"Why didn't you drive your own car?" he asked.

"It was blocked in the driveway. I looked for Ceci but she'd gone to bed." Sofie prattled on nervously, "Her boyfriend Eric was still out by the pool. He told me to take her car."

Detective Anderson had seen the Corvette and seemed to find the story hardly believable.

"I know what you're thinking," she said. "It's a brand new car. What if I wrecked it?"

It wasn't necessary for the detective to know Eric had told her to leave her car keys in the kitchen and take the Corvette, because when Ceci crashed she could sleep for days.

Sofie didn't like lying, especially to a cop, but she didn't want to get her cousin, or Eric, in trouble, so she opted for the middle road.

Feeling guilty, Sofie recalled one of her mom's favorite sayings: *La verdad a medias es mentira verdadera, mija—Half of a truth is also a lie.*

Ignoring the words, she recovered and smiled at the detective. "Ceci and I are really close. Like sisters. Thanks so much for taking the report and not thinking I'm crazy. It's such a bizarre story, I didn't know if you'd believe me. I'm so glad Mr. Garcia showed up."

Detective Anderson cleared his throat, took out another sheet of paper, and clicked his pen. "I'd like to ask a few, more personal, questions."

Oh, great, she thought.

"Sure. If it will help."

The detective scribbled a few notes and said, "Miss Davis—Sofie—I can tell you're a nice girl. But do you have any enemies?"

"No."

"Do you have a boyfriend?"

"Yes. His name is Ben Stevens. He's a student at CSUN. He rents a house here in the Valley with some friends."

"He wasn't with you last night?"

"It was his poker night with the boys."

"And you were out all night?" Detective Anderson tapped his pen on the desk. "Does he push you around? Is he a jealous or violent kind of guy?"

"You think he came looking for me and we had a fight? That I made this story up?"

9

The detective watched her carefully.

"Are you kidding? That's ridiculous!"

"It happens all the time."

"I don't give him any reason to be jealous." She met the detective's eyes. "I love him. I've been seeing him for over a year."

"Okay." Detective Anderson sighed. "Were there any suspicious guests that might have followed you from the party?"

Suspicious guests? No. Coked out guests who were suspicious and paranoid? Hell yes. It was the ugly part of the druggie deal. But that wasn't the detective's question. She couldn't imagine anybody finding a reason to follow her from the party and hunt her down.

"No," she answered. "Don't you remember? I told you about the other man who came up to the car. He said I wasn't the one."

"Yes." Detective Anderson put his elbows on the desk and laced his fingers. "Tell me about your cousin, Cecilia. Does she have enemies?"

Ceci had nothing but friends. Sofie thought about the house full of people last night and wondered if she had too many of them.

"No. I can't think of one. And she's not only my cousin, Ceci's my best friend, so I'd know."

He studied her closely. "Are you *sure* you're not involved in drugs?"

"No. I don't do drugs." Sofie was grateful she could honestly answer the question.

She glanced up to the ceiling panels, toward heaven, *Now Mom, here I answered the detective with the truth, the whole truth and nothing but the truth.*

Sofie didn't think it was necessary to add that the last, *and first*, time she smoked pot was in high school. It left her paranoid for days. Ceci had talked her into trying coke too. But as a struggling student, Sofie found it too expensive to become a habit. Lately, as she watched what went on all around her, the exorbitant price seemed like a blessing.

At the end of the interview, Detective Anderson walked her to the front of the station. "This sounds like a planned hit over a bad drug deal to me. If you and your cousin aren't involved in drugs, it's probably a case of mistaken identity."

Sofie protested, "I swear I'm not," and wondered if he believed her.

"You're one lucky girl." He opened the glass door.

Yes, Sofie guessed she should feel lucky, but she was too numb to feel much of anything.

"Here's my phone number in case you remember something else," he said, handing her his card. "And if anything comes up, we'll be contacting you."

❦

Sofie found a gas station on Devonshire and used the pay phone to call Tía. Hating to lie, but doing it anyway, Sofie told her she was having car trouble and wouldn't make it to Mass. Her aunt wanted to send Tío to help. Sofie said they were already changing the battery.

Tía bought it, which only made Sofie feel worse. When she asked about her daughter, Sofie used their original excuse—Ceci had started her period last night and had really, *really*, bad cramps.

Now, terrified to drive and particularly nervous of the freeway, Sofie used surface streets to get to Ben's place across the Valley. He met her at the door, and she fell into his arms, sobbing.

When she finally opened her eyes, she noticed one of his roommates peering at her over the front page of the *Los Angeles Times*, worried and curious.

Ben hustled her into his bedroom and they sat on the bed. Sofie told him the story of her morning, adding the details in disjointed bits.

Later in the bathroom, when she reached for the handle to turn on the shower, she heard low, serious voices on the other side of the wall. She opened the door a couple of inches and listened for a few moments while Ben shared the story with his roommates in the kitchen.

Exhausted by the rush of adrenaline and lack of sleep, she stepped in the tub and stood under the shower, letting cool water rain over her body. One thought kept cycling through her mind, as she massaged shampoo through the mass of her curls: *If I'm not the one, who was the gunman after?*

It might have been Ceci.

She picked up the conditioner and wondered why she hadn't considered this sooner. It was possible her party-girl cousin did have enemies. And Jaime, Ceci's ex, was a loser. She'd been attached to him in a crazy, addicted way Sofie couldn't quite understand…

Paralyzed by fear, she sunk to her knees in the tub.

The bullet may have been meant for my cousin.

This had to have something to do with Jaime. Everybody who loved Ceci was glad he was out of her life. *Who knows where the two-timing creep is?*

And who cares? Eric, a lawyer and also a genuinely nice guy, was definitely a positive distraction.

But…

Sofie turned off the water and grabbed a towel. She went into Ben's bedroom and used the phone on his nightstand to call her cousin.

Ceci didn't answer.

The girl who did was a new favorite in Ceci's crowd of friends. Sofie wasn't impressed. With a groggy, surly attitude, the girl clearly wasn't happy to be awake. Sofie didn't care.

She asked to speak to her cousin. But the girl flatly refused, stubbornly insisting Ceci was fine, asleep in her room. Trembling all over again and near hysteria, the most Sofie could convince the girl to do was crack Ceci and Eric's bedroom door to make sure she was really there.

Sofie heard the girl set the phone down and disappear.

Just about the time Sofie decided the girl had blown her off, and left the phone off the hook, going back to bed—wherever that was—the girl returned, assuring Sofie that she'd seen Ceci and everything was fine. Before Sofie let her hang up, the girl reluctantly agreed to write Ceci an urgent, but cryptic, message.

Sofie collapsed on the bed. Ben came in and sat with her while she tried to nap and waited for her cousin's call.

It was past noon when she woke up to find Ben at the dresser, stuffing his wallet into his shorts.

She leaned on her elbow. "Where are you going?"

Startled, Ben turned and adjusted his blue and white cap. "I told you yesterday. There's a Dodger game this afternoon. I'm going with the guys."

"You're still going? I was hoping you'd stay with me."

Ben, busted trying to make a quiet exit from the room, lowered his head sheepishly. Regrouping, he said, "It's a big game. The Braves." He picked up his keys. "You know my mom's from Atlanta. It's a tough choice, who do I root for?"

"I don't want to be alone and I can't leave. I'm waiting for Ceci to call."

"Like Eric said, that could take days. And you're not alone. Someone will be around the house today..." Ben glanced toward his closed bedroom door. "I think."

"It's not the same." Sofie felt the back of her throat constrict, the panic resurfacing. "What happened this morning was *really* scary."

"Yeah, I get that. But they weren't looking for *you*."

"I don't want to be alone!"

"Then go back to your dorm. There's plenty of people there."

Disgusted, she said, "Thanks a lot, Ben."

"Valenzuela's pitching," he whined.

Ben came to the bed and kissed her on the forehead. "You'll be fine. If you're not here when I get back, I'll call you."

Feeling tears materialize in the corners of her eyes, Sofie couldn't speak.

He opened the bedroom door and hesitated. "It might be late. There's this little bar near Elysian Park where the players hang out at after the game, we're thinking about stopping by there on our way home."

It was hard to believe he could be so insensitive.

Later, alone in her dorm room, Sofie locked the door, and secured a chair against the knob. Turning both lamps up high, she left several messages for Ceci. It was dark outside when Ceci finally called. Sofie sat on the bed and relayed the details of her horrific morning.

"I swear I don't owe *anybody* money," Ceci said. "I don't have enemies either."

"Okay then. I think this might have something to do with Jaime."

"No. *Jeez*, Sofie!"

It wasn't often she was the recipient of Ceci's irritated, big sister tone.

"Thanks for the support. Like everyone else in the family, I know you didn't like him. But that's impossible. We're not even together anymore." Ceci sighed. "I'm getting a divorce."

"I know. It's just…"

"I'm with Eric! I don't even know where Jaime is…"

Sofie detected the subtle collapse in Ceci's voice, "The last I heard, he'd moved to Pacoima with the trailer trash he's been sleeping with. That's where my lawyer sent the papers. But who knows what puta he's with now."

"What about the coke you've—"

Ceci laughed. "Give me a break. I swear you're paranoid. Nobody's looking for me. Or you. And come on, this is LA, I'm not the only girl who drives around town in a new red Corvette."

CHAPTER TWO

Las Brisas

The Breezes
Thursday, July 5, 1984

Alex held the telephone handset to his ear, propped a pillow against the pink tiles of the headboard, and waited to check in with his boss.

There was a delay. In El Paso, Karen was busy sweeping the line.

After the all-clear, he said, "I made it."

"I'll put you through to Dean."

Alex picked at a piece of pink lint on the striped bedspread. "Thanks."

"Good luck." Before Karen passed the call along to their boss, she added, "Have a good vacation."

Smiling, Alex said, "I will."

"Wakefield, how was your flight?" Dean asked.

"Too long."

"Aren't they all?" He chuckled. "Settled?"

"As settled as I'm going to get." Alex kicked his duffle bag away from the bed. The duffle skidded across the floor and hit the wall with a thump.

"Are they in town?"

"I'm having dinner with them tonight."

"Excellent," Dean replied.

Adrenaline sent a familiar rush of anticipation that built in Alex's chest and vibrated throughout his body. He silently reined himself in with one word—*patience.*

The plush accommodations consisted of a pink and white hotel overlooking the stunningly blue Acapulco Bay. Surrounded by lush tropicals and hot pink bougainvilleas, his casita had its own tiny bean of a

14

swimming pool, sprinkled with fresh hibiscus blossoms every morning. It was a leap up from the Travelodge in San Ysidro, the housing where he'd spent months shadowing the Mendoza operation. Alex decided that when you haven't had a vacation in years and pay for it yourself, you get to choose something with a comfortable bed and flowers in the pool.

"How's your room?"

"Thanks for the recommendation," Alex groaned. "It's nice if you like Pepto Bismol, I'm surrounded by pink. What really sucks is the striped Jeep. I should have gone to the Princess and rented my own car. "

"Suck it up. I'm doing you a favor by saving you some cash. The Jeep came with the room."

"I don't look very competent or successful. I'm driving around in a clown car."

"You'll be fine," Dean said.

"The Jeep is no different than the pink car my nieces put their dolls in—except this one's on steroids."

"You need to be there. The house is nearby and you're right in town."

Alex heard the smile behind Dean's voice and sighed. "I know."

He imagined Dean looking out the window with his cowboy boots propped up on the desk. Alex glanced out the sliding glass doors, past the rippling palms, and down to the postcard bay.

"And you've got a great view."

Alex wondered if Dean had read his mind. "Yeah. But it still doesn't make the Jeep worthwhile. What about the guys? Are they still around?"

"You know how it goes. We've got a light staff next week. A group of them are going fishing. This time of year it seems like everyone's on vacation."

Yeah, Alex thought, July *is* a great month for vacations.

Dean couched his words carefully. It was unlikely, but neither of them wanted to leave any thorny tails that might eventually whip back and sting them all in the ass.

His words told Alex everything was in place. Nick would have agreed too. The agency had infiltrated the Mendoza family once again, and this time there'd be no Washington mistakes—and no Mexican officials around to tip anyone off.

While Dean detailed everybody's bogus plans, Alex drew fireworks across a pad of paper he found on the nightstand, turning the patriotic doodles into ominous explosions.

In an Albuquerque bar on the night of Nick's funeral, rage and frustration had bonded a group of his fellow agents. Gluing them together for the past three years was Nick's memory, the dedication to find justice for his wife and sons, and a commitment to do the hard work it took to take the Mendoza family down.

There'd been no choice. Nick had moved from being a person who lived, loved, and gave his life for the job, to nothing more than a file continuously waved in Mexico's direction and shuffled between Washington bureaucracies.

The DEA didn't have jurisdiction outside of the United States. So they'd stitched a team together who were operating out of the country, under the radar, and on their own time. Everyone's career was on the line. If the execution wasn't flawless, they might be left hanging by the short hairs and in a shitload of trouble. The last thing they wanted was an international incident. Even worse, they could lose another man.

Massaging his forehead, Alex tried to rub away the beginnings of a headache. "I'll keep in touch."

"You do that. I'll be around through next Wednesday, then the wife and I are going to Galveston for a long weekend. Go have a drink at the bar. Or have room service deliver one to you. The sunsets over the bay are beautiful."

Alex said goodbye and dialed again, California this time.

"Happy birthday, Mom."

"I'm glad you called."

Though she tried to sound cheerful, he noted her disappointment.

"I was hoping you'd be around. Everybody's here," she said.

Familiar voices could be heard in the background as his mother's trailed away, "Carl! It's Alex on the phone!"

"Where are you, honey?" his mom asked when she returned, "I hear static on the line."

"Working."

"Are you out of the country?"

"Mom. You know I can't—"

"Just tell me this: are you far away?"

"It's not too bad. I'm on the same continent. South."

"We miss you. Teresa and the girls ask about you all the time. I haven't seen you in months."

A short sigh escaped before he caught himself. "I miss everybody too."

"You sound tired. How've you been feeling?"

Shit. Here we go. "I'm fine."

"You don't sound like it." If his mom were half Indian, like Nick, her name could've been Eagle Ears.

"I hate it when you do that," Alex said. "Don't worry. Seriously, I'm fine."

"It's my job to worry. Wait until you're a parent. You'll understand."

He ignored his mom's subtle, well maneuvered remark.

Even when the need for his family grew into a deep ache he couldn't shake, he dreaded going home. It didn't take more than a day or two before his mom started in with questions about his long-term plans.

It always began with her standard interrogation: When did he plan to give up his chaotic, nomadic life to come home and help his father on the ranch?

Lately, Alex asked himself the same question.

Then she'd move to her second favorite topic, asking when, if ever, he planned to find a nice girl, fall in love, settle down, and get married. She'd invariably mention his sister, who was younger and already two children ahead. He'd remind his mom that he'd been there once and it hadn't worked out.

Kim was years ago. Thank God she didn't get pregnant. They'd been too young.

After more than a decade with the agency, it seemed unlikely a woman could ever understand his past. He'd never be able to explain it anyway.

In the last year, these uncomfortable clashes with his mom had dwindled into indirect remarks that he answered with stubborn silence.

"When are you coming home?" she asked.

Alex hadn't lived with his parents since he left for college. Technically, home was an often empty duplex he rented in Santa Monica that spawned a litter of dust balls and a coven of mice that moved back in every time he left. When he wasn't working, it served as a spartan crash pad, a place to sleep, watch TV, and listen to his extensive music collection—sometimes all at once. He hadn't been there in months, except to stop by overnight to repack his suitcase on his way in and out of Los Angeles.

"Relax, Mom, I'll be back soon. It's a quick project. I promise I'll drive up and spend some time with you when I get back to LA."

"We're barbecuing tri-tip. Your dad finally mastered the garlic bread. You grill it twice."

"I'll remember that." His stomach began to grumble. Besides hunger, a thick soup of homesickness, guilt and regret, melted into a lead ball that expanded and burned in his gut. "Next year, I'll be there for your birthday."

"Promise me, Alex."

He felt personally responsible for the distress he heard in her voice that sometimes bordered on hysteria. She'd flip if she ever found out about Nick.

Alex laughed, trying to soothe her concern over a pathetic telephone connection. "I promise. And Mom, will you do something for me? Don't worry. I'm doing great. We're just finishing up some last details, and then I'm coming home. I'll be there in a week or two and we'll celebrate. Tell Dad to have the barbecue ready."

"Okay. Where is your dad? He must be on the patio, I'll go get him."

"No, don't. I'll be in LA soon. I'll talk to him when I get into town."

"Well…" She hesitated as if she wanted to say more but realized it was pointless. "I love you, honey. Be careful."

"I'm always careful," Alex lied. "You too, Mom."

Suddenly, he wished he'd said how much he loved them all. But it was too late, the connection was dead.

Alex took Dean's advice and called room service. When it came, he took his beer out to the balcony.

Dean was right. The sunset was spectacular.

Earlier in the afternoon, when the stewardess opened the cabin door, Alex had been greeted with a blast of steamy humidity. A breeze drifted through the palms now. He watched a cruise ship ferry human sardines to shore… Why tourists paid to be herded onto a shrunken Vegas, deluding themselves into thinking the experience was romantic and fun he'd never understand.

A pretty blonde came out onto the balcony from the casita next door. Built exactly to his personal specifications—tall and thin. A wisp of hair blew across her face as she looked past the flat rooftops down to the sparkling bay. She brushed it away with her hand and gathered her hair into her fist at the nape of her neck. Arching her back, she thrust out a pair of magnificent breasts.

She caught Alex's approval, smiled and nodded. He lifted the beer in appreciation, but that was all. This was a working vacation.

Alex wasn't interested in distractions.

Together, they silently watched the sun begin to slip into the horizon. A few minutes later, a man called from her casita and she returned to the room.

The Love Boat gradually lit up after the sun set, spilling its reflection onto the water. He'd been to Acapulco before and was certain he'd see the ship's passengers around town this evening. They'd never be mistaken for the locals. Scattered throughout the waterfront, the women roamed the stalls in resort wear, rifling through jewelry and colorful, embroidered clothing. The guys called it "junk," too arrogant to care whether the locals understood, more interested in finding the next bar.

It was one of the things that disgusted Alex about Mexico. There was a giant divide between those who did well—tourists and the local, wealthy elite—and the rest, who struggled. Alex wasn't surprised so many illegals poured into the United States.

Most people who lived in this hellhole couldn't afford a cruise. They were more likely on board, slave-laboring to feed their families.

The Mendozas were one of the exceptions.

Alex took a sip of his beer. There'd be no Mexico or Love Boat when he got around to taking a real vacation. And lately, he'd been thinking about making it a permanent one.

He'd landed over a decade ago in San Francisco and hadn't stopped moving. In those days, he was ready for more, too angry and wired by war to go back to the monotony of a rancher's life along the rolling hills of California's central coast. Alex chose instead to accept a job doing what the United States Army had perfected in him—using his skills working for the DEA. No ties, no commitments, just the rush of getting the job done.

Alex smiled. They were so close tonight. Soon, he'd be having dinner with the Mendoza brothers. Alex and the team were determined to destroy the family. In addition, the Mendoza's first attempt at trafficking Colombian cocaine into the U.S. would never make it past the border.

As point man on the team, Alex was the closest to the family. Getting here hadn't been easy. He shut his eyes and imagined the sinew of Ramón Mendoza's neck beneath his hands. Alex squeezed, intertwining his fingers, and dug his nails into his skin. He didn't stop until he felt the pain.

The moon poked up over the mountains while he finished his beer. He said a silent prayer, asking for justice from a God he wasn't sure if he believed in anymore.

Alex felt nothing.

He couldn't blame God if God had given up on him long ago. The silence could be God reminding him justice was Alex's responsibility. He gladly accepted the assignment.

Lights began to flicker until the crescent of the city grew into a luminous oasis. Alex stretched, feeling the hum of excess energy buzz through his body. He grabbed the empty beer bottle from the table and crossed the threshold into his dark hotel room. Turning on the lamp, he unzipped his duffle bag. The humidity was already a bitch; he'd need another shower before dinner.

CHAPTER THREE

Estrella de la Noche

Evening Star
Thursday, July 5, 1984

"You must be Alex. Please follow me," the host said, and led him through the foyer of the elegant beachside restaurant towards a private area in the back.

Alex stopped at the doorway and took in the scene. By sight and resume, he knew almost everyone there. One by one he counted several of the Mendoza brothers and the family's entourage off his mental checklist. A year of surveillance and communication had finally paid off. He took a deep breath. This was the best part of the operation: When it all came together and, one way or another, the deal was going down. Tonight was special. Dinner with the Mendozas gave Alex a high he hadn't felt since he and Nick were deep into making their last big drug bust.

The opportunity to pull the underpinnings of the Mendoza family up by the roots would make all the painstaking investigation and crappy legwork worthwhile. Ramón and his brothers were unaware their dossiers were already full. The physical introductions were the last pieces to fall into place.

Mexican pottery decorated the walls. Palms choked the corners of the room, and comfortable chairs lined its perimeter. One waiter poured water while others placed baskets of bread and butter on a long table. Men stood in small clusters along a wide window that framed the bay. Outside, city lights made an arc against a pupil of black water.

The oldest Mendoza brother and leader of the family, Ramón, stood in close conversation with a man who wore a short black tuxedo and appeared to be the maître d´. Ramón laughed and glanced in Alex's direction.

"Good evening, Alex. We have been waiting," Ramón said, crossing the room.

"Am I late?" Alex checked his watch.

"No, no. You are right on time. How was your flight?"

"Fine. It's good to finally meet in person." Alex held out his hand.

Ramón grasped it with smooth, uncallused fingers. Closing in on forty, he wore a custom, well-tailored suit. His dark hair and coffee colored—almost black—eyes accented an aristocratic nose above a generous, trimmed mustache.

There was no doubt Señor Mendoza would be considered a gentleman. Alex itched to reach up and clutch his nemesis by the throat. He checked the urge, conquering the impulse. *Relax*, he told himself, we worked hard for this and it's finally here.

Alex gave Ramón Mendoza his most expressive smile. *Oscars are wasted on actors*.

"Come," said Ramón, leading him towards the window. "I would like you to meet my brothers. You remember Esteban."

A large man in several ways, Esteban stood a good head taller than anybody else in the room.

"Of course, I remember."

Esteban beamed. "Amigo!" He took Alex's hand and shook it vigorously. "How's it going?"

"Bueno, good. Chicago?" he asked.

"Warmer than the last time you were there. You'll have to visit again this fall…" Alex turned to Ramón. "You should come too. It's the best time of year in the city."

Ramón nodded but didn't commit, then summoned a man who stood near the edge of the window, apart from the others.

Alex recognized Felipe, the family's lapsed priest, from his photograph. His right arm hung useless at his side. Years ago, Nick reported the disfigurement hadn't been an accident; Felipe had been born that way.

Ramón draped his arm around his slight, unassuming brother, made the introduction, and added, "Felipe is the true secret of our family's success."

Felipe glanced at Alex, then stared at his feet. Ramón laughed and the rest of the men joined in.

"It's a pleasure to meet you, keeper of the family secrets." Alex chuckled, toying with one of his prey.

Felipe mumbled as Ramón's eyes settled on Alex, hesitating for a nearly imperceptible second.

Alex shot both men his best Americano grin, deciding there should be a hall of fame for liars.

"Marco is back at the ranch. You will meet him tomorrow. And Gabriel…" Ramón looked around and frowned. "It appears he will be joining us later."

"This is Alex Wilson from Chicago," Ramón announced to the rest of the men in the room.

Everybody gathered, and Alex shook hands until his own began to cramp. All of the Mendoza brothers knew how to speak English, and so did several others. But the bootlickers, whom he didn't recognize, could only smile.

"Come,"let us get you a drink. Esteban tells me you have quite an operation in Chicago."

"My staff and I have worked hard to build the business. It's great to see it beginning to pay off. The warehouse—"

Ramón reached out and put his hand on his shoulder. Alex had to steel himself not to flinch.

"That is good to hear. But we will have plenty of time to talk business at the rancho," Ramón said.

It was a relief when Ramón finally removed his hand. As much as Alex had prepared himself, the proximity of the man still clenched his gut. Surrounded by the enemy, he wondered if he'd made the right decision to keep his gun hidden at the hotel.

"I am anxious to show you la finca, or our rancho, the facilities, and to hear more about yours. However tonight is a night for celebration. You will enjoy seeing a bit of our beautiful city."

A tuxedoed waiter delivered Alex's whiskey. Alex nodded and took a long sip. How civilized of Ramón Mendoza, providing amusement before he moved to business. The brothers knew their manners of course. They came from what Alex's grandmother called "good breeding"—in this case, Mexico's upper class.

They ate steaks with béarnaise sauce—an American meal in the heart of Mexico—and Alex sailed through the evening in his manufactured role. Seemingly careful to avoid subjects that could lead to anything potentially unpleasant, Ramón and Esteban asked questions about Chicago and the

United States. Esteban relayed his impressions of a visit north earlier in the year—pizza, the Sears Tower—when Alex played host and tour guide. Further down the table, Felipe and the rest of the men ate in silence.

By dessert, Ramón joined the men at the other end of the table who'd started an animated conversation Alex couldn't understand.

He had lobbied hard to become the point man for this operation. Dean, and a few others on the team, thought the logical choice should have been Greg Herrera, who spoke Spanish fluently, and not Alex, who only knew the basics. But Alex insisted—Nick had been *his* partner. Alex convinced the team the language barrier would be a better fit in the end, because the Mendoza family would never expect the DEA to send someone into Mexico so hindered by the language. It wouldn't matter anyway. Alex had argued; by the time he flew into Acapulco, everything would already be in place and ready to go.

And it was.

Esteban leaned to one side as a waiter set a dish of flan in front of him. "They are discussing fútbol, or what you call soccer. Do you follow soccer?"

"No. We have basketball, baseball and our own version of football. Soccer hasn't caught on with Americans."

"Interesting. There are fútbol fans all over the world. I'm sure someday it will immigrate to the United States." Esteban took a bite of the custard. "I enjoyed my visit to Chicago, I hope to visit again soon. Maybe someday I can convince Ramón to open an office there." He glanced down the table. "The facilities you have in the city are impressive. Like you, we have a large warehouse. We need more offices. Ramón has an office here in Acapulco, but at the rancho we are already quite overcrowded. How many people do you have on your payroll now?"

"Still just three of us. Myself, Joel, who works in the warehouse—you met him, plus the girl I have to answer phones and get coffee. You remember her?"

Esteban nodded appreciatively. "Muy bonita—very pretty and nice too."

Alex would have to tell Karen she has—well, had—an admirer.

"I have drivers lined up I use from job to job," Alex said. "Used them for years. I've always been very selective about who I hire. When a delivery comes in, I make it a point to work in the warehouse myself alongside my employees. My old partner, who moved to New York, loans me some of his staff when big shipments arrive."

Alex noticed Esteban's forehead wrinkle with concern.

"There's nothing to worry about. They're all people I've worked with before," Alex explained. "We don't outsource anything. Never have. We're easily handling the workload and shouldn't have any problems incorporating your business."

Esteban seemed satisfied.

Returning to his chair, Ramón said, "Enough business. Did Esteban tell you about the rancho? *Now that is impressive.*"

Of course, Ramón had been listening.

"Our ancestors have lived on this land for generations," he continued. "The Mendozas have answered to many masters. First Spain, then the leaders of our own Mexican Independence and generations of political upheaval. Our ancestors even helped send the great Benito Juarez to lead our country. Through it all, the one constant has been our connection to the land. We have nurtured it and the land has sustained us. The secret to our success is not only Felipe..." He looked down the table toward his brother.

Felipe snapped to attention while the rest of the men chuckled.

Ramón laughed too, then added seriously, "It is our ability to grow and change with the times."

Esteban and Ramón both nodded, sharing a glance.

"We are ready to begin a new era of Mendoza family excellence." Ramón lifted his glass and everyone at the table found theirs.

Riveted by his host's arrogance, Alex wanted to applaud. *Slowly.* Instead he raised his whiskey too.

"You can be confident when you do business with us, that we are not... what do you call it in the United States? Country pumpkins? We also move freely, here in the city. Our connections are very powerful. We are in control now." Ramón brought the glass to his lips and swallowed.

Pumpkin or bumpkin, your days are numbered, you arrogant fuck. Alex followed his host's lead and lifted his drink. *I'll toast to that.*

Later, while Ramón gave instructions to the waiter, Alex sat back in his chair and silently congratulated himself with another sip of Jack Daniels. He had worked tirelessly to win over the Mendoza brothers, and tonight he'd taken the first steps to insert himself as a new addition to their entourage.

The only curiosities so far had been Felipe—the keeper of the family secrets—who seemed innocuous, but was buried so deep in the organization the team knew very little about him, and Ramón's youngest brother, Gabriel, who had yet to make an appearance.

Most of the men at the table lounged in their chairs, talking in small groups. Every man's life would be unalterably changed within a week. Many of them would be dead.

Alex had no regrets.

Well, there might be one. Esteban. Alex met him in Chicago last winter, when Ramón, smart enough to be skittish about traveling to the U.S., sent Esteban to check out and photograph the team's operation.

In Esteban, Alex had discovered a friendly, intelligent man. Around his own age, Esteban was full of questions about the United States. He'd been instantly captivated by Chicago and took dozens of pictures—more photos of the skyline and the city's sights than the warehouse facilities the team had set up for his inspection.

Difficult to read, Felipe sat quietly in his chair halfway down the table. The confessionary, who'd observed plenty of family secrets, was the son who had been given to the church for the priesthood. He'd inexplicably left the seminary a few years ago, moved home, and into the family business.

Alex believed people's lives were shaped but not driven by circumstance. On the surface, he had to admit the Mendoza brothers didn't seem to be such a treacherous group of men. *If* you pulled Ramón out of the line-up and shot him in the head not once, but twice, maybe more—and left him for dead. That was a special pleasure Alex saved for himself. Anticipation flooded each nerve, electrifying his resolve.

He sent a satisfied grin to his new business partner.

Ramón, on the other side of the room, smiled.

Many of the men settled in cushioned chairs scattered against the walls after dinner, enjoying brandy and Cuban cigars—impossible to acquire in the States.

Through the window, Alex watched the dinner cruises dock for the night. The Love Boat glittered, the star of the bay. She pealed her siren and dories began to ferry the first wave of tourists back aboard.

Alex drew his cigar, and smoke drifted toward the ceiling. A huge drug bust with the satisfaction of revenge was the perfect way to finish up his career.

Ramón turned from the window, and slapped his palm on the table. "Let us find Gabriel," he said.

The city was enveloped in a rich haze of golden light. Traffic stalled and moved forward only a few feet at a time as cars snaked their way down the crowded La Costera. In the interior of the new limousine, Alex, Ramón, and his brothers, along with a lieutenant named Victor, waited. Alex took note of the Cadillac's plush appointments, running his palm along supple, camel-colored leather. Ramón had been busy collecting all the trappings of wealth while he built his empire.

Ramón grumbled. Even one of the most powerful drug lords in the country couldn't get the traffic to move.

Taxis, a few other limos, and outdated cars rarely seen in the United States anymore, crammed the pavement. A striped Jeep, pink and white—a sister of the one Alex been given—kept pace with the limo.

Through the tinted glass, he watched the dark-haired gringo grip the steering wheel. His body rigid, he pushed forward as if determination alone would help him get wherever he was headed quickly. Alex understood. Persistence had been his method of operation for years now.

When the Jeep fell behind, Alex turned to look and realized just how ridiculous he'd appeared earlier driving around town. He silently cursed Dean. Besides the obvious humiliation, it was as if once you hopped behind the wheel, "tourist" had been tattooed on your forehead.

Orchestrated by horns and music, the Costera was a circus thriving beneath flashing neon. Alex not only heard, but felt, the pounding reverb through the closed window. He pressed the control to lower the glass, and the city assaulted him with the stench of dirt and hot rubber, cooking smells, and trash. The smell, simmered in humidity, melded with the salty air into a steamy, pungent broth.

The limo pulled up to several nightclubs and waited while Victor went in to find Gabriel. Further up the coast, the bottleneck gave way, and they stopped at yet another club. Alex watched the clientele move in and out of the doors and decided this establishment had been invisibly tagged, "locals only."

A group of gringos went in, and Alex realized at least a few tourists were determined to find a more native Acapulco experience. He wondered if they were looking for drugs or just incredibly naive. Probably both.

Victor stuck his head into the limousine. "He's here. Sofia and the girls are with him," he reported.

Sofia?

The only Sofia Alex knew was a cousin in California and she went by

Sofie. Could this Sofia be someone he hadn't been briefed on—maybe one of Gabriel's or Ramón's girlfriends?

A thumping bass line greeted them before they even reached the entrance. Inside, "Billie Jean" throbbed through giant speakers, energizing the club. Beneath muted light, Alex scanned the smoky, packed room. Small round tables, that barely held more than a couple of drinks, surrounded the perimeter of the dance floor.

Alex hated Michael Jackson, dancing, and disco. Classic rock, like Zeppelin and The Who, were more his speed.

A crowd stood around the bar, two and three deep. Most appeared to wait for drinks, and surprisingly, some seemed to carry on conversations over the music. The vague headache he'd noticed earlier began to pound behind his temples. He was getting too old for this.

Ramón stepped into the interior of the club and the sea of people parted as if Moses had arrived. Alex followed with Felipe and Esteban. Several booths had been hastily cleared. The rest of Ramón's entourage, who'd arrived in another, older limo, had already taken up residence in the building. Some were seated at one of the tables, while others stood around the edges of the room monitoring the crowd.

Alex took note of Ramón's men and their positions by habit. At the door, one of the men adjusted his weapon and nodded to his partner who manned the hallway that led to the bathrooms. A family as powerful as the Mendozas needed protection. But this show was merely a reminder someone influential had arrived.

Gabriel left a group of women along the bar and came to the table. When the music transitioned, introductions were made, and he took Alex's hand with a disinterested grasp.

Felipe moved over and made a spot for Gabriel in the booth. A poorly bleached blonde in black hot pants took their drink order.

"Jack Daniels on the rocks," Ramón said, ordering drinks for the table.

Alex studied the youngest Mendoza brother. Catalog handsome, he'd be twenty-three in March. His whole life was ahead of him. *What a waste.*

Conversation wasn't possible. Felipe appeared bored, this obviously wasn't his scene either. Gabriel thrummed his fingers on the table, mildly agitated.

There had to be problems, the team didn't know about, between the brothers. Alex wondered what they were. Settling into the booth with his drink, he mulled over the possibilities and watched the dance floor.

It was impossible *not* to notice the young woman under blue lights in the center of the room. Reflections from the disco ball bounced over her fluid movements. Her long, black hair had been pulled away from her forehead and gathered into a thick ponytail of curls cascading down her back.

Ramón's California cousin, Sofie, was more attractive in person than in her photos.

Graceful on the floor, she matched her partner, move for move. In tight pants, the guy was a caricature of the disco scene. Beneath his unbuttoned shirt, gold chains decorated his dark, pelted chest. He was a dancer too. *A real Travolta.*

Alex scanned his memory. The agency kept track of the Mendozas north and south of the border. Sofie Davis lived on the periphery of the immediate family, but she still fell into their circle and had been investigated. He'd seen the report. She had no connection to the family business and had limited contact with them in the last five years. A student in Los Angeles, she spent most of her free time with her boyfriend.

The guy she was with tonight couldn't be the Valley boy she dated. Maybe they'd broken up and she'd found somebody new.

Why hadn't Alex been notified of this development? Someone in the agency had to have known she'd left Los Angeles. Alex hadn't been here for a day; already somebody had fucked up and there was a glitch in the plan.

When the music faded, her partner leaned in close and Sofie laughed. She flashed an infectious smile, and Alex wondered what it would take to get Sofie to share her secrets with him, several of which had nothing to do with his job. He willed the thoughts away. This girl wasn't going to interfere with his mission.

Travolta put his arm around her waist and led Sofie to a table where a group had collected. Alex had seen a few of the clique in photos. Others, he didn't recognize.

Why was she here? Was this a vacation or something more permanent? Had she left school and relocated?

Sofie said a few words to her friends, sipped from her wine glass and glanced around. She seemed to notice the club had been cased, and stopped. Alex watched her seek Ramón out and scrutinize each man who sat at their table. When Alex met her eyes, she stalled for a second before moving on.

She spoke to the gold-chained Travolta and left her friends. Wearing tight black bellbottoms that hugged her hips, Sofie, who couldn't stand much over five feet barefoot, strolled across the floor in high heels with the confidence of a woman who knew she was hot.

"Ah, mi amor," Ramón greeted her, "I wondered when you would notice me. You are always lovely, but this evening you look especially beautiful. A Spanish princess."

The rest of the men nodded.

Sofie's eyes sparkled and she blushed.

"The whole room is watching you." Staring across the table, Ramón said, "This is Alex Wilson. From Chicago. We are going to be working together."

Ramón turned to his cousin. "This is my cousin Sofia... who prefers to be called Sofie. We are very proud of her," Ramón almost crowed. "She has just graduated from UCLA, a prestigious university in California, with a degree in accounting. Sofia is our newest addition to the family business."

Her eyes weren't twinkling anymore. With lithe fingers, she politely touched Alex's hand in a quasi handshake.

So that's her motivation. She's come to work for the family.

Glancing Alex's way, Sofie leaned into Ramón and spoke. Ramón replied, sending Alex a curious smile.

Sofie's shy but inquisitive stare put Alex on edge. What had they said? Was this some kind of trap? Had Ramón been so leery of the team's set-up he'd brought in an accountant to look over Alex's books? Rachel, from the agency's finance division, had sworn the books were solid. They'd even had them audited.

Sitting in a virtual nest of Mendozas, Alex had to remind himself to keep his cool. The music pulsed again and didn't give them a chance to speak. He'd have to make time for that later.

Sofie remained at the table for a minute or so, then spoke to Ramón, excusing herself. She returned to the dance floor, now with another dark-haired and bejeweled suitor.

Felipe seemed relieved when Ramón appeared to tire of the noise. He stood and spoke to Gabriel, who dutifully remained seated, and moved to Alex.

Leaning in close, Ramón said, "We are leaving. You can come with us and we will take you to your car. Or you can stay here with Gabriel."

Ramón pointed to his brother, who sent Alex the required smile. "And he will take you when you are ready."

Alex didn't want to miss an opportunity to discover the mystery of the remaining Mendozas. "I think I'll stick around and enjoy the music for awhile." He avoided glancing toward Sofie on the dance floor.

Ramón opened his wallet and pulled out a business card. Esteban fished a pen from his jacket and handed it to his brother.

"Here is the address. It is not far from your hotel. Meet me at the house at one tomorrow. From there, we will leave for the rancho."

Alex hadn't mentioned his hotel. Ramón clearly knew about the Jeep, and Alex couldn't help but be embarrassed. At the same time, he wondered if Ramón already had sent someone to search his room.

"We can talk business once we get to the rancho. I look forward to you joining us."

"See you tomorrow. Thanks for dinner. It was great." Alex stood and shook Ramón's hand.

"My pleasure. When you get to the hacienda and taste Rosa's cooking, you will have a traditional taste of Mexico unlike any other."

"I can't wait."

Ramón glanced at his men and both tables began to clear.

"Well, goodnight then. Adiós."

"Adiós," Alex uttered his first Spanish word of the day.

The entourage followed Ramón out of the club, leaving Alex and Gabriel alone.

Scooting closer, Gabriel called the waitress over. "We need a drink. Another whiskey or something else?"

"Jack on the rocks."

Gabriel spoke to the waitress in Spanish.

Then he turned to Alex. "Pardon, I'll be back." Apparently, he'd pick his drink up at the bar. Gabriel motioned to the crowd dancing beneath the shimmering disco ball. "We have plenty of beautiful women here, don't you think?"

Alex nodded, focusing in on one.

"Enjoy yourself."

It wasn't a surprise when Gabriel walked toward the bathroom. Alex sat with his drink and tried to concentrate on monitoring the nightclub. In the meantime, he watched Sofie and wondered about the implications of this new, unwelcome complication he hadn't anticipated.

Would he eventually have to kill her too?

Ramón's bodyguards had left with him. Even surrounded by the enemy,

Alex had felt oddly insulated. Now, he noticed other men scattered around the room, packing heat, men who made him wish he'd worn his gun.

The heavy bathroom traffic proved business was brisk. Things could get dicey if he needed to take a piss. What if he ran into Gabriel? Alex didn't want to spend the night trying to burn off an obligatory coke high, swimming frantic laps in his minuscule pool.

Gabriel wasn't a surprise; of course one of the brothers would end up a coke-head. At least the guy who'd prepared Gabriel's dossier had been worth his pay, better than the California idiot who'd missed Sofie's arrival altogether.

Between the sketchy crowd and Sofie, the self-assurance he'd felt earlier evaporated. Alex kept close tabs on the temperature of the club, dividing his time between the drug trade going in and out of the head, and watching Sofie—Señorita Butterfly—flitter between her friends and the dance floor.

Ramón was right, beautiful Sofie had no trouble attracting admirers. She wasn't Alex's type; he preferred long-legged, big-busted blondes—like the woman back at the hotel. But Sofie had an allure Alex couldn't deny.

Occasionally, she'd glance at him, especially when she sat among her gaggle of girlfriends. Once, when another young woman who was several inches taller and attractive—but not quite as pretty as Sofie—spoke, all the girls turned and openly stared.

Amused, Alex nodded and took the last sip of his drink.

The women giggled. Apparently embarrassed, Sofie looked away.

Gabriel returned, sniffling. "Are you doing okay? Need another one?" he asked, motioning towards Alex's glass of skating ice.

"I've already ordered. Should I call her over?"

"No. I can wait." Gabriel tapped his fingers on the table in time to the music. Inhaling, he sucked in deep, trying to capture the hazy remains of the white powder around the lip of his nose. "You doing okay?" he repeated, his knee now bouncing rapidly as well.

Alex thought about asking the same question. He wanted to place his hand on Gabriel's arm and tell him to slow down. Instead, he said, "Enjoying the view. Watching the señoritas."

"Good." Gabriel grabbed a handkerchief from the pocket of his blazer and blew. He glanced around, distracted. "Tell me when you want to leave. I see some friends at the bar."

"I'll let you know when I'm ready."

As the night wore on Alex sat alone and surveyed the scene, trying to imagine what possessed Sofie to give up an opportunity for a decent career in the States for this corrupt hellhole.

A couple of women came over and asked him to dance, including one of the girls who'd eyed him from Sofie's table. He lifted his drink and politely turned them down.

The need to piss made him take the chance of losing his vantage point from the booth. Fortunately, the bathroom traffic had thinned and Gabriel was laughing with a woman at the bar.

Alex passed through the hall on his way back into the club and realized being an acquaintance of Ramón's had perks—the booth was empty and another glass of whiskey had been delivered to the table.

Sofie had disappeared from the dance floor.

He saw her just beyond the entrance of a dark hallway, wrapped in the arms of a guy he hadn't noticed before. They were kissing.

Wow, Sofie, you seemed so shy at the table.

Glancing away, he scanned the rest of the club. Soon, she was back under the blue lights with yet another Romeo.

Alex watched her until their eyes met, and the connection didn't break until she turned. He waited to catch her gaze again. It wasn't long before he did. Alex told himself it was work, but he heard Nick's voice echoing in his head, warning him—*Look away, buddy, don't let this get messy.*

Mid-song, she spoke to her partner and left the dance floor, purposefully walking toward Alex. She sat down in the booth and scooted to his side as the music faded.

"You're sitting all alone. My friend Lucy came over to ask you to dance," Sofie said with a clear, California accent. "Why'd you turn her down?"

"I was waiting for you." Alex took a sip of his whiskey.

She stared, as if trying to read him. A pair of diamond studs sat poised beneath the elegant shells of her ears. Between the lapels of her turquoise blouse, a silver necklace with a lacy heart rested within the crests of her petite breasts.

Alex had to remind himself he liked them bigger.

"Okay. Let's dance." The sultry voice fit her perfectly. Sexy with sass.

Dancing wasn't what Alex had in mind. He needed information. "I don't dance."

"Everybody dances." She grinned.

The music started again and he had to lean in to say, "Not me."

She grasped his hand and tugged.

Her warm fingers were too enticing not to follow. Ironically, "Stayin' Alive" blared through the sound system.

They danced. She was pretty good. He was pretty bad.

Halfway through the song, she laughed and yelled over the Bee Gees, "You're right, maybe you shouldn't dance."

Alex stopped moving and felt the color rise on his face. He didn't have thin skin, but something about Sofie made him chafe under the sarcastic dig. He should have been happy she wasn't impressed. He needed information from her. Nothing else.

So why was he standing here, feeling insulted? Because against his better judgement, Alex was attracted to Sofie and he didn't want—*couldn't afford*—to be.

With a firm grip, he grabbed her arm and led her to the booth.

Snatching her arm away, she rubbed her wrist. "Why'd you do that?"

"I told you I don't dance."

"I was joking. Sort of." Her brow wrinkled. "*Sorry.* I thought you wanted to dance."

"Did I say that?"

"You kept staring at me." Sofie's voice, when full of sexy promise, was much more intriguing than this petulant whine.

"Was I?"

"You know you were."

He heard her indignation and didn't care. She pissed him off. With just a few words, Ramón's tiny cousin had grazed his masculinity, further shaking his confidence.

"Okay. We'll talk instead." She settled into the booth. "Your name is Alex, right?"

"Yep."

"And you're from Chicago?"

"Yep."

"What do you do in Chicago?"

It was Alex's job to ask the questions. "What are *you* doing here, in Mexico?"

"Why do you care? No. You answer my question first."

This wasn't going the way Alex had planned. Frustrated, he refused to speak. It was juvenile. But at this moment, it didn't matter that she was a Mendoza and he was supposed to be charming the family. Alex wasn't in the mood to play games. He wanted answers. He hadn't met a woman who'd irritated him this much in years, possibly ever.

Sofie's eyes were wide and intense. "Do I know you? Have we met before?"

"Ever been to Chicago?" *Shit. Why am I still answering her questions?*

"No."

"Then you don't know me."

"Well, Alex. You don't like to dance, and even if you did, you're not very good at it."

"I warned you." Alex wondered how long he'd have to listen to Sofie bitch about his dancing.

"It's too loud in here to carry on a conversation. This obviously isn't going well for either of us. You're not even my type."

She turned to slide out of the booth, then stopped. Her warm, minty breath kissed his cheek, and her sultry voice returned, "It's been nice, but —"

As the song ended, one of Zappa's songs flashed through his mind. Alex didn't bother to filter his thought: "You need to decide which dancing fool you're going to fuck tonight?"

Alex didn't expect the words to come out so loud. He didn't expect the words to come out at all. *Shit.*

"What did you say?" Sofie's eyes blazed. She lifted her hand to slap him, but didn't. "You're an *asshole bastard*!"

Sofie Mendoza, accountant to one of Mexico's biggest drug lords, was such a lady she didn't even know how to cuss. Alex couldn't help but laugh.

Dismissing him, she scrambled out of the booth, collected herself, and strolled into the crowd.

❦

Alex Wilson was an asshole, Sofie decided, pulling Damián onto the dance floor. Her friend had been talking with the boys but didn't seem to mind the distraction. Ramón must have found Alex Wilson under a rock. At first, there was this mysterious quality about him that sent a rush of anticipation rippling through her belly. She decided it must have been her imagination; because, after close inspection, there was nothing mysterious here at all. Jerks like him were just one more reason she wouldn't be working for her cousin, no matter what Ramón thought.

Monica's radar had been off the map this time. She'd been so sure Ramón's new business partner was scoping Sofie out from across the room.

When she declined Monica's challenge, Lucy, who also thought Alex was hot, took charge and made her way to his table, only to be rejected. Sofie wished he had turned her down when she asked him to dance too.

Lucy and Monica had moved to the bar, so she'd have to wait to tell them what happened. The man may be hot, but the appeal ended there. She'd warn her girls to stay away from his lousy moves and filthy mouth.

She navigated the crowded hallway on her way to the restroom. Coming out, she rounded the corner and an arm draped her shoulder, pulling her in.

"Hey, foxy lady," a stranger drawled.

Sofie turned. *A Southern boy.*

Over the Southern boy's shoulder she saw Alex's eyes bore into her. She flipped her ponytail, ignoring Alex's steely gaze.

Ramón wouldn't have asked Alex to keep an eye on me—would he? Sofie shuddered, wondering if that was why he'd watched her all along.

Determined not to let Alex—or Ramón—ruin the night, she took a good look at the Southern boy and smiled. "Texas?" she asked.

He was cute. Not "fuckable." She wasn't looking for "fuckable" men. But cute enough to hopefully piss off the gorgeous asshole from Chicago.

"Alabama," he said. "You speak English. Where are you from?"

"California."

"What are you doing here?"

"I'm on vacation."

"Hey," he said, "We're on vacation too." He kept his arm on her shoulder and nodded toward two guys nearby. "Meet my buddies."

Introductions were made, but it was too loud to decipher names. She couldn't decide if the guy who'd cornered her said he was Mike or Mark, so she named him Alabama in her head. It was easier that way.

"Come on, let's dance," she said.

By the end of the first number, she realized Alabama was *really* drunk. And now, he'd become a sticky shadow.

She tried to make a polite getaway. "I need to find my friends."

"No you don't," Alabama said, squeezing her arm.

"My cousins are here. They'll worry." She glanced around the room.

"Why?" Alabama's eyes were lacquered and his breath hot, soaked in alcohol.

Great, she thought, searching for her cousin Monica, Lucy, and the rest of her friends. *Where'd everybody go?*

Finally she dipped out of his grasp. "I need to go to the restroom."

Alabama reached for her, teetered, and stumbled. "I'll be here when you get back," he slurred.

"It might be awhile, it gets crowded in there."

"I'll wait."

Fifteen minutes passed before she chanced it and made her way out of the restroom. When she saw Gabriel at the bar, she considered making a stop, but she could catch up with her cousin *after* she dodged Alabama. Thankfully, she spied him against the wall and slipped past him, returning to the table where Monica, Lucy, Damián, and the rest of her friends had regrouped.

Sofie let the crowd encircle her and avoided the jerks she'd met tonight, both from home; one from Chicago, the other Birmingham.

Oh, there was Tomás as well, who stared all googly-eyed from across the table. Unlike her new disappointing acquaintances, she'd known Tomás for more than one night. It didn't make him any less of a pest. No, it made him more persistent. She still fumed about the stolen kiss in the dark hallway.

Are all men jerks? She quickly excluded her cousin Gabriel and Damián from the list. Tonight in particular, Damián, her effeminate friend—who had yet to come out of the closet—came in handy. She clasped his hand and coaxed him back onto the dance floor before Tomás got any new ideas.

Distractions kept her from losing herself in the music. She watched for Alabama and stole glances—she couldn't help it—in Alex's direction, trying to avoid his eyes.

The music transitioned again. She didn't want to return to the table and a possible face-off with Tomás, so she checked the bar. Gabriel had disappeared. He'd been doing that a lot lately.

Evading the glut of objectionable men, she moved around the perimeter of the room, hoping to find her cousin. Getting nowhere, she stopped near the hallway Tomás had lured her into earlier. There, she found the perfect spot to monitor the bar.

She checked her watch. It was past midnight. Gabriel still couldn't be found. Alabama's friends had taken up residence at one of the small tables around the dance floor. Alex still sat in Ramón's booth. Their eyes met, and he turned away. He seemed to be looking for someone too.

Who?

Sofie recognized Alabama's hot alcohol breath when he grabbed her arm. Spinning her around, he pulled her into the dark hallway. He slammed against her body, pinning her to the concrete wall.

"Hey, where'd you go?" Alabama swayed, his grip still tight.

She struggled to escape, and realized that, even drunk, he was surprisingly strong.

He ground his pelvis into hers, pressed his open mouth against her lips, and assaulted her with his thick, disgusting tongue.

Gagging, she turned her head. "No! Stop!"

Alabama pushed in hard. He pinched her breast with one hand and clutched a handful of her bottom with the other.

"Leave her alone," Alex Wilson growled.

Instantly, she was free, and she began to back out of the hallway toward the light of the club.

Now, Alex had Alabama pinned.

"Hey, man! What's it to you?" Alabama said. Pulling away from Alex, he stumbled after her.

Before she could scramble out of his reach, Alex had Alabama by the neck. He shoved Alabama into the concrete block, lifting him off his feet. "I said, leave her alone."

Alabama tried to pull Alex's hands off of his throat. They wouldn't budge.

Sofie watched, horrified, until Alabama raised his arms in surrender.

Alex let go, and Alabama's feet hit the floor.

He choked and sputtered. Rubbing his neck, Alabama croaked, "Hey—hey man, that wasn't necessary."

"Get out of here," Alex demanded.

Alabama wasn't drunk enough to argue. He staggered out of the hallway, holding his throat.

She couldn't read Alex's expression in the dim light.

Who is this guy?

Crossing her arms, she said, "I don't need your help."

"Go back to your friends," Alex said, shaking his head.

Sofie heard his disgust and stood her ground. He couldn't tell her what to do.

Alex grabbed her arm and walked her toward the dance floor. "Stay out of dark hallways, Sofie. Your cousins aren't here to protect you."

He didn't release her until they were beneath the blue light.

Trembling, she made her way to the table. Gasping for breath, she sat down and tried to focus on breathing evenly.

No one noticed her, or that she'd been gone. They were all enraptured by some inconsequential, silly drama.

The only time she'd been this shaken up was on a California freeway almost three years ago. But tonight, she wasn't flooded with fear. No, this was a tsunami of embarrassment and anger.

Alex Wilson was too full of himself. She could have handled Alabama on her own.

She didn't need—or want—a man acting all macho, swooping in to save her. He wasn't her white knight. *We don't live in the Middle Ages, Alex Wilson. It's the 1980s now. Women have been liberated for God's sake.*

❦

Tonight Alex had learned a few things about Sofie Davis. First, she was an ungrateful little bitch. Second, no matter how pretty she was—and she was beautiful—she could be irritating as hell.

When the gringo she'd danced with earlier pushed her into the shadows, Alex had looked around, expecting Gabriel to appear and come to her rescue. But Gabriel hadn't, and Alex had no choice but to handle the situation.

He hadn't signed up to babysit any Mendoza brats.

Unfortunately, Gabriel had been missing in action again, probably in the head, sucking more powder up his nose.

A little late, he sauntered over to the booth.

"Amigo." Gabriel squared his shoulders in a pathetic attempt to appear threatening. "There are plenty of hot, *available*, women around here to choose from. My cousin Sofia is *not* one of them."

"Don't worry. That's not going to happen," Alex snapped. "I'm ready to leave. Will you take me to my car?"

CHAPTER FOUR
Bahia Vista

Bay View
  Friday, July 6, 1984

In the bathroom, Alex opened his shaving kit, shook two pills from a bottle of aspirin, and chased them with a handful of water. By the time the sun came up, his headache had settled into a dull, relentless beat. Bloodshot eyes bid him good morning in the mirror. "Shit."

When he'd returned to his room last night, he'd checked—his .45 caliber was still hidden, untouched, and his briefcase unrifled. There'd be plenty of time for the Mendozas to go through his things at the ranch.

The clock hit seven, and he dialed the phone. Karen swept the line and put him through.

Dean's voice was clipped, "What's up?"

"Why didn't you tell me about Ramón's cousin Sofía?"

"What about her? She's in California. With her boyfriend."

"No, she's here. Without the guy. I met her last night."

Alex heard a hitch in Dean's breath and imagined the gears turning in his head.

"I'm supposed to know this ahead of time." Alex leaned against the headboard and pinched the skin between his eyes.

"If we'd known, we would have briefed you."

"That's the problem. We didn't know," he hissed. "No surprises, remember? How could the LA office drop the ball? The last time somebody fucked up, I lost my partner." He squeezed the handset and wished it was the California investigator's neck.

"Whoa. Hold on. So his cousin shows up. She's—"

"I didn't come this far to end up in the trunk of a car in downtown Acapulco!" Alex stood and opened the empty bedside drawer. He didn't know why, so he slammed it shut.

It wasn't the first time Alex was sorry he'd quit smoking. He could use a cigarette.

"She's a non-player."

Pacing the length of the telephone cord, Alex said, "She's graduated and gone to work for the Mendozas. She's an accountant now. Somebody forgot to put that in the report too."

"The books are clean."

"Screw the books. It's not having all the facts that pisses me off. We don't know anything about her. She's going to fuck up the plan." He could hear Dean give instructions over the intercom to Karen.

"Cool down. You're overreacting. I'm already on it from this end. You work on it from yours. Give me twenty-four hours."

"I'll call when I can—not sure when. I'm going to the ranch today." Alex rubbed his aching head. "And Dean? *No more surprises.*"

❧

A winding mountain road led Alex into the neighborhood where the Mendozas had their Acapulco retreat. The property sat nestled in a hillside above the bay. This location was more secluded than the estate the Mendozas owned north of the border in La Jolla, where Alex had spent countless hours doing stealth curb duty.

This afternoon, he had trouble finding the address hidden among the natural overgrowth of ferns and palm fronds. Finally, a little after one, he found the tiled number and tried to pull off the road, but the ass of his pink and white Jeep jutted out onto the street, between two tight curves. He half wished someone would speed around the corner and take him out of his misery.

Black wrought-iron arches were just wide enough for a limousine to pass through. Alex pressed the buzzer attached to a metal pole nearby. A woman's voice answered and the gate slowly opened. There wasn't much of a drive, just a few empty parking spots tucked into the corner.

Surrounded by lush vegetation, the courtyard steps led to a trickling fountain and glass front doors. When he looked back towards the Jeep, he noticed the driveway angled off to the right. The rest of the estate was hidden among the cultivated jungle. Bits of blue-tiled rooftops, identical to the main house, were scattered throughout the property that flowed down the hillside.

Before he could knock, a maid met him at the door and led him through a modern fishbowl of a house with an expansive view of the sparkling bay. She sent him down tiled steps, through the living room and out an open wall of glass onto the patio.

A swimming pool seemed to cling to the edge of the hillside. Sofie and a girl he recognized from the nightclub were draped on two lounge chairs.

Sofie wore a tiny lime bikini and her friend had on an identical suit in yellow. There wasn't enough fabric between the two of them to make a large napkin. Alex didn't complain. With a perfect figure, Sofie glistened, luscious under the sun.

Alex had to keep telling himself she wasn't his type.

But there was this thing about her... It didn't matter. They'd gotten off to a rocky start and disliked each other already. That wasn't bad. Alex didn't need to remind himself of his first self-imposed rule: Never get involved.

Not only irritating, Sofie was Ramón's cousin. She shared his blood. That was enough to sour him for good.

Lifting her sunglasses for only a moment, she repositioned them along the bridge of her nose, making no move to greet him.

He stood over her and let his shadow spill across her body. "Where are your cousins? Ramón told me to meet him here at one."

"Something came up at the ranch. They left this morning." She drew her mouth into a tight line and slid the sunglasses up into her dark hair.

Alex waited for more, wondering if she planned on giving him any details.

Ignoring him, she picked up a magazine from a nearby table.

She still must be pissed.

He noticed the faint bruising on her wrist and felt bad for a second, knowing he might be the one responsible for the marks.

So what? Alex wasn't going to apologize. If he hadn't shown up when he did, the guy with the Southern drawl would have left more than a few bruises.

Didn't Sofie realize she owed him gratitude for saving her ass last night? "Well?"

"Well what?" She lowered the magazine and stared at him.

For the first time, he noticed her eyes were a mossy, emerald green. A striking contrast to her caramel skin and black hair.

She may have beautiful eyes, but Sofie *Mendoza* Davis was still a bitch. "Is there a message for me?"

"Hmmm." She cupped her chin as if deep in thought, supposedly making an attempt to recall any possible messages she may have forgotten.

Alex crossed his arms and waited. Ramón's little cousin really was a piece of work.

Finally, she exhaled a long, deep sigh. "You're riding with me. We're supposed to be there by dinner. But I'm not done tanning yet. Then, I need to shower and pack. So I won't be ready for an hour or two. You can wait for me here, by the pool." She examined him, taking in his shorts and T-shirt, and pointed toward the covered patio. "Or, if hanging around the pool is uncomfortable for you—you can wait for me over there."

Her eyes shimmered with contempt and a glimmer of something he couldn't quite place. *Delight?* No problem. He considered this a stroke of luck, realizing how he could make this new development work to his advantage.

Alex sprawled out on an empty lounger, leaned against the white terry-cloth cushion, and cradled the back of his head with his hands. "I might go swimming. I think I'll get my suit from the car."

Sofie didn't respond.

But the yellow bikini, her interest peaked, rolled over and lowered her sunglasses. If she was waiting for a formal introduction, she didn't get one.

"Hi. I'm Monica, Sofie's cousin," she said. "I remember you from the club last night."

"I'm Alex. From Chicago."

Grinning, Monica looked at Sofie. "Isn't this the guy you think is so hot?"

"Monica!" Sofie turned her head toward her cousin, mouthing "Stop!"

Alex couldn't hear Sofie's whispered, agitated reply. At least there was satisfaction in knowing the initial attraction had been mutual.

"I can see why." Monica leaned closer and gave him a perfect view of her ample tits. "Nice to meet you, Alex from Chicago. Are you here for business or pleasure?"

"It's a business trip. My first time down. Wish I could stay longer than a few days," he said, appreciating the view. "It's beautiful here."

Monica seemed to catch the double meaning and smiled without blushing.

Sofie skewered him with disgust. He couldn't help it if she wasn't as well-endowed.

Grabbing her blouse, Sofie buttoned the gauzy cover-up. Alex had to admit that in contrast to her cousin, he found Sofie's modesty refreshing.

She hid behind the gossip rag.

Monica sat up and got comfortable on the lounger. "So, tell me about Chicago."

"What do you want to know?" he said.

Just to piss Sofie off, he focused all of his attention on Monica, and they fell into comfortable conversation.

It was too easy. Sofie threw the magazine onto the concrete with a slap, stood and grabbed her towel, stumbling over it as she stomped into the house.

Alex smiled.

"What's up with her?" Monica asked.

"Have no idea. It could have something to do with what happened last night."

"Oh, I haven't heard about that." Monica raised her eyebrows mischievously. "Yet."

He shrugged. "Maybe she's just not into being my chauffeur."

"I'd be happy to take you there myself." She seemed disappointed. "But I have to be in town today."

Alex was disappointed too. Monica was tall and willowy, more his type. Having to endure several grueling hours in the car alone with Sofie wasn't going to be the most pleasant way to spend the afternoon. On the other hand, it was a prime opportunity to get the answers he needed. Dean said he'd work on the riddle of Sofie Mendoza Davis from his end. In a car, Alex would have the whole story just inches away.

❦

Showered, packed, and reluctantly ready to go, Sofie closed the front door. Hesitating for a minute in the courtyard, she took a deep breath and listened to the water trickling in the fountain. She tried to internalize the calm, needing all the self-restraint she could muster for the trip.

Ever since the incident on the freeway three years ago, she'd hated to drive. Especially alone. Now, she couldn't decide what was worse—driving solo or traveling with Alex.

Earlier in the afternoon, the scene by the pool with Alex had been humiliating. Shaking the memory away, she closed her eyes, trying to block it out. Yes, at first, she thought Alex was hot—emphasis on *at first*—but

Monica didn't have to relay private information.

Then, Alex ogled Monica's boobs, like every guy did between here and Mexico City. When it was finally clear he planned to ignore her—even though Sofie was busy ignoring him—Sofie tried to make a pointed, but graceful, exit. That's when she tripped on her towel. *Ugh.*

And now, she'd be riding in the car with Alex all afternoon. Sofie was tempted to fish a coin from the bottom of her purse and toss it into the fountain, making a wish for a magical reprieve, and frowned instead, knowing it was pointless.

The day had gone south before Alex even arrived. She had already made plans with Monica and Lucy for another night out when Ramón came outside and announced he had to leave for the rancho early. He couldn't find Gabriel, so he needed Sofie to take Alex down to the ranch. She'd groaned.

Curious, Ramón tilted his head. Sofie quickly recovered and said, "Sure."

She did consider telling Ramón how rude and overbearing Alex had been at the club. If he knew, family loyalty would overrule any business deal, and her cousin would see to it that Alex was on the first plane headed north.

But since her uncle passed, Ramón had taken on the role of the family's patrón. He'd ask questions, lots of them, and make judgments. And if Alex mentioned the guy from Alabama, Ramón would probably assign one of his men to be her constant chaperone. Sófie hated being monitored, so she kept quiet.

Sofie stepped into the driveway, saw Alex's Jeep, and forgot her earlier agitation. She laughed, imagining him cruising around Acapulco in a pink-and-white-striped Barbie car.

Not wanting to pass up the golden opportunity to embarrass Alex, she abandoned her plan to walk to the gatehouse and have Juan bring the Mercedes around. Alex, a wayward Ken, could be the driver.

While she silently formulated sarcastic thoughts into the perfect comment, Alex met her in the drive.

He held up his hand. "Don't say anything about the Jeep."

She snickered and delivered the perfect remark, "Oh come on, Ken. I think it's cute." Throwing her overnighter into the back, next to his luggage, she jumped into the passenger seat.

Alex climbed into the Jeep and put both hands on the wheel. After a long pause, he put the key into the ignition and stared at her with his blue eyes.

It didn't fit. Alex didn't appear to be the typical, pale Midwesterner, spending long dreary winters in the snow. He resembled the guys from college that surfed Southern California's beaches all year 'round.

Brown, sun-bleached hair fell floppy over his forehead and, in the heat, a few sticky curls clung to nape of his neck. Sofie fought the urge to touch them. She wondered where the thought had bubbled from, before she pushed the idea back down. Her Tía Sofia would say he needed a haircut. As gorgeous in daylight as she'd found him the night before, this new view didn't change her opinion. Alex was still an asshole.

She smoothed her yellow sundress and asked, "What are you waiting for?"

"I thought we'd take your car."

"Don't have one." A small lie. Sofie didn't actually own a car in Mexico, but there were several available down the hill in the garage.

Lowering his sunglasses into place, he exhaled and turned the key.

The Jeep wouldn't start. There was nothing except a rapid succession of clicks.

He tried the ignition again. "Shit!" Alex smacked his hands on the steering wheel. "You sure you don't have a car stashed someplace?"

"Is it out of gas? Or does it run on strawberry Kool-Aid?" She giggled.

Alex frowned and leaned back. "The tank's full. See?"

Detecting the intoxicating mixture of musky aftershave and sweat, she caught her breath. Trying to ignore Alex, she focused on the gauge. "What about oil?" she asked. "You're a guy. Don't you know anything about cars?"

"Oil isn't the problem. It sounds like the battery to me."

Can't you wiggle a wire or something? she thought. "Maybe you can fix it. Why don't you get out and check?"

"I'm not a mechanic."

Even her dad, a doctor, knew the basics. She crossed her arms, finding it hard to believe this hunk of a man didn't have at least some knowledge of how an automobile engine worked.

Grumbling, Alex climbed out of the Jeep. She could see his big hands fumble around beneath the open hood. He closed it after a minute or two, and wiped his fingers on his khaki shorts.

He shrugged. "I can't see anything."

"Try to start it again," she instructed.

Back behind the wheel, Alex turned the key. Nothing.

Irritated, she bit the inside of her lip, climbed out of the Jeep, slammed the pink door, and stormed down the path toward the garage. "Juan!"

"Right. No car," Alex said, when Juan brought the new Mercedes up the driveway.

Staring at him, Sofie refused to comment.

Alex grabbed his own luggage, hopped into the passenger seat, and waited.

Could he have found it within his ability to get her luggage and open the door for her? She wondered if this Neanderthal had any manners. As a liberated woman, she wouldn't have let him, but he could have offered.

In the back seat, she stowed her luggage next to his, and opened the driver's door. "Didn't your mother teach you to be a gentleman?"

He looked at her. "Didn't yours teach you to act like a lady? She should have told you to stay out of dark hallways."

"Don't talk about my mom," Sofie snapped.

They pulled out of the driveway in silence. He didn't know anything about her mom. Sofie's mom had gone to finishing school. She didn't think they existed anymore, but clearly he could use a crash course at one, polishing his own manners.

She doubted Surfer Ken had ever heard of finishing school. Sofie had been taught to treat others with respect and kindness. Some people, like Alex, made that *really* hard to do.

Turning onto the main road, she headed south, driving past the golf resorts, and followed the beach beyond the airport.

After awhile she couldn't help but look his way. Alex stared out the window. Unlike anyone she'd ever met, he had this mysterious quality she couldn't gauge. It was as if he were two sides of a magnet. Both pulling and repelling, tying Sofie into knots. The ripple in her belly returned. *Had it ever left?*

They'd already turned inland when he spoke, "Mind if I turn up the air?" He reached for the control before she could answer.

Sofie rolled her eyes. "Go for it."

He took off his sunglasses, lowered his visor, and lifted the mirror. Communing with his reflection, he grinned. "So, what made you decide to move down here?"

Her glance caught his in the mirror. "I haven't moved here. I'm on vacation."

Alex returned to his reflection. "That's not what Ramón said."

She decided Alex was not only rude, he was narcissistic too.

"Why do you care?" she asked.

When he didn't answer, she added, "If you must know, my boyfriend and I broke up. I needed to get away for awhile. He was as much of a pain as you are. How far do I have to go to get away from annoying men?"

"It's your charming personality that attracts us."

"Shut up, Alex."

He returned to the mirror, but he soon seemed to tire of amusing himself. Closing it, he leaned back and shut his eyes.

"Didn't you get any sleep last night?"

Alex didn't bother to open them. "Hmmm…"

Further south, the jungle began to creep toward the edges of the road. While Alex slept, Sofie decided not to let some stupid guy ruin her favorite part of the trip. Ahead, between two plantations, lay a familiar small shack, with wood panels doubling as both shutters and awnings against the hot sun.

As Sofie approached, local children began to gather along the side of the road. Some wore threadbare pants and dresses, many had on little more than dingy underwear, and the tiniest wore nothing at all.

She slowed down.

Alex sat up. "What's going on?" he asked, glancing around. "Why are they waving?"

"They're hungry. Got any change on you?"

He checked his pockets and pulled out a handful of quarters.

"Throw 'em."

The children called out hopefully, "Señorita! Señor!"

Sofie smiled at the children and slowed to a crawl, while Alex hung out the window flinging quarters into the strip of grass edging the road. The children scrambled. She followed them with her eyes in the rear-view mirror.

Alex turned to her, grinning. She discovered a single, adorable dimple she hadn't noticed before and couldn't help but beam back, bridging the canyon between them.

Checking his pockets again, he dug deeper, and pulled them inside out, before he stuffed them back into his shorts. He shrugged. "That's all I've got."

"Get my purse from the back seat," she said, praying he'd focus on the coins. She hoped he wouldn't think digging through her purse was permission to peruse her life. It was a risk, but the thought of hungry children tipped the balance in their favor, so she decided to take a chance and let him dig for the change anyway.

He pulled her large handbag from the back seat. "Cute," he said, lifting it up for inspection.

Made from seagrass, it was one of Sofie's favorite bags, with its bouquet of colorful straw flowers embroidered on the front.

"Damn, it's heavy. What do you carry in here? Bricks?"

She sighed.

Alex unzipped the purse and rummaged through its contents. Pulling out a plastic rectangle, he opened it before she could stop him. Two Tampax fell onto the floorboard.

"Sorry."

Sofie felt color blossom along her cheeks. "I don't have a change purse or anything. Check the bottom and leave the rest of my stuff alone. Do you think you can manage that?"

Pinching his thumb and index finger, he picked up the Tampax as if it were contaminated. Handling as little of the pink plastic wrapping as possible, he returned them to the container and dropped it into her bag.

Sofie rolled her eyes again. *Did Alex think holding a wrapped Tampax was going to turn him into a girl?*

"Where'd the kids go?"

"They'll be more when we pass the next village."

"That fruit stand was a village?" he asked incredulously.

"They're not fruit stands. They're little stores where the locals get supplies."

Alex scavenged nickels, dimes, quarters, and a few pesos, from the bottom of her bag. He stashed them in the empty ashtray.

"Don't forget the pennies. I always have lots of them."

"No wonder your bag is so heavy. You carry around a cash register of change in the bottom of your purse."

"These people are poor. Every coin helps. They say there's poverty in the United States, and I guess there is, but it doesn't compare to the destitution here. It hurts my heart. We're driving in a big air-conditioned car, plenty of everything, and these kids…"

Alex peeked over her purse, and she wondered why he seemed so surprised. Did he think she couldn't honestly evaluate the conditions in her second home?

"There's a huge discrepancy between the wealthy and the poor here, I've never been able to reconcile," she said. "The middle class in Mexico is small and underrepresented. It's a terrible stain on such a beautiful country. My family is one of the lucky ones. Then again, maybe it's not luck. They've worked hard for generations to build all they've acquired." She hoped he couldn't hear the guilt prickle the edges of her family pride. They were blessed with so much while others had so little.

"It's the best part of the trip." She smiled, keeping her eyes on the road. "Throwing change probably isn't much. But it's something. And I love to see the kids get so excited."

Alex raccooned his way through her purse. He found a few more coins and unfolded her wallet.

"Hey! Just get the change. This isn't an invitation to inspect my life."

"So, your middle name is Morgan." He laughed, ignoring her. "You don't look like a Morgan. That's a big man's name for a tiny little girl like you."

Sofie raised her eyebrows. "I'm not a *tiny little girl*. I'm a *grown woman*. Anyway, it's a long story."

"We've got time."

"You really want to know?"

"Yeah."

"It's from a Welsh myth. It's the name of an enchantress on the mythical island of Avalon."

He lifted his eyebrows. "An enchantress?"

"You've heard of King Arthur and Excalibur?"

"The guy who pulled the sword from the stone." He searched her wallet. "I'd imagine your middle name would be Magdalena, or something exotic."

Their eyes met, and Sofie quickly turned hers back to the road. "Isn't Morgan unusual enough?"

"If you were born here in Mexico, why is your last name Davis?"

"Quit snooping! I was born in California. My father is from Detroit, Michigan. My mother was a Mendoza, born on the ranch we're going to now."

"Was?"

"She passed when I was twelve."

"I'm sorry. That must have been hard."

"Yes," Sofie said, deciding it was time for some fair play. "What's *your* middle name?"

"Don't have one. My dad wanted it to be Austin. My mom refused. She said my initials would be AA—like Alcoholics Anonymous. I guess she didn't want to imprint me with any destructive ideas." He chuckled. "I found those all on my own."

"Austin sounds like some Texan's name. Are you from Texas? I thought you said you were from Chicago."

"I was born in Texas. My parents moved to Chicago when I was a kid."

She imagined him as a toddler. He must have been a terror. Alex was this weird conglomeration—a Texan, who lived in Chicago, and looked like a California surfer.

"Do you speak Spanish?" he asked.

"My Spanish isn't as good as it used to be. I get by," she answered. "I learned it living here when my mom had cancer. My father's a doctor and couldn't handle it when she gave up on American medicine and came to Mexico, so they separated."

She'd made peace with her childhood years ago, but it was still painful to verbalize. Sofie looked to Alex. He wasn't just listening—he seemed genuinely fascinated.

Sofie couldn't decide if this interest in her personal life was good or bad. Maybe she'd pegged him as an asshole too soon. "Why are you so interested?"

"I can keep you company or I can sleep. You choose."

Rambling about her life made more sense than compulsively stealing glances, watching him nap. "At first, my mom agreed to treatment in California. When it didn't work, she came home and got involved in alternative cures—apricot pits, coffee enemas, bizarre crap... I stayed here after she died." Sofie realized she was anxiously massaging the steering wheel and forced herself to stop, uttering the hardest words ever, "My mom's buried in a small graveyard on the ranch."

Armies of papaya trees lined the roadside and sank deep into the landscape. She watched the speedometer and kept an eye out for more shacks.

"So you went to school here in Mexico?"

She nodded. "Monica and I were sent to a private all-girls, Catholic school. When it was time to go to high school, my dad convinced me to move up to Sacramento, where he lives. I stayed there until I went to college. My father and I got along great. His new wife, her girls and I, not so much."

Through the corner of her eye, she spied on him. He'd lifted his sunglasses and studied her intently. *Let's change the subject,* she decided, feeling overexposed underneath such close scrutiny. "Are your parents still married?"

"Yeah."

"Do they live in Chicago?

"Outside the city."

"Brothers and sisters?"

"A sister. What about you?" he asked.

She navigated a section of uneven pavement and watched for potholes. A few splats of rain hit the windshield, but afternoon showers never lasted long. "My cousin Ceci was like a sister, but I'm an only child. I don't see my dad much. He created a whole new story for himself and moved on without me."

"It must be hard trying to fit into a new family."

She turned on the windshield wipers. "You get used to being the odd man—in my case girl—out." It was a sudden lie she didn't bother to retract. Actually, giving up her dad to a whole other group of females really hurt.

I'm giving Alex too much information. I need to ask the questions. "Anyway, I have a whole extended family down here. What about you?"

"Not much to tell," he said. Now deep in her life, he went through the pockets of her wallet.

"What did I just say about rummaging through my purse?" She glared, trying to split her attention between his investigation and the glimmering asphalt.

"I come from a typical American family. My parents have been married for years," he said, concentrating on sorting through her pictures. "Nothing is perfect I guess. But they love each other, and they've made it work. My sister's married; I have two nephews. One is in third grade, or is it fourth now? And the other is in kindergarten."

"Do you get to see them much?" she asked.

"Not often enough." Alex glanced out the window. "I miss them."

Interesting. Apparently there was a heart, that pumped blood, not ice, inside that hot body. A faded pickup truck passed in the opposite direction, one of the few vehicles they'd met along the two-lane road. Driving didn't seem daunting at all with Alex beside her in the car.

He returned to the picture sleeve and held up an assortment of silly faces Sofie and Ceci made in a photo booth. It had been taken on the pier in Santa Monica, the last summer Sofie was in high school. "Who's this?"

"Ceci. My cousin. My best friend."

"She lives in the States?"

Sofie held up her hand to silence him. "I don't want to talk about her," she said quietly, her memory still too raw for any explanations.

"Why?"

"I said *no*." Sofie knew she'd end up crying if she shared that loss too. His incessant questions felt like sandpaper rubbing against her heart. She'd revealed too much already. "You married?"

"No. I'm single. Why do you ask? Interested?"

"Don't be silly. We already established last night you're an asshole."

He laughed. "I thought I was an *asshole bastard*. But come on, I think you owe me some gratitude."

"For what!? You didn't need to go all macho on that guy. I could have taken care of him."

"Yeah. That's what it looked like."

"I told you last night that I can take care of myself." She stared at him. "It's none of your business what I do."

Alex raised both hands in surrender. "Hey, you're right. It's the eighties. You're free to get into as much trouble as you want."

"Didn't you get the memo? Women have been liberated. What I do, or don't do—and who I do, or don't do it with—is none of your business!" She gripped the wheel. "You *really* are a pain. And put my purse away! What are you? Some kind of detective?"

A moment passed before he answered, "I study people. That's all. Sofia Morgan Mendoza Davis. You intrigue me."

He'd said her name as if it were a caress. I intrigue him? Sofie couldn't help but notice the catch in her heart. But still…

"*Enough!* Give me my purse." With one hand she grabbed it from his lap and threw it into the back seat. "And give me my wallet."

Alex held it in the air so she couldn't reach it.

"Hey, keep your eyes on the road! Don't freak out." He replaced the sleeve, snapped the wallet shut—something she never did—and tossed it into the back seat with her purse. "There. Satisfied?"

The chasm between them returned. Sofie kept her attention on the road. Alex alternated between gazing at the scenery and napping. The only respite was the children along the way. Then he would hang his body out the window like an oversized sun-bleached dog, yelling *Hola!*, throwing every coin in the car he could scrounge. Their collection was exhausted by the time they reached the river.

Sofie pulled the Mercedes into the dirt near the bridge, parked, and got out of the car. Stretching her legs, she walked to the riverbank.

When she returned, Alex stood beside the car, his arms crossed over his chest.

"It really is beautiful here. What are we doing?" he asked.

"Waiting."

"For what?"

"The boat."

He looked up and down the empty river. "What boat? Nobody said anything about a boat."

"I didn't think I needed to. The boat is going to take us to the ranch. Otherwise, we'll never make it in time for dinner."

"How do you know we haven't already missed it?"

"The boat would be waiting. They know we're coming."

"You're going to leave a new Mercedes here?" he asked, glancing around the deserted lot. "What about the poverty stricken neighbors?"

"Nobody would dare touch the Mercedes. I could leave it here a week unlocked and no one would bother it. But don't worry. Somebody will drive the car down to the ranch when the boat comes."

He seemed satisfied. "Sounds good. I'm hungry. Will anybody else be joining us?"

"Not that I know of. But I didn't think we were expecting guests in the first place."

"Will all of your cousins be there?" Alex asked.

"I guess so. I had plans in the city tonight, but now I'm babysitting you."

"Then we're even." He leaned against the passenger door. "Don't worry, sweetheart, it will be over soon."

"Not soon enough... *Darling.*" Sofie teased, joining him at the car.

With Alex only a few inches away, she could detect his mesmerizing scent and see the sun-bleached hair on his forearms. He stared straight ahead, and she wondered what he watched behind the sunglasses.

Last night, when he'd pulled Alabama off of her in the hallway, she had no doubt Alex could be downright scary. Today, she'd discovered a softer side of him.

Sofie didn't know what to think. Turning to him, she asked, "What kind of business do you have with my cousins anyway?"

He took off the sunglasses. "The usual."

The blue irises of his eyes widened as his pupils constricted in the sunlight.

Sofie wasn't psychic. "What do you mean by *the usual?*"

Birds called across the surrounding jungle. She refused to look away, demanding an answer.

After a few moments he blinked. "I have a warehouse in Chicago. I'm importing goods from Mexico to sell in the Midwest."

"I know my cousins have moved into the import-export business. Ramón told me last night. What I'm asking is—What. Exactly. Do. You. Import?" she said firmly. "You have so many questions for me. Why is it so hard to get answers from you?"

Alex stepped away from the car. With his back to her, Sofie watched the seductive play of muscles underneath his black T-shirt.

Picking up a handful of flat rocks, he skipped them, one by one, into the sluggish river. It took awhile for him to speak. "Dry goods. Fabric. Furniture. Sometimes even coffee. Things manufactured or grown in Central and South America."

When the rocks were gone, he walked back to the car. "We've found there's a growing demand for Latin imports in the United States and want to tap into the market. I've brought the financials. I'd be happy to let you go over them when we get to the ranch."

Something felt off. But she didn't have the right questions to get a straight answer. "Why would I want to do that?"

"Ramón gave me the impression you've joined the business on the financial end last night."

The nerve of some men. Particularly Ramón and his unrelenting assumptions. Of course Alex would think she was going to stay down here and work for the family.

"Ramón is pressuring me to. But I already have a job lined up in Los Angeles that I'm supposed to start in the fall. I'm not sure what I'm going to do. The only thing I know for sure is I'm tired of meeting everyone else's expectations."

"USC right?"

"UCLA," she corrected.

"SC has a better football team."

Sofie smirked. "Why am I not surprised?" Then she remembered last fall's game. She took the tiny pleasure and savored it. "We beat SC by ten points last November."

Alex blew her off. "Your team got lucky. You don't want to go into accounting?"

"I didn't say that. I've spent four years busting my bottom for the grades to stay on the dean's list. I want to take some time off before I begin the grind of building a career. I haven't taken the Certified Public Account's exam yet. I'm supposed to be back in LA to start the prep classes in the fall, and I'm not positive I'll even make those. I needed a break this summer. This is the perfect place to take one… That is, until you came along."

Alex settled his eyes over her head, onto the river. "I won't be here long. Your chauffeuring days are over unless you plan on piloting the boat too. Here it comes."

CHAPTER FIVE

Rio del Paraiso

River to Paradise
Friday, July 6, 1984

Buzzing with excitement, Alex stood at the bow of the fishing boat and watched the river wind in front of him. Other than Nick, no one from the agency had ever been this close to the family's inner circle, and by Alex's estimation, he'd been on their property for miles now.

It didn't appear many fish had been snagged off this remarkably clean vessel. The lazy river was a surprise. Deep enough for the boat to navigate upstream where they'd parked the Mercedes. Along the bank, trees, low palms and shrubs grew in tangles, dipping branches into the soupy green water.

The pitch of the engine broke through the jungle as the boat churned toward the ocean. Sofie stayed in the back, near the pilot. She'd begun to mellow some in the car, answering his questions, thanks to the kids who ran alongside the road and thawed the silence between them. And even though Sofie had been pissed when he went through her wallet, she'd opened up, shading the lines of her story with details only she could provide.

Alex had learned several facts so far: Sofie was here on vacation; she'd been born in the United States; her middle name was Morgan. He still thought it was ridiculous, giving a man's name to such a tiny girl. But there was no denying she had grown into a stunning woman. A strong dose of women's lib permeated her consciousness. However, she seemed vulnerable. And even though Ramón said she was working for the family, Sofie disagreed and seemed confused about her direction. She spoke Spanish, and had spent years living in Mexico when she was younger.

Obviously, she had stronger ties to the family than the team anticipated.

Some of Sofie's revelations made him wonder if they had more in common than he'd realized. Alex also had questions about his future, and was disconnected from his parents too, although they were both alive and long married.

Sofie seemed clueless about the drug trafficking. She wasn't sure where she'd be in the fall. Alex wondered if this was a ruse, and she'd already chosen to stay and work for her family, deliberately hiding the information from him.

He needed more answers. But it was as if they'd been airline seat mates who'd bonded in flight and now had gone back to being strangers at the baggage carousel.

Thick with heat, the air was moist, and the surrounding jungle was rich with the earthy smell of living vegetation on the threshold of decay. Sweat dripped beneath Alex's T-shirt, shellacking his arms and legs.

Sofie stood at the railing wearing her big sunglasses. Alex watched the black curls swirl around her beautiful face as she struggled to manage the chaos against the wind. His imagination clicked into gear when she discretely lifted the skirt of her thin sundress to fan herself. Alex suspected the tawny skin of her thighs would feel as silky in his hands as they looked.

Light caught one of her diamond earrings and bounced a tiny ball of reflection whenever she moved. Unlike any woman he'd met before, she had an allure he couldn't deny. He turned and focused on the river. She wasn't his type. This thing—this attraction he instinctively felt for this girl —couldn't get in the way and distract him from his mission.

Her perfume, a clean, tropical mixture of flowers, announced her arrival before she laid her hand on his shoulder. When Alex turned, she quickly pulled it away, as if she suddenly remembered he wasn't her type either.

She pushed the sunglasses into her hair and pointed out the clay tiles of a rooftop on the bank ahead. "That's the hacienda my great grandfather built."

"It looks like the jungle has already reclaimed it."

"I know. My mom grew up here. She died in the bedroom on the left. See that crumbling door on the balcony?"

The whitewashed building, with dilapidated wood doors, had deteriorated into a shell of its once modest grandeur.

"It's where we lived before Ramón built the house by the ocean. I'm not complaining, the new location is beautiful. But it isn't really a house—it's more of a compound."

Her black eyelashes glistened. Alex couldn't tell if it was caused by the boat pushing against the wind or her grief.

"I have so many memories here. I love this place. And the jungle is stealing it away."

Of course the loss of her mother had scarred her. *How could it not?* And it hadn't been the only tragedy. She'd refused to discuss her cousin Ceci in the car. He'd recognized the girl's face from the strip of photos and couldn't blame Sofie. A fresh wound, barely scabbed, didn't tolerate picking.

Alex could relate. Whatever sympathy he had for Sofie's grief disappeared when his mind flashed on Nick's wife and boys.

She wiped at her eyes. "Avalon."

"What?"

"This was my mom's Avalon," she explained. "My mom was fascinated with Arthurian legends. She used to read them to me. There's so much more than the famous love triangle between Sir Lancelot, Guinevere, and King Arthur." She swept a handful of hair away from her face. "Avalon is the mythical island I told you about. It's where Arthur is buried."

"Yes, the enchanting Morgan, the king, and his sword."

"Morgan ruled Avalon. It's where Excalibur was forged."

Alex caught the warmth in Sofie's clear, emerald eyes. "How's this your mother's Avalon?"

Sofie seemed fixed someplace beyond the bank. "Avalon was an island paradise where everything was provided. It's how my mom thought of this place. The land, the river, the sea. My mom said it was all she needed," Sofie whispered.

Alex leaned in close, careful not to distract her.

"Sometimes I wonder why she came to the United States in the first place, if she loved it here so much. I guess my dad lured her away. Or maybe she didn't learn to appreciate home until she left. Maybe she didn't realize what she'd lost until she didn't have it anymore. Now it's too late to ask. I'll never know."

Alex wondered if Sofie realized she'd spoken out loud. Who was she really talking about—her mother or herself?

Was this the connection that made her willing to take such a big risk and go to work for her family? She must be motivated by a need to return to her heritage—la familia—her mother's home. Was it a place she believed she'd be provided for and protected, like this mythical Avalon she talked about?

There was no way Sofie could be that naive.

She seemed lost, hugging her sides while she searched the jungle. He wanted to comfort her, but he wagered she'd push him away after last night, embarrassed and angry. So he gripped the wood railing of the boat.

"Morgan brought King Arthur to Avalon so he could recuperate from a battle. She was his half-sister."

Sofie moved toward Alex and brushed against his arm. A jolt of desire shot through his body.

"Like Arthur, my mom came home to her family. King Arthur had Merlin. My mom searched for her own magician. She didn't get better because there is no magic. There's just death, and the rest of us, who have to keep on living."

Amen, he thought. *You're right, Sofie. But you forgot one more thing. Justice.*

Alex, the cynic, had to consider the possibility her memories may be manufactured. He rejected the idea, deciding he projected his own conscience—if he had one at this point—onto her.

Earlier in the car, he surprised himself, giving her bits of truth weaved into his fabrications. He wasn't worried. Millions of other Americans had the same history. His facts were so intertwined with fiction, there would be no way anyone could track him down once the operation was over.

The best lies always held a kernel of truth.

Sofie stood trembling next to him. It would be such a simple act to place his hand on top of hers. But he couldn't. A vague sense of guilt? Trepidation? *Something* he didn't understand wouldn't let him.

Across the river, on the bank, Alex spied the saw-toothed ridges of a crocodile sunbathing along a thick branch dipping into the water. Shattering the melancholy moment, he pointed it out. "Look!"

"Gross." Sofie shivered. "They are so creepy." She wiped beneath her eyes, leaving sad smudges behind. "When we were kids, my cousins and I stayed away from the river, afraid of crocodiles. Slimy river bottoms freak me out. I'd rather have sand under my feet." Turning to him, she added, "I've never actually seen one along this river before... Maybe I wasn't paying enough attention."

"If you do, you'll find surprises everywhere."

A gull circled above, and Alex smelled the briny scent of the ocean ahead. The sun had already begun to slide into the horizon, shading the lonely dock emerging in the distance.

❦

When they arrived, Esteban waited for them at the landing with Victor and a young man who appeared to be one of the houseboys. Alex ushered Sofie out of the boat. She didn't flinch when he touched her, and her skin was velvet beneath his fingers.

Taking her hand, Esteban gave her a kiss on the cheek.

"Welcome. I hope your trip was pleasant," he said. "Ramón wanted to meet you, but he had to take a call. He'll join us for drinks before dinner."

Alex grabbed his briefcase and started for the luggage. The houseboy was already working his way up the stairs with his duffle. The pilot held Sofie's small overnight bag. Apparently, she didn't plan on staying long. Why should she? A whole city awaited her.

Esteban noticed too. "That's all you brought?"

She shrugged. "It's all I thought I needed."

He led the way up the stairs, past the sweeping lawns of the impressive estate. Sitting on top of the plateau, several sand colored buildings, of varied heights, were connected by latticed walkways. Surrounded by lush tropicals, brilliant pink bougainvilleas climbed up the walls and across the latticework, not only providing shade, but giving the modern structures a distinctly Mexican feel. Tall glass panels, two stories high in some places, showcased the main building.

Ramón had chosen the location wisely. Well-placed, the property had a spectacular vista of the ocean, the river, and the surrounding area.

At the top of the stairs, they followed the pathway past the main building and came to a large courtyard. As Alex took in the shimmering pool, groupings of patio tables, and an outdoor bar, he decided he'd seen swanky resorts with less elegant set-ups. Esteban sent Alex off with the houseboy, toward a low, complementing rectangle, which appeared to be the guest quarters. Glancing at Alex, Sofie silently followed Esteban into the main house.

The houseboy showed Alex the eccentricities of the ultra-modern room and said he'd be back in an hour to escort him to dinner. The illusion of a high-end hotel was so disconcerting, Alex instinctively reached for his wallet to give him a tip, then kept his hand in his pocket, thinking better of the gesture.

Behind the curtains, sliding doors led to a generous lawn. Waves broke onto blinding white sand at the bottom of a cliff. He already knew the warehouses were secured further inland. Alex was impressed. Straddling both the Pacific and the river, the property was not only protected, but a perfect location for the Mendozas to monitor activity.

After Alex showered, he unpacked and put his briefcase on the dresser. He kept it unlocked, knowing his luggage would be inspected when he went to dinner. Checking the room for surveillance equipment and finding it clean, he took the pocketknife from his shaving kit, then unscrewed an air-conditioning vent, hiding his .45 caliber and magazines there. If all went as planned, he'd have no need for the gun over the weekend anyway.

He lay down on the bed and cradled his hands behind his head. Instead of resting, Alex cataloged everything he'd brought with him, down to his socks and toothpaste, considering once again if any of it could provoke suspicion.

Soon, his thoughts gravitated to the irritating, lovely, and *confusing* Sofie. Alex had to admit that more than once, he'd found himself infatuated, mulling over possibilities that had nothing to do with his job.

He might not be able to help the attraction, but it was up to him to monitor his response.

Sofie's sadness along the river seemed genuine. On the other hand, it occurred to him again that he might not be the only actor playing a role. If she had been acting, she was flawless. Ramón may have planned to have her drive him to the ranch all along. Her questions may have been designed to test him, possibly to catch Alex off guard and give him a false sense of security.

Alex wasn't worried. The books were airtight. He'd every reason to believe his company would be accepted and the deal would be made. His life literally depended on it.

Whatever her motivation, Sofie, Ramón's newest star, was in the thick of the production—and a puzzle Alex had yet to solve. Why did she dump her boyfriend and choose to move to Mexico to be under her cousin's thumb? Was it really all about family?

Alex wondered if she realized what she'd gotten herself into. Sofie couldn't be oblivious to what went on all around her. The city was saturated with dope, her cousins directing the trade.

Despite her protestations, he didn't believe for a second she hadn't planned to join the family business. If Sofie didn't want to be involved, she should have stayed in California. Ramón didn't accept refusals from anyone, even family. Alex tried to untangle these knots until, exactly one hour later, Mendoza's man arrived to escort him to dinner.

CHAPTER SIX

Calor de la Noche

Night Heat
Friday, July 6, 1984

Sofie slipped off her sandals and opened the closet doors, looking for something to wear to dinner. There were only a couple of outfits in her size; the rest of the closet was cluttered with Monica's more voluptuous things. The choices were slim: A black rayon jumpsuit Sofie loved and forgot to pack from her last visit, and another sundress in a different style, red this time. Unable to decide, she left the doors ajar and unpacked the rest of her clothes.

The spacious bedroom had been selected by Ramón for the girls in the family, and he'd let Monica have a hand in the decorating. They'd done a remarkable job. Like the rest of the house, the bedroom was modern but comfortable. The massive bed was surrounded by an exposition in white. Splashes of lavender had been used in the linens and accents throughout the room. An excellent palette, Sofie decided, because purple had been her mom's favorite color.

A bouquet of fresh flowers filled the room with delicate perfume. She turned up the air-conditioning and opened the curtains. One of the houseboys waved his skimmer through the azure pool in the courtyard below. Not far in the distance, down a concrete walkway, was the ocean, where clusters of thick, bowed palms shaded the edge of the sand.

Countless afternoons had been spent playing on this beach with her cousins. Since summer began, she'd let the city bewitch her, and she'd forgotten how much she loved the ranch. She watched a trio of dolphins play beyond the surf line and promised herself she'd spend more time in the countryside near her mom. Here, she could clear her head and make sensible decisions.

Unlatching the sliding door, she stepped out onto the balcony. The whisper of a cool breeze passed by and promised some relief when the sun set.

The guest quarters were shaded by well-maintained tropical plants along the walkway to the beach. What was Alex up to? She let her imagination run wild, starting with the smooth line of his masculine jaw. Would the faint stubble create the perfect mixture of rough satin against her skin, she wondered, before pushing the rebellious thought aside.

Yes, it was nice to have a quasi guy friend again, but that's all Alex was. At times, he could be almost nice, at others, well, predictably exasperating. She knew so little about him, but that hadn't kept her from answering his incessant questions, revealing more of herself to Alex than she had to any man in months.

The reason wasn't a surprise. Sofie valued the honest companionship and perspective of the men in her life. Ben, not only a lover, had also been a friend. It was over. And she and Gabriel had been close in the past. However, he was distant and withdrawn this summer.

The tide eased its way back in for the night along the beach. Earlier, when they went by the old hacienda, she'd been unprepared for the rush of feelings that had emerged. Alex hadn't done a thing to comfort her as the boat passed the house.

Emotional needs made her try to massage Alex into someone he wasn't. Embarrassed, Sofie had to admit she didn't feel as liberated as she pretended to be. *What am I thinking?*

"Grow up, Sofie," she whispered.

She opened the slider and stepped back into her room. A shock of icy air raised goose bumps on her arms. Noticing the crystal bowl filled with sea glass on the dresser, Sofie picked up a handful and trapped a large amethyst nugget in her palm, letting the others filter through her fingers. Some claimed Avalon was an island made of glass. Sofie, with thoughts of Arthurian legends, rubbed the smooth chunk of violet, knowing her mom watched over her.

Crossing the plush carpet to the closet, Sofie again considered her choices. The jumpsuit was wrinkled, so she left it on the doorknob for the maid to press. Snatching the red dress from the hanger, she made her way to the shower, and remembered—with the tiniest glimmer of hope—that

Monica had once said the color made Sofie stand out in a crowd.

❦

Wrong again Monica, Sofie thought. No one seemed to notice her, or the red dress, when she entered the living room. Alex stood by the windows, deep in a conversation with her cousin Marco.

As the ranch foreman, Marco spent most of his time on the property. His new wife, Estella, had yet to arrive, making Sofie the only girl in the room. She liked Estella, an intelligent and friendly, but quiet, girl, who spoke little English. Now Sofie wondered if she'd be joining them for dinner at all.

Alex had cleaned up well. A white cotton dress shirt highlighted his surfer-boy tan and Levi's hugged his hips. He didn't have the physique of someone obsessed with himself—like she'd assumed earlier in the car— spending hours in front of a mirror, and wasting time in the gym all day. More likely, Alex had honed his broad shoulders and taut body with hard, physical labor.

Then why didn't he know anything about cars? Something about him didn't add up, but she couldn't nail it down.

When she'd come into the room, he hadn't even bothered to nod. Apparently, Sofie was invisible. Pushing away the disappointment, she smoothed the front of her dress and wondered where Gabriel and Ramón were. Gabriel had better show, because if he didn't, he'd be facing Ramón's inevitable wrath.

Esteban waved to her while mixing drinks behind the bar. His size, hair, and full beard invariably reminded Sofie of a friendly bear. She met him, and he poured her a glass of California Chardonnay before they crossed the expanse of the room with everyone's drinks.

Marco took his whiskey, set it on the credenza, and hugged her. "Sofia, it's good to see you."

Sofie greeted him, slipped out of his embrace, and glanced at Alex.

"Alex." Unable to shake the anticipation, Sofie tried to sound disinterested. *I can play this game too.*

He nodded and asked Marco, "Did you build next to the old warehouse?"

"We found a new location close to the river…"

She should feel relieved Alex was ignoring her. Sofie took a sip of wine and sat down on the edge of a butter-colored couch, nestled in one of two seating areas at each end of the room. This was her second favorite area of the house. Ramón had chosen a perfect blend of color and materials—a collage in various shades of white and cream. A two-story wall of glass overlooked the countryside. A pair of large area rugs, commissioned by Ramón and brought down from the States, covered polished mahogany floors. Splashes of color were displayed in the original art hanging on the walls. Priceless Zapotec statues and artifacts Ramón had acquired tastefully adorned the rest of the room.

Uninterested in the men's discussion, Sofie toyed with the chain of her silver heart, checked the V of her neckline for modesty—*good, nothing exposed* —and spied Alex from the corner of her eye. Her enigma, so close yet so distracted, hadn't even smiled in her direction.

Ramón came into the room greeting everyone, and joined the men near the window. Felipe followed, quietly slipping through the doorway. Esteban went to the bar for more drinks.

Gabriel was still missing.

"Alex, did you enjoy the drive?" Ramón asked.

Surprisingly, Alex glanced her way, nodded, and grinned.

Their eyes met, and Alex held her gaze. There was a twinkle in them that told her he'd been acutely aware of her presence all along. Or maybe it was the dress working its magic. Whatever the reason, Sofie was delighted.

He looked away and focused on Ramón. "My chauffeur was exceptional."

She blushed and wondered if the compliment contained a hidden gibe.

Sofie's cousins noticed her reaction and laughed.

"Your home is spectacular. Marco is telling me about the rest of the ranch. I'm looking forward to a tour," Alex said.

The men thankfully returned to their earlier conversation. Sofie didn't want to get caught studying Alex, so she moved to the far side of the window. Below, the village began to twinkle as the evening unfolded. The only other sign of civilization was the occasional bead of light miles away.

Gabriel finally arrived. Sofie met him at the bar, watching him while he rummaged through the refrigerator. His wet, black hair had been combed back from his forehead. Had he come from the pool or the shower?

"When did you get in?" she asked in Spanish.

He opened a beer, glanced at Ramón, and took a gulp. "A half-hour ago."

Watching, Ramón arched an eyebrow from across the room, then returned his attention to the men.

Gabriel brought the beer to his lips again.

Even in the air-conditioned room, Gabriel's cologne was thick, stifling. "Where have you been? Ramón was looking for you today." She tilted her head in Alex's direction. "I got stuck bringing surfer boy, over there, out this afternoon. Isn't that your job?"

"I'm busy. It couldn't have hurt that bad to spend a couple of hours with him."

"After last night—"

"So you had to do the Hustle with a cowboy who can't dance. What's so hard?" His voice had an edge of impatience she hadn't heard before. He took another swig and glanced around the room.

"Are people still doing the Hustle?" Sofie didn't expect an answer. "I don't think he could Hustle if his life depended on it. You know how much I hate driving."

"Grow up. Get over it."

The comment stung.

"Alex Wilson can be arrogant and controlling." She didn't mention the magnetic pull that recharged whenever he was nearby.

"I saw you two in the shadows. What happened?"

Taking a step back, she glanced towards the windows. This wasn't the time or place to explain.

"Never mind. I don't want to hear you whine about your problems." Gabriel's pupils were tight in flinty eyes. "So you did Ramón a favor. Try living my life. He rides me constantly, wanting to know where I am and what I'm doing. He gives me odd jobs to do with no authority to make a decision—'check with me first' or 'run it by Esteban' is all he says. I'm sick of being just another houseboy."

Sofie *really* took in Gabriel's appearance for the first time in weeks. Her cousin was pale. Purple pools of skin settled in deep crescents beneath his eyes. Something was wrong.

She touched his shoulder. He flinched but didn't move away. "You seem tired."

"I am. Long days, even longer nights. I need some sleep."

"Get some."

"I would have if Ramón hadn't insisted I join the family for dinner."

"You could use a good meal. You're looking pretty thin these days."

"Don't start in on me too." he growled.

"I'm sorry, Gabriel. I don't mean to hassle you, I just want to help.

Don't you feel well? You look exhausted. What's going on?"

Moving away, he finished his beer, bent down, and buried himself in the refrigerator, pulling out another one. "I'm not sick. Nothing is going on. I need some *sleep*."

Teodoro, a member of the staff who'd been with the family for years, entered the room and announced dinner was served.

Gabriel slammed the refrigerator door and his voice boomed through the room, "And I'd like to get this fucking dinner over with so I can get some!"

"Perfect timing," Ramón sarcastically replied in Spanish.

❦

Ramón ushered Sofie to a chair across from Alex in the dining room. She had no choice but to sit down. Alex sent her a polite smile, and the undeniable, familiar flutter in her stomach intensified.

She had hoped to sit next to Gabriel, who'd moved to a seat at the other end of the table. If she could explain her concern and figure out what was wrong, maybe he would grace her with his wicked grin, the one she'd rarely seen this summer.

The dining room sat high above the ocean. Down the hillside, a canopy of palm fronds were underlit by landscape lighting. Beyond that, the glow of a ship cruising towards Panama spilled starlight on the water, while a sliver of vermillion sank into a remnant of the day.

One of the staff placed a bowl of Rosa's delicious Albondigas soup in front of Sofie, and she picked up her spoon.

Halfway through her soup, Ramón addressed her from the head of the long glass table. "Sofia, tell us about the drive down."

Placing her spoon by the bowl, she said, "Not much to tell."

"I found it quite interesting," Alex piped in, leaning back in his chair.

Sofie prayed he wouldn't describe the ransacking of her purse.

Alex had everyone's attention. He grinned and said to Ramón, "We threw coins to the kids alongside the road. She had me clean out my pockets. Then we emptied her purse of change too."

It wasn't a surprise when Ramón's smile collapsed.

Great. Thanks, Alex. Here we go…

"Sofia. I am disappointed in you," Ramón said, as if on cue. "We have already had this discussion. I do not want you encouraging beggars."

Turning to Alex, Ramón said, "Leave them be. We try to handle the poverty here, but I have discovered there is a certain class stubbornly reluctant to work. They make their living by begging instead. And they encourage their children to do it as well. It is pathetic. Some guests who come to our beautiful country say the beggars frighten them. I can understand."

With his fork, Ramón cut into a meatball swimming with vegetables in broth. He popped half of it into his mouth, chewed and swallowed. "In Acapulco, when visitors take a boat tour around the bay, there are boys at the dock begging for you to throw coins in the water so they can fish them out. There is some honor there, entertaining the tourists for pesos. But children running along the side of the road chasing cars? There is no honor there. *Dogs* chase after cars."

Ramón laughed and nearly everyone laughed along with him. Except Sofie and Alex. Felipe, with one arm resting useless on the table, kept his head low, spooning soup into his mouth.

Sofie felt a crimson burn rush up her face. Ramón was pathetic, not the children who were reduced to begging. They had argued about this before, but never in front of guests. The embarrassment was hard to place. It was humiliating to be dressed down at dinner by her cousin, particularly in front of Alex. But Ramón's arrogance was disgraceful. With plenty of influence and money, their family had at least some responsibility. They could do more to help the situation if they wanted to.

Crossing her arms, she sat quietly fuming. Even though Mendoza blood flowed through her veins, ultimately, she was a guest in this country too.

Alex grinned, winked at Sofie, and turned to Ramón. "It's a trend these days in American universities for students to feel it's their responsibility to stick up for the *underdog*."

Sofie kicked at Alex beneath the table, missing his shin.

"After spending the afternoon with Sofie, I've realized she's a generous young woman. First, she gave up her plans for the day to drive me here. Then, when we saw the children, well…" He smiled in her direction.

Yeah, right, I was so gracious around the pool. Sofie wondered where he was planning to go with this.

"Her enthusiastic charm couldn't help but rub off and I'm sure I egged her on," he said diplomatically.

Sofie couldn't believe it. Alex was rescuing her again.

Before she could speak for herself, Alex changed the subject, "What were all of those groves we passed? Are those papaya plantations?"

Papaya plantations?

Ramón schooled Alex on the history of the papaya while the ceviche was served.

Drumming her fingers on the table, Sofie seethed. Yes, it had been kind of Alex to stand up for her, but…

A quick pass through her wallet and Alex thought he knew everything, including her college experience? More importantly, Alex didn't think she could hold her own with Ramón. Of course she could. But not here, not now. With no other choice, she did her best to concentrate on the meal and ignore the rest of the room.

The men soon returned to the subject of education. Focusing on the merits of a college diploma in the business world. It wasn't a surprise when Ramón didn't bother to ask for her opinion, even though she'd just received a diploma of her own.

Sofie watched Gabriel, further down the table. A group of the younger cousins had forged a camaraderie many of their elders couldn't understand. In the past, Sofie and Gabriel might be separated for years, but once they reconnected, it seemed they'd only been apart for hours.

She accepted all of the blame for the distance. Their ties had unraveled because she'd been preoccupied by her own recent challenges—senior year and the crisis of her breakup with Ben—to pay much attention to his.

Tonight, Sofie and Gabriel sat at opposite ends of the room, and no chatter or funny faces passed between them like the old days. Hopefully, she would get a chance to talk to him and clear the air.

Sofie returned her attention to Alex and found him studying her. Their eyes met, and he smiled. Some of her anger towards him couldn't help but fade away. Her stomach felt like she was at Magic Mountain, cresting Colossus. Shy under such close scrutiny, she felt a blush rise, the heat spreading across her cheeks.

Ramón's pontification shattered the intimate exchange.

"…It's been beneficial for a farmer and businessman like myself to forgo higher education and move directly into the family business, learning the— how do you say it in English?" He looked to Alex and Sofie for an answer. "I remember—ropes." Seemingly satisfied, Ramón pointed his finger into the air, creating a visual exclamation point. "Learning the ropes from the ground up…"

Between courses, Ramón stood and moved to the window.

It was hard to pay attention to his words with Alex so close. She didn't have to look; Sofie *sensed* the intense connection build between them.

Sofie had to be imagining things. She glanced in his direction for confirmation.

Alex's gaze was fixated on her.

A moment passed before she looked away. She attempted to focus on Ramón's back, when Alex was the only man in the room who mattered.

What was he sending? Admiration? Speculation? Tentatively, she glanced at him again and Alex's eyes conveyed the palpable message—*I want you.*

I want you too.

In her belly, the roller coaster crested the peak, plummeting into a delightful abyss. The revelation left her exhilarated, then so confused, she had to look away, taking a sudden interest in the smudges on the glass table.

Ramón said something. The men laughed. Except for Alex, who pulled her in again with his eyes.

The spell didn't break until Ramón returned to the table.

"...Like my father and grandfather, I found it highly valuable to spend time in each aspect of the family business, from start to finish. This is how we have succeeded. Another secret of our family's fortune," Ramón said.

"Felipe is only our spiritual protection. A gift from the church," he explained. "Our own personal priest in residence."

Sofie had heard it all before.

Felipe shifted in his chair, covering his withered arm with the healthy one, uncomfortable as usual with being the focus of Ramón's attention.

"None of my brothers, nor I, have college educations, and look around you," Ramón said, expanding his arms, "We've become quite accomplished."

"However, the old methods of business are on the decline. A college education will be much more valuable in the future, actually necessary. We have Sofía here—"

She choked on a forkful of chicken.

"Our cousin has a fine degree from an outstanding university. Sofía will become a valuable asset to our business and its future success," Ramón said proudly.

Sofie had been pushed to the edge. "I haven't decided what my plans are yet."

"Of course, *mi amor*," Ramón said with a wave of his hand. "I have great faith in your capabilities and your commitment to our family. All of the

Mendozas have been given this legacy. The love you have for your mother, my Tía Olivia—may God bless her soul—and her home, *your home, Sofia*, is evident to us all. You are an intelligent young woman. I trust you will make the right decision."

❦

Sofie stood barefoot on the balcony and let the cool air waft around her thin cotton nightgown. Below, within the subtle illumination of the foliage, dreamy shadows danced around the perimeter of the courtyard. In the center, the breeze stippled the swimming pool. The trip past the old hacienda, Ramón's dressing down, and Alex, left her unsettled.

On nights like this, the hint of lingering grief that always throbbed below the surface intensified, and Sofie missed her mom more than ever. Tía Sofia provided an open door and understanding when Sofie felt this way over the years. But she was in Los Angeles, two thousand miles north.

Much of Sofie's normal childhood disappeared when the cancer exploded in her mom's body, eating it away. Each night before bed, Sofie would visit her mom's room to get her unruly hair braided. In a house full of family, it became cherished private time. Her mom would soothingly rake her fingers through Sofie's hair, laying one plait over the last, while Sofie shared her day. Friends. Cousins. Missing her dad. Adjusting to life on the ranch. Sofie's mom always delivered welcome advice. And afterwards, while her mom dropped off to sleep, Sofie would read to her the Arthurian legends Sofie had grown to love too.

Tonight, she looked around the courtyard. Most of the rooms were dark. Apparently, everyone else had retired. Sofie willfully put aside an attempt to define what was happening with Alex and concentrated on something less confusing—how to maneuver around Ramón's manipulation. For the millionth time, she wished her mom was still alive to help her sort things through, because she was getting nowhere on her own.

She surveyed the blizzard of stars and silently called to her mom, asking for some clarity, a sign that would help her focus on a future with some direction.

Breaking waves, reverberating up from the beach, were the only answer.

Suddenly, she shivered, as if a breath of frigid wind had blown in off of the ocean. She leaned against the railing and crossed her arms, trembling with dread and the certainty that big changes were coming, a personal earthquake of a magnitude she wasn't sure she could endure.

Then she reminded herself the shake-up had already arrived—

graduation and the breakup with Ben. She'd crossed those waters, bruised by love maybe, but not scarred. Making it this far, she tried to convince herself she'd be able to handle whatever challenges she'd yet to face.

And it's time I design my own future.

She watched the door open to Alex's room. He quietly closed it and followed the path down to the beach.

What's he up to now? Returning to her bedroom, she replaced her nightgown with a T-shirt and shorts. No shoes, no bra, no panties. No time to rationalize her behavior.

❦

Sofie stepped onto the sand and saw Alex, a lone shadow walking the beach. She hesitated for a moment, unsure if he'd welcome her company.

Finding her courage, she ran to catch up with him anyway. "Hey."

Startled, he turned. "What are you doing here?"

"I couldn't sleep." She kicked at the sand caking her feet and let a foamy wash of saltwater pull on her toes. "You too?"

Alex had changed into shorts and was barefoot now.

"Yep."

"The breeze is nice. It's a relief."

"Hmm."

Maybe it had been a mistake to join him. Now, she wasn't sure why she'd decided to come down in the first place. But she didn't want to go back. Not yet.

They walked in silence while a silvery band of moonlight began to widen across the water.

"Wanna talk?"

He stopped abruptly. "You don't want to work for Ramón?"

Sofie kept walking. She didn't want to talk about her cousin.

Once Alex caught up, she said, "Let's talk about you. Haven't you already heard enough from me?"

He didn't answer.

Sofie sighed. "I told you. I haven't decided what my plans are." Her college degree had been so highly praised at dinner, it occurred to her Alex might want to pull out of the deal if she wasn't on board. "If you're worried about going into business with Ramón, whether I work for him or not shouldn't be a concern. He knows what he's doing. Always has."

"That wasn't the question."

Sofie tried to dodge a breaking wave, and Alex switched positions with

74

her.

He can be a gentleman after all, she thought. "Why do you care?"

Taking her arm, Alex turned her toward him. She could feel his sweet, warm breath on her face. It was difficult to decipher his expression in the moonlight. "I'm curious."

Moments passed before he added. "Like I said, you intrigue me."

When they were driving in the car, Sofie believed this might have been one of Alex's standard lines. She suspected he truly meant it now. Her heart did a somersault. *I intrigue him.*

Alex let go—Sofie wished he hadn't—and continued walking down the beach.

She called after him, "I don't really know why I don't want to work for the family."

Sofie caught up and reached for his arm. "That's the most truthful answer I can give. I don't have a good reason except I feel the equal pull of two lives: one in California, and the other here in Mexico. My mom's memory draws me here. California? It's my home. I thought I'd built a life there—my future was there. I'm not so sure anymore."

"What happened in California?"

"It's an old story. Ben and I dated through college. I thought things were more serious than he did. When I graduated this spring, I wanted to take the next step. Apparently, he had other plans."

As she walked along the beach with Alex, a life with Ben seemed a long, long time ago.

"How—"

Sofie waved the next question off with her hand. "You've explored my purse and rummaged through my whole life. I hardly know anything about yours."

"There's nothing exciting to tell."

"Is it so weird that I'd want to know something about you?"

A sizable swell came in and Alex nudged her up the beach. Even so, warm water rushed in and swirled around her knees.

They both laughed.

"I can't figure this out," she said.

"What's to figure? I can't sleep. You can't sleep either, so you met me down here. If you want small talk, you ask the questions."

She smiled, assuming it was too dark for him to notice. "Hmmm."

"Shoot."

"Well, since college was a big topic tonight and you're so well-informed, did you go to college?"

"Yes."

"Where?"

"Boston University."

Sofie took her turn and gently nudged Alex back. "East coast. Interesting. I've only been to Manhattan. My Tía Sofia took my cousin Ceci and I there once. A forest of tall buildings. Great shopping."

"Who's Tía Sofia?"

"She's my aunt. Ceci's mom. No wonder you said colleges were preoccupied with social issues. Isn't Boston a hotbed of Liberalism?"

"So they say."

"Are you a Democrat?"

"I'm not sure what my politics are anymore," Alex answered. "Lots of things liberals do piss me off, but conservatives bother me too. Lately, I consider myself an Independent. Don't know how I'm going to vote in November."

"Isn't an Independent more or less 'live and let live'? Don't get involved? You seemed pretty willing to be involved when you emptied your pockets today." Grinning, she gave him a sideways glance. "Actually, you enjoyed it. That seems pretty liberal to me.

"*By the way*," she added, "I can hold my own with Ramón. Remember 'don't get involved?' Once again, you didn't need to jump in and rescue me."

"Sorry. I was trying to keep the dinner conversation pleasant."

"Yeah, you did." She laughed. "You changed the subject. To papayas."

"It worked."

Sofie stepped on a small, sharp shell. "Ouch!" Hopping, she rubbed her foot. "How did you get into the import business?"

"Are you okay?"

"I'm fine. Don't try to change the subject."

"A roommate from college and I started out in the business a few years after graduation. We worked hard. It grew. We sold it. He packed up and moved to New York. I stayed in Chicago and opened my own company."

"How long have you had it?"

"Three years."

"How old are you?"

"Thirty-two. You?"

"Twenty-three."

"I'm an old man, feeling older by the second." Alex chuckled. "Too old for you."

"I agree. But who said anything about the possibility of there ever being an *us*?"

"Just in case you were thinking along those lines. All of these questions are beginning to feel like an interview."

"No way." Sofie grinned, tempted to push him into the waves.

"Admit it, you're having a good time." Alex said.

"It's more exciting than counting sheep."

"You're comparing me to farm animals? I'm stoked."

She could see Alex's dimple in the moonlight. "You're not that old. You just think you are."

"Tell that to my mother. She thinks I should settle down. I travel a lot. She also wants me to have kids. Two grandkids don't seem to be enough for her. My mom wants more and my sister swears she's done making babies. Expectations…"

Sofie sighed. "People have expectations of me too."

"I've noticed." He grasped her arm just in time and they sidestepped another pool of shallow water rolling in. "Want my opinion?"

His hand was warm and Alex's viewpoint had to be better than trying to decipher the stars. "Sure."

"Don't let your family manipulate you.

"As for me, kids are okay, but I'm not sure if I'll ever have them. They were always some day on the horizon. As I get older, I wonder if it's such a good idea," he said. "The world can be a dangerous place."

"What do you mean?"

"And you. You're at a crossroads. I'd weigh my choices carefully."

How could Alex be so perceptive?

They'd almost reached the mouth of the river. It was time to turn around, and Sofie didn't want to. She could walk along the beach with him all night.

Alex stopped.

Sofie tugged on his hand. "I'm not ready to go back."

"Come here." Alex laced his fingers into hers and led Sofie to the edge of the trees. Lowering her to the sand, he sat down as well.

Sets of ghostly whitecaps rolled in. He smelled delicious, a mixture of deodorant, cologne, and something uniquely *Alex*. She'd noticed it before, and now realized it was a scent she'd remember forever as his own.

"My life is full of options," she said with more confidence than she felt. "I have a degree in a field that's just beginning to open its doors to women. Believe it or not, I'm highly marketable."

Alex brought his hand to Sofie's cheek.

She couldn't help but press her lips into his palm.

"I know you're capable. The world is yours to shape." Alex's face was so close. His breath, minty and hot. "I want you to be smart."

Their lips met, and his mouth was perfect, soft, inviting. Slowly his tongue brushed against hers, and when Sofie responded, the kiss became more intense. Her body molded into his and they both fell back onto the sand.

Here they were beneath palm trees, making out in the middle of the night. Sofie didn't think she even liked the guy this morning, but she had been so wrong.

Alex slid his hand under her T-shirt and caressed her breast. A jolt of electricity shot through her, and she pressed against him, wanting more. She felt his own need hot and firm against her hip. Bunching her T-shirt above her chest, Alex moved away from her mouth, and with a sigh, he brought his lips to her breast, cupping the other with his palm. Warmth spread throughout her being and pooled in her core.

With lightly calloused, perfectly masculine fingers, he started to pull the T-shirt over her head and she moved to reposition herself to help him slip it off.

Suddenly, he groaned and pushed her away. "We need to stop."

"Why?" He'd left her trembling, breathless, and neither her mind or her body understood.

"We just do." He got up and grabbed her hand. "Let's go back."

She snatched it away, hurt and confused.

Alex sighed, turned, and began walking back along the beach towards the compound.

What the hell just happened?

Sofie couldn't believe this. *I'm not a yo-yo!* She'd opened herself to him and he'd rejected her.

Finally, she got up.

He only turned back once to see if she'd followed.

When Sofie arrived at the path to the compound, she was ready to scream. She didn't care who she woke up when she gave Alex a well-deserved piece of her mind. But the courtyard was empty, and the guesthouse dark.

☙

Alex sat on the edge of his bed and waited for Sofie's footsteps to pass on the walkway.

He held his breath when he heard her pause, silently warning—*Keep walking, Sofie. Don't stop. Don't knock. I won't answer. Let's forget about this and go to sleep.*

Alex counted the seconds until he heard her footsteps begin again, then fade.

Shit. This was a first. He'd really fucked up this time. *Royally.* Getting emotionally invested with a Mendoza could lead to nothing good. But this didn't qualify as emotion. Raw desire twisted him into knots, nothing more.

Running his fingers through his hair, Alex knew this was his fault, he hadn't been able to keep himself from watching her at dinner.

It seemed she could barely tolerate his presence most of the time.

Ben was an idiot to let her go. Alex still could feel the memory of her silky skin beneath his hands. When his lips found the pebble of her nipple, he'd heard Nick's voice in his head, saying—*Get your mouth off her tits and get a grip, brother.*

He'd lost his cool and his purpose. Sticking to the basic plan proved easy, but when it came to the details, Sofie had become a major distraction. Alex couldn't let that happen.

On the beach, he'd filled her with more bullshit. There'd been no East Coast college. The only long-term East Coast experience he'd ever had was a miserable tour of duty in Washington. He'd quickly requested a transfer, unable to get out of D.C. fast enough.

Sofie Morgan Mendoza Davis lived up to her namesake; she was enchanting. She had this way of worming into him. With her tiny, perfect body, she'd been compliant, opening herself to him, and eagerly returning his kisses. He'd wanted to take her right there on the beach, and started to, until his common sense—or maybe it really was Nick—reminded him who she was. And where he was.

He'd left her in the dark, bewildered and alone on the sand. No explanation.

With any luck, she'd be pissed again and gone before breakfast. It would be a relief. He could finish the rest of this deal without her around. That is, if he had any luck.

CHAPTER SEVEN

El Rey de las Palmas

The King of the Palms
   Saturday, July 7, 1984

When Ramón entered the courtyard, Sofie looked up from her breakfast, grateful she'd remembered to hide her bleary eyes and wild hair beneath sunglasses and a hat. She hadn't slept much, and she didn't want to answer any of Ramón's probing questions.

Most of the night had been spent staring up at the ceiling, listening to the tide peak and recede, trying to understand what had happened on the beach. Alex had manipulated her with magnetic looks and encouraging words, leading her on. Sofie knew better, but she allowed him to seduce her anyway, even before she'd walked down to the beach and right into his arms.

Sofie was furious with him. But she saved some anger for herself too, for so thoroughly misreading the man. She'd spent the night cycling through a seesaw of emotions. Confused and frustrated, she then switched gears, concentrating on how to avoid Ramón's persistence, contemplating what path she'd follow in the fall. Finally, when dawn began to clarify the shadows in the bedroom, she was finally able to get some sleep.

"Buenos días." Ramón sat down at the table, picked up the carafe of coffee, and refilled his cup.

"Where is everybody?" she asked.

"Esteban and Marco took Alex fishing," he said in Spanish, glancing at the front page of the *New York Times* folded nearby. "When you are finished with breakfast, I would like to see you in my office."

"Can't we talk now? I'm driving back to the city this morning." Despite

80

her fear of driving, especially alone, one decision had been made. There would be no Alex in Acapulco—*Thank God*. She'd deal with Ramón later.

"No. Mi amor," Ramón said, covering Sofie's hand with manicured fingers. "Can't the city live without you one more day? There is a quinceañera this evening. In honor of Teodoro's youngest daughter, Claudia. I am her padrino," he boasted. "The whole village will be coming to celebrate, and you should be here too."

His eyes full of warmth, he watched her carefully.

It must seem like such a small request to Ramón.

Living beneath the umbrella of his hospitality, she decided to give him this simple win. "Okay. But I'm leaving tomorrow morning."

Ramón nodded. "I am going to make a call. I will see you shortly." He tucked the newspaper under his arm, picked up his cup, and disappeared into the house.

Sofie shuffled a plate of Rosa's delicious huevos rancheros around with her fork and wondered why he wanted an office meeting. He could still be irritated over the incident with the kids along the roadside, but then again, it was most likely her lackluster enthusiasm during dinner. He probably planned to cajole her with another round of soft-sell tactics.

Or maybe someone saw me on the beach with Alex.

The first two scenarios should be easy to handle. She was more than ready to discuss the kids, and recently she'd become an expert at being evasive when he tried to wheedle her into joining the family business. Explaining Alex would be difficult. Sofie prayed someone hadn't followed her down to the beach and spied on them in the moonlight, wrapped in each other's arms under the palm trees, Alex's hand up her shirt.

All of her male cousins, excluding Gabriel, who understood these things, were positively Victorian in regards to dating and sex. Especially Ramón, who tolerated only some of Sofie's American habits. In this culture it was expected Ramón would receive reports on her activities. But fortunately, there seemed to hover a silent understanding between the two of them: Never push anything in Ramón's face, and he'd let denial work its magic.

It hadn't been a problem this summer. That is, until now. Ben had been her first and only. Many of her friends coupled like bunnies, so she considered herself practically virginal. Since Ben, and before last night, she'd done nothing except kiss a few of the local boys, young Latin men who'd always been respectful and, like Tomás, controllable.

If Alex hadn't jumped to her rescue at the club, she could have even handled the asshole from Alabama.

After breakfast, Sofie knocked on the closed door of Ramón's office. Situated on the main floor, his office was located down a long corridor where clerical space took up the whole southern wing of the building.

"Come in," he commanded in Spanish.

Entering the room, she recognized Alex's briefcase open on Ramón's desk. He was sifting through its contents.

"I took the liberty of having Victor bring me Alex's briefcase," Ramón said. "These are his financial statements and some additional records I requested. I wanted to get an early start, before I met with him."

With a flash of relief, Sofie realized this was going to be a business meeting. She sat on the edge of the leather couch against the opposite wall. "Won't he be upset you lifted his briefcase from his room? You couldn't wait for him?"

"He will not mind. I am busy this afternoon. And no, I did not want to wait." Ramón's arrogance lingered beneath the familiar veneer of courtesy. "Would you oblige me with a small request? I would like you to look these over. See if you find any discrepancies. Something we might need to explore before we make a final decision on going with him."

"I thought you'd already decided."

"Almost. That is why he flew down here, to finalize the deal. We have had our people up there looking things over too. But everybody plays with their books a little."

"You want me to see if I think he's played a little too much?" Sofie smiled and moved to the chair in front Ramón's desk.

"Do not act so shocked. It is the way business works."

"I know. I'm just surprised to hear you admit it so freely."

"His books have been audited. Alex did it as a favor to me. For assurance. I make it a practice to be very careful who I do business with."

"That's a good practice."

Ramón leaned towards her. "Your experience will bring a fresh eye and may pick up something I have missed." He looked down at the stack of papers in front of him. "As far as I can see, everything is fine. César has seen them also and has not found anything. But he might have missed something too."

"I'll be happy to look at them…this time."

Ramón watched her carefully but didn't respond to her qualification. "It is all here. I will be gone for most of the day. You can use César's office.

Alex should return before lunch. Victor will send him around afterwards to answer any questions. If you find anything that concerns you, please report to me first."

"Of course."

"I will be back late this afternoon. We can talk then."

The sound of a whirling machine led Alex down the hall to the office where Sofie was huddled over his financial records. Running her fingers across a calculator keypad at high speed, she didn't look up when he arrived.

His empty briefcase sat open on a chair next to the desk.

"Are you the one who took this from my room?" It hadn't been unexpected to find his briefcase missing, but it was still annoying.

"No. Not me. That was Ramón, or I should say it was taken at his direction. He said you wouldn't mind." She finally glanced at him with her startling green eyes. "Is it a problem?"

"No." He snapped the briefcase shut, placed it on the floor, and sat down.

Sofie, what a little liar you can be, Alex thought, shaking his head. "So, you already are working for Ramón?"

"No. This is just a small favor."

Alex wasn't sure what to believe. She'd been so accessible last night. Today, the switch had been flipped and the girl from the club was back, all of Sofie's defensive walls erected again.

"Did you find everything you need?" he asked. "We don't have much of a payroll. I'd be happy to send that detail too, if you're interested." Alex relied on the crash course from the agency's accounting department to sound convincing.

A narrow strip of white paper continuously trickled from the back of the adding machine.

"So far, the information here is sufficient," she said nonchalantly.

Alex felt the tension weighting the room. She seemed to have trouble looking at him. It *was* pretty shitty of him to leave her alone on the beach. "Last night…"

"What about it?"

He tried again, "I'm—"

"Alex, I'm so over this. I went down to the beach last night to make it clear I don't want or need your help. What happened afterwards *obviously* was a mistake. Let's just forget it."

She sighed. "The balance sheet and profit and loss look great. It appears Hanover Imports is in good financial shape. How'd you come up with the name?"

Okay, Sofie, we'll do things your way.

"A friend suggested it."

She glared at him.

He didn't elaborate.

"Well. The receivables are healthy, payables manageable. You own the warehouse and there isn't much of a mortgage. Plenty of liquid assets. No serious debt." She collected Alex's records, shuffled them into neat rectangles and drummed them on the desk. "Ramón will be pleased."

She stood. "If you'll excuse me, I'm going for a swim."

Alex watched her stride out of the room. He should have been delighted to have passed this test. It was a relief to know the books were flawless. Everything was right on track. He was one step closer to his goal, and two steps further away from the girl.

❦

The afternoon temperature had again crested at "sauna" when Alex stepped into the courtyard on his way down to the beach. Sofie didn't bother to look up from her magazine. Yesterday, poolside in Acapulco, she'd worn a tiny bikini; now, she was dressed more conservatively in a black, one-piece bathing suit. She had on a big floppy hat he hadn't seen before, and her enormous sunglasses.

He knew she was furious. It would be pointless to try to talk to her, so, as planned, he went down to scout the beach by daylight. This time, he would go all the way to the river.

Last night, he'd stopped before he reached the river mouth, positive it was being watched. Now, he waved to the armed guard in the tower and turned to walk the beach in the opposite direction, stopping every once in awhile to pick up a shell and chuck it into the Pacific.

The plan required a boat coming in from the ocean. A small squad from the team were flying into Acapulco early next week and commandeering a fishing rental that would eventually be abandoned along the beach. The first order of business would be taking care of security before they moved upriver. That shouldn't be a problem. A large shipment would be coming in, and thanks to Nick, the team knew that when a big project was undertaken on the ranch, Ramón pulled every available man to assist.

High-altitude surveillance had spotted a new warehouse and airfield.

The warehouse had been nestled among a cluster of older outbuildings along the river, where the cocaine would be delivered and repackaged for distribution. Less than a quarter of a mile inland, an airstrip had recently been carved into a clearing.

It had been Ramón's arrogance that gave the team the opening they had been anxiously awaiting. Thrilled to be breaking into the Colombian dope trade, Ramón had invited Alex to participate in the inaugural process, warehouse to warehouse.

Alex still needed to see the warehouse and airstrip in person. They could revise the operation from there if necessary, looking for mistakes in the strategy and considering their best options. Alternatives had to be weighed and measured. Something unexpected always happened.

He'd already screwed up enough with Sofie. Today, he concentrated on refocusing. She was hurt—he could see it in her eyes—and pissed, but collateral damage was common in this business. And it wouldn't be long before she truly hated him.

❧

Sofie heard Alex's door open and his footsteps fade on the concrete. She kept her eyes glued to a caption below a photo of Princess Diana. Distracted, she compulsively reread the words. No telling where he'd gone this time. She told herself she didn't care. At least he wouldn't be hanging around the pool, bugging her.

It had been excruciating to hear him stumble through his half-assed apology, so she cut him off, keeping the meeting professional, and her dignity—what was left of it—intact. Alex said he was curious. Intrigued even. *So what?* He'd played with her emotions, and there was nothing he could say that would make the incident on the beach any less humiliating. Hopefully, now he understood she didn't want *anything* he had to offer, especially his protection.

Sofie hated him. But her own body betrayed her sensibilities, stubbornly drifting toward Alex. She ignored the familiar coaster flip in her belly and the desire to once again run her hand beneath his shirt and feel the smooth muscles along his back. No one before Alex—not even Ben—had made her melt like this and ache for more.

God, I despise what he's done to me. Maybe he'd gone down to the beach for a swim. It would serve him right if he drowned, or was eaten by sharks.

She shouldn't have agreed to stay for the quinceañera. If she had any sense, she'd pack up and leave after her meeting with Ramón. He would

85

never permit Sofie to drive alone. And she didn't want to, especially at night.

Managing the evening with Alex around could be tricky. Then again, tonight would be a fiesta, and the whole village would be there, so it should be easy to elude him in the crowd. Planning a vague strategy, Sofie turned over on her stomach and tried to get some sleep...

Someone tapped her on the shoulder.

"Mi amor, you might be burning." Ramón said in Spanish. "How long have you been sunbathing?"

Sofie opened her eyes to find her cousin sitting on the edge of a nearby lounge. "Huh?... What time is it?"

"Around four. You need to get out of the sun. Did you see Alex's reports?"

"Yes." The heat, humidity and suntan lotion had left her skin gooey. She yawned and rubbed her eyes, leaving smudges of mascara on her fingers.

Apparently, Ramón noticed it too. "You need a shower. I will be in my office. Meet me there."

An hour later, she sat across from Ramón and gave him her analysis.

"I thought so." He smiled. "I did not see anything that caused me concern. The receivables are up to date?"

"Yes. One small invoice sixty days, the rest all within thirty."

"Excellent. I appreciate your help." Ramón returned the reports to Alex's briefcase and snapped the lid shut. "What about Alex? Do you like him?"

"Not particularly."

He frowned. "I am hoping you will give him a chance."

Sofie laughed. "Why?" It wasn't his style to encourage her with any man.

"Oh, mi amor, you mistake me." Ramón chuckled. "I did not mean it the way you are thinking. I am asking if he seems to be a man we can trust?"

"I didn't catch him playing around with the books if that's what you mean."

Cocking his head, he studied her. "Has Alex been inappropriate towards you?"

Her breath caught and she swallowed. Maybe he knew about the beach and was waiting for a confession. This was her opportunity to tell him everything—*the edited version.*

"Of course not!" she said. *Was it really a lie?* If she'd chosen to be truthful, Sofie thought she'd been the one inappropriate on the beach. When Alex had pulled away from her, she was so lost in the moment, she'd reached for him, not wanting to stop.

She focused on the journals lining the bookcase, hoping Ramón wouldn't notice the color rising on her face.

"Good. Then what is your concern?"

"I don't know. Nothing." She exhaled. "He seems okay to me. I wouldn't have any reservations working with him if I were you... You're asking for a lot of assurance from the guy. More than what's customary. A lot more. Is there a reason?"

"I am cautious. That is all."

"I haven't been an accountant that long. Remember, I only got my degree a few months ago. I hope I've helped."

"You have." He lifted his chin. "You should spend more time with him."

This wasn't a request, it was a demand. But Ramón would have never asked this of her if he had been aware of what happened last night.

"I'm going back to the city tomorrow morning."

"Alex likes you. I can tell. You are both American—well he, more so than you, but you two have that in common." Ramón toyed with his pen, repeatedly clicking the nib's lever. "I am hoping you will stay a while longer. Just for a few days. Get to know him. He seems pleasant enough. The two of you could work well together. Let me show you around. It has been years since you have taken a tour of the ranch. We built a runway for shipping. I am tired of paying bribes to the authorities in Acapulco."

"I need to get back."

"Why, Sofia?" Ramón's why was a heavy word, holding more than one question.

She knew what came next.

"I am hoping you will reconsider." The subject had shifted and Ramón was pushing again, talking about much more than extending her visit.

Sofie wasn't interested for so many reasons. The first one? The torturous possibility of having to work with Alex.

"You would be a great asset to the family." Ramón leaned back, resting his arms on the leather. "We need your education and qualifications. An education *I* have subsidized. I'm sure you have not forgotten." Ramón discarded the pen on the desk. "Give it a try. You will enjoy working with us. Your job would require traveling all over the Americas, meeting clients and helping us build our operations."

Ramón stood and came to Sofie's chair, towering over her. He was so close she could see flecks of steely glint in his eyes. "Papa expanded the rancho and made it a profitable endeavor, something that has helped us all, including you. The import-export business is growing rapidly. Now is the time to expand."

Sofie was cornered. "You have César."

"César has served the family well. However, the responsibilities have grown beyond his abilities."

"No. I'd like to help, but..."

Ramón didn't pay attention. "I have tried to entice you to consider us. Now, I must insist. You owe it to the family for the investment we have put into your education."

Sofie *had* let Ramón help with her college expenses. Stupidly, she'd thought the gestures had been driven by benevolent concern. Now, she was discovering the true meaning of the word "manipulation."

"You didn't have to help me with school. I could have asked my dad when I was short on money. I could have managed—gotten a part time job." She couldn't help but sound desperate.

"But you did not," Ramón's voice was razored.

Recoiling from the verbal slap, Sofie closed her eyes.

She heard his carefully measured sigh. Ramón placed his hand on her shoulder, and his voice warmed again. "You are family, Sofia. We wanted to help."

"Why don't you send Gabriel to college? Let him be your new accountant."

"He does not have your intelligence, or the American advantage. You move freely between both worlds. Gabriel moves freely up and down La Costera."

"I don't want to make a decision yet." Sofie's eyes began to sting with tears.

"Then mi amor, I will decide for you."

Trapped, Sofie scrambled. "I haven't even taken the test. What makes you think I'll pass the CPA exam? There are several sections. It's very difficult. Lots of people don't pass the first time."

"I am sure you will succeed. I have great faith in you, Sofia. You have no need for American licensing here anyway. Although it would be an advantage. That is why I am willing to let you go to California in the fall.

Study, pass the exam, then you will return to us."

"You're telling me I have no choice?"

"Of course you do." He smiled. "Do you want an office here or do you want to take one of my offices in the city? I would suggest both. I know you chicas get bored on the rancho. You choose. What do you prefer?"

Dumbfounded, Sofie realized Ramón had stolen her options.

She remembered a warning Tía Sofía had given her a few years ago: *You don't get something for nothing. Remember, mija, everything has its price.* At the time, Sofie assumed she had been speaking about life in general. Now she wondered if Tía had been specifically referring to their family.

Ramón had been generous in offering his help with her college education, and Sofie had been too eager to accept it, grateful for his insistence that he'd cover any costs, that she'd want for nothing.

At the time, she'd been thankful, loathing the idea of calling her dad and groveling for money beyond tuition. Worst of all, Sofie had hated listening to her stepmother on the extension, complaining that Sofie's needs were taking resources away from her own girls, while her father remained silent.

Sofie had come up short and asked Ramón for help. Once. Soon, a generous check began arriving monthly in her campus mailbox.

"Well?"

"I don't know what to say." Sofie blinked back tears.

His face was rigid. "How about, 'Thank you for the opportunity'?"

Standing in front of her, Ramón massaged her shoulders with a firm grip, and his face began to relax. "I remember all of the wonderful times you had with us when you were young... I am aware we are not a big accounting firm in a large American city. You told me once, you were not interested in that. Trust me, you will again learn to love this life." He smiled. "What is not to love?"

Where should I start?

"We need to gather to walk down to the church soon. Go upstairs, mi amor, and find something pretty to wear."

CHAPTER EIGHT

Fiesta de la Flores

Festival of the Flowers
Saturday, July, 7, 1984

While everyone else sat in the village church and watched Teodoro Garcia's daughter, Claudia, leave flowers on the altar of the Virgin Mary, Sofie sat in front of her mother's grave. She lit a match and sparked the candle resting in a tall glass cylinder.

Determined to retain the last trace of personal control—what she chose to wear—from Ramón's grasp, she hadn't changed her clothes. It was silent refusal. A weak personal protest she'd eventually have to discard.

Only after the sun set, underneath the barest hint of daylight, would she make her way back to the compound. Sofie didn't care if she got lost. Trapped by naive choices, she was already lost, alone in a crowd. Sofie believed being part of this family meant something unconditional—not a contract with inescapable strings attached.

For Ramón, it had been so easy. She'd fallen into his plans like one of the sailfish he caught offshore—lined and hooked.

An assortment of ornate crypts surrounded her mom's miniature, snow-white cathedral. Most were painted boisterous yellows and blues, with a few blinding fuchsias scattered around. It was quite different from the cemeteries in the United States. Sofie understood; most of her mom's ancestors were buried here. But she still found it hard to comprehend why her mom had chosen this garish circus over a more peaceful, pastoral scene.

In the center of the small graveyard, a concrete arch protected the nearly life-size rendition of the Blessed Virgin who overlooked the remains of the

90

family's delivered souls. The Virgin had her arms extended, welcoming all who wished to receive her comfort. Sofie sat on a short stone wall, skimming the soles of her bare feet along thick blades of green grass, and discovered she could find no consolation at all.

❦

There'd been no sign of Sofie before the quinceañera mass. Alex discretely watched for her as long as he could, until Esteban ushered him to the front of the church, where he sat as Ramón's guest during the ceremony. At the end, when Alex turned to leave, he expected to find her—a late arrival—along a back pew. She wasn't there.

Church bells pealed as the procession moved up the hill toward the compound in the dark. Holding a blaze of torches, Claudia's male escorts led the way, while Claudia and her female attendants, along with her parents, the priest and Ramón, followed. The village trailed behind. Joining the middle of the parade, Alex trooped up the dirt road with the rest of the Mendoza family. Sofie was still nowhere to be found.

The courtyard had been decorated for the fiesta, overflowing with candles and flowers. Tiny white lights snaked up the palms and ribbons of pastel banners had been strung from tree to tree across the patio. Local women from the village served platters of food while a Mariachi band circulated throughout the crowd.

Esteban motioned for Alex to join a group of guests seated at one of the long tables. Felipe made room for him on the bench. Alex recognized only the rice and beans. Felipe pointed out Cabrito—the roasted goat—and other regional dishes. Everything was delicious, Alex decided, with the exception of the goat.

Surveying the courtyard for the rest of the Mendoza clan, Alex found Ramón at the head banquet table with Claudia's family and her entourage. Monica, who had arrived at the church just before the Mass, sat next to Victor, across from Marco and his wife, near the pool. Victor had mentioned his engagement earlier in the day while they were fishing. And now, as if to ward off any possible competition, he protectively draped his arm around Monica.

Alex couldn't find Gabriel. Maybe he was with Sofie, boycotting the party altogether. He wouldn't be surprised if she'd enlisted Gabriel to drive her back to the city. The thought should be a relief.

It wasn't.

Esteban passed Alex a shot of mescal, saying, "Salud."

91

Alex replied in kind, swallowing the harsh, fiery liquid. It would be too obvious to ask about Sofie. He didn't think he should go search for her, so he tried to focus on the festivities.

Gabriel finally appeared without Sofie, just as Claudia, wearing a gigantic pink, ruffled dress, stepped into the center of the patio with her father for a waltz.

Soon, many of the guests began to dance. Esteban brought Alex a beer and offered another shot of mescal. Alex scoured the crowd for Sofie and couldn't find her.

He was worried. It would have been dangerous for her to have taken a car and gone back to Acapulco alone, unbeknownst to Ramón. What if she hadn't made it back to the city? What if the car had broken down and she sat stranded along the jungle road in the dark? Alex's gut clenched. This was his fault. He'd tried to apologize to her this afternoon, and she hadn't let him. He should have insisted.

Alex frowned. *How can I explain the unexplainable?*

Ramón held court, laughing with a group of villagers. He seemed unconcerned about—or maybe he was unaware of—his young cousin's disappearance.

The evening settled in and the crowd thickened, spilling throughout the estate. Alex excused himself from the table.

Inside, a more elaborate party was in full swing. Marco manned the bar in the living room, pouring drinks from a fifth of Jack Daniels. More Jack and several bottles of expensive tequila were lined along the back bar, ready to go.

"Come join us." Marco grinned. "Let me make you a drink. Whiskey or tequila?"

Alex smiled and lifted his beer. "Got one here. Thanks anyway."

Standing near the windows, he searched an expanse of ink-black countryside. Sofie could be alone out there somewhere, and no one seemed to care.

Maybe she'd gotten sick. She could be holed up in her room for the evening. Maybe everybody else knew this and felt there was no need to relay the information. Why should they?

He went to find a bathroom. Afterwards, he worked his way through the crowd, canvassing the unexplored areas of the spacious home.

An extravagant arc of stairways met along an upstairs landing. He decided to explore the left corridor and bumped into Gabriel as he came out of one of the bedrooms, startling them both.

"Sorry. I was looking for a bathroom."

"The bathroom is back there." Gabriel pointed in the opposite direction. "Third door on your right." He moved past Alex, rubbing his nose as he walked down the hall toward the stairs.

Alex scouted around the second floor, not sure where Sofie's room might be, and found a pair of carved mahogany doors. He was tempted to investigate, then reminded himself he'd come too far to be caught prowling around what was probably Ramón's bedroom.

He turned to leave and heard the clap and scatter of billiard balls behind the doors.

Sofie cursed.

Beneath a trio of lights in the center of the room, she played a solitary game.

Her strappy high heels had been abandoned in the corner of the room. She wore a black jumpsuit with elastic around the waist and ankles. Large turquoise, red, and purple Chinese dragons paraded in the cotton across her thighs.

Alex wanted to explore her thighs.

She leaned over the ornate pool table and lined up her shot on the red felt. As if aware of his presence, she glanced up. "No boys allowed."

Entering anyway, Alex closed the doors.

The billiard cue slid through the crook of her fingers. Balls clanked and clacked, spreading around the table. None were pocketed.

He smiled. "I think you may be better off on the dance floor than handling a pool cue."

"I've had more practice in clubs. My chauvinist cousin, Ramón, doesn't believe girls should be in here. This is his domain. It's why he put the billiard room on the second floor, by his bedroom."

"You skipped the quinceañera, and now you're missing the party."

"I'm having my own fiesta here, see?" She held up a glass and walked unsteadily to the bar at the far side of the room. Lifting a wine bottle, she filled her glass, emptying the bottle. "I need more chardonnay."

"It looks like you've already had enough." Alex moved toward the open doors that led to a balcony. Guests gathered on the lawn as fireworks began to explode above the river.

Ignoring him, she swallowed a gulp. She walked to the pool table and stood directly across from him. Her eyes were glassy and her voice stern,

"Don't tell me what to do. I've had enough of that today."

With no clue what was bugging her, Alex backed up, set his beer on the credenza, and raised both hands in surrender. "Suit yourself. You'll be the one fighting the headache tomorrow."

He checked his pockets. The change was gone, compliments of Sofie's generosity, so he pulled out his wallet and removed a dollar bill, sliding it underneath a square of blue chalk that rested on the edge of the pool table. "You in?"

Sofie appeared to study her own game, then looked at him. "I don't have any money on me. It's in my room."

"I'll front you." He took out another bill. "You can pay me back tomorrow."

"You're on." She set her glass down next to his beer and found the rack.

They both collected the balls.

Alex chose a cue.

"Break?"

"Ladies first," he said, giving Sofie a small bow.

She snorted and glared. "That's how you reel us in."

Sofie was obviously a little drunk, and still pissed, but was it his fault this time? She bent over to take her turn, and he could see she wasn't wearing a bra. The swell of Sofie's small, perfect breasts made him wish he was back with her on the sand.

Her cue hit the billiard ball with such force he thought others might fly off of the table. The yellow thirteen slid in.

Looking up, Sofie smiled. "Stripes."

Alex suspected it had been beginner's luck when she missed the next shot.

The fireworks intensified outside. After every boom, the oohs and aahs from the crowd drifted up through the balcony doors.

He scouted the table searching for the best shot. Whenever he glanced up, Sofie followed him with her eyes, holding her pool cue like a sentinel. Alex pocketed a pair of solids and grinned.

One strap of her outfit slipped off her shoulder and he was disappointed when she absently flicked it back into place.

He missed his second turn, leaving the ball well positioned for her.

"I think you did that on purpose. *Don't rescue me!*"

"You're crazy. I'm not that good. Anyway," Alex said, smiling. "There are two bucks at stake here. Take your shot."

"I'm going to," she said, looking for the best position. "Do you mind?"

Nudging past him, she eased her butt along his leg. He hadn't thought he could get any harder than he already was.

"Stop rushing me. People always do that." Sofie said, so close he could smell her flowery, tropical perfume. "I don't like to be pushed into things."

"Nobody does," he said. "So tell me, why didn't you make it to the village for the quinceañera?"

Whether she concentrated on the question or her next move, he couldn't tell.

The eleven ball slipped into a corner pocket. Sofie grinned, meeting his eyes. But she missed the next shot.

A thin cloud of sulfur drifted in from the balcony, stinging his nose.

"I didn't feel like seeing Ramón."

"You two have a fight?" Alex asked casually, searching for the best angle. Four solids found pockets in quick succession.

She glared at him. "Not quite an argument... A disagreement?" Crossing her arms, she pursed her lips. "I have an explanation—a coercion."

He looked over his pool cue. "Coercion?"

"Ramón had more than one reason to ask me to look over your financials. Which I told him passed with flying colors by the way..."

"Thanks. I expected them to." Alex took pity on her and missed. "Your turn."

"He wants me to come to work for him. But you knew that."

"Did you make a decision?" Alex asked.

"The decision isn't mine anymore." The spark in Sofie's eyes flashed hard and angry. "Apparently, it never was. My own stupidity put me in this position. I let Ramón help me through school. He insisted I put my efforts into my grades, and I gladly accepted. And now I owe him. He told me so this afternoon, and he refuses to take no for an answer."

She worked her way around the table, leaning on the red felt to study the angle of her next shot.

The revelation didn't surprise him. But her reaction did. Sofie should have known Ramón would want a return on his investment. The team should have been on top of Sofie's situation and noted the possibility too. Could she really have had no idea what was expected of her?

Alex wondered if he'd walked into an elaborate charade. Had he been marked before he even arrived in Mexico? Was Ramón using Sofie as a femme fatale to pull him in? Then again, if his cover had been blown, he wouldn't be upstairs, next to Ramón's bedroom, playing pool. Alex would never have gotten this far. He'd be at the bottom of the river by now, crocodile food.

He chose his words carefully, "International import-export is the wave of the future. There's a lot of money to be made. Plenty for everybody. You'd be a great asset to the family." His words were loaded. If she were tuned into the truth, Alex would see it in her face.

There was no recognition in her incredulous stare.

Without blinking, she said, "Don't you guys get it? I am not interested in the exportation of coffee, furniture, or anything else." She turned and focused on the table, concentrating on the best possible shot. Sofie took it and scratched.

"That's the trouble with you men!" she exploded. "It's like with Claudia. Why would I want to go watch a fifteen-year-old in this dirt-poor village officially reach womanhood? Do you have any idea what that means? She's finally marriageable!" She hesitated. "Is that even a real word?"

She didn't wait for an answer. "Whatever. Claudia's now old enough that her parents can barter her off to the highest bidder. Which they will do soon. What if she dreams of something different? Has an inkling something else might fulfill her life instead? She's so blind to the possibly that she could have any other choice, she's out there right now in the courtyard—smiling!"

Alex retrieved the cue ball. When he looked up, Sofie was so close he could see flecks of gold in her emerald eyes.

"What hope is there for this girl? For her life? She's had no education, no opportunity to make any kind of future with her own choices. She's out there naively opening up pretty trinkets. Eating cake with a stupid doll on top—*what an irony*—with her friends and family. Celebrating her greatest achievement—turning fifteen! And the best of all, her *padrino*—her godfather—my cousin Ramón, is her host and benefactor!"

"You're yelling at the wrong guy. I'm from America—land of the free. Remember?"

She snatched the ball from his fingers and dropped it on the table with a thud.

Alex didn't mention it wasn't her turn.

Sofie shuddered and inhaled, so close he could see tears on the verge of spilling over, glistening in her long, black lashes.

"And then there's me. I like to think I'm different, but I'm not. I tell myself I love it here. But my mom searched for a miracle in Mexican hocus-pocus. A witch doctor probably could have kept her alive longer. When I moved away, I turned my back on a life grounded in ignorance and superstition. And where am I? Right here in the thick of it. Trapped. Like poor little Claudia, my host and benefactor is Ramón too."

She wiped the tears away with the back of her hands. "Here's the difference: I know there's a much larger world out there with opportunities Claudia will never see—opportunities I probably won't see much more of either."

An explosion of fireworks echoed throughout the room. The finale had begun. "Ramón can't force you to do anything you don't want to do."

"This is my family. They're all I have. If I lose them, I have no one."

Even with the mixture of makeup and tears sliding down her cheeks, Sofie was still beautiful. Alex gathered her into his arms.

She snuggled into him, her sobs soaking his white dress shirt.

They were a perfect fit. He kissed the top of her head and smoothed the soft curls of her hair.

Her arms settled at his waist. After a while she sniffled and backed up a little, looking first at his chest, then up to him.

"I got mascara on your shirt. I'm sorry."

Irresistible Sofie. He couldn't stay away. Alex gently wiped the makeup off her cheeks and pulled her close.

"No problem." Bending his head, he kissed her, discovering the true reason he'd searched for her tonight.

Sofie tasted like she had before, sweet, a heady mixture of cherries and a hint of chardonnay. The kiss started slow. He knew she wasn't in the mood to be rushed. But when her mouth opened and she ran her tongue along his bottom lip, the kiss intensified. Alex couldn't hold back anymore.

"I know I should, but I can't stay away. I want you." he whispered, and buried his head into her neck, inhaling her sweet perfume.

"Me too." Sofie smiled. "I mean…"

Alex laughed quietly. "I know."

Loud voices coming from the hall separated them seconds before the doors opened. Leading a group of young men Alex recognized from the living room, Marco stopped talking mid-sentence.

Marco seemed to take in the intimate scene with curiosity.

"Sofie. Alex—"

Alex quickly recovered. "I hope you don't mind. Sofie mentioned you had a billiard room, and I insisted she bring me up here." He walked over to the pair of dollar bills sitting under the chalk. "She's even trying to make a couple of bucks off me." Laughing, he waved them into the air. "Line up, guys. She says she's not very good at pool. But be warned, I think she might be a shark."

Several men reached for their wallets. Others moved to the bar for drinks.

"Sofie, your turn," Alex said. "Pick your pocket." Several stripes were still scattered across the table. All of his solids had been pocketed. The eight ball remained. He counted on Sofie to understand the switch.

She seemed a little dazed, but grasped his instruction with a slight smile. Choosing a corner pocket, she positioned the white ball in front of the black and lined up a straight shot. The eight ball slid into the leather net. She looked up and beamed.

"What did I tell you? Watch out for her. This girl is dangerous." Alex chuckled.

Sofie left the bills on the table and one of Marco's friends added to the pile.

"Rack 'em up!" he said in broken English.

While Sofie chalked her cue, Alex leaned into her ear and whispered, "Be careful when you bend over. I don't want you giving them a show. You're mine."

Sofie blushed.

Melting into the crowd, Alex left the room to change his mascara-smeared shirt.

When he returned, the billiard room had grown into a teeming stag party.

Sofie had eluded him again.

Alex spent the rest of the evening trying to track her down. Apparently, he'd scared her off and she didn't want to be found.

Confident Sofie had no idea what the family business entailed, he knew she was on the edge of making a huge, life-changing mistake. The trick was how to talk her out of it, keeping her uninvolved and away from the ranch for the next week, without blowing his cover.

CHAPTER NINE

Fiesta de la Luna

Festival of the Moon
Sunday, July 8, 1984

Before Marco and his friends arrived, Alex had dominated the pool table, so it wasn't a surprise when Sofie lost the game. He was still in the room when her new competition racked up the balls. She took a shot, and when she looked up Alex was gone.

It wasn't the first time he'd left her, and any interest she had in winning disappeared along with him.

She checked the balcony, hoping he waited there, but it was empty. The fireworks had come and gone, leaving clouds of smoke that lingered among the guests who remained on the lawn. In the moonlight, the river became a black ribbon unspooling toward the ocean.

As Alex had predicted, headache loomed behind her temples. Whether it was from the wine or the second abandonment by him in as many days, she couldn't tell.

Inside, the noise jumped a few decibels, indicating the arrival of even more testosterone. Anger and alcohol had given her the courage to invade Ramón's male domain. Sofie recognized the look in Marco's eyes as he politely humored her, his American cousin who didn't quite know her place in their world. Thankfully, the men ignored her as she made her way through the crowd to retrieve her heels from the corner of the room.

Expecting to find Alex, she went downstairs and into the courtyard for the first time this evening. On the edges of the patio, women from the village gathered, traditionally cloistered from their men. They stood in small groups talking, and monitored the children who bounced around the guests on the dance floor.

Estella's crystal laughter erupted from a cluster of young women standing across from the band. Catching Sofie's glance, she called her over to join them. Sofie waved her off, not interested in company. Only one person had captured her attention, and he couldn't be found.

Sofie's hair began to misbehave, so she unhinged a bobby pin from the frizzy mess and tried to steer the curls into submission, sliding a few tendrils behind her ears. The chardonnay high had vanished along with Alex. She was grateful she'd listened to him and quit drinking when he arrived; her headache could have been worse.

It was a reassuring—and elating—to discover the electricity that surged between them was mutual. *But where did he go?*

After searching for half an hour, she went upstairs, discouraged. She washed her face in the bathroom. Downing a couple of aspirin, she chased them with a glass of water. Fluffing a pillow, she settled on top of the lavender bedspread and listened to the village band. The music drifted up from the courtyard and through the open door. She fell asleep wondering if Ramón had waylaid Alex, or if he'd just decided on his own to disappear.

When Sofie awoke, the sliding door was still open. It was late, and the only music filtering into the bedroom was the subtle chink and chime of movement, underscored by hushed conversation between the staff as they cleaned up. She oriented herself, and realized she had no memory of Monica waking her when she came in.

Monica rolled over, tugging on the covers. Sofie listened for her slow, measured breathing to resume. Lifting her head, Sofie glanced at the bedside clock. She'd been asleep for hours. Dawn would be arriving soon.

The headache was gone, but her mouth felt thick from sleep and wine, and she was thirsty. In the bathroom, she filled her glass, pausing at the sink to brush her teeth. Sofie studied her reflection in the mirror and grinned, recalling each detail of her most recent encounter with Alex. For the first time, she let herself revel in the hum of attraction that had sprouted in her heart and now vibrated throughout her body.

She took the glass out onto the balcony. Most of the candlelight had sputtered and died. The remainders spread a subtle glow over the nearly deserted patio. In the corner, the band packed up their gear. The household staff was busy below, collecting scraps from the party and gathering scores of empty beer bottles into clusters on a planked table.

It had been a long night for everyone. Even longer for those expected to restore order by sunrise. Carrying trays and cleaning supplies, the staff wore a path between the courtyard and the kitchen. A boy she recognized as Teodoro's son, Eduardo, who lived with his family in the village, hosed the concrete, while another young man she hadn't seen before skimmed flowers and debris from the pool. More thoughtful patrons would have sent their staff home and let them clean up in the morning. Sofie had compiled a vocabulary of words to describe Ramón. *"Thoughtful"* wasn't one of them.

Standing barefoot on the balcony, Sofie observed the scene and congratulated herself. She'd accomplished her goal: She'd made it through the night without bumping into Ramón. Glancing toward the darkened guest quarters, Sofie decided it was her only success of the evening.

Eduardo noticed her and waved. Sofie waved back. Uncomfortable overseeing the scene as if she were a princess, supervising her minions, she went inside, changed into a sundress, slipped on sandals, and headed downstairs to help.

The courtyard was spotless within an hour. She sent Eduardo and his friend down the path toward the village and the rest of the exhausted staff to bed.

A warm, calm breeze rustled though the palms. Slipping off her sandals, she sat at the edge of the pool, listening to the lullaby of gentle, lapping waves arriving along the beach. She hiked her dress, tucked it under her thighs, and strummed her legs through tepid water.

Overhead, wisps of clouds obstructed her view of the heavens. Sofie wasn't looking for advice tonight. She'd already decided to return to Acapulco in the morning. Ramón had suggested a tour of the ranch, but she would leave before he roped her into any more of his schemes. She needed time away from him, to clear her head and think things through—something she'd wished she could have been able to do here, but found impossible.

Men. Once in the city, she'd decide her next move. She could buy a plane ticket back to California, turning her back on her Mexican family south of the border, or she could reluctantly agree to give Ramón and a Latin career a shot.

Her conundrum slept just yards away. Sofie debated whether she should lightly tap on Alex's door, remembering the kiss earlier tonight that sent a jolt of excitement racing through her. What else could he do to her body if they had the opportunity to further explore the undeniable charge between them?

To her delight, Sofie knew he wanted her too. If she went to him, he'd let her in and they'd make love.

Why can't a girl have a one night stand? Guys do it all the time with no remorse whatsoever. *And so do women these days.*

Sofie had never considered being one of those women before…until now.

There was a first time for everything, *right?*

No, it wasn't in her nature. *But,* if she knocked on his door, tomorrow morning he would finally be out of her system, and she could leave with no regrets. It could only be a win-win that would help her move forward.

She could think of this as a test. A night with Alex could help her decide what her next move should be.

Sofie had never done anything this bold. Conflicted, and basically a coward, she remained on the ledge of the pool.

What difference did it make? If she decided to go back to California, she wouldn't ever see him again anyway. As a liberated woman of the eighties, she was in charge of her own sexuality. She could do want she wanted.

And I really want Alex.

Gathering courage, Sofie focused on his door. She hadn't contemplated doing anything this daring. *Ever.*

She climbed from the pool and sat on a lounge chair, drying her legs with a towel.

Then she stood and straightened her dress.

Taking a deep breath, Sofie walked a few steps toward the guest quarters. She stopped, wondering if she'd misread his signals again.

But, tonight he said… Alex says a lot of things. Then he changes his mind.

She returned to the lounge chair but didn't sit down.

It's now or never. With shaky legs, she walked towards his door.

Alex walked up the pathway from the beach.

He hadn't been in his room all along.

Smiling, Alex came to her, standing just inches away. Close enough for Sofie to see the rise and fall of his chest.

To make sure she hadn't conjured him up, she touched his cheek with her finger, and followed the small curve of his one adorable dimple in the moonlight.

Enraptured by the beginnings of a beard, she kept her hand on his face, anticipating the seductive feel of his skin moving against hers. She wanted him so badly, blood rushed to her head, making her a little dizzy, and settled deep below her belly.

"Where did you disappear to?" he asked.

"Where'd you go?"

"To change my shirt. When I came back, *you* weren't there."

Sofie found the complaint endearing. "I couldn't find you, so I went to my room. You were right about the headache," she said, moving her hand away. "Walking the beach again?"

"Couldn't sleep. Again."

"Me neither," she said.

His breath was hot and sweet, and she yearned to press her lips to his. But she held back, aware she was toeing an invisible line. *Would one night really be enough?*

"How's the headache?" he teased.

"Better. A couple of aspirin and few hours sleep helped."

"You whip their asses playing pool?"

"Hardly. It's cheating in reverse when you let me win. Like I keep telling you, I can handle myself. You don't need to cover for me."

"Somebody needs to watch out for Señorita Sofía."

She wanted to move into his arms.

As if he could read her mind he said, "Come here."

Sofie didn't hesitate.

Alex put his lips to her forehead. "It's your fault I can't sleep," he whispered into her hair. "You smell so good, like tropical flowers."

His kiss sent a shock of liquid fire coursing through her veins. Sofie reached up to put her arms around his neck. She let his tongue tease hers, encouraging Alex to deepen the kiss, offering herself to him.

He took her hand and led her toward the pathway.

"Where are we going? Back down to the beach?"

"No. Someplace with no sand. Spend the night with me. What's left of it."

Sofie glanced around the dark, empty courtyard and followed Alex behind the palms, into his room.

❦

Alex closed and locked the door. Earlier tonight, he'd told himself he'd let Sofie lead, decide what was enough, and where they'd stop. He was long past that point. As much as he'd tried to avoid it, he'd known this would happen. It was inevitable that she'd wind up in his arms, and somewhere, somehow, they'd fuck.

I have to have her.

He didn't switch on the lamp or attempt to find the bed in the dark. Alex pushed Sofie against the wall, needing to be inside her. Now.

She didn't protest. Standing on her toes, she kissed him, sliding her soft tongue into his mouth.

Alex ran his hand up her thigh and found her sheer panties. Sofie was already soaked. This was exactly how he'd imagined she'd be, hot and ready. He slipped a finger underneath the elastic and found her slick nub. She moved against him, eager for more.

"You're so wet." He put his other hand under her butt and hiked her higher against the wall.

"Aah…" Without breaking the kiss, Sofie eased her body onto his palm, adjusting her legs around his waist to welcome his hand, encouraging the exploration.

He was more than willing to comply with the request. Wanting to see her face, Alex wished he could turn on the light. She seemed to be holding on to him for dear life, pushing her body against his while she kissed him with wild abandon, using her hips to capture his thrumming fingers.

Tonight, Sofie was a delectable snare he wasn't going to fight. He pushed her thin dress up past her waist. With one hand, he ran his fingers along the silky skin of her smooth bottom. She cried out, protesting when he moved his other hand away.

Alex wasn't going anywhere. Running his palm down her stomach and beneath her panties, he heard Sofie's moan. Coaxing her, he said, "It's okay, baby. Let's just get you out of these."

Lowering the lingerie so she could step out of them, Alex slid two fingers into their new home.

They both laughed as they stumbled in the dark toward the bed. He stood at the edge and unzipped his shorts, while she reached out from the mattress, running her warm fingers along his side. Moving to the front of his boxers, she slipped her hand into the slit and found him.

He was about to explode.

With her other hand, she tugged Alex's arm, urging him to join her. "Come here."

Dipping his fingers into her soft, warm folds, he moved above her, anxious to replace his fingers with the true source of his passion. There wasn't time to remove her dress, but it didn't matter. They were both naked enough, and he knew she wanted him now.

Alex helped Sofie spread her legs as she welcomed him, bending her knees and arching her hips to meet his. She placed her hands underneath his shirt and guided him into her body, meeting each of his thrusts with her own.

He pushed deeper, finding exquisite comfort in her tight, silky sleeve. His heart pounded, while the familiar pressure began to build and intensify as their pace increased.

"Oh, oh, God. I'm co—", Sofie cried out.

Alex's lips met hers, and he felt the tender contractions milking him, urging his own release.

Gripping the sheets, Alex orgasmed inside of her. In a moment of clarity, he realized this was something different, more powerful and intimate than anything he'd experienced before.

Spent, he cradled Sofie in his arms and ran his hands along the silky skin of her thigh. He stared into the black ceiling, overwhelmed with dread and the realization he'd discovered valuable property in desperate need of protection.

Alex told himself Sofie wasn't his problem. But she was.

He knew he should be feeling satisfied and relaxed, ready to send Sofie back to her room, roll over and get some sleep. But he wasn't. They'd both just crossed a very dangerous line. If they were busted, the fallout would be catastrophic.

There was more. He'd slipped out of her just moments ago and he already was getting hard again. Once wasn't going to be enough.

Once would have to do. There was no other option.

Cool air from the ceiling fan whispered over their bodies. Alex faced Sofie in the evaporating darkness and pressed his index finger on her thumb, drawing an imaginary line up her arm and back down to her breast, wishing he'd taken off her dress. Finding a long silver chain with his fingers—the one she always seemed to wear—he followed it from her neck all the way to the heart puddled on the sheet. "You really waited for me by the pool?"

"Not at first. I went downstairs to help clean up. After I sent everybody off to bed, I wasn't tired. So, I sat by the pool—contemplating."

"What?"

He could see a hint of her features in the moonlight.

Grinning, she answered, "Things."

"Things?"

"You." One by one, she opened the buttons of his shirt. Placing her palm on his chest, she found his nipple and lightly skimmed it with the flat of her hand.

A shot of renewed desire coursed through Alex.

"Then you came along and saved me a trip."

"Where?"

"Not far." Sofie confessed. "Just across the courtyard to your door." Smiling, she ran her fingers past his belly button, lower. "I'm glad you came up from the beach when you did."

"Me too." Alex grabbed her hand and pulled Sofie on top of him, taking her again.

❧

Sofie wondered if it was luck, or maybe it was just Alex turning away from her on the bed, that jostled her awake. It was light outside, and she needed to go.

The experiment—a one night stand—had been a complete failure. One night hadn't been enough. Somehow, she'd always known it wouldn't be.

She checked the bedside clock—a quarter past five. Sofie couldn't get caught sneaking out of the guesthouse.

It might already be too late.

But the supple skin of Alex's back held constellations she wanted to map and explore. She looked toward the window and frowned. This area of his body would remain unfamiliar territory. The rest of him a memory.

Sofie mouthed a silent goodbye, pressing her lips on a small scar she'd found near a cluster of freckles, and slipped out of bed. Searching for her panties, she found them on the floor, and slipped them on. Alex had disappeared on her twice before, now it was her turn.

She closed his door and tried to smooth her horribly wrinkled sundress before she stepped onto the pathway. Scurrying across the courtyard, she stopped by the pool to retrieve her sandals.

If anyone saw her they'd know she'd been out all night and probably would report it to Ramón. It wouldn't take much sleuthing for him to figure out exactly whom she'd spent it with. Even though he'd encouraged her to get to know Alex, he wouldn't approve. Sex wasn't what Ramón had in mind.

Sofie smiled.

CHAPTER TEN
Cambio de Arenas

Changing Sands
Sunday, July 8, 1984

"Where were you last night?"

Startled, Sofie looked down to find Ramón questioning her in Spanish from the middle of the stairs. Had he tired of waiting for her to come to breakfast, or now brunch?

Sofie planted her feet in the thick carpet of the landing. Unsure of his question she opted for a safe answer. "I took a walk and forgot to wear my watch. When I got back I had a really bad headache. For awhile I suspected it might even be a migraine... Do you remember my mom used to get them too? Anyway, I thought I'd lay down." She shrugged. "By the time I came downstairs everybody had already gone to the village."

Ramón raised a skeptical eyebrow.

Crossing her arms, she forced a smile and hoped he'd buy her bogus explanation. He wouldn't want to hear the truth. She'd refused to attend the quinceañera because she wasn't going to be pushed around by his manipulations anymore. Ramón could be overwhelming. Direct confrontation proved to be futile. Retrieving her power was essential. Alex had been right. Her life was her own to design.

What she'd done with Alex... Well, that was none of Ramón's business, no matter how much she wanted to tell Ramón that she'd spent the early morning hours making love with his new business partner—just to see Ramón's stunned reaction.

The experience was a special pleasure she intended to keep to herself. Had one night been enough? As tempting as Alex was, for her own sanity,

107

she convinced herself this morning it had to be. Alex and Ramón were a package deal.

"Remind me to invite you upstairs after dinner tonight. I hear you know your way around the pool table. I would like to see this myself." Ramón pressed his lips into a firm line. "Have you started drinking whiskey too?"

"I don't like whiskey." Sofie took a breath, leveled her eyes with Ramón's, and lifted her chin in defiance. "I'm leaving this morning. Back to the city."

"Yesterday we agreed you would stay on for a few more days so I can show you around. I was coming upstairs to get you. We are taking a tour of the ranch."

"Another time."

"Why?"

She tightened her arms and kept her gaze steady. "Monica will ride back with me. Or Gabriel. Maybe both. I already mentioned it to her this morning. I'm going to talk to Gabriel at breakfast."

Ramón sighed. "I will be in Acapulco next weekend. On Saturday, we will go to the downtown office and I will show you around. If you plan to work from the rancho instead, you will need to pack your things anyway."

He turned his back and moved down the stairs. At the bottom he hesitated. "You will begin to work with César after next week. A big shipment is coming in Thursday and until then he will be unavailable. He can help familiarize you with our operations."

"We'll talk this week." Sofie slid around the truth, not up for an argument in the foyer. She needed space, and time, to decide how she planned to respectfully, *but firmly*, decline his offer.

Ramón nodded and opened the front door.

Outside, a small caravan was lined up along the drive. Everyone, including Monica and Gabriel—and, Sofie assumed, Alex—waited in a pair of Chevy Blazers. For the second day, she ate breakfast alone.

❦

Alex stood in front of Ramón's office and faced his closed door. Today, he'd been able to compartmentalize his complicated feelings toward Sofie and focus on this crucial moment. For the first time, he would be alone with his target.

Steeling himself, Alex repeatedly clenched his fists. Never had the stakes been so high, or so personal.

Scanning the empty corridor, he listened for sound. All was quiet. It would be so easy to take Ramón out now. Alex's heart raced, his mind overflowed with enough suppressed rage to do the deed silently.

I'll wrap my fingers around Ramón's neck and I'll squeeze hard enough to watch the blood vessels burst in his eyes. He'll gurgle, and I won't let go until the last bit of life flows out of his body.

Alex closed his fist a final time and knocked, mentally grasping his mantra: *Keep your cool, man. Keep your cool. Stick to the plan, and let it play out to the end.*

"Come in," Ramón called.

The familiar screen muted his consciousness as he entered the room. He'd maneuvered in and out of this state before. When he looked into Ramón's dark eyes, Nick never existed. Alex Wakefield didn't exist.

And Sofie was just another girl.

Alex Wilson did exist. With his company's first major cocaine deal just days away from completion, Hanover Imports would then be on its way to opening its doors to massive wealth. This morning's tour had given him all the information he needed.

Gathering Hanover Imports' financial records into a stack on his desk, Ramón said, "I will hold on to these."

"Of course. They're yours."

Ramón snapped the locks on the empty briefcase and passed it to him.

"Please, have a seat." Ramón motioned to a chair on the other side of the desk. "Cigar?"

When Alex nodded, Ramón turned to the humidor on the credenza and cut two cigars, passing one to Alex.

"Thanks. The Cuban I had the other night was excellent." Alex set his briefcase down and settled into the comfortable leather. The room wasn't large but it was expertly decorated. He suspected the massive walnut furniture had been chosen to make an impression. A dazzling view of the mountains spanned the length of one wall. More Zapotec figurines, similar to the ones that had been pointed out to him in the living room, sat upon the shelving behind Ramón's desk.

"These are Cohibas. I have been told Cuban cigars are illegal in the United States. I will send some home with you," Ramón said, charring his before he handed the gold lighter to Alex.

"Thanks." Alex ran the cigar under his nose. Inhaling, he let the honeyed aroma tantalize his senses.

"Magnífico." Ramón took a puff and laughed. "Contraband," he said, waving the cigar in the air. Fragrant smoke billowed through the room. "Our association will have many benefits for both of us."

Ramón, you are so right. Alex's mind flashed to early this morning with Sofie in his bed.

"It has been a pleasure to meet you in person, Alex," Ramón continued. "Esteban and I are impressed with your operation. You have worked hard and jumped through many circles to do business with us."

Yes, I have. Alex nodded, noting the cigar's near-perfect draw and its slow, razor-straight burn. Cuban cigars couldn't compete with Ramón's beautiful cousin, but they were another added bonus of this job. "Any questions?"

"Just a few. Everything seems to be in order. Your company will be an outstanding complement to our organization. Have your backers been coordinated? Is the money ready?"

"My office is awaiting my call. It will be on the plane."

"Good."

"Have you heard from Colombia? Where's the boat?" Alex asked.

"On the way. Scheduled to arrive Wednesday night or early Thursday morning."

"Good. When I get back to Chicago, I'll investigate the other ventures we've discussed to dispose of the cash on my end."

Ramón smiled. "It is advantageous for us the attention is currently on Caribbean traffic. This gives us time to establish ourselves in the market. Let the U.S. authorities chase the Medellín shipments in and out of the cays. By the time they realize we are here, we will be firmly entrenched and our pipeline will be running smoothly. In the meantime, we will have worked out our minor weaknesses, and we will demonstrate to the Calis that we can get their cocaine safely delivered."

"The Cali family's decision to investigate another route is a brilliant move," Alex said. "Some say Carlos has confiscated a whole island for his own personal use."

"Carlos has created an empire."

"People call him the Medellín Megalomanic."

"Even within his organization, some think he is out of control." Ramón snorted. "He will soon go too far and either the Colombians or the Americans will catch up with him. We can fill the vacuum with a new, more rational business model."

Alex nodded in agreement.

Ramón took the cigar and gestured with it to establish his point. "Make no mistake, Alex, I know the Cali family well. We are very privileged to get this opportunity. Colombians prefer to work with their own kind. At home and abroad, they are their own form of insurance. I know this from personal experience. We had a small situation a few years ago. No mistake on our part," Ramón said. "Nevertheless, it took some time for us to rebuild their confidence. It is a great honor they have put their trust in us."

When Ramón set his cigar down in an obsidian ashtray, Alex got a good look at his Rolex; dozens of diamonds encircled the gold face of the watch.

"I have to pay for this shipment in advance. Therefore, I have placed a great amount of confidence in you. And never forget: Although they are not as brutal as the Medellíns, if something should go wrong, they are just as deadly." His dark eyes flickered. "If necessary, the Mendoza family can be deadly too."

Alex accepted the warning with a nod. Content to play the role of Ramón's subordinate. For now.

Gazing out the window, Alex studied the landscape and, for a moment, the screen of his persona lifted. Ramón had no idea his grandiose plans were doomed. It was almost impossible to face the truth of the man—what Ramón had done—and not lunge at him from across the desk. Alex slipped back into his role and turned, meeting Ramón's eyes. "I guarantee you won't be disappointed."

"Good." Ramón cleared his throat. "I have great hopes for Sofia. As a courier, she will make an exceptional addition to our operations, easily traveling between both countries and eventually using her expertise to help create new and better ways to dispose of our major headache—cash. A welcome but troubling problem." He chuckled. "I am confident the two of you can work together to find creative ways to rectify this mountainous issue. It is rapidly becoming unmanageable. Sometimes, we have had to use the banks in the Cayman Islands. The two of you together can probe for more lucrative options."

Probe? Alex and Sofie had done their fair share of probing, and it had been quite lucrative. He stifled a smile, this wasn't what Ramón had in mind.

Ramón paused and checked his waning cigar.

Alex watched as he clasped the smooth ribbing of the lighter between his fingers and sent a new wave of smoke into the air.

"However, at this moment, Sofia is unaware of our true activities.

Comprendes?"

He already had this figured out, but it was relief to have confirmation. "Comprende," Alex didn't care if he butchered the response.

"I am sending you back into the city with her today. Let her give you a tour. Come back on Wednesday, when the boat is due to arrive. Schedule your pilot for Thursday. In the meantime, enjoy our beautiful country. See its sights and attractions. My hope is that someday you will think of us as your second home."

Surprised, Alex wondered what Sofie thought of this new plan. She'd disappeared from his room, and he hadn't seen her all morning. He wasn't even sure she was still around until now. Did she know she'd be taking him back to Acapulco? Would she—*could she*—say no?

"There is a flight to Chicago on Wednesday at six-fifteen in the evening. Have Sofia drop you off at the airport. Wait in the bar. Hector will pick you up at seven and bring you back here."

"You're the boss." Alex wondered if Ramón had planned to throw them together all along.

"And one last thing..." Ramón locked eyes with Alex. "Sofia was a favorite of my father's. My Aunt Olivia's only child. She is exceptional. I can see she has an attraction to you, and you may feel the same about her. You will work closely together in the future. I discovered long ago that a mixture of business and romance does not work."

Too late, Ramón.

But Alex knew this too. Nick's ghost had been breathing down his neck all morning, saying the same thing. A part of Alex hoped Sofie had wised up for the both of them and already gone back to Acapulco. A different part of him, primarily centered below his stomach, needed to see her again.

Ramón's mustache twitched, and he appeared to measure his words, "Our culture is quite different from yours. We take honor and family very seriously. A woman's virtue is highly valued here. Sofia claims to be American and parades around with many of her crazy American ideas. However, she belongs to us. Like many young women, she is emotional. Her wishes are sometimes erratic. I trust that you will not betray our hospitality by taking advantage of any fleeting crush she may have for you."

Alex Wilson should be worried. Alex Wakefield was elated.

"Of course." Feigning respect, Alex hid his exhilaration. He couldn't help but wonder if his hatred for the man sparked the intense desire he felt

112

for Ramón's sexy, emerald-eyed cousin.

In Sofie, Alex had already taken something important from Ramón, and had begun to chip away at the foundations of all he held dear.

Alex hadn't anticipated this complication, and literally overnight, sweet Sofie had become a major one. He didn't want to use her to get to her cousin. But, for the deal to go down, it might become necessary.

❦

Sofie heard the knock. Ramón entered the bedroom without an invitation.

"We have a small problem. One only you, Sofia, can help me resolve," Ramón said in Spanish.

She zipped up her overnight bag and left it on the bed. Turning to face him, she pressed her lips together.

Standing just inside in the doorway, he smiled. His eyes were soft, full of benevolence. "I have worked all morning, trying to assist you on your mission to get back to Acapulco today. Unfortunately, I need Gabriel here with me. And Monica... Victor is in need of Monica... Or, should I say Monica needs Victor, and I need him. Well, you see how it goes." He laughed. "They have begun to plan their wedding—I am sure you are aware of all this. What you may not know is Victor would like to convince her to have the celebration here, on the rancho. I recommend it of course, a home wedding—a fiesta—done in the traditional manner. But, it seems Monica needs to be persuaded."

Ramón walked over to the dresser and glanced down at the bowl of sea glass. Picking up a frosty white shard, he frowned, and immediately dropped it back into the bowl.

Sofie suspected he couldn't understand the value in collecting colored bits of tumbled and sand-washed trash.

He looked up and grinned. "And you, my little cousin, are determined to make it back to the city. Alex would like to get back too. Would you mind taking him to his hotel this afternoon? And while he's in town..."

Minutes after Ramón left, Monica bounced into the bedroom. Pulling a clean pair of shorts from the dresser, Sofie tried to entice her with the promise of a girl's day at a salon. Manicures, pedicures, a facial, *anything*. "We can have lunch. My treat. Come back to the city with me," Sofie pleaded.

"Victor wants me to stay here." Monica shrugged. "What's the problem? So what if Ramón asked you to show Alex around? Take advantage of the situation. I think Alex is a fox. You do too. And I know how you hate to drive alone."

Sofie averted her eyes, focusing on the sea glass.

"What?" Monica said, curious. "Alex said something happened at the club. Tell me."

"It's complicated."

"In the end, romance isn't complicated at all. It's undeniable desire driving two people toward their destiny."

They both laughed.

"I didn't realize you were such a philosopher."

Monica smiled. "I didn't either. But I've noticed how you watch him when you don't think anyone is looking," she teased. "Don't bother to lie to me. Victor says you'll eventually spend a lot of time working together anyway. As long as Ramón doesn't find out, why not make it enjoyable?" Her chestnut eyes twinkled below her thinly penciled brows. "I won't tell."

More alone time with Alex only played into Ramón's manipulations. But, that wouldn't be the worst of it. "Thanks a lot," Sofie muttered.

CHAPTER ELEVEN
Viento de la Montaña

Mountain Wind
  Sunday, July 8, 1984

Nothing today had gone the way Sofie imagined. A simple plan to drive back to the city was now designed by Ramón. Again, she sat behind the wheel of the Mercedes. They hadn't taken the boat this afternoon, but drove the long dirt road that led to the paved, one-lane highway. In the distance, jungled hills climbed inland and cradled the river. Sofie pressed her bare foot down on the accelerator and a cloud of dust billowed in the wake.

Ramón had no idea what he had done by sending Sofie and Alex back to Acapulco alone. And Monica had been so eager to throw them together. Sofie had been careful not to mention anything that had happened already. Monica loved to devour good stories, and this one would be too juicy not to tell.

Sofie still couldn't believe she'd followed Alex into his room and pulled him down onto the bed with her. She'd never done anything that brazen before. Running her fingers through the chaos of her hair, she slipped a wayward curl behind her ear and smiled, remembering just how amazing the sex had been.

Her stars were definitely aligned for punishment; because now Alex was acting as if she'd dreamt the whole thing. Ever since they'd pulled out of the compound gates, he'd silently watched the dusty landscape. He hadn't even glanced her way. *Great.*

One night in bed should have been enough to diminish the sizzle of attraction. For her, the opposite had happened. The sizzle had sparked a

115

full-blown blaze.

Alex was hot. *Too hot.* At other times, cold. Like right now. Her intuition kept blaring defense sirens—*stay away, a major scorching is inevitable.*

And this morning, when clarity surfaced with the sun and finally clicked into gear, she'd planned to head back to Acapulco.

Then Ramón stepped in, sending Alex back too.

Alex had invaded her life in just a few days. However, he seemed only interested in the contemplation of pastured cows this afternoon. Sofie frowned and tried to concentrate on the road.

"We need to talk," he said.

I swear, I think he can read my mind.

"Oh, God. Don't try to apologize again." Glaring at him, she raised her hand, not in the mood to hear his remorse or willing to make any confessions of her own.

"I wasn't going to. No regrets. You?" There wasn't a smile attached to his steady, penetrating gaze.

"None." She quickly turned her attention back to the road, surprised by his response and confused by her own.

They drove in silence for miles, past cultivated fields and giant, canopied trees, with massive, knuckled trunks. When they neared the cut-off to the old hacienda, she didn't bother to point it out. Her stomach twisted when she saw the three overgrown palms marking the long driveway. She promised herself, she'd go back and visit the abandoned homestead some day.

As the road began to curve around rising hills, she noticed one of Ramón's black Chevy Blazers far behind. Normally, Sunday was a day off, and people didn't leave the rancho to run errands.

It was possible Ramón sent a chaperone to tail them.

She glanced at Alex, his eyes were closed, his head turned toward the passenger door. How he managed to sleep while she navigated this washboard of a road was a mystery. Between the curves and the dust, she slowed and watched the Blazer through the rear-view mirror, seeing it decelerate too. She tried the test several times with the same result, and wondered if the driver avoided her choking trail or was following them.

This didn't make sense. Ramón had mentioned a big shipment coming in next week. All available hands would be needed. How could he afford to send someone to follow them? He wouldn't hesitate if he thought it necessary. *Who doesn't he trust? Alex or me?*

At the intersection, she parked between a small cluster of buildings. A rusted gas pump stood in front of one, its nozzle lying in the dirt. Beneath a corrugated tin roof, a doorless entrance welcomed customers into a gloomy storefront. A single light bulb, hanging from a long cord, illuminated the interior.

While she slipped on her sandals, Alex lifted his head, wiping his eyes. "Where are we?"

"At the highway. There's a restroom behind the store, and I need to stop. Will you go in and get me a soda?" She pointed to the chipped blue building, whitewashed by the sun. "Whatever they have. Just make sure it's cold. Please don't bring me anything warm."

"Yes ma'am," Alex answered, as if ready to give her a salute. Instead, he grinned, flashing his adorable dimple.

She followed the path to the restroom and smelled the block outhouse before she discovered it. Too gross to enter, she held her breath, thankful she didn't really need to go. Sofie waited against the wall until she heard the Blazer come up to the intersection.

Hiding, she skirted around the outside of the building. The Blazer made a left onto the lonely highway, headed towards Acapulco. Within a minute, she heard the Blazer's return. It made several maneuvers in the dirt before it parked.

Sofie peeked around the cinderblocks and saw the black truck hidden on the north side of the garage, facing the road. Hector, one of Ramón's lower-rung lackeys, stood next to it, smoking a cigarette.

She found Alex in the room, which was thinly disguised as a market. Moist, spongy air stirred beneath a wobbling ceiling fan. His broad shoulders were bent over an aged cooler as he rummaged through the galvanized tub of sodas, swimming in water and ice.

"Come on, let's go."

Alex seemed confused, but paid and followed.

Back at the Mercedes, he held up two drippy Cokes as if he'd scored first prize.

Once he closed the door and settled into the seat, she gunned the engine. The Mercedes spit dirt and gravel as she pulled onto the pavement.

Running his wet hands along khaki shorts, he whipped his head around, asking, "Is this the right direction?"

"I've been thinking. Ramón wanted me to show you around. Give you a tour. Have you ever heard of Monte Albán?"

"What is it?"

"It's this mesa of ancient Zapotec ruins, thousands of years old. Near Oaxaca, overlooking the city."

"Where?"

"Not far. Inland about sixty miles, maybe eighty."

"The difference between sixty and eighty miles over mountains can—"

"We go south and pick up the road at Puerto Escondido, then over the mountains to the Oaxaca Valley."

"Sounds like a long drive."

"We'll make it by sunset."

He frowned, unconvinced.

Southbound, she gave him a tour of Mexico per instructions—country style. They passed more green groves of papayas, with clusters of fruit hugging the trunks, small towns, larger than the "fruit stands" they'd seen further north, and miles of unspoiled landscape yet to be cleared and cultivated.

As they approached the ocean, tin shacks began to appear, surrounded by busy clotheslines strung between the trees. Here, they discovered horses grazing in fields of green grass. Alex pointed out elegant breeds he said would be coveted in Kentucky.

In Puerto Escondido, a town bigger than she remembered, they stopped at a Pemex station to get gas. She used the restroom, this time for real.

Alex was leaning against the car when she returned. With folded arms, he studied the mountains. "We're gonna cross those?" He raised his eyebrows. "By sunset? Hope you brought Dramamine."

"There's some in the glove compartment. It's not too far. A couple of hours."

He shook his head in disbelief.

Sofie looked up and down the road, checking.

"You lost him."

"Why didn't you say anything?"

"You had it under control. But that dirt road..." He laughed. "I don't think I'll be able to forgive you for destroying my kidneys."

"You saw him before the highway?"

"He brought the truck around before we left the ranch."

"Very perceptive." She wondered if Alex ever missed anything.

"I try to be," he said seriously. "Is this an issue of trust or control?"

"Probably both."

Alex looked delicious in a black T-shirt that fit snug across his contoured biceps. The coaster in her stomach made another dip, and she felt the catch in her heart. She couldn't decide what to do with her hands, fighting the urge to reach out and touch him, slip into his arms and feel the hint of his beard against her cheek again.

"Who is he?"

Lost in salacious thoughts, it took a moment for Sofie to regroup. "Hector. A new employee. The first time I saw him around was a few weeks ago."

"Well, I'm up for anything. Let's go for it." His grin was clearly skeptical. "You said we'll make it over the mountains by sunset."

She nodded, hoping childhood restlessness had grossly distorted the emerging memory of an interminably long and winding road.

Hours after the sun had set, they still hadn't reached the summit. Climbing another crooked finger of the trek, Sofie drove around a switchback into a tight corner, meeting a crowded transit bus barreling down the mountain. She screamed, slamming on the brakes.

"Jesus! Shit!" Alex yelled as she swerved into the low rock wall at the edge of the cliff. Thankfully, the Mercedes came to a stop and didn't hurtle hundreds of feet down the mountain.

Already queasy, she put her head on the steering wheel, gulping thin air.

"Forget sunset," Alex said. "We won't live to see sunrise with you behind the wheel. Before you get both of us killed, let me drive," he demanded.

She didn't argue, grabbing the gear shift to put the car into park.

"Not here. Keep going. At the next opportunity, pull over."

Shaking, Sofie righted the Mercedes and continued the crawl up the mountain to a tiny village, where they were finally able to make the switch. Alex found a flashlight in the glove compartment and inspected the damage.

"It's just a scrape on the wheel," he reported.

"I forgot to tell you how much I hate to drive."

"You should have mentioned it before. You're looking pretty green." He replaced the flashlight and shoved the box of Dramamine into her hand. "Take a couple of these. It will make you drowsy. With any luck, you can get some rest when we get back on the road."

Exhausted and sick, it was a relief to settle into the passenger seat. Sofie swallowed two pills and hoped the lulling effects would kick in soon...

Sofie startled awake when Alex touched her shoulder. Still surrounded by black mountains, they'd begun their descent into the Oaxaca Valley. In the east, the moon started its journey across the nighttime sky.

His voice was full of awe. "Look at that," he said, pointing into the distance.

A thunderstorm hovered over the city. From their vantage point, they watched brilliant bursts of light emanate from within the clouds, sending jagged shafts of electricity across Oaxaca and its suburbs. Sofie rolled down the window and let a blast of heated air envelope her. The nausea had disappeared and she felt much better, inhaling the pleasant petrichor of a fresh storm.

"I love summer storms," she said, listening to the music of thunder rumbling across the basin. "This is magnificent."

They dropped further down into the valley. It was as if Midas spread his palms below the clouds, fanning a golden city ahead of them. Oaxaca had been one of her mom's favorite places, and since Sofie's first visit, she felt its charisma too.

"Sorry. I guess I'm not as good as I thought at judging distance."

"You're forgiven. But only because I like the light show you ordered for the end of the trip," Alex teased.

Sofie smiled. Tonight, she was in control, traveling a road she'd chosen. Alex sat behind the wheel, following her directions, not Ramón's. There'd been no sign of the Blazer since they'd left the store at the crossroads hours ago. Sofie and Alex were alone and on their own. Maybe, sometimes, things work out better than intended after all.

CHAPTER TWELVE
Luna de Limon

Lemon Moon
Sunday, July 8, 1984

"It's near the zócalo and the cathedral. I can't remember the name, but I'll know when I see it," Sofie said, determined to find the bougainvillea-covered hotel where she'd stayed with her mom years ago.

Alex kept both hands on the wheel of the Mercedes and moaned, shaking his head. "You're driving me in circles. It's almost eleven. I'm *hungry*."

The rainstorm had moved on, but it depleted the Sunday night traffic along the city streets. Under street lights, the asphalt glistened, and as a reminder of the deluge, tiny rivers flowed down Oaxaca's gutters. She inhaled the honeyed air of the refreshed metropolis and smiled.

When they drove by a hotel and it wasn't the one she searched for, she endured Alex's heavy sigh.

"We'll be there by sunset? Yeah, right. Ever since we left the ranch, you've been steering me wrong. *Find a hotel.* At this point anything will do."

Feeling guilty, Sofie focused on the empty sidewalk. Her confident promises *had* translated into hours of corkscrewed mountain roads with little relief, and now they were in town, navigating a grid of narrow, one-way streets. She tried to ignore his complaints. "The hotel I stayed in before will be perfect. It has a beautiful courtyard and fountain."

As they passed yet another, he protested, "What about this one? All I want is a comfortable bed."

"The one I'm thinking of has those too—here's the zócalo!"

The plaza was surrounded by an ambitious cluster of shops and restaurants with archways along the ground floor. Upstairs, many of the buildings were decorated with ornate wrought iron, giving the square a distinctly European feel. Sofie wondered if the intent was to pay homage to Mexico's Spanish influence or to stamp out the city's ancient Meso-American history. Probably both.

"The cathedral is just up ahead. The hotel is around the corner from there."

"What's a zacowlo?"

Sofie swallowed a giggle as Alex mangled the language. "Zócalo. It means the main marketplace."

It looked like the shops and restaurants around the plaza were closing early, but light bulbs strung between the trees were still shining bright. An ornate bandstand sat in the center of the square, deserted and forlorn, a causality of the storm. Small groups of revelers lingered underneath covered patios. Fountains, brimming with water, splashed the already wet pavement.

Laurel trees had been planted in the last century to provide welcome shade from the sun during the day. Tonight, they released their own residual rain shower above deserted benches.

"There are wonderful artists. And the jewelry..." She watched the vendors shutter their stalls. "Oaxaca is famous for its gold."

"Seriously, Sofie, I don't want to shop." He continued to complain, "It's late and I'm hungry. I'll compromise. Let's park and eat. We can find your hotel later."

"The food's not great in the zócalo. The restaurants a few blocks over are better. There's this one, La Casita Diaz. It might be closed too—"

"Sofie! Come on! I'm starving!"

The cross-traffic cleared and the Mercedes moved forward.

"Here's the cathedral!" A pair of stately towers flanked an ornate crown, all bathed in brilliant gold and enhanced by the afterglow of rain.

"Isn't it magical, all lit up at night?" The massive Catholic cathedral appeared to be the Baroque rendition of Heaven. "Make a right."

Alex made the turn. She wasn't sure if he'd found the cathedral impressive. Apparently, he wasn't speaking to her anymore.

Sofie didn't mind. She loved driving through the city. Each block flooded her with fragments of newly discovered memories. On this street, the buildings had been ornamented with swirled, wrought-iron balconies. "There it is—no—that's not it," she said, shaking her head.

Frowning, Alex sent her a sideways glance.

"Sorry," she mumbled above his grumbling.

Finally, she recognized the intersection. "Left. Here!"

He spun the wheel and made the turn, his mouth pressed into a thin line.

The hotel's flower-draped entrance came into view. "Stop! Let me out," she said.

At the curb, she climbed from the car and stuck her head into the open passenger window. "There's parking in the back. I'll meet you inside."

Beyond the lobby of the hotel, Sofie stood in a courtyard surrounded by tall archways. Water rippled into a star-shaped fountain. Its tiles were a delicate blue and orange design, and as lovely as she'd remembered. She held the key to their room and waited for Alex, rubbing the pad of her thumb across the number twenty-seven etched into the smooth brass.

When he walked through the door with their bags, she hid the key, nervously twirling the metal skeleton on its ring behind her back. Minutes earlier at the front desk, she'd purposefully slipped her left hand below the counter and signed with her right, hoping the middle-aged man wouldn't notice her bare finger.

The clerk had met her eyes and hesitated for a moment before handing her the key.

She was relieved Alex barely understood Spanish when the clerk called from the lobby with an exaggerated, "Good night, and congratulations on your marriage, Mister Wilson."

Never mind, it was too late to be embarrassed.

Seemingly clueless, Alex nodded and mumbled, "Hola." Ignoring the clerk, he asked, "Where can we eat?"

"The clerk said the courtyard restaurant is getting ready to close, but they're holding a table for us while we take our bags up to the room." She gestured toward a waiter, busy wiping puddles off a pair of chairs on the patio.

"Do you like molé? Oaxaca is famous for its molés."

"I'll try anything. Once."

Sofie held up the single, large key. "How about twice?"

Alex cocked his head. He studied her as his grin spread, enveloping his features.

Captivated by his dimple, and satisfied that she'd been able to please him for the first time in hours, she fought the urge to stand on the tip of her toes and kiss him. With promises of food and sex, he was too easy.

"There was only one room left with a private bath," she explained. Sofie had left the accommodations up to fate and was thankful the stars seemed to be shining on her again. "With all of the others, you had to use a bathroom at the end of the hall."

Surveying the courtyard and the surrounding buildings, he said, "Good choice. Nice place."

"I told you so."

Many of the rooms were dark. Apparently most of the guests had retired for the night. "Isn't it beautiful?" she whispered.

"Is it how you remember?"

"In some ways, better." Having Alex with her made it perfect.

He stared over her head. She turned and followed his eyes to discover a tall, skinny silhouette. A man stood in one of the private balconies that overlooked the courtyard, watching them. Backlit by the lamplight in his room, he had no distinguishable features. He was just a man, wearing a wide-brimmed hat, holding a smoldering cigarette.

Turning toward Alex, she realized he was silently questioning her. The man didn't have Hector's compact stature, so she shook her head. Moments later, the guest stubbed the cigarette on the railing and flicked it down into the bushes.

"Just give me a blanket and a pillow. I'll sleep on the floor," Alex offered.

The man went inside, and the lamplight faded behind curtained French doors.

She kept her voice low, "That won't be necessary. It isn't as if we haven't slept together before."

Alex winked. "Technically, we didn't sleep much at all."

Sofie laughed and tried to take her bag.

With his duffle on one shoulder, a briefcase in one hand, and her overnighter in the other, he refused to let her carry anything. "Lead the way."

Inside the hotel room, she turned on the lamp and waited as he deposited their luggage onto the scuffed wood floor. The room was shabbier than she'd remembered, although the iron bed that took up most of the area was inviting.

They didn't bother to change or wash up. Instead, they made their way down the stairs, past arches illuminated by flames in filigreed sconces, and into the courtyard restaurant.

White lightbulbs had been strung across the patio, mimicking the zócalo, creating a pleasant ambiance. The waiter greeted Sofie and Alex, taking them to their table.

Sofie followed Alex's eyes above the courtyard again. Trellised bougainvilleas, their trunks as fat as trees, framed the same balcony they'd noticed before. Now, a rocking chair creaked in the shadows. The man had returned, smoking another cigarette. She studied him a second time, just to make sure. He still wasn't recognizable. There was nothing to worry about, so she concentrated on her menu.

The waiter moved slowly as the evening waned. He took a sip of beer from behind the bar, probably upset they'd waylaid an early close. Sofie squirmed in her chair, wilting in the pair of white cotton shorts and blue T-shirt she'd put on this morning, wishing she'd had time to take a quick shower. But her stomach had growled as well, and if she hadn't followed, Alex would have gone downstairs without her.

A couple occupied a table on the edge of the patio, finishing their meal. Otherwise, the courtyard was empty. Occasional laughter erupted from the Mariachis sitting at the bar. They were still dressed in the traditional black garb, their sombreros and instruments abandoned nearby.

Returning with a pencil and tablet in hand, the waiter apologized. They were out of this evening's special. Most of the menu was written in Spanish. Alex set his down and rubbed his eyes. Sofie ordered the drinks. Two cervezas.

"Do you want me to order for you?" she asked.

"You mentioned moles. What is it? Never tasted it. Only seen it on a menu."

"It's not a rodent," she teased. "It's a sauce made with chilies and chocolate. Do you like chicken?"

"Chocolate and chicken?" He scrunched his face then waved his hand. "I'll eat anything at this point. Surprise me."

The waiter brought their drinks and she placed their order in Spanish. When he left, Alex took a sip. "What's this beer?"

"It's local."

"It's good," he said, and took another drink. "I like these European hours. But still, we lucked out. Made it just in time. Nice of them to stay open after the storm chased everybody inside. Did you have to bribe the chef?"

"I used my extraordinary charms. Works every time." She grinned. "Worked on you."

"When you charmed me into driving over those mountains I didn't know we'd embark on a hair-raising trek halfway across the country." He faked the frown, his dimple gave him away.

"Oh come on. The drive was worth it. We're here and it's beautiful." Sofie glanced at the starry sky. "And we saw an amazing thunderstorm. Now, it's dry—more or less. We're relaxed, the drinks have arrived, and dinner will be here soon. What more could you want?"

"A shower and a comfortable bed." Alex tilted his head toward the rocker on the balcony. "Our friend, do you recognize him?"

"It's not Hector. No one else could possibly know we're here. I didn't make the final decision myself until I pulled onto the highway," she said, happy to have found some breathing space away from Ramón.

"Hector didn't know what he'd signed up for when he agreed to keep an eye on you…or us."

"Ramón means well." She tried to define her conflicted feelings. "He's just… He's protective of me. Our parents were close. My tío, Ramón's father, only had sisters. He was very protective too." At the center of the table, the flame flickered in the syrupy candle. "When my parents met, the family didn't like the idea she'd fallen in love with an Americano."

Alex picked up his beer and smiled.

"My mom ran away to be with him. Both my mom and tío have passed, and I think Ramón is trying to carry on family tradition."

She wasn't sure why she defended her cousin.

"No. That's not the only reason. He likes to be in control. It's all he knows."

"What year did your mother—?"

"In 1973. I was twelve. My uncle died several years ago; he's buried alongside my mom. My tía, his wife, rests next to him on the opposite side." Flooded with memories, Sofie didn't want to share anymore. As much as she loved being in this courtyard—at this hotel—it was emotional too. Sofie wondered if the need to repave bittersweet moments had been a factor in her impulse to bring Alex to Oaxaca.

"I'm sorry…" He covered her hand with his. "That sounds weak. I wish I had something more meaningful to say."

"It was a long time ago," she replied, shaking her head.

Sofie had been with her mom the last time she'd visited Oaxaca. They'd been on vacation; and her mom had appeared healthy, miraculously cured. Inhaling the city, they'd taken in everything Oaxaca had to offer. One afternoon, they lit candles at the cathedral, and later, here in the courtyard of the hotel, Sofie's mom had taken Sofie's cheeks into her hands and kissed her, saying she felt blessed with luck. They'd made wishes at the starred fountain, and, turning their backs, they tossed pesos into the water.

Just a few weeks after they returned to the rancho, the cancer had attacked her mom with a vengeance. She had been so brave while Sofie helplessly stood on the sidelines and watched her mother slip away.

Crossing her arms, Sofie sat back in her chair and steered the subject to her living family. "It's the family drama that sends me over the edge. Ramón can be so manipulative."

Alex watched her closely. "All families have their problems."

"Some are worse than others."

"You'd be surprised how screwed up most families are. They just don't talk about it. A few freaky limbs have branched from my own family tree," he confessed.

"I'm intrigued." She raised her eyebrows. "Elaborate."

Alex fell silent as the waiter delivered two platters of shredded chicken in a spicy chocolate sauce heaped over a bed of rice, with beans on the side. The waiter left and returned, placing a plate of fresh corn tortillas, wrapped in a warm towel, between them.

After Alex took the first bite, he seemed surprised. "This is good." He scooped another forkful and swallowed. "My uncle once climbed a transmission tower. He had to be extracted by the fire department. He said he could hear God communicating through the power lines. The miracle was he didn't get electrocuted. I think he got tired of waiting for the Rapture. I know the rest of us were tired of hearing about its imminent arrival."

She smiled and demonstrated how to stuff the molé into a warm tortilla.

Between gulps of beer he said, "It must be exhausting trying to work your way up to God," adding, "This food is good, *really good*."

He groaned, delighted this time. One more reason Sofie was glad they'd found the hotel. The molé *was* delicious, and so was the rest of the meal. She laughed, pleased he was pleased.

Alex laughed too.

"Worth the wait?"

Busy eating, he could only nod.

"Was this on your mom's side of the family?"

"No, one of my dad's brothers. For that stunt, my uncle spent some time in the hospital." Alex took the last sip of his beer. Getting the waiter's attention, he lifted the bottle, holding up two fingers.

She sensed the occasional waft of cool air in the pleasant breeze. Between the storm and the mountains, it was finally cooling down. "They released him?" she asked.

"Yep. I think he's a preacher in Florida. We 'heathens' haven't heard from him for awhile. I'm not sure if the Lithium is working or not."

"You have one person. We've had a few nut cases in our family."

"That's just my dad's side. On my mom's side, I have a cousin, Lisa, who went to prison." The waiter delivered the beers, and Alex thanked him. "Like most families," he continued, "crazies sprout in both directions."

"What did she do?"

"Embezzled fifty thousand dollars from her employer. The stolen money helped support her drug habit for over a year." Alex scowled in disgust.

He's sharing with me, so I should be willing to share my cousin too, Sofie thought. *What the hell, he's already seen the photo strip from the Santa Monica Pier.*

"Well, if we're talking about drugs, I think I have you there. My cousin Cecilia..." Sofie crumpled her napkin and dropped it on the table. Anger still propelled the words, "Ceci was my best friend. She died from a drug overdose."

It happened over two years ago, and the anger should have dissipated. But the rage lived, simmering in the center of Sofie's body, somewhere below her heart, above her stomach, boiling to the surface whenever she ruminated over the tragedy. Anger towards whom? Ceci, for her stupidity? Sofie herself, for not being able to see the impact of Ceci's destructive dance with cocaine and her downward spiral into addiction? God, who had stolen from Sofie not just the one, but the two most important people in her world?

Sofie bit her lip. Full of sympathy, Alex seemed to be waiting for more. She realized she didn't have anything else to give. The explosive emotions were still too raw, somewhat embarrassing. He couldn't understand.

Alex reached for her hand and gently rubbed her fingers with his, and they were warm and comforting. Their eyes met and she looked away. Exposed.

"Hey, I didn't get to finish my story," he said, finally breaking the silence that weighed heavy between them. "It gets better. My cousin fell in love with one of the prison guards while she was incarcerated. They're married now. Live in New Mexico. Made two kids."

Sofie felt her eyes widen. "Really?"

Smiling, he set down his beer and lifted his right hand. "Swear to God."

"I think you might win. Your family is pretty screwed up," she teased, knowing hers was just as dysfunctional. "Holidays must be interesting."

"My mom and dad are relatively normal. My sister, her kids and husband are great. Don't see them much. That's the problem. I haven't been home for the holidays in years. I'm usually working."

"The import-export business doesn't allow for holiday time?"

Alex shrugged, folding his napkin.

Clearly, he wasn't going to explain, so she changed the subject. "Cocaine. It's seductive. Several years ago, in LA, a friend of ours went to work for two guys who started this exclusive business installing custom stereo systems in people's homes. They did great. One had sales experience. The other had the technical brains. The technical guy—the guy who knew how to create these amazing sound systems—got strung out on coke. He would do anything to get it. Including cleaning out the business and family bank accounts. His wife left him. They lost the company. The last time I heard of him, he was at Ceci's, trying to find a dealer so he could score more coke to free base. Even Ceci realized he'd gone over the edge."

"You do drugs?" Alex asked, his voice grim.

Alex had rapidly become a comfortable friend, easy to talk to under exquisite starlight and over a few beers. "I tried pot once, in high school. It made me hungry and super paranoid. It's never been my thing. Coke? Occasionally, Ceci would get me to do a few lines. I remember the first time, we stayed in the kitchen talking most of the night. The guys sat in the living room, on the couch, watching TV. I know they hoped at some point we'd shut up—in retrospect, I can't blame them. But we didn't. We were full of energy and plans. It felt great. Coke was fun. Each idea seemed the most brilliant we'd ever had. Somehow, by morning, all those brilliant ideas lost their luster."

Almost imperceptibly, he moved his hand away. She noted it and continued with the truth, "Thankfully, coke is expensive and people who really get into it don't like to share. I didn't have the money. And it quickly became clear coke is a sneaker. It seriously lost its appeal when I started noticing the damage it did to Ceci and her friends. Horrible, terrible things."

She called the waiter over and asked for coffee. After he left, she asked Alex, "What about you? Any *Fast Times at Ridgemont High?*"

Alex slowly shook his head.

"Never?"

"No," he answered.

"Not even pot?"

"Not even pot."

"You're such a surfer boy. I'm surprised."

"Who said I surfed?" He leaned back in his chair.

"When I think about it, I guess there aren't great swells on Lake Michigan. I would have pegged you as the Spicoli, loadie type."

Alex laughed. "It's your fault I've been driving for hours. Give me a break!. I'm just tired."

"Seriously. I'm impressed. You made it through college without experimenting?"

"I'm more the ROTC type."

"Really? That would be my last guess."

"I'm older than you. Sometimes, it seems like a whole different generation." He finished off his beer and reached for the last of hers. "You mind?"

"It's all yours."

He took a drink. "Things were simpler then. Us older guys—us squares —believed in all America stood for. Fighting Communism. Going to Nam —"

"Well, you kept yourself from blowing a hole in your nose."

"A hole?" He lifted his eyebrows.

"You can blow a hole through your nose if you do too much cocaine. I thought my dad was trying to scare me when he told me. But coke constricts your blood vessels. If you snort a lot of it, the drug starts to cut off the blood supply, and that's when your nose begins to rot off."

Sofie watched Alex grimace.

"Seriously, I know several people who've had, or need, reconstructive surgery to repair their noses. Right here." She touched the small cleft on the side of hers.

Alex caressed her cheek and their fingers met. "I'm glad you made the right choices. Yours is still pretty."

A rush of warmth spread through her body.

"My dad's a doctor; he knows these things. But I didn't believe him until

I saw it for myself," she said. "You went to 'Nam?"

He pulled his hand away. "I did some time there."

Sofie looked down at the table. They'd devoured their meal, talking between forkfuls the whole time, and now both plates and the tortilla platter were clean. The waiter delivered coffee.

"You want anything more? Dessert?" she asked.

"I'm full. You?"

"Me too." Sofie hesitated, unsure whether the next question would be welcomed. "The war. Do you feel like talking about it?"

He appeared to choose his words carefully, "Not much to tell. Nothing interesting."

Like Ceci was for her, Viet Nam may be Alex's own dark well of emotion. Sofie willed herself to respect that. But she wanted more, eager to learn everything about him—the good stuff and the bad.

"How was it when you came back home?" She'd heard the stories of soldiers coming back from Southeast Asia being treated badly. Some were called "baby killers," others even worse.

"I did a lot of traveling back in the States."

"Where?"

Alex ran his finger along the rim of the glass candleholder. "All over. Lots of places. No place as nice as home."

"Do you still believe?"

"In freedom and American pie?" He chuckled. "Isn't that a song?"

"Believe in what America tried to accomplish over there?"

"I don't know." He contemplated the remains of the beer, appearing to search for one last swallow.

"We have to protect ourselves. As for exporting the American Way, in the sense that we should dictate how the rest of the world should work?" He shrugged.

The waiter brought the bill. Alex signed it to their room, and once again they were alone.

"I used to believe this, now I'm not sure. The cost is too high," he said.

Alex hesitated, as if he wanted to say something more.

She paid attention and focused on his beautiful face, knowing the classification would offend his masculine sensibilities.

He put the empty beer bottle down and closed his kissable mouth.

"Anyway," he said, sighing, "Americans don't want to watch the realities of war on the nightly news. Public support fades. Heroes, men more courageous than I, were ordered to withdraw like cowards from Viet Nam. We lost the country, and good friends, good men, died for nothing. The battle has been reshaped and continues on multiple fronts. It's a losing one."

Sofie didn't quite comprehend. "What do you mean?"

"It's complicated."

"I think the United States has a lot to say for itself," she argued. "And a lot to teach the rest of the world. I can't help but wonder if my mom would still be alive if she had stayed in California and taken advantage of the first-class medical treatment available there. We've been driving for hours through villages unchanged in a hundred years. Nothing advances. They love their mothers too. Don't they deserve a chance?"

"Your family benefits from this society."

"That doesn't mean it's right. If I'd ever intended to live here, I wouldn't be an accountant, I'd teach. The village near the rancho doesn't even have a teacher for its school most of the time. Without education, nothing will ever change."

"Wouldn't Ramón disapprove?"

"The upper class has an investment in perpetuating the status quo. Ramón doesn't approve of much I've done lately, except get my degree. I have no intention of letting him, but *if* he manages to hold me hostage in Mexico, I'll start teaching in the village. Maybe I can use my college protest skills to cause a local uprising and secure my freedom," Sofie said with a wicked smile. Glancing around the deserted restaurant, she pumped her arms in mock protest. "Start a new revolución!"

Sofie and Alex laughed. The waiter, chatting with the bartender drying glasses, ignored them.

"Ramón would appreciate that." Alex's eyes sparkled.

"I'm sure he would. With me, he'll get more than he bargained for."

"You are more than anyone could bargain for."

A rush of pleasure washed over Sofie, full and content.

"Tell me about your cousin Felipe?"

"What about him?"

"He's around, but he stays on the sidelines, looking uncomfortable," Alex said.

"Felipe has always been painfully shy. I think it's because he feels different. You noticed his arm?"

"Yes."

"It's some kind of birth defect. My mom told me that when he was born, my aunt was in labor for days. It was a difficult home birth and, for a while, they thought my aunt would die—but thankfully, she survived. Felipe is really, really intelligent. If he had more confidence, he could give Ramón a run for his money. When I left Mexico, he was headed for the seminary. I discovered he'd come home when I got back this summer. It's a mystery. I'm not sure what happened. What did you think of the molé?" she asked.

"It's great. Rich. I never imagined a mixture of chocolate, chilies, and chicken could taste this good." He wiped his mouth with the napkin.

"As far as crazy family goes, I still think I might win," she said. "You missed a spot." She licked her thumb and ran it across a tiny speck of sauce on the corner of his mouth. "Well, on second thought, it could be a tie."

"My family is little strange." He grinned.

"You still haven't heard all about mine. But I want to ask you a question."

Alex nodded. "Shoot."

"The other night in the club, did Ramón ask you to keep an eye on me?"

"Seriously, how can you think that? We're the ones who need a chaperone, and you lost him."

"I was just wondering." She lifted the hair from her sticky neck, let the breeze do its magic, then ran her fingers through her curls. "I have a confession to make."

Alex spoke slowly, "Yes?"

"I'm glad you were there. In the hallway."

He chuckled. "It's a relief to know I'm not an asshole bastard."

"I wasn't looking for 'fuckable' men."

"I know."

"All I wanted to do was dance. Then you came along."

"I can't dance."

Remembering Alex last night, she blushed. "But you've mastered all the important moves."

Alex reached for her hand.

It was getting late, past midnight now, and she shivered—from anticipation or the drop in temperature she couldn't tell. She looked up into their room. Lamplight filtered onto the balcony from behind closed curtains. "About the room—"

"Yes? Another confession?"

"Well… It was a little awkward at the front desk. Here, people still are very traditional, even in the city." She hesitated, trying not to stumble over her next words. "I had to sign us in as Mister and Misses." Quickly, she explained, "I hope you don't mind. It's a culture thing, and this is one of the nicest hotels in Oaxaca."

"So, we're on our honeymoon?" Alex said, amused.

Even in the dim lighting, she could see the hint of fine lines crinkling the skin around his eyes. Embarrassed, she said, "You know what I mean."

He appeared to be enjoying this too much. "What do you want, Sofie?"

"I want you," she whispered.

Sofie didn't sound as sophisticated as she'd hoped. She wanted to be liberated enough to maintain a casual sexual relationship. Alex, years past college romances that held any expectation of commitment, wouldn't want a crier—a girl who collapsed into his arms, begging him not to leave after a few days of fantastic sex.

Determined not to humiliate herself, either now or later, she took a breath and said, "But let's keep this light and fun. Okay? No expectations."

"Sofie..." Alex frowned and studied her with wary eyes.

Catching the scent of jasmine in the cool breeze, Sofie crossed her arms, realizing she'd need a sweater if they didn't go inside soon. "I was in a relationship for a long time. I don't want commitments or expectations. I want right now."

She hoped she'd spoken the truth and not told another lie like the others, designed to deflect Alex—and sometimes even herself—from what really went on in her head. She wanted him. Needed him. For how long? That might take time to decipher.

Alex sighed. "*Listen.* I'm not in a place that I can offer anything more than a couple of days."

Though not unexpected, these weren't the words she'd secretly hoped to hear. Suddenly, she imagined a woman who loved him, someone he loved too, waiting back in Chicago. Her stomach twisted with dread.

"I should have asked this earlier. You said you aren't married. But are you involved with anybody?"

"No, that's not it. My life... This isn't a good time..."

Silence fell like a blanket over the table between them. He didn't owe her any more explanations. Their eyes met, and she read unmistakable desire in his.

Finally, he said, "Are you *sure* you can handle no expectations?"

"Of course."

Yes, Sofie was risking her heart, but she needed to see how long this blaze between them could burn.

"Sofie. You intrigue me. You're bright, interesting, beautiful—"

"Stop." She raised her hand. "You're embarrassing me. And not paying attention. Wasn't I the one who insisted we keep it light?"

"You didn't let me add 'a pain in the ass,'" Alex teased. "Are you sure? No promises? No expectations?"

Sofie nodded.

"We have a deal then?"

"Deal," she said, lacing her fingers into his.

He gently massaged her thumb. "I'm ready for bed."

"The candle first." Sofie nodded towards the candle on the center of the table.

"What?"

"Let's blow it out. Together. Make a wish."

"I don't believe in magic. You said you didn't either."

"I've given up believing in the magic of water. Tonight, I'll take my chances on fire."

He seemed confused.

Sofie puckered her lips and blew. The flame flickered and died. Her wish consisted of one word.

Alex.

CHAPTER THIRTEEN

Amor en la Sombra

Love in the Shade
  Monday, July 9, 1984

Sofie set the brush down and wiped her hand across the mirror, watching a new wave of condensation blur the glass. She had no idea how she'd walk into the bedroom, climb into bed with Alex, and keep her heart from spiraling out of control.

I'm such a liar.

Full of dread—and at the same time, anticipation—that he'd join her, she'd sent Alex into the shower first despite his protests. What she'd needed most was time, to calm herself and sort her feelings. To reach conclusions that never seemed to arrive.

Alex waited for her on the other side of the wall. All of a sudden, she felt shy and a little afraid. Dropping her towel to the floor, she slipped on a fresh T-shirt and panties. She wiped the mirror again, brushed her teeth, and hung the towel on the bar.

Another crossroad, never or... *Now.*

Opting for the latter, Sofie opened the door.

He had made a heartwarming attempt to set a romantic scene. Using the thin, red scarf that decorated the dresser, he'd covered the bedside lamp, muting the light in the room.

His boxers were on the floor beside the bed.

Everything was perfect.

If he'd only been awake.

Alex was asleep on his side, the gentle rise and fall of the sheets belied his heavy, rhythmic breathing. The drive must have done Alex in.

She climbed in beside him, covered herself with the sheet, and stared at the cream-colored bead board on the ceiling.

Shit. All that anxiety for nothing.

Sofie got up and switched off the light. Returning to the bed, she listened to water trickling in the starred fountain, thankful she'd left the French doors ajar so a cool breeze could flow into the room. Alex began to snore. Not an irritating rumble, but a benign cadence that made her smile, glad there'd only been one available room. *I can get used to this*, she thought, letting the music of Alex and water lull her senses...

Surfacing from a sleep, Sofie felt Alex's hands move up her legs and gently spread them apart. For a moment she thought she might be dreaming.

No, this was real.

She kept her eyes closed, reveling in the spark and the slow, exquisite burn. His fingers lingered, caressing her inner thighs, stopping at the elastic of her panties. One finger slid under. Another. Using his palm, he cupped her mons.

Sofie raised her hips, wanting more.

His calloused fingers teased, not quite slipping inside. Instead, he moved his hand away, lifted her hips even higher and disposed of her panties. She heard the fabric land on the floor.

"I always knew your skin would be this silky," Alex whispered. Licking the shell of her ear, he stopped to suck on the lobe before pulling the T-shirt over her head. "I want you naked."

Raising her knees, Alex spread her legs wide. Hot breath on her thighs sent waves of sizzling passion flooding through her, as he positioned himself on the bed, cradling her bottom between his arms so his hands were free.

Starting midway up her legs, he lowered his head and ran his tongue along her thighs, dividing his attention between both, before moving higher, using his fingers to find her core.

An achy desperation, demanding friction, gathered at the source and rippled through her body, soaking Sofie in desire.

Pleasure built in measures, calculated and controlled by Alex. Finally, Sofie opened her eyes, needing to see his expression.

It was still dark outside. Inside, scarlet light filled the room. Earlier, while she slept, he must have turned on the lamp.

Alex looked up into her face, smiling. "Did I wake you up?"

Fully open to him, Alex was nestled between her legs with an unadulterated view of her most intimate parts. Ben had never taken time to study her so closely.

She blushed, feeling shy and overexposed, and reached over to turn off the light.

He grabbed her arm, and brought it down to the bed, holding tight. "No, don't. You're beautiful. Everywhere."

Their eyes locked. His harbored fascination as he licked the inside of one thigh, then moved to the other. Up. Closer.

Sofie scooted into the iron headboard, and grabbing a pillow, she propped herself up on her elbows.

Stopping, Alex grinned. "Good. I want you to watch me taste you." He lowered his head, and with the tip of his tongue, he flicked the pearl between her legs. A jolt of exquisite electricity ricocheted through her body and settled into a vibrant hum.

He smiled. "I need to investigate," he said, framing a better view. He bent his head, licking her pearl. She inched closer to his lips. His magnificent tongue.

On the edge, pulsing in anticipation, Sofie bowed her body to meet him, seeking maximum contact. Wanting—no, *needing*—more.

Burning all over, her breath came up short as his fingers moved inside. Wet, her own juices mixing with Alex's saliva, his mouth was now fully on her. She'd do anything—*anything*—so long as he didn't stop, as she edged closer to her own personal cliff, ready to free fall into ecstasy. *Here I go, I'm coming, right there, yes, yes, yes...*

Explosive waves of pleasure shuddered through her body. She cried out, unable to stifle the complete release.

Undecipherable tears formed, collecting in the corners of her eyes.

Alex began to work his way up, covering her with kisses. Starting at her hips, he planted one on each side, then one on her stomach, her breasts, neck, eyelids. Finding her lips, he blessed her with a deep soulful kiss, she tasted herself as he slipped his tongue into her mouth.

"That's never happened to me before. It was amazing."

"No, Sofie. *You are amazing.*"

Fluffing his floppy, surfer-boy hair, she said, "Thank you."

His blue eyes glittered with satisfaction. Poised above her, Alex was hard and ready.

She arched up to meet him, wanting him inside of her, now.

With a slow thrust, he melded into her body.

It wasn't just the magnificent fullness of Alex being inside of her, or the irresistible response he could conjure with his hands and mouth, there was something more in their coupling. For the first time in years, she felt she belonged. There was no denying it: In his arms, she'd found home.

Alex began his sweet assault and Sofie arched up to meet him, move for move.

Abruptly he stopped.

"What?"

"Take your necklace off. I don't want anything between us."

"But…" How could she explain? Sofie had worn the silver heart every day for years. How could she turn down this request?

"Please?"

Relenting, Sofie lifted her head and let Alex remove the necklace.

Alex slipped it on the post of the iron bed and thanked her with a kiss, lifting her bottom back into position.

Intuitively, Sofie's body relaxed, and she adjusted her hips to find the perfect spot for maximum sensation. And while Ceci's necklace jingled against the bed, Alex drove her to another shattering climax.

Breathing heavily above her, Alex seemed lost in the moment. She felt his heart, a rapid beat against her breast, as the spasms of his desire spilled seed into her body.

Afterwards, both sweaty and spent, Alex propped himself on his elbows, and Sofie followed him with her eyes. With his nose he touched hers, kissing it before he rolled away. Lying on his back, he placed the back of his hand on his forehead and sighed. With his other arm, he adjusted her body, cradling her into him.

Sliding her leg over his, she ran her fingers along the fine, masculine hair of his chest. Sofie beamed. She'd never experienced two orgasms in succession. Usually, one wasn't so easy to achieve.

Sofie hadn't known it could be like this. Ben had never been so attentive. She'd always held a part of herself back, unwilling to let go.

Maybe she hadn't been with the right person. *Until now.*

Alex had not only *made love* to her, it was as if she'd been cherished. This was extraordinary. Their two bodies had become fully intertwined and they'd become one.

The afterglow was a lush, elemental sensation, awash with the pleasure of their bare bodies folded together, *skin on skin.*

There was no guilt. *None.* Instead, Sofie felt wrapped in a timeless, sacred privilege. Every bit of angst and confusion drained away, her soul being replenished with a serenity she'd never felt before. Sofie realized she'd been waiting for Alex, all of her life—even in the moments when she believed she didn't need anyone or anything.

How could I know where I needed to be if I've never been there before?

Sofie was in big trouble. Already she was falling in love with a man who'd told her, up-front, love wasn't an option.

When Sofie felt the tears begin to pool in her eyes again, she moved out of his arms, so he wouldn't notice, and turned her back to him.

He rolled over, spooned her into his body, and whispered, "You okay?"

"Yeah, fine. Just tired."

Alex kissed the back of her hair. "Let me hold you, baby. Go to sleep."

CHAPTER FOURTEEN
Bailarines de la Mesa

Dancer's Mesa
Monday, July 9, 1984

It's night and we're in the Mercedes. I don't recognize the road or the surrounding flatlands, but somehow I know we're in Mexico. Ceci is driving. Alex is sitting behind us. He lights up a joint. I know this because I can hear the exaggerated, sucking sound coming from the back seat and smell thick, sweet smoke filling the interior of the car. He passes the joint to Ceci and she takes it. She purses it to her lips and inhales.

They're both laughing. I'm the only one watching the road, and I don't have control. Ceci and Alex are high, really high. They have that flinty, lacquered look people get that frightens me, because they aren't in control either.

Ignoring me, they joke with each other and my panic intensifies, scrambling up a flight of stairs toward hysteria.

"Jeez, Sofie!" Ceci says, "Lighten up! It's fun!"

I'm begging her to slow down. She won't stop and careens across the edges of the pavement.

Headlights appear from the opposite direction and saturate the road. I open my mouth to scream, but can't move the sound past my throat. At the last moment, Ceci dodges the blinding glare.

"Chicken!" Ceci squeals with glee.

Alex is in the center of the back seat, perched on the edge of it, egging her on.

The headlights are back, on our tail.

I turn to look.

It's the black van.

Pushing. Pushing. Pushing us. Until the Mercedes skids against a low rock wall, then up, over, and down the cliff...

141

Sofie woke, breathing hard and flooded in panic. Her heart beating a rabbity patter, she clutched the thin sheets and realized it had only been a dream.

Relieved, she focused, letting her surroundings sink in.

Alex was sleeping next to her, his arm draped over her hip.

Ceci is gone. Sofie gasped, feeling a final hitch of panicked pain.

Alex and Ceci will never meet.

The van was a horrible, scary mix-up. A long-ago memory she'd tucked away, only to surface infrequently in her dreams.

In fact, it had been almost a year.

A small, lemon-colored bird welcomed Sofie when she opened her eyes, fluttering around the bougainvilleas framing the balcony. She watched him through open French doors, searching for breakfast among the magenta flowers.

There'd been nothing of the real Alex in her dream. Before dawn, he had used his hands to wake her, plying her into intense, pleasured awareness, before he eased into her yet again. Sometime after the cathedral bells chimed five, Sofie, wrapped within Alex's arms, drifted back to sleep, splendidly satiated.

Sofie concentrated on shaking off the dream and focused on last night's dinner. She smiled, adding a second wish to last night's extinguishing candle: *Please, Alex, give us a chance to explore this—whatever this is—happening between us.*

The little lemon bird landed on the rail, bobbing its tiny head, on alert, waiting. A minute later, his less colorful mate joined him, and they flew off together.

Easing out of Alex's arm, she checked her watch—eight-fifteen.

Still half asleep, Alex sensed her movements and spooned her body back into his, ruffling her hair with his breath.

They needed more time. Time they didn't have.

Like the birds on the balcony, Sofie wished they could fly off together. *No complications. No expectations.*

Then she remembered. *Don't some birds mate for life?*

Sofie waited for Alex's slow cadenced breathing to return before she slipped from the bed and went into the bathroom.

Just as Sofie finished rinsing shampoo from her hair, Alex opened the shower curtain, naked and grinning.

"Want some company?" he asked. Not waiting for an answer, he climbed into the tub.

They soaped each other up, and when they rinsed off, Alex pressed her body against the blue Mexican tiles and they made love beneath the spray of water. Afterwards, he soaped her up again.

She left him in the shower and grabbed a towel. After drying off, she fastened the towel across her chest and opened her makeup bag, looking for deodorant.

Alex peeked from behind the shower curtain. "Hey, where are you going?"

"Back to bed. I need rest," she teased.

As she left the bathroom, Alex sang, "Won't Get Fooled Again," slightly off key.

Sofie smiled, his voice was endearing, but The Who wouldn't be calling Alex to replace Roger Daltrey anytime soon.

Below, a new day was getting started. Hotel guests ate breakfast in the courtyard; their murmurs and occasional laughter filtered up into the room.

Not ready to put clothes on just yet, Sofie closed the French doors and settled herself within the rumpled linens.

The pipes creaked and steam began to seep from the bathroom.

Hmmm… He must like his showers hot. There's so much of him she'd yet to learn.

Discarding the towel, she nestled within the cool bedding, enjoying the luxurious sensation of cotton against her skin. She was a little sore *down there*, but their time together was limited, and she hoped he'd want her once more before they dressed for the day.

It occurred to her that the negativity she'd felt toward Alex in the beginning may have been a form of self-protection—that somehow, after their first meeting, she had innately known it would eventually come to this. The realization sent a fresh wave of panic coursing through her body.

They were headed back to Acapulco today. These would be their last hours alone. Soon, Hector would be around, with watchful eyes. Others might be spying too, happy to report to Ramón.

Here, they were wonderfully free.

Sofie adjusted both pillows against the headboard and tucked the sheet under her arms, remembering Alex's words last night: *I don't want anything between us.*

She found her necklace hanging on the iron bedpost and slipped it on, returning it to its home between her breasts, while she waited for her lover.

It would be devastating if she lost the silver heart.

Sofie realized if she had to let Alex go, that would be devastating too.

Alex shut off the water and the pipes groaned again. Appearing in the doorway, his long hair was slicked back—dark, wet and already beginning to curl at the ends. He had the shadowy beginnings of a beard, and was definitely delectable with the towel wrapped low on his hips.

"Ready for breakfast?" he grinned.

"What do you have in mind?"

Alex raised his eyebrows. "Is that an invitation? I thought I'd give you a break."

"Isn't there a song called 'Afternoon Delight'?"

"I'm more of an early morning guy, myself. But, don't get me wrong." Alex winked. "Any time will do."

"I'll be out in a minute," he added, and vanished behind the open door.

She imagined him ogling himself in the mirror, then conceded he deserved a bit of admiration. She'd done a fair amount of ogling of her own.

"I've decided you sing better than you dance, but either way, don't quit your day job," she called.

Alex laughed from the bathroom. "What? I'm no Sinatra? No Astaire? I'm offended. You haven't seen my moonwalk yet."

He turned on the faucet and popped his head around the corner. "Can you do me a favor, beautiful? Will you get the shaving kit from my duffle bag? It's right on top."

Alex has said it twice now. He thinks I'm beautiful.

Elated, Sofie found her T-shirt on the floor and slipped it over her head. His bag was on the ground in the corner of the room. She bent over, unzipped it, and pulled out the small black leather case.

When she stood, she accidentally kicked the duffle bag, and her big toe connected with something solid. Rock hard.

"Ouch! Crap! That hurt"

He'd teased her about bricks in her purse. Apparently, he owned one.

She limped to the bathroom doorway. The water was still running in the sink. He must not have heard her yelp.

Alex reached for his shaving kit. As an afterthought, he peeked his head around the corner, kissed her cheek and mumbled, "Thanks," before he closed the door.

"Don't think I didn't notice the T-shirt. I'll be out of here in a few minutes," he called. "I'd like you back in bed, preferably naked."

Sofie slipped off the T-shirt and climbed onto the mattress, massaging her foot.

What does he have in the bottom of his bag?

Too curious to stop herself, she crossed the room to his duffle.

❦

"It's all yours, if…" Alex said.

Sofie sat on the bed, pale and glowering.

He stopped just outside the doorway. "What?" he asked.

"Why do you have a gun?"

Fuck. Fuck. Fuck. He'd opened the door to one more mistake in a succession of stupid moves.

What am I thinking?

His loud mouth in the nightclub, kissing Sofie on the beach, running off with her to Oaxaca—a list of fuck ups.

He should have known she'd look through his bag. Mistrust inflamed his own suspicions, and he turned it around. "You searched through my luggage?"

"I didn't *search* through your luggage. My big toe found it when *you* asked *me* to do *you* a favor."

Deflect, and buy time.

"Are you hurt?" He took a step into the bedroom.

Shaking her head, Sofie cringed, shrinking into the headboard.

Alex could see fear and misgiving in her eyes. She studied him as if she didn't know him at all.

She doesn't.

"You don't need to be—"

"I hate guns!" she exploded, her voice shaky, on the verge of tears. "You have no idea what it's like. Have you ever had a gun in your face? Felt cold steel against your nose?"

He was stunned by her admission. At the same time, he had to stop himself from saying. *Well, Sofie, actually I have.*

The question was, who held a gun on her? *Ramón? Unlikely. One of his thugs?* It wasn't the time to ask. When he regained her trust, he'd discover the story.

Watching her, he wondered if he'd ever get the chance to do either. His beautiful Sofie sat on the bed, her fist fearfully clutching the sheet to her throat.

She was the one snag he'd never, *ever* considered. Alex took another step into the room.

"Don't."

He froze.

Sofie continued to stare, her emerald eyes narrowed. "Who are you?"

"I'm the good guy."

Alex saw her attempt to read him. Covering, he silently tried to deliver all the compassion he could muster. Seconds seemed to turn into minutes, minutes into hours.

"Ramón put you up to this, right? He gave you the gun before we left, for protection."

Clearly, she needed an acceptable scenario.

Alex nodded, relieved she'd been able to manufacture one.

"Ramón knows I hate to drive, so when I've travelled he's tried to get me to carry a gun too. But I hate guns even more than driving alone," she explained. "He's worried that I'll have car trouble or something. Afraid of the dreaded *peasants* coming to get me. I had enough common sense to refuse him. Obviously, you didn't."

"It isn't loaded."

"Well, *that's* a relief."

Adjusting the sheet, she revealed his .45 caliber. It was a stark, metallic contrast against the white cotton.

Considering her hatred of the weapon, Alex was astounded—and a little worried—that his gun had been laying beside her all along, beneath the sheets.

Sofie motioned to where it lay, and moved to the far edge of the bed. Dismissing it, her lips curled with distaste. "Come get it. Put it back in your bag. Don't let me see it again. If I do, you'll be taking a bus back to Acapulco."

Alex crossed the room and picked up the gun, returning it to his luggage. He zipped the duffle, went back to the bed, and sat on the other side of the mattress.

He didn't think her eyes had moved from him since he'd stepped into the room.

Reaching across the bed, he wrapped his fingers around her trembling hand. He wanted to help. "Tell me."

"It was a long time ago," she answered. "I don't want to talk about it."

"Tell me anything. I'll listen. I promise, you can trust me."

He watched her body relax as her defenses noticeably crumbled.

Pulling her into his arms, Alex rubbed her sweet, silky back until finally —finally—her tremors began to subside.

He kissed her forehead, despising himself for having said, "*You can trust me*," because he knew he could never keep the promise.

Sofie moved back and let the sheet fall between them. Taking off her necklace, she placed it on the bedpost and slipped into his arms, just the way Alex liked it, *skin to skin*.

"I do," she said. "I do trust you."

❦

As Alex's tour guide, and in an effort to steal a few extra unmonitored hours, Sofie planned a late morning visit to Monte Albán, which sat on a plateau high above the Oaxaca Valley.

After they had eaten a quick breakfast of pastries and hot chocolate, Sofie went downstairs and asked the hotel to pack them a lunch so they could picnic on the site.

Within an hour they'd packed, and once they were in the hotel lobby, Alex had tossed Sofie the car keys and sent her around the corner for the Mercedes.

Now, Alex placed the small, white box from the hotel in the back seat. He loaded their bags in the trunk, shut the lid, and climbed into the passenger side, tucking two orange-colored bottles of soda in the top of her purse.

Shrugging, Alex said, "I don't really understand Spanish. I'm not sure what flavor these are, but they're cold."

Though the road to Acapulco should be an improvement over yesterday's trek, it still promised another long and arduous day of driving. On their balcony at breakfast, they'd already agreed to avoid the sights of the city. The cathedral wasn't nearly as impressive in the daylight, and even on a Monday, the zócalo was already over-crowded with people.

Monte Albán loomed ahead along an expansive mesa. They parked in the lot nearby. Luckily, the tour buses hadn't arrived yet, and the lot was nearly empty. Good. That meant they should have most of the ruins to themselves.

Sofie and Alex climbed the path to the mountain's plateau. Green grass covering the area struggled to blanket the long-lost city. Decayed stone buildings, steep stairways leading to giant platforms, and the remains of pyramids were positioned around the site.

Alex surveyed the scene. "This is huge."

"I know. Isn't it amazing?"

As predicted, they were nearly alone. They came across only one other couple, who weaved in and out of the openings that tunneled into the stone walls.

"It's so quiet now. Can you believe this was once a thriving city?" she asked.

"No," he said, inspecting designs along a wall of the North Platform before he slipped into one of the entrances.

Fearful of snakes, she waited outside and called into the foundation's depths, "There are tombs scattered all over the area. They found a fortune in jewelry here. Most of it is in the Oaxaca museum—beautiful gold, turquoise and coral pieces nearly two thousand years old."

"Is this where Ramón got the Zapotec statues?" Alex asked from inside.

Sofie shrugged. "My understanding is they came from an art dealer here in the city."

Materializing into the sunlight, Alex took her hand, pointing. "Let's go up those stairs."

They explored the grounds without a map. Sofie stood above the I-shaped ball court. "No one knows for sure the exact rules of the game, but apparently the competitions were pretty grisly. The losers were executed."

Alex grimaced. "Sounds like a Superbowl of death. You know a lot about this place. You've been here often?"

"My mom used to bring me here whenever we came to Oaxaca." She playfully nudged him. "You thought I was joking. Seriously, no trip to the valley is complete without a visit to Monte Albán," she said, adding a tour guide's enthusiasm to her voice.

At the top of the Gran Plaza, a magnificent pyramid with a fantastic view of the valley, Alex pulled her into his arms. "Thanks for bringing me up here. This is spectacular."

She stood on her toes for a kiss.

"I get the funniest feeling whenever I'm here," she confessed, loving the already familiar comfort in the way Alex draped his arm over her shoulder as he gazed out into the valley. "The only other time I've felt this way was when I was in New York City. My Tía Sofía, Ceci and I got the chance to visit Ellis Island. Another abandoned site."

Sofie hesitated, wondering if she should explain. "You're going to think

I'm crazy, but I can feel the people who once lived here. Not individual ghosts, just this collective humanity. I'm not quite sure how to explain it."

Alex ran his fingers along carvings etched into the stone. "This *is* a ghost town."

"Can you feel it too?"

"No. Don't feel a thing."

She started down the steps into the heart of the plateau. "Follow me. I'll take you to a building that's connected through an underground passage to another across the field. During religious ceremonies the priests would *magically* emerge on the other side."

Distracted by the ruins, they separated at the observatory. It was the only building on the mesa that wasn't part of a larger rectangle, receiving its coordinates from the stars.

She found him studying a group of stone slabs nearby. "There you are."

Sofie walked over to a slab carved with a crude depiction of a broad-shouldered man with protruding lips. The man in the etching wore a necklace and wheel-shaped earrings. "Aren't these incredible?" she said, "These are the Danzantes."

Alex raised his eyebrows. "Danzantes?"

"That means dancers," she explained. "But take a closer look—I don't think they're dancing. Many of them are really grotesque and violent. Archeologists think they represent conquests."

"Who did these?"

"I believe it was the Zapotecs. Their civilization peaked around the time Christ was born."

As they walked around the rest of the grounds, climbing up and down the ancient ruins, Alex disappeared again. Minutes later, he jumped out from behind a tall stone stele.

She shrieked and he pulled her to him, laughing.

"Watch out. I'm going to drop our lunch," she teased.

They stopped to picnic on the South Platform, along a low wall above the valley.

Sofie unwrapped two carne asada tortas and gave one to Alex.

He took a bite. "This is good. Why do they call this place Monte Albán?"

"No one knows for sure. Some believe a Spanish conquistador named it. Others think it's an extrapolation of a Zapotec word."

Wisps of brilliant white clouds floated across a vivid blue sky. Sofie opened the sodas, passed one to Alex, and took a sip of hers.

They ate in comfortable silence, not needing to fill the empty spaces, as if they'd been together for years.

Finally, he said, "There is something special about this place. It is peaceful. Even with all of those sadistic carvings."

"They are haunting." She laughed. "In a good way... Does that make sense?"

He looked at her and Sofie saw the dimple she'd fallen in love with. It faded away as his mood changed. The edges of his mouth turned grim and he seemed to study the mountains across the valley.

Sofie wished she knew what he was thinking.

Buses worked their way up the road toward the parking lot. In the distance, the sporadic pitch of tourist's voices began to filter through the mesa.

She scooped up their empty wrappers, stowed them in the picnic box, and finished her orange soda.

"Being here, I can't help but think about my mom and Ceci. Maybe it's the altitude, perched high on a plateau, on top of the world. Like this might be the first step on a stairway to heaven." She smiled. "I know that's silly, but my mom loved this place. I've never heard my Tía Sofía talk about Monte Albán. She followed my mom to the United States when she turned eighteen and hasn't returned. So, I don't think Ceci ever visited Mexico.

"But I feel connected to Ceci and my mom here. More connected than usual..."

Sofie wondered if she had Alex's attention. He still appeared to be focused somewhere in the charcoal-blue mountains across the valley.

It was a long time before he spoke. "I buried my best friend three years ago."

How was it possible they shared this same history?

She saw the desolation on his face and knew it was true. Hurting for him, tears gathered in her eyes.

His shoulders slumped, and he swallowed, "There have even been a few times I've picked up the phone to call, thinking, 'I've got to tell Nick this'... and then I remember..."

Subtly closing in, Alex sighed and crossed his arms.

Unsure of the best way to comfort him—if any comfort she could offer would even be welcome—Sofie kept her hands in her lap.

He looked down into the valley, offering no details.

"What happened?" she asked, wiping the corners of her eyes with a napkin.

"Nick was killed in a work-related incident. He had a wife and three little boys."

Unmistakable grief etched his features. She'd felt it—and seen it—before.

"I try to check in on them when I can. Not often enough."

"Did he work for your company?"

"No."

Collecting a pile of small rocks from the surrounding dirt, Sofie erected a pyramid of pebbles. Aiming at nothing in particular, she tossed one down the hill and watched it arc into the brush below. "Was he a friend from Chicago?"

"He died in Texas."

That's right, she thought. Alex said he was born in Texas. Nick must have been a childhood friend.

"Nick and I were different," Alex explained. "He rarely spoke, and when he did, people listened. Nick was a perfectionist, taking the time to make sure any project he tackled was flawless. He was a frustrated cabinetmaker, so good he could have done it for a living. You should have seen his garage. He built his own workbench and installed hand-crafted shelving along the walls. There was this old broom closet in his kitchen… When he married Danielle, he tore it out and built her this elaborate pantry."

Alex cleared this throat before he spoke again. "We met after I came back from 'Nam."

Nick wasn't a childhood friend after all. There was so much about Alex she needed to learn.

"It took him a while to make friends. He could be disconcerting, because you never knew what he was thinking. Nick was selective, but once he befriended you, you had a friend for life."

Alex's smile was bittersweet. "I didn't realize it at the time, but it was a gift to watch him with his boys, just roughhousing around their living room. I know they'll never forget their dad."

Picking up one of the small rocks from her pyramid, Alex pitched it down the hillside. It landed, a bull's eye, centered on the trunk of a tree. "Nick and Danielle were one of those couples really committed to each other. They fought sometimes—everybody does—but what they had was… special."

"Nick never took unnecessary risks. With one exception. His only guilty pleasure, his wild streak, his Indian."

"His Indian?"

"His motorcycle." Alex laughed. "An Indian who owned an Indian. Danielle tolerated it when she met him, calling it the 'Other Woman.' After they started having kids, she hated that bike, even when he finally broke under her constant nagging and agreed to wear a helmet.

"Nick hated helmets. He kept his hair long and usually wore it in a braid." Alex smiled. "Once, in a moment of weakness, he told me he liked the feel of wind blowing through his hair."

Alex's jaw moved as if he were grinding his teeth. Sofie knew exactly how painful this was for him.

"Danielle was sure he'd kill himself on the thing… But that wasn't the way he died."

Alex was somewhere else, someplace far across the valley, beyond the mountains. "I should have been there with him. I was busy at the time, working. Nick called and said he needed some feedback in regards to a situation he was dealing with at his job. I returned his call, but got no answer. By the time I got there, it was too late."

"I don't understand. Was it an industrial accident?"

"It's hard to explain."

Alex glanced up and closed his eyes, when he turned back they were shaded. "Some day, I'll tell you the whole sordid story," he said. "Not now."

"Hey." She reached up to touch his cheek. His skin was smooth beneath her hand. "I know the feeling. If you had done something different, you could have changed what happened."

"I could have."

Detecting the guilt in Alex's blue eyes, she understood. But, from experience, she also knew how insidious guilt could be.

"No." She ran her fingers along his chin, and held it. "Listen to me. It doesn't work that way. When it's someone's time, it's out of our hands. There's nothing left for us to do except move forward. Your friend Nick is fine. My mom and Ceci are fine." She slid her hand through the crook of his arm and rested it on his thigh. "I believe this. I have to. It's how I make it through each day.

"I guess, like Nick, Ceci had a wild streak too. Hers was different. She was a few years older than me, and growing up we were always in some kind of trouble with Tía Sofía. Nothing serious, but whatever it was, it was usually Ceci's idea."

Sofie sighed. "Then she fell in love. My tía almost had a heart attack when Ceci married Jaime, a guy from Colombia who lived in East LA. Everybody saw the mistake but Ceci. The best thing I can say about him is that he's really handsome. She worked and went to school and supported him. He used her. He cheated on her while he skated through a succession of jobs. The whole time they were married, I don't think he ever had anything steady. I think he was the one who introduced her to cocaine.

"It ended one afternoon, when she couldn't lie to herself anymore. She came home from work early and caught him in bed with the next-door neighbor."

Sofie tucked the empty soda bottles back into her purse. "After they separated, Ceci seemed to make better choices. At work, she met a lawyer, Eric—a decent guy—and moved in with him. And in the beginning, coke was cool, everybody was doing it. Doing it a lot.

"Well, not everybody. But Ceci gradually slipped into addiction, falling deeper and deeper into the drug scene. She got super thin and looked like hell. Eventually, my tía and tío found out and tried to get her help. Eric and I did too. Ceci insisted she had it handled."

Hurling the remainder of the pebbles, Sofie watched them cascade over the ledge and skitter down the hillside. "Ceci began to disappear for days, doing coke. A housekeeper found her in a motel room on Sepulveda Boulevard in the San Fernando Valley. The coroner said it was a speedball that killed her. At the time, I'd never even heard of a speedball. She shot up a mixture of heroin and cocaine."

Sofie shrugged. "The thing is, Ceci was terrified of needles. I still don't get it. No one suspected heroin. If any of us knew, she wouldn't have had a choice; we would have locked her up in rehab."

She thought she might have found the same spot across the valley Alex was fixated on, because it didn't feel like she was in Mexico anymore. "I was stupid. I was her best friend. I should have known."

Alex put his hand on hers. "There's nothing you could have done."

She'd told herself that too. It didn't always resonate. "If that's true for me, it's true for you as well."

Alex squeezed her hand and held it tight.

Another tour bus drove up the road, heading toward the parking lot. "Most of the time, I can convince myself it just *is*," Sofie said. "We have to find a way to make peace with this and go on. We'll never have all the answers."

Untangling her hand, Alex put his arm around her shoulder. She leaned into him and he kissed her forehead.

A middle-aged couple came up the stairs, disturbing their refuge, and began to explore the area. The man lifted the camera hanging around his neck and snapped a few pictures—thankfully, starting on the other side of the platform.

"Should we go?" Sofie asked.

"In a few minutes."

She nestled her body against his and waited for his cue.

CHAPTER FIFTEEN
Camino Hacia el Paraiso

Road to paradise
Tuesday, July 10, 1984

It was past midnight when Sofie and Alex began their descent into the city. She saw the lights of Acapulco and sighed. Things would change once they entered Ramón's domain.

They'd been driving for hours, only stopping to gas up the Mercedes and get something to eat. Then, once again, to switch drivers about two hours ago in the middle of nowhere.

The glow of the dashboard permeated their tranquil cocoon. Sofie felt more comfortable driving than she had in years, with Alex sleeping beside her. It seemed as if they'd been riding together her whole life. He was easy to talk to. Easier to make love with. She had never felt this safe with any man. But in minutes, she'd be back in her bed. Alone.

And there was nothing she could do about it.

"Hey, wake up," she said softly. "We're coming into town."

He smiled, but kept his eyes closed, shaking off sleep with a lazy yawn.

Finally, Alex looked around. "Where's the light show? This isn't as spectacular as the Oaxaca Valley during a thunderstorm."

"Where's Thor when we need him?" She laughed.

"I'll take you to your hotel. Go to the front desk with the keys tomorrow, and I'm sure they'll come fix the Jeep," she suggested.

He grinned. "Just take me to your place."

Alex wants to come home with me.

Ecstatic, Sofie realized he wasn't ready for this—whatever *this* was—to wind down either. "As much as I'd like you to stay with me, you can't," she

155

explained. "Monica's mom, my Tía Angélica, lives in the house with us. And Hector will probably be around. I need to check in. Alone."

"What are you going to tell Ramón if he calls and asks where we've been?"

"The truth. I've been showing you around the city as he requested." She smiled. "I just won't mention which one."

"He'll buy it?"

"Ramón has no choice, unless he decides to tell me he sent our misguided friend, Hector, to stalk us. And Hector...I don't know him well enough to guess what he told Ramón. Don't worry. Seriously, I can handle my cousin."

"The Jeep runs fine by the way. I removed the distributor cap."

Sofie raised her eyebrows. "What?" She had assumed he'd wanted more time together too. Now, she felt stupid. In reality, he just needed to pick up his car.

"You lied to me about the Jeep?"

"I wasn't giving in to your degrading attempt to get me to drive to the ranch in a doll's car."

"You were being an asshole."

"You were being a bitch."

"Touché."

"Don't go French on me. Spanish is bad enough," he teased. "Technically, you lied first. You said there wasn't a car—one we could use on Friday." Alex leaned across the console and gently rubbed her shoulder. "Really? You wanted to bounce around the countryside in that ridiculous Jeep," he asked, smacking his palm on the padded roof, "when we have this comfortable, air-conditioned Mercedes?"

Sofie didn't want to admit he had a decent argument. Instead, she asked a question, one that bothered her ever since she found the gun in his bag: "What other secrets have you hidden from me?"

"Tell me yours and I'll tell you mine." Alex winked.

She wanted answers, but Sofie wasn't ready to make any confessions of her own.

Once in the city, they followed the Costera along the beach, drove up the hill, and turned into the Las Brisas neighborhood. Soon, the headlights of the Mercedes lit the familiar foliage fence. Sofie punched in the code and the iron gate skimmed over the driveway.

The Jeep sat parked where he'd left it.

She shut off the ignition. Finding the release for the trunk, Sofie got out of the car and met Alex in the shadows. Heated moisture, nearly as thick as rain, hovered in the air. "Well, here we are."

"You and your skewed sense of distance." Alex pulled her into his arms, resting them loose against her bottom.

Sofie reached up and laced her fingers around his shoulders, once again reminded they were a perfect fit.

"You were worth every kilometer," he added.

Running her hand along Alex's chin, she brought her lips to his, and tugged lightly on his hair. "I'm not ready. To go in."

"Then don't." His breath, sweet and hot, sent chills down her spine. "Come with me to the hotel," he murmured into her ear. Lowering his mouth, he nibbled her neck.

Torn, she moaned, "I can't... Hmmm... I shouldn't. I'm probably in enough trouble already."

Alex leaned back and met her eyes. "You said you could handle this."

Sofie wasn't certain if he was talking about Ramón or their blossoming relationship.

"I can. It won't be a problem," she answered both possibilities and bit her lip. "Ramón told me you're going back to Chicago this week. When are you leaving?"

"Wednesday afternoon."

"Oh," her voice wilted. Sofie wanted to say more, something like, when will you come back? Or, will I ever see you again?

No commitments. No expectations.

She snuggled herself into his arms, inhaling the distinct Alex scent, intent on burning his memory into her consciousness.

What an unliberated liar I am.

"Can you take me to the airport?"

Wednesday was less than twenty-four hours away. She couldn't stifle a frown. "Of course."

Trying to hide her disappointment, she stood on her toes, kissed him, and said cheerfully, "I'll show you around the city tomorrow. Have you ever seen cliff divers?"

"No."

"They're pretty amazing. If we go at night, it's even more impressive. This time, let's take the Jeep. There are so many around the city, Hector will never be able to find us."

"I guess I'm willing to look like an ass for some privacy. What time should we meet?"

"Early."

"That was a long drive. You got to sleep most of the way." Alex massaged her shoulders and chuckled. "I didn't."

"You can sleep on the plane. Tomorrow is our last full day together. I'll be at your hotel around nine. Will that work? We can decide where to go from there."

"I'll order breakfast," he offered.

"You do that."

Alex opened the door of the Mercedes, fished a pen and paper napkin from the glove compartment, and wrote down his room number. He handed it to Sofie and rested his hand on her hip.

Sofie put it in the pocket of her shorts and caressed his arm. Their lips met, gently at first, then the kiss intensified, their tongues meeting in urgent exploration. She didn't want him to go. She wanted to go with him. She knew neither option was possible.

Alex pulled back. "Are you sure you can't come with me?"

It was such a sweet, honest request. Sofie felt the roller coaster rush through her belly and the catch in her heart. "Tomorrow. I'll be there early."

A few kisses would never be enough; she wanted more. She leaned against the side of the Mercedes and wished they could go back to the privacy of Oaxaca and the cool mountains.

But that wasn't possible. Folding her arms, she watched him take his briefcase and duffle bag from the trunk and stow them in the back of the Jeep.

Beneath the yard's decorative lighting, he opened the striped hood and jiggled a few wires. Alex knew exactly what he was doing. Glancing up, he grinned.

Sofie shook her head while he wiped his hands on his shorts and climbed behind the wheel.

The Jeep sputtered to life. Alex waved, and the pink-and-white-striped Jeep slipped past the open gate into the sticky night.

As much as he wanted Sofie to come back to the hotel with him, Alex was relieved she declined the offer. The girl had become a major problem and, as alluring as she was, he needed an escape for a few hours. Dean would be looking for a report, and Alex had been out of contact with the team for days.

At least there'd be time to make the call before she'd come knocking on his door to spend their last full day together. And it would be their last. He couldn't figure out how to make any other possibility feasible.

In the bathroom, he stepped into the shower and let water flood over him, taking mental inventory. He berated himself for sharing private details of his life with Sofie. Still, he felt secure in the knowledge he hadn't betrayed the team or compromised the plan.

He felt a jab of guilt for having told her so many lies, but it was unavoidable.

There'd been lies on both sides. Alex never bought her claim that she was ready for casual sex. Despite her protests, Sofie was a traditional girl who would eventually want a commitment—one she could build a life on.

Shit! He was involved too. Against his better judgment and meticulous strategy.

With any luck, by next weekend he'd be gone. He'd be back in California. And even if she wanted to—*and she wouldn't*—she'd never be able to find him.

Alex left the shower, dried off, and picked up his toothbrush, squeezing a blob of toothpaste across the bristles. *Fuck.* Lousy timing.

He'd found the right girl in the wrong family. *The worst.* If only Sofie hadn't accepted her family's money, hadn't come down here this summer.

If only we'd met some other way... This was ridiculous—screwy—thinking. It would never have happened.

In the end, Alex was certain Sofie would wish she'd never seen his face, much less shared his bed. While he would relive these mind-blowing moments for years...

Alex left the bathroom and lay down on the bedspread, listening to the ceiling fan whir overhead.

Even though he was exhausted, he found sleep impossible. He opened the patio door, hoping a breeze would come up off the bay. Alex adjusted the pillow, rested his hands beneath his head, and mulled over the facts.

Why do I care?

Alex couldn't answer the question.

Where did this irresistible need to protect this woman come from?

It could be because Sofie was naive and, in a weird way, he loved that about her. Her ability to trust was something he'd lost a long, long time ago.

Sofie was naive, but not stupid. Alex saw the doubt in her eyes occasionally. Obviously, she didn't know the true nature of her family's business. She must have an inkling of something though, because somewhere in that pretty little head, she had the good sense not to get sucked in.

Ramón might have noticed the attraction between them, but he wouldn't have sent Sofie to Alex as a gift. And Sofie wouldn't let herself be used that way.

If Ramón suspected how far it had gone, Alex knew for certain he'd be furious.

Good.

Then again, Alex was lost, and he wondered why, after only two nights with the girl, he couldn't sleep without her.

Sofie was unlike any woman he'd ever met. Maybe it was because she understood the pain of losing a best friend. This connected them in a way he'd never thought possible.

She was extraordinary, moving him in an entirely unexpected direction. With her innocent, emerald eyes and mass of black hair, she wasn't the tall, busty blonde that turned him on in the past. Instead, Sofie stunned him in her own dark, erotically exotic way. With grace and a combination of spirit, compassion and vulnerability, she was a slow drip seeping into his soul, eroding his spotless resolve to keep work—*work.*

There was a knock on the door, and Alex's eyelids snapped open.

Did I dream the sound? Or was it real?

He heard a succession of raps again.

It could be Sofie. Or Hector, checking up on him. One of Ramón's guys with an unexpected—maybe ominous—change of plans?

Alex leapt from the bed, found his khaki shorts on the chair, and grabbed the .45 caliber from his duffle.

The knock became persistent.

He loaded the magazine by moonlight and entered the foyer of his hotel room.

"Who is it?" Alex asked from behind the door.

"It's me," Sofie almost whispered.

"Give me a minute." He went back to the bed and slipped the gun into the nightstand drawer.

He opened the door to find Sofie leaning against the wall, her overnight bag held tight in front of her waist.

"Hey. I missed you."

Alex walked past her and inspected the entryway.

"It's just me," she sounded confused.

The area around his room was clear. He followed her through the door and locked the deadbolt.

Pulling her into his arms, he kissed her hair. "I thought you needed a night at home."

"My tía wasn't there." Sofie shrugged. "I'm not sure where she is. She may have gone to Taxco to visit her sister. Hector isn't around either. If I'm in trouble, I'm in it already."

Sofie locked her arms around his neck and rested her head against his chest. "You're leaving soon, and I know you're exhausted, but I want to sleep here. With you."

"Sofie. I don't..."

Surprise caught her sultry, sexy voice, "You want me to leave?"

"No. I'm glad you're here. But I don't want to hurt you."

"You won't. Remember our deal? No expectations? I can keep it light... casual."

He slipped a curl behind her ear. "It's already more than that."

"All I want is right now."

Alex really didn't mind the change of plans. Tomorrow, he'd find a way to ditch Sofie for awhile. He still needed to call Dean.

"Come on, let's go to bed," he said.

Spooned around Sofie's bare, silky body, Alex had one thought before he drifted off to sleep: *This is how it always should be.*

❦

Alex rolled over and checked the bedside clock—noon. Hot, heavy air beat slowly around the room beneath the sluggish ceiling fan. Sofie's side of the bed was empty and the sliding glass door open.

Beneath a pink-and-white-striped umbrella, a newspaper was splayed across the patio table. Studying it, Sofie played with a wet curl that had escaped from the haphazard mound gathered on top of her head. Breakfast had arrived. Several Mexican sweet rolls lay on a plate nearby, surrounded by scattered crumbs.

He picked up the coffeepot. "Good morning. Or afternoon. Why didn't you wake me up?" he said, bending to meet her lips.

Sofie smiled and returned the kiss, ruffling his disheveled morning hair.

"You needed your beauty sleep."

Settling into a patio chair, Alex asked, "What's the plan?"

He tore apart a roll and noticed a new batch of fresh hibiscus floating in the minuscule pool.

"Well, we could go down into the city and check it out... or shop..."

Alex grimaced. "We could. But did I tell you I hate to shop?"

"No souvenirs to take home to your family?"

"What can we do instead?"

Sofie, wrapped in an oversized robe provided by the hotel, stood and took a few steps to the rail, surveying the bay.

Turning, she leaned against the railing. "It's your tour. What would you like to do?"

Exquisitely bathed in the midday sunlight, Sofie, with wisps of her hair gently blowing in the breeze, was so beautiful it hurt. Alex had to blink.

Soon, she's going to despise me.

"I have an idea. Come here."

She came to him and Alex put his hands on her waist. Pulling her onto his lap, he buried his head into her neck, breathing her in.

"Well, we could... Stop that, you're giving me chills!"

Alex sensed her mock protest when she snuggled even closer.

Loosening her belt, he pressed his palm to her tawny stomach. He explored her silky skin and ran his hand lower, smiling when he discovered Sofie wore nothing beneath the robe.

"We'll decide later," Alex said. Nudging her off of his lap, he led her by the hand toward the room. "I'm already hot, let's take a shower."

❦

At the La Concha Beach Club, Alex swam the length of the natural pool, coming up for air near the bar. He searched for the pay phone and spied it next to the bathroom. Soon, he'd find a chance to slip away.

Convincing Sofie to endure the heat of the afternoon near water hadn't been difficult. Originally, he'd suggested going back to her empty house. Her pool would have been a great cover. At this point, it was unlikely Hector would expect to find them around the blue-tiled estate. After she'd vetoed the idea, they'd driven the Jeep down to the hotel's beach club instead.

Alex considered it a point of accomplishment that he'd finally made peace with the Jeep. The Barbie car had come in handy after all. It was the perfect cover, with dozens of them driving around the city.

He swam back and climbed the steps of the rock-lined pool. Alex grabbed his towel and found Sofie tanning where he'd left her. The diamonds sparkled in her ears, and her necklace—the silver heart that she'd taken off for him—hung between her breasts. Other than the jewelry, she wore nothing but the tiny lime bikini she had worn on Friday.

Alex kissed her, picked up his sunglasses, and sat on the adjoining lounge chair. "Where's the nearest deserted beach? Someplace we can be alone."

Sofie smiled slowly. "We're in the city now, Alex. Privacy is tricky."

He tilted his head toward two loungers surrounded by curtains, near the pool. "Let's go into that cabana and close the curtains. I want you again."

"You're incorrigible." She laughed.

Reaching over, Alex gradually let a lock of Sofie's hair slide through his fingers.

"Don't," she said, snatching it away. "I hate my hair."

"Why? I like it."

"You wouldn't if you had to deal with it every day. It's my nemesis. It never behaves…"

Alex winked. "You never behave."

She raised her sunglasses and grinned. "Neither do you," she said, glancing meaningfully toward the cabana.

Sofie sat up in the lounge chair. "Come here. You're burning, let me put some sunscreen on."

He moved over and let Sofie slather lotion on his body. The feel of her deft hands applying sunscreen onto his back wasn't quite the experience he'd had in mind. However, in public, it made a decent substitute.

She was so distracting. But Alex focused, working on a scheme to slip away. Ten, fifteen minutes was all he needed. That should be enough time to go over the plan with Dean. And, if he could get a few details from Sofie, Alex might be able to ask Dean to do him a favor.

"Can I ask a question?"

"Sure," she said, rubbing more lotion into the skin along his shoulder blades.

"Can we talk about guns? Why you're so freaked out by them?"

He heard Sofie's sigh. "I had a really terrifying experience several years ago…in California."

Alex started to turn around, to see her face.

"No, don't."

He'd follow her instructions, as long as she willingly shared the story.

"I was on a freeway in Los Angeles, in the Valley... This guy chased me. He ran me off the road. Then, I wasn't the one he was looking for... It was awful."

"Did you go to the police?" If she made a report, Dean could get the record.

"Yeah. They never caught the guy. For months afterwards, I had the sinking premonition I was going to die. Then, I realized something: I almost had."

"Oh, Sofie..."

"Ceci used to tease me about 'dodging a bullet—literally.' I'd laugh, but it wasn't funny."

"It's not."

"It was a fluke thing. A weird experience. One I hope to never have again." Sofie placed both of her hands on his shoulders. "There. You're protected," she said, lightly pressing her lips to his back.

Alex wished he could have been there when she'd needed protection.

"I've been thinking."

"Yeesss," he replied, turning around. Sofie's delicious body glistened, and Alex, distracted by her petite, perfect breasts—his new obsession—wondered how he could convince her to go back to the hotel room.

"I'm thinking of working for the family."

Surprised, Alex asked. "Why'd you change your mind?"

"Well," she hesitated, "It's a good opportunity. I'll get my feet wet—I'd guess it'd be more like diving in—working in all aspects of accounting. I'll be my own boss—except for Ramón. I'm the one with the degree and, to him, that should count for something."

Just what is happening here? Alex's suspicions clicked into gear, and he wondered if she'd planned to take the job all along.

He stood and walked to the edge of the pool. Turning, he studied her closely. That wasn't it. Sofie appeared to await his approval.

This had to have something to do with their intense attraction to each other. She seemed to have trouble keeping her hands, and mouth, off of him. Alex wasn't any better. Like today, in the shower, when he'd lifted her up, wrapped her legs around his back, and slid into her sweet, willing body.

He had started to wonder if there could be a way to keep this going beyond its inevitable conclusion, navigating a minefield of unpredictable *ifs*.

This could only work, *if*, after she delivered him to the airport tomorrow, he could pull the operation off without her ever finding out about his involvement.

With some skewed idea of working for the family, the last thing he needed was for her to show up at the ranch this week and find him there. No. He needed Sofie to commit to return to California and pursue her original goals. Soon.

If she did, when—or *if*— she ever discovered the true nature of Ramón's activities, it shouldn't be that hard to convince her of Alex's own innocence, that he was an honest businessman.

"You aren't saying anything," she said.

After the death of her cousin, Ceci, Alex knew *if* she ever had an inkling he'd been involved in drugs or trafficking himself, he'd never be able to eradicate her suspicions.

Naive, yes. But Sofie wasn't stupid. *If* she got any closer to the family business, she would quickly discover Alex's involvement and she'd make him answer for it. No explanation would satisfy her, no matter how the deal went down.

And worse, after Alex's call to Dean on Friday morning, Sofie had been implicated in the Mendoza family business by Alex's own words. *If* anything happened to him in the next few days…

Shit, I need to talk to Dean.

"I thought it was important for you to get your CPA license. Can't you work anywhere if you have one?"

"Yeah. But I can get that later."

"Wouldn't it be easier to pass the exam and get it over with? You've come this far, I'd hate for you not see it all the way through."

Sofie looked past him.

Alex hoped he'd finally given her a reason to reconsider.

"I'd see you more." An unmistakable blend of hope and need filled her sultry voice.

This was exactly what Alex *didn't* want to happen. Sofie had thrown her good sense out the window and was relying on emotion.

"We'd be working together. I could go up to Chicago, you'll be back down here—" Trying to sell him on the idea, he heard her stop just short of sounding desperate.

"Sofie…" Alex hesitated, "If you went back to the States we'd both be in the same country. I could come see you in LA and you could visit me in Chicago."

"I'll be busy with work and prepping for the test. I won't have any time."

"We'll make it happen."

"I'm willing to take the job with Ramón. It would give us an opportunity to see if this—whatever *this* is that's happening between us—is going anywhere."

Alex walked back to the lounge chair and gently moved her legs so he could sit next to her. Using his best ammunition, he said, "Don't take a job, one you don't really want, because of me. And don't put your life on hold, or your dreams, because of a couple of great nights in bed."

The words were harsh. Alex knew they registered when he saw the color bleed from Sofie's face.

"I'd like to think of what has happened between us as something more than *sex*." She made the word sound filthy.

He reached for her.

She flinched and pulled back.

"You know it's more than that. But what's happened in the last few days isn't enough to constitute making a life-changing decision. Don't be impulsive."

"I know what I want."

"I was an asshole bastard just a few days ago." Alex smiled.

Sofie pressed her lips together into a thin line. "You're being one right now."

A tear slid down her cheek. Lifting her sunglasses, Sofie wiped it away and retrieved her magazine from the table.

People magazine became the Great Divide, shielding Alex from any insight into her thinking. Dismissed, he searched for the right words to make her understand something he couldn't explain. Something she'd never find comprehensible.

All of a sudden, she slapped the magazine down. "You're right."

Her personal armor seemed to have been reconstituted.

"So what, if the sex is good? It surely isn't an indication of the potential of a relationship. Or its future. A little fun fucking is all this is."

"Don't use that word, it's not you. We both know it's more than that."

She picked up the magazine, shutting him out again.

After a minute, knowing there'd be no way to make her understand, he pointed out a middle-aged man stepping into the water with white athletic socks hiked up over his calves, and chuckled. "Look at that guy over there."

She ignored him.

Alex placed his hand on her warm thigh. Sofie moved her leg.

He waited while she continued to read the magazine.

The front cover faced him, featuring a picture of Harrison Ford and an actress hawking his new movie. Apparently, Sofie was engrossed in a mesmerizing article on the other side. Alex tapped the cover. "Have you seen *The Temple of Doom?*"

"Stop," Sofie ordered.

He did. Instead, he grasped the pages, blocking the print.

She lowered the magazine and scowled.

Alex grinned and tried to coax her out of her crappy mood. "Let's talk."

"There's nothing more to say." She snatched the magazine away and buried her head behind the cover.

Sofie was right. Alex gave up and left the lounge chair to find a phone.

CHAPTER SIXTEEN

Los Amantes de la Puesta del Sol

Lover's Sunset
Tuesday, July 10, 1984

Sofie sat in the lounge chair and listened to a group of kids fight in the pool over a beach ball. She'd tried to read the cover story in *People* magazine, but it was a futile attempt to ignore the man she found irresistible.

It appeared she'd been right about him in the beginning. Alex was just another stereotypical jerk—totally happy with no commitments, no expectations. *Men.*

Yes, she'd agreed to the arrangement. But the spark between them had grown into something more. Alex admitted he felt it too.

This new development made working for Ramón a viable plan. Surprisingly, Alex had shut her down. She wanted to argue, talk it out, and come to a resolution. That way, she wouldn't have to drop him off at the airport tomorrow with a few kisses and only a remote possibility of meeting again in the future.

But Alex's push-pull magnet was back, pushing her away this afternoon.

Sofie had been naive and let her defenses down. Just days ago she'd chosen to rationalize her attraction to him instead of following her intuition. She'd lied to Alex, and to herself, because she wanted him.

Casual sex had never been her thing.

It was hard to determine where to place the anger, but she decided Alex was her best target. There'd be plenty of time for self-criticism tomorrow evening.

Another thing bothered her too. Ever since they'd arrived in the city, he'd seemed overly cautious. Last night, he'd been seriously—and unnecessarily—on edge when he opened his hotel door, even checking around the corners of the walkway to the room.

Sofie had tried to reassure Alex this morning. Telling him they needed to avoid Hector, otherwise, there was nothing to worry about.

But the hyper-vigilance hadn't subsided. She'd gotten the distinct sense he was waiting. He couldn't, *or wouldn't*, explain. And, it was even more confusing when he inexplicably suggested they spend the afternoon around her pool, where Hector would surely check in.

Maybe he was having flashbacks to traumas he'd experienced in Viet Nam. Maybe his odd mood could somehow be related to his friend, Nick.

No wonder Alex is so resistant to letting me into his life.

Ultimately, they were strangers. In just a few days, how could she expect anything more? But didn't he realize she understood grief, that she could be there for him when he needed compassion from a woman intimate with its roadblocks and switchbacks?

Sofie was afraid Alex would be able to see what she was thinking if she looked at him. So, embarrassed, she'd reread a caption in the magazine over and over again.

Alex finally got up and left. *Thank God.*

Because she'd been about to say the really stupid words she'd been stuffing down for hours.

I'm falling in love.

❧

Alex got change from the La Concha Bar and found the pay phone next to the men's bathroom. Despite the bewildering instructions written in Spanish, he deposited the required coins and dialed the number. Karen swept the line and Alex heard his boss's voice.

"Wait a minute. Let me close the door," Dean said. He came back and erupted, "Where the hell have you been?"

"It's complicated. We took a detour on our way back to Acapulco."

"Who's we?"

Dean would freak if he knew Alex had bedded the enemy. "I'm with Sofia Davis."

"Ramón's cousin? The new accountant?"

"One and the same. She—"

"Explain later. We haven't found anything on her from our end yet. But first, is everything okay?"

"I'm fine."

Dean exhaled. "You had us worried. How'd it go?"

"Great. Give Rachel in accounting a raise. They liked the company's books."

"Good. Are we on for Thursday or Friday?"

"Thursday afternoon. We're unloading the boat in the morning. Repackaging afterwards."

"Excellent. Is Ramón okay with the cash coming down on the plane?"

"He thinks Karen is working on it as we speak."

"Our source confirmed the Cali connection flew into Oaxaca on Sunday. He went by helicopter to the Mendoza compound to pick up their money. The boat has already entered Mexican waters, but they won't deliver until they're paid."

"How long was the connection in Oaxaca?"

"A couple of hours. Why do you ask?"

Alex wondered if the man on the balcony who watched them Sunday night was just a curious guest or a Cali operative. "Nothing."

When Sofie decided to steer the Mercedes toward Oaxaca, it had been at the last minute. The Calis couldn't have known.

Could they?

Alex felt sick, realizing he may have unintentionally betrayed his boss. The team. Nick's memory.

Sofie *was* trustworthy. Alex would stake his life on it.

Then again, he had to admit she'd clouded his judgment, prompting him to contemplate a crazy scheme full of *ifs* he knew were unlikely to succeed.

Guilt clenched his gut and burned. Leaning against the wall, Alex silently sighed and rubbed his forehead. On the other side of the wall, a toilet flushed.

"I saw the airstrip. Tell Travis it's paved. It should be a smooth landing."

Pulling the cord of the pay phone around the corner, Alex spied on Sofie near the pool. She'd abandoned her magazine and appeared to be looking for him.

Serves her right for ignoring me, he thought. *Let her wonder where I am.*

Alex returned to the phone. "I walked the beach. It's heavily monitored from the river. There's a guardhouse. If you decide on another entry point, come in from the south."

"Good to know. We're ready."

"He's really proud of his operation. We spent Sunday morning taking a tour of the ranch."

"Ramón?" Dean asked.

"That's right." Alex checked on Sofie again. She was standing now, seriously searching for him. Panic flashed across her face as she nervously fingered her necklace.

Did she really think I'd abandon her?

She spotted him and raised her hand. He waved back, rounded the corner, and leaned against the wall.

Dean gave him a rundown on the team. Then he asked, "What are you doing with Sofia Davis?"

"Dean, like I said it's complicated." Alex checked poolside one more time.

Sofie had disappeared.

"And I need to talk to you about her, but I gotta go. I'll call when I can."

"Who are you talking to?" Sofie asked.

Alex snapped the handset down in its cradle and whirled around.

She stood before him, weighted down by their stuff.

"Work." The last time he'd sounded this guilty was right before his senior prom, when his mom had caught him with a six-pack of Coors behind the seat of his pickup truck.

Eyeing him with suspicion, Sofie opened her mouth as if to speak, then closed it. She grabbed him by the elbow and said, "Let's go. Hector's here. I'm not sure if he saw me, but I saw him."

❦

Sofie wanted answers. "Why didn't you come to me when I waved? I needed you."

She stared at Alex and slipped the strap of her red sundress—a different style this afternoon—back on her shoulder. They'd just pulled into a parking space and were waiting for the sunset performance of the La Quebrada cliff divers. "Who were you talking to?"

Earlier, as the Jeep whizzed through the city, it had been fruitless to try to get her questions answered. Any words were drowned by a clattering engine and downtown noise. After they'd left the beach club, the best she'd been able to do was motion directions, and guide him through the heart of Acapulco.

"Alex, are you going to answer me?"

Both of his hands still gripped the wheel. "Work. I had to call my office," he explained. "I've been out of touch with them for days.

"As distracting as you are, once in awhile I need to check in." His face relaxed and he grinned, revealing his Get Out Of Trouble Free Card—at least the one that always worked on her—his lone dimple.

Not this time. "Who's Dean?"

The Hotel El Mirador sat directly across from the parking lot. Alex wouldn't look in her direction, seemingly more interested in the hotel's red-tiled rooflines clutching the rocks.

A young family walked out of the entrance. The mom clustered her chicks under her wing.

Sofie focused on Alex. It didn't matter if he didn't like her questions, she deserved answers. "What did you mean when you said, 'I need to talk to you about her?' Who were you talking about? Me?"

Alex's face suddenly stiffened.

Although it wasn't unusual for his answers to be non-existent or pathetically vague, she frowned, waiting for a reply.

The mother gathered the children while her husband lifted his camera for a family photo.

When Alex bolted from the Jeep to help, Sofie knew he'd found his escape. Surrendering the camera, the dad smiled and joined the family.

The mom put the children through several photo switch-ups before they posed. It was such a happy scene, Sofie had to stifle a pang of jealousy.

When Alex returned to the Jeep, she persisted, "You didn't answer my questions."

Alex sighed. "No expectations. No commitments. Wasn't that our deal?"

"I never agreed to no questions."

"I didn't abandon you. I needed to check in." For the first time he looked at her. "We need a sign."

This was a surprise. "A sign? For what?"

"You said you needed me. If you want me, and I'm not close by, we need a sign."

"Like if Hector finds us again?"

"Exactly. Any ideas?"

"Waving won't work. I waved and you just waved back. Then you ignored me and went around the corner."

"What about your necklace?"

"What about it?" She pulled the silver heart from beneath her sundress and ran it along its chain.

"You wear it all the time. Play with it, like you're doing now. That way

172

I'll know something's up."

"What's your sign? You might need me too, you know."

"Between now and tomorrow afternoon, I'm not leaving you alone again." He grinned. "How's that for commitment?"

"Better." She smiled.

"Don't get greedy," Alex teased. He put his hand on her thigh and squeezed it gently. "No more questions, okay? We don't have much time left, and I don't want to fight."

Sofie placed her hand over his knuckles and laced her fingers through his. *I don't want to fight either,* she thought, wishing they were back in his hotel room.

But the cliff divers were getting ready to perform. "Let's go so we can get a good spot before the crowd gets here."

Alex held her hand as they walked down the steps to the upper spectator pavilion. Umbrellas were scattered along the pavement, where vendors sold cold drinks from red carts. In the sea below, beyond the breaking waves, boats began to gather, bobbing in the water.

The sun sank toward the horizon. On the edge of the bleached blue sky, a curtain of clouds billowed across the tangerine sunset. Alex bought two Cokes and gave one to Sofie.

A spray of salt air wafted up from the cleft in the rocks, and she led him down the steps, deeper into the narrow chasm.

"See that arch up there?" She pointed to a rock altar. "The Virgin of Guadalupe is inside. The clavadistas pray to her for luck."

"Is she really a virgin?" Alex teased.

Sofie gave him a sideways glance. "She's made of plaster. What do you think?"

"Is that what a clavadista is—a virgin?"

"Guadalupe is probably the only virgin up on the rocks. The clavadistas are men. They're macho cliff divers."

Alex laughed. "You never mentioned what a clavadista was."

"Sorry. I forgot you don't speak Spanish. Anyway, the Virgin must be doing a good job protecting the divers, no one has died in all these years. Just broken bones and busted eardrums."

They descended the last set of stairs to the lowest pavilion. The undulating tide filled and drained the narrow gorge. Nearby, barefoot divers assembled in a cluster, waiting to swim the divide. One of the older men climbed over the low stone barrier, down the rocks, and dove into the water. Once across, he scaled the other side, slowly navigating the rock face until he stood on the staging area, high above the sea.

The crowd grew. Sofie and Alex moved to the far edge of the platform to find the best vantage point.

After studying the sea, the clavadista knelt before the Virgin while the rest of the divers scaled the wall and gathered near the top of the craggy outcropping.

Carefully moving down the cliff, the first diver found a perch along the rocky face and stood, calculating.

Sofie explained, "He's checking the depth. It's important to time the dive with the tide."

As the crowd swelled, Alex moved behind her, wrapping his arms around her waist. She leaned into his body, supremely content.

The diver made the Sign of the Cross. He arced his body and aimed. His call echoed through the cavern as he sailed, bird-like, through the air, clearing the jagged rocks. Mid-dive, he knifed his body and sliced into the sea with a clean splash.

Applause exploded from the crowd. Sofie joined in while Alex howled with approval, and the next diver began to shimmy down into position.

"What'd I tell you? Pretty amazing, huh?"

Alex bent his head to kiss her. "Pretty amazing."

Emerging from the sea, the first clavadista climbed the rocks to the viewer's pavilion. He toweled off amid cheers from the audience. Beaming, the diver soaked in their adulation. Alex pressed a few American bills into the the diver's palm as he worked his way through the crowd, collecting tips.

The rest of the divers took their turn. The sun had slipped into the ocean by the time the performance ended. Night was coming fast. The crowd began to thin as the sky deepened into a rich sapphire, edged with swirls of violet and pink.

A little girl, one of the children from the hotel, bolted from her family, working her way down the steps. Her father followed, scooping up the laughing toddler. Smiling, he waved, tossed the child over his shoulder, and climbed the stairs.

This would probably be the last sunset Sofie would ever share with Alex. It wouldn't be long before their time together would unspool into shady memories. She looked at him. His floppy, sun-streaked hair fell shaggy below his ears. Alex needed a haircut and someone to take care of him.

Earlier in the day, she'd sat on the bed, watching him through the open bathroom door as he shaved. A hint of his beard had already grown back. Sofie remembered the feel of his skin against hers and shivered. Standing on her toes, she pressed her lips against his jaw one more time.

He put his arm around her shoulder. "How can you be cold in this heat?"

"I'm not," she answered. "The sunset is beautiful."

"Yes. And you're beautiful too," he said, pulling her into him.

Kissing her, Alex grazed his fingers across the back of her neck, and down, along the skin of her spine.

Ignoring the smattering of bystanders who remained on the pavilion, Sofie returned his delicious kisses, running the tip of her tongue over his lips.

Alex groaned. "Look at me."

She did.

He lifted his sunglasses and positioned Sofie's in her hair.

"Whatever happens, this has meant a lot to me."

Sofie began to say the words she'd stifled since they'd travelled down the mountains, "I love—"

"Don't." Alex slowly shook his head.

"Why?"

"You don't know me."

"I know enough. I don't want you to leave without telling you how I feel."

"Shh…" Alex put two fingers to her lips. "Not yet."

"What are we waiting for?"

"Nothing… Everything." He hesitated. "I know this doesn't make sense."

Thoroughly confused, she stared at him.

"Back in California, you may decide you don't like crazy Lake Michigan surfers from Chicago."

They both laughed.

"Please, just answer one question and I'll let the others go. Are you feeling this too?"

"Of course I am. I don't want us to end like this. I don't want this to end at all. But I didn't expect this to happen."

"It's not that complicated."

His eyes flashed a hint of something she didn't understand, then he squeezed them shut, closing her out altogether.

She asked the only logical question she could fathom. "You lied to me, didn't you? You're married? Engaged?"

"*No, Sofie*, it's not that. I told you before I'm not involved with anyone… I've done things I can't talk about."

The war again. She sighed. "I've done things I'm not proud of either. Everybody has. What's important is the future. Not the past."

"If I tell you something, will you make me a promise?"

Sofie was slow to agree, unsure of what would be asked of her. "Deal."

"I haven't been completely truthful about being married."

"I knew it!" She recoiled from him, squirming away.

Alex tried to pull her back.

Scrambling, she turned and headed for the stairs.

He's such a liar.

Alex caught up and grabbed her arms. He faced her and put his hands on her shoulders. "Wait. Let me finish. *Before*. I've been married before. I'm divorced. It was years ago. We met in college."

Sofie stopped wrestling. "What happened?"

"I joined the Army. We got married. When I came home from 'Nam, she'd moved on. At least she'd had the decency not to send me a Dear John letter while I was still there."

"Oh."

"Kim was young. I was young."

Alex's breath felt warm in her hair. "You're nothing like her," he said, running his fingertips along the length of her arms.

She stood on her toes and planted a kiss on his chin. "Her loss is my gain."

Holding her body at arm's length, Alex smiled and gazed at her with his beautiful blue eyes. "It's my turn. Our deal, remember?"

"That isn't much of a confession." Sofie grumbled. "What do you want from me?"

"Take the job in California and get your CPA license. Promise me you won't join the family business."

Sofie nodded, figuring she had all the answers she needed for the time being. They'd work the rest out later.

The sky deepened into a rich, salmony pink. Swelling clouds had turned purple, bruising the horizon. As long as they had each other, they could conquer anything. She leaned into him, ran her finger down his arm and tilted her head, kissing him again, this time meeting his lips. "Come on, I'm hungry. There's this great place for dinner. It's just up the road."

CHAPTER SEVENTEEN

Musica de la Luna

Music of the Moon
Tuesday, July 10, 1984

Sofie paused on the steps into the delightfully quaint patio of Casa Luna. Delicious aromas from the restaurant kitchen greeted her, and she suspected Gabriel had been right about his newly discovered find.

The restaurant sat high above a small inlet outside of the city. Colorful lanterns, rocking gently in the breeze, peppered the area. A friendly man, who probably was the owner, welcomed them and escorted Sofie and Alex to a table, suggesting the special of the evening.

Resting over the ocean, the moon was nearly full, spilling shimmery light onto breaking waves. Sofie smoothed the tablecloth. "He said the Dorado —that's Mahi-Mahi—is especially fresh tonight."

Alex looked around the patio, taking in the scene. Tiny sun-weathered lines around the edges of Alex's eyes crinkled as he grinned. "Great. I love fish."

A trio of red votives, flickering in the center of the table, promised three wishes. As if Aladdin read her mind, one wish had already been granted. All of Alex's earlier tension was gone and, tonight, he appeared completely at ease.

Her heart soared. Finally, outside of the bedroom, they seemed to be in sync.

She unfolded her napkin and spread it on her lap. "This is Gabriel's new secret hangout. I've been curious and wanting to give it a try."

"Secret hangout?"

"He thinks Ramón has people who watch him and keep track of his every move. I think Gabriel's a little paranoid." She smiled and pointed to the battered boats anchored for the evening in the small harbor below. "He says the food here is good and the fish is excellent. All they have to do is somehow get the daily catch up the cliff."

A pretty girl, who might have been the owner's daughter, arrived and took their drink order.

"I think Gabriel's tired of being the baby in the family," Sofie explained. "He says Mexico is a fishbowl. I tell him it's a fish tank. But I'm beginning to understand what he means. Just for some time alone, I had to take you on a crazy chase. It's been exhausting."

"It's the time alone that's been exhausting." Alex teased. "Lack of sleep." She raised an eyebrow. "You're complaining?"

"No." He laughed. "Though the side trips were interesting. I just didn't realize they'd involve treacherous mountain passes and dilapidated roads. I don't know how you slept through the potholes. The next time we get into a car and you tell me it's not far, I'm bailing out."

"I think all that drive time together served its purpose."

"You slept most of the time."

"Not always. And sometimes you did too. Don't forget the arguing. I figure we've worked out most of our differences by now. We'll never fight again."

"Don't count on it."

"I slept because I needed rest after the mental sparring. You even rifled through my purse. I had no choice. I needed to put you behind the wheel."

Alex winked. "Now, I know all your secrets." He took a gulp of his newly delivered beer and looked around. "Aren't you glad you've decided against living in a fishbowl?"

"That promise really wasn't a fair trade. You told me you were married *before*. That's something about your past, not the present." She tasted her margarita, a perfect blend of lime and tequila. "There'll be a lot of things I'll miss about Mexico. It's home to me in many ways."

"It'll be better for us in the States. I'll spend more time in California than you can imagine. You might get sick of me hanging around after awhile. My family is there—"

"You said your family lived in Illinois."

Instantly, Alex's eyes clouded. "They used to live in Illinois. They moved to California a few years ago."

He was lying. *What is he hiding?* She was afraid to think he might be reluctant to introduce her to his family because she was half Mexican—a subject they hadn't even talked about. Yet.

That discussion would have to wait, because she needed to find the restroom. She'd discover the truth when she returned. "I'll be right back."

"Remember our sign." He grinned.

She touched the silver chain with her fingers. "Of course."

Sofie disappeared into the interior of the restaurant. *Shit.* Alex had blown it *again.* He imagined Nick sitting at a nearby table, shaking his head, asking, *Hey brother, what happened to no complications? No commitments?*

Alex was finding it impossible to stay in the Alex Wilson role when Sofie was around. His goal was to get through tonight and keep the personal details to himself. He needed time away from her to formulate a coherent plan. Only then could he rewrite and edit the story to fit the elements of his real life.

On the other hand, he studied the candles on the table and wished time would slow down. Their future together after Thursday proved highly unpredictable, possibly explosive.

He hadn't mentioned the particulars to her yet, but with any luck, he'd be able to patch together a seamless reunion in LA in a few weeks. If he could wrap things up in El Paso, he might even get into town a day or two early.

Alex looked up just in time to see Gabriel walk down the steps onto the patio. He didn't wait for a table. Instead, he glanced around, searching for someone. A waiter nodded, and Gabriel left the restaurant as quickly as he'd arrived.

No wonder he liked this place so much. Alex knew exactly what he was fishing for.

He stood when Sofie returned to the table.

"Where are you going?" she asked.

"The bathroom."

"Where's my sign?"

"It's not far, yell if you need me."

She seemed vaguely bewildered as she sat down.

Just past the bathroom and beyond the kitchen, Alex found the back door. In the parking lot, Gabriel slipped the waiter the cash and pocketed the stash, making the deal.

The family sat on a mountain of coke. *Why did Gabriel have to make his buys from a waiter?* Maybe Ramón didn't know his little brother was tapping into the product.

Alex wondered if he cared.

Sofie would. Had she figured out yet that Gabriel was an addict?

Returning to the table, Alex sat down, and asked, "Did you see Gabriel?"

"No." She looked up from her menu, scanning the restaurant.

"He already left."

"You didn't call him over?"

"No."

Her eyes widened with surprise. "Did you tell him I was here?" She questioned him with the palms of her hands. "Did you talk to him at all."

"No."

"Why?"

"He was doing a little business."

Sofie froze. "What do you mean *a little business?*"

"He went into the parking lot with one of the waiters."

"I thought you went to the restroom."

Whether or not he went to the bathroom wasn't the information she needed to digest. He waited for the reality of his words to sink in.

"You're wrong," she said firmly.

"No. I watched them do the deal."

Sofie raised a skeptical eyebrow.

Alex met her stare, silently willing her to believe in him. The emotional turbulence warring just below the surface pushed the rigid lines of Sofie's features toward collapse, wavering between acceptance and denial.

She bit her lip and glanced away. Then spoke in a rush of words, "If he was making a deal, he did it for a friend. After what happened with Ceci, he wouldn't touch the stuff. I know it. Gabriel spent time in California. He knew her. She was his cousin too."

Moments passed and Alex watched the lines of Sofie's face soften. Her expression shifted from denial to concern as the pebble of doubt settled.

"Gabriel was devastated when she died. He swore to me he wouldn't do drugs," Sofie said softly, then buried herself behind the menu.

Alex pretended to study the selections, written in Spanish and a haphazard version of English.

Sofie carefully set down her menu and tapped her fingers on the back of one hand. "It's not that I don't believe you. But you must have the context all wrong." Motioning the waitress to their table, she asked. "What are you having? I'm ready to order."

As if he'd taken a long needle and popped a balloon, he'd deflated her mood. He felt bad, but there weren't any more questions. They ate the meal in silence and Alex suspected her thoughts had nothing to do with him.

❦

Sofie, though still disturbed by Alex's supposed sighting of Gabriel at the restaurant, didn't argue when Alex suggested they take a walk along the beach. They drove through the city along the Costera and found a place to park in an ocean-side lot. Unfastening the straps of her leather sandals, she tossed them onto the floorboard of the Jeep. She passed the deserted palapas scattered on the sand and made her way to the water, sure Alex would follow closely behind.

Her mind whirled with possibilities, unsure of what Alex had seen while he was supposed to have been in the restroom. He had to be mistaken... But it made sense. Gabriel's paranoia. Disappearing for days at a time. His mood, exhausted sometimes, manic at others. The explosive irritation. It was all too familiar. *Not again.*

Wasn't Gabriel supposed to be at the ranch? If he was back in town, she prayed he'd have an innocent explanation. Either way, she'd discover the truth.

Tomorrow. After Alex boarded a plane back to Chicago.

She slowed down a little, purposefully shaking off the negativity, and concentrated on making their last night in Acapulco a night to remember.

The vibrant city cast an incandescent aura across the sky. Underscored by street traffic, a pulse of music emanated from the bars and clubs along the Costera, filling the beach with muted noise that competed with the soft whoosh of the waves.

Alex caught up and clasped her hand. Occasionally, they'd greet and sidestep another couple traveling in the opposite direction. Above, the nearly full moon spilled light across pebbles and shells scattered along the shore.

"I remember the first time we walked the beach," he said.

"That seems so long ago. When was it? Friday night?" Sofie spotted an opaque hunk on the ground and untangled her fingers from his.

She gasped, delighted. *What a surprise.*

On second thought, she'd never known anyone who'd found sea glass along the beach at night, and decided it could be a pale rock, or more likely just a piece of quartz.

The next wave captured the bauble and it glittered in the moonlight, rolling with the tide. She caught the large chunk when it returned to shore and discovered it really was a piece of worn glass, almost half the size of her palm. "Look at this."

"What is it?"

"Sea glass. I think it's white." She ran her fingers over the piece, inspecting its edges, and handed the tumbled jewel to him. "See? Feel it. This one is smooth all over—well cooked—just the way I like 'em."

"It's just litter. What's the big deal?"

Alex gave it back.

"Sea glass is more than that." Slipping it into the pocket of her shorts, she worry-stoned it between her thumb and finger. "The ocean catches discarded bottles with the tides, and between the rocks, the sand, and stormy waves, it breaks up and gets all mellowed. Then, the ocean regifts the small treasures to the beach."

"Women collect things like dolls and plates. And I find a girl who collects broken glass."

Sofie deemed this particular find a gift from her mom. It contained a message: *Trust him.* "This one's special. I've never discovered sea glass in the moonlight before."

Alex chuckled. "I'll keep on the lookout for more to add to your collection."

"I'll tell you a secret about me, and this one's a freebie. I expect nothing in return..." She clarified, "Right now."

Sofie hoped he could see her smile in the moonlight. "Remember when you laughed at me because my middle name is Morgan?"

"Yes. But don't hold that against me." He put his arm around her, and said in a low, seductive voice, "You were being bitchy then. Now, you can press anything against me you'd like."

Sofie laughed. "Seriously. Remember when I told you Morgan is the name of the patroness of the island of Avalon? The woman who nursed King Arthur back to health?" She didn't wait for his answer. "Avalon, according to the legend, was an island made of glass. I figure there must have been plenty of sea glass along its shores. So, I collect it. Makes sense, huh?"

"You have legendary powers too?"

"I am legendary," Sofie teased.

"I think you are." Alex pulled her into his arms and kissed her. The city seemed to melt away, and there was nothing left, except Alex, the warm ocean, and the gentle breeze whispering through the palms. Sofie opened her lips, welcoming him in.

He touched his forehead to hers and asked, "Do you remember on Friday night when we talked about expectations and decisions?"

"Of course. Our first date."

"Then we made out like teenagers."

She nudged him playfully. "I'd like to think of it as our first kiss."

Alex found her hand and they continued to walk. "You got angry when I stopped us."

"Angry? Yeah. But I was more confused than anything."

There was a somber timbre in his voice. "I was confused too." He stopped, turned and, in the moonlight, she saw his eyes. "I'm not anymore."

Sofie wrapped her arms around his waist. His confession, these words—though just short of *I love you*—were what she'd wanted to hear. She put her head to his chest and listened to the comforting beat of his heart.

Alex held her as if he didn't want to ever let go. All of her life, she'd waited for him, needed to love him. Maybe she hadn't realized it in the beginning, but Alex was her destiny. And she knew, without a doubt, meeting him in Mexico was a gift from her mom. These were two inexplicable certainties she knew to be true.

Snuggled against him, she looked up into the night sky, and felt the piece of sea glass in her pocket, pressing into her thigh. For the first time in a long while, she sensed her mom smiling down. All of her unanswered questions would eventually get answered. In his arms, she finally found home.

She pressed her lips against his collarbone and said, "Let's go back to the hotel."

❦

Sofie, her bare feet planted on the tile floor, stood in the hotel room. Alex sat on the bed in front of her, slowly unzipping her sundress. Removing the straps, he let them slide down her arms and placed his lips on her shoulders. Anticipation began to build and settled in her core with a thick, almost itchy, ache that clamored for release.

"Weren't you wearing another red dress a couple of nights ago?" he asked.

His hands skimmed along Sofie's skin, igniting a delightful, incessant hum.

"I didn't think you noticed."

He traced the trail with his lips, his eyes holding a devilish gleam. "You're impossible to ignore, Sofie. And you look great in red."

Smiling, she stepped out of the dress and let him unhook her bra.

She eagerly undid his shirt and tugged at his shorts with shaky fingers.

Grabbing them, he stopped her. "No. Not yet, I want to look at you first."

Alex finished undressing her and positioned her body to stand before him, gliding his hands along the curve of her waist. "So I can remember," he whispered.

Gently twisting her fingers through his hair, she drew him close. He pressed his lips to her belly and traced a line of kisses to her navel, making her giggle.

Laughing, he glanced up and met her eyes. "Lower?"

"It's my turn." Pulling him up to stand, she unfastened his shorts and ran her palm along the hot, rigid length of his penis.

Alex stepped out of his shorts, while Sofie pushed the shirt off his shoulders, letting it fall to the floor. Beneath the waistband of his boxers, she skimmed her fingers along his flesh and freed him, lowering her mouth.

Sofie kissed the velvet tip. "I love this."

"Me too."

"No, this." Sofie bent her head again and tasted a salty droplet of anticipation. She looked up at Alex, meeting his eyes. "You're hard velvet. The essence of a man, both rigid steel and silky soft at the same time."

Alex grinned, his eyes sparkling as he maneuvered out of the boxers.

When he was naked, she nudged him onto the bed and Alex pulled her on top. Astride him, she tossed her hair, caught it with her fingers and tied the curls into a knot. She flipped the necklace to her back, hoping it would stay there and out of their way.

Leaning forward, she arched her neck, and lacing her fingers though his, pushed his hands onto the sheet. Sofie lowered herself to him, soaring with the sensation of being on top, in control. Hesitating, she only allowed his hot flesh to press against her labia, sending warm honey pulsing through her veins. Wet and distracted, she couldn't help but glide her pearl against his silken length.

Alex grasped her hips, trying to move inside. She stopped him, regaining self-control. As much as she needed him inside her, she wanted to give Alex something he wouldn't forget.

Ever.

Sofie looked into his smoldering blue eyes, and began with a kiss. One on the cheek, another brushing against his eyelids, one on his forehead, and finally on the tip of his strong, patrician nose.

His lips met hers, their tongues flirting. She gently licked his lip and moved lower, using her mouth to discover the rugged silk of his chest and find his nipples. She drew them past her lips, sucking each into a small, hard nub.

"I love your chest. The downy fur," she said, totally turned on by the masculine texture of his skin. She used her teeth to lightly nip Alex's flesh and felt her own body quiver with need.

Alex moaned as Sofie eased his legs apart, licked his navel, and began to gently kiss her way down, teasing the velvet tip with her tongue, then moving up again. Running her fingernails along the sides of his stomach, she lifted her gaze, and watched his eyes darken and flicker, reveling in his heady expression, intent on pleasing him with her mouth.

I love this man, she thought, *And I know he's falling in love with me.*

Her hair was already unraveling, so she stopped for a moment to reknot it and reposition the wayward necklace before moving down his legs.

Gently, she stroked her nails along the skin of his inner thighs.

Alex groaned while his penis moved, straining against her cheek.

She kissed the trail down from his navel again, and licking her tongue across her lips, filled her mouth with saliva. Finding the head of exquisite velvet and steel, she sucked him in, and felt tiny spasms begin to build in his body.

"Slow down, baby, I want to remember this. Make it last," he murmured.

The most sensitive part of his body was a treat, one to be essentially savored. She wrapped her lips around her teeth and teased her tongue back and forth across his tip. Using her hands, she stroked his shaft and cupped his balls, then altered the technique, gently taking them into her mouth. His pulse sent a rush of wet, warm desire flooding into her already soaking core.

Pulling her up, Alex kissed her, and said, "Come here, beautiful," trying to position her on top of him.

"No." Sofie lowered her head again. This was a simple gift of giving.

Holding his penis, she traced the underside of her tongue along the vein. Reaching the ridge that led to the head, she licked the shaft, bringing him to the brink.

He moaned. "You feel so good."

Opening her mouth wide, she took the velvet shaft in. Her lips met the base and she began to move, varying the speed. Soon, he pumped deeper into her mouth, and she took him in, all of the way, his length tickling the back of her throat.

His hands moved to her hair, pushing her head down and undoing the precarious knot. The mass of curls were suddenly everywhere, a curtain hanging between them. Her heart raced with the heady, erotic power, the privilege of pleasuring the most vulnerable, intimate part of Alex's body. It sent waves of sparks that built, sending Sofie to the brink of climax herself.

She tasted the hint of salt just before his seed shot into her mouth.

"Sofie!"

Glancing up, she watched the twisted beauty of a climax briefly mold his features. Sofie didn't stop moving until he put his hands on her shoulders.

After a minute, he said, "Come up here."

The covers had fallen to the floor, leaving only one sheet on the mattress. Sofie crawled her way to the pillows.

They faced each other, side by side. Alex ran his fingernails between her shoulder blades and down her back, tickling the sensitive triangle near her bottom. "You're incredible."

Elated, her breath caught in her throat. Sofie knew she'd remember these words forever.

"You have nice legs," Alex said, moving his hand along her thigh.

Sofie was damp and achy, needing her own release, but as long as he was giving compliments, she could wait. "Ceci's brother, Rich, used to call me the Hanes Chicken. He said I had skinny legs." She laughed.

"He's wrong. You should wear dresses every day."

"Shorts show my legs too."

"I like you in a dress." He found the curve of her back and picked up a strand of dark hair, letting it curl through his fingers. "Your hair is almost black and your eyes are so green. I know why your parents named you Morgan." He grinned. "You've enchanted me."

Blushing, she traced his lips with her finger and Alex caught the tip in his mouth, sucking. A jolt of electricity rocked her body and settled in her core.

Alex lifted the necklace, holding the silver heart in his hand. "Take it off," he instructed.

"I can't." Sofie teased, "I need you. *Now.*"

"I'm right here."

"I never take this heart off."

Alex smiled. "You did for me."

"You're the only exception. My mom sent this necklace to Ceci on her fourteenth birthday. After Ceci's funeral, my Tía Sofia gave it to me." She held the filagreed heart, feeling its weight in her palm. "Why is it so important to you?"

"You're so soft." Alex ran his hand along her clavicle. "I like your skin on my skin with no distractions." He brought his lips to hers. "I want nothing between us when we're in bed. Not Ceci, not Ramón, not Gabriel. It's just us." Alex took his finger, tapped his heart, and placed it between her breasts. "You and me."

Inspired by his heartfelt words, she lifted her head and let Alex remove the necklace.

He put it on the nightstand. "It will be right here, waiting for you in the morning." Alex pulled her on top, hard and ready again.

She opened her legs, inviting him in.

He held her hips and slid into her core, stroking his body against hers.

They'd entered new territory. If he wanted her body and soul, she would gladly give it to him.

CHAPTER EIGHTEEN
El Deseo de Engano

Desire's Deception
  Wednesday, July 11, 1984

The clementine moon sank into the horizon while the confederate light of an inevitable new morning began to bloom gray along with Sofie's trepidation. The first time they were together, she never thought she'd get the chance to map Alex. Now, having just begun to learn his nuances, she didn't want to let go.

Where had all of her Women's Lib rhetoric disappeared to?

The undeniable tide of love washed it all away.

Alex exhaled, mumbled, and rolled over onto his side. She stared at his back with a bittersweet smile and wished she knew his dreams.

She'd deliver him to the airport this afternoon. Yet no real decisions about their future had been made. Doubt planted an unwelcome seed. Alex obviously knew his way around a woman. He may not be in a relationship, but it didn't mean he'd been celibate. With his beautiful eyes, adorable dimple, and laid-back, surfer-boy appeal, he must have left a string of women behind in the States.

Could this be his M.O.? If he told each woman exactly what she needed to hear, was it easier to leave, making vague promises he never intended to keep? Sofie frowned. After they'd spent their last night together making love, Alex probably disappeared from their lives too.

The thought of Alex with another woman, even Kim, his long-ago ex-wife, sent an arrow of jealousy spinning through Sofie. She felt like tracking each woman he'd ever been with down, to pluck their hair out, strand by strand.

What do I really know about Alex?

Enough, she decided. Enough to believe this was different. Special. Precious. The fire that ignited between them and burned, sometimes against her will, was strong enough to spark a future.

Ramón became an afterthought. She didn't have to buckle beneath his underhanded demands. He wouldn't ever stop his manipulations; it wasn't in his nature. Sofie belonged in the States anyway, so she'd follow her original plan, returning to California like Alex wanted. They *could* make this work.

Trust him.

Sofie mouthed the words and spooned herself into Alex's back, kissing it lightly. Sliding her arm underneath his, she followed the taut muscles of his stomach with her hand. Her thighs rested against his legs and she savored skin on skin, cataloging to her memory the things she loved about him. The stubbled beard against her flesh, the fine hairs scattered across his body. How adorable he'd looked throwing quarters to the kids along the side of the road on the way to the ranch, and how he had turned to her, laughing with boyish glee.

She pressed her hand against his heart, determined to imprint the cadence of the beat into her memory. Sofie was glad she hadn't stopped taking the pill, but someday she wanted to have his baby.

Using the flat of her palm, she found his nipple, felt it bead and moved lower, down the supple trail past his navel.

Alex caught her fingers, laughed, and rolled over. "We just fell asleep. It can't be morning already."

He pushed her hair away and met her eyes.

"Rise and shine." She grinned.

"Again? Okay, Sofia Morgan Mendoza Davis, I aim to please," Alex said. "I'm on top this time, even though I love the sparkle in your eyes when you're in control."

Later, she lay on her back, slick with sweat, her limbs melted to jelly, his seed seeping between her legs. Another exquisite, soul-sapping climax left her wrung out and bursting with love. It explained the tears that trickled paths down her temples and soaked the pillow.

Alex drew her close, and when he did, he must have realized she was crying, because he pulled away. His intense blue eyes studied her in the morning light.

Sofie tried to smile while he wiped away her tears.

"I'm sorry. I don't know why I'm so emotional... I can't help it."

"Don't be sorry." Alex kissed her forehead. "Are you sad? I hate to see you cry."

"I'm happy. Sad it's Wednesday. Filled with..." She stopped just short of the word: *Love*.

He tucked her body into the crook of his arm and said into her hair, "It'll be okay. We'll work it out."

❦

Sofie pulled Alex by the arm through the cluster of palapas on the crowded beachfront. Every item she picked up—an embroidered white cotton dress, colorful pottery or trinkets—Alex stubbornly said, "No."

He'd announced he needed a last-minute birthday gift for his mom at breakfast, and Sofie, having whittled shopping down to a science, knew just where to go.

Now, in exasperation, she arranged a colorful bouquet of crepe paper flowers.

Alex raised his eyebrows in disgust. "I won't walk around an airport with those."

They worked their way into the street-side bazaar. Deep in the aisles, she asked for the nth time, "What does you mom like? Does she have a hobby? Collect anything? A favorite color?"

Alex didn't answer. But it wasn't the first time he grumbled. "I told you. I hate to shop."

Finally, Alex—on his own, surprisingly stopped at a jewelry stall. While he browsed the selections, she decided this was a good time to slip in a question, "Why did you tell me your parents lived in Chicago—when now, you say they live in California?"

His eyes were clear, innocent. "You misunderstood. My parents *lived* in Chicago. They moved to San Diego two years ago. You have them confused with my sister. She lives in Naperville—it's a suburb, about an hour outside of Chicago." He turned back to the jewelry. "How about a bracelet?"

Sofie didn't have time to speak before the vendor pounced.

"Señor, we have lovely pieces—"

Finally, some direction. She steered Alex by the elbow. "Let's go. I know the perfect place."

Driving along the Costera, she told Alex to turn inland and they traveled through one of the nicer parts of town. She had him pull up to the curb in a commercial neighborhood, in front of Ramón's favorite jeweler.

A little bell jingled over the door. Señor Aguilar, a friend of Ramón's, looked up from his desk and his eyes twinkled.

"Señorita Sofía, it is a pleasure to see you," he said in Spanish, his smile wilting as he scrutinized Alex.

Señor Aguilar turned to Sofie. "But where is your cousin today?"

"At the ranch this week. This is Alex Wilson, a guest of Ramón's and a friend of mine. He's looking for a birthday gift for his mother."

"Excellent," Señor Aguilar said, switching to English.

Several years had passed since she'd last seen him, and she noticed the graying edges of Señor Aguilar's hair. He gave Alex his full attention and introduced himself. "Welcome," he said, extending his hand over the glass countertop. "I am sure we can find a gift your mother will cherish. Do you have anything in mind?"

"Maybe a bracelet?"

"Right over here."

Sofie and Alex followed him to a display case. He pulled out an assortment in a velvet-lined box for Alex to examine.

Alex picked up a few pieces and shrugged, searching for guidance.

With no clue as to what his mom would appreciate, Sofie scoured the store with her eyes for an answer. Finally, she suggested, "What about earrings?"

"That might work."

Señor Aguilar said, "Follow me."

Across the room, he pulled out another tray. Sofie focused on a beautiful, classic pair of gold hoops nearly the size of silver dollars. She adjusted the oval mirror perched on the counter and held them up to her ears.

Alex picked up a smaller gold hoop molded into a thick wreath design.

She thought his selection might be a better mother-style choice. "It kind of resembles a Greek laurel. Will she like those?"

"Which ones do you like?" he asked.

"These hoops." She set the classic ones down, next to the wreath.

Alex picked up the second wreath and laid each pair side by side. "What do you think?"

"They're both pretty, just different styles. The larger hoops are simple. Maybe too plain. There's more going on with the laurels."

"The big hoops go well with your diamond earrings."

Sofie grinned, surprised he'd bothered to notice. "Yes. But I have only one set of piercings. And we're looking for your mom, not for me. Does she have diamonds? Two sets of holes?"

"On my parent's thirtieth wedding anniversary, my dad surprised her with diamond earrings, so she got her ears pierced. Doubt if she'd do it again. She doesn't wear them very often."

"Why? I wear mine all the time."

"She says diamonds are too extravagant to wear every day. That's why these might work."

Sofie's smile faded and she touched the diamond in her left ear.

Alex caressed her shoulder. "I'm not talking about you. It's just the way my mom is. She's a country girl. Into simple things. Don't worry. When you two meet, she'll love you."

Thrilled, Sofie felt relief sweep through her body. This was a big step, talking about their future. And hopefully, Alex was right about his mom.

Glancing at Señor Aguilar, she realized he watched them both carefully. Sofie wondered if he planned to mention their visit to Ramón, telling him, "Sofia and her Americano boyfriend came into my shop."

Ramón would undoubtedly be angry. *With me. With Alex. Would it screw up their business deal?*

Alex must have noticed too. But he didn't drop his arm from her shoulder. Instead, he massaged it protectively as if to stake his claim.

Sofie had never been more in love. *Ramón will have to get over this. We're out of his control.*

Alex picked up the gold hoops—Sofie's choice. "Maybe that's why I should buy these. They're simple."

"Actually, the wreaths are more understated."

"You're right." Alex handed Señor Aguilar the earrings. "We'll take both pairs."

"Both?" she asked.

"The laurels for my mom, and the hoops are yours."

"Mine?"

"When you get to California, get your ears pierced again. Wear them with the diamonds."

Back on the street, in the Jeep, Alex handed her the box containing the gold hoops. "I know how sentimental you are." He gave her a sweet kiss. "Wear these and think of me."

She touched his already stubbled cheek. "I'll never forget you."

Alex opened the second box and slipped the wreaths into the pocket of his wallet. Sofie glanced at his Illinois driver's license. She didn't realize she searched for inconsistencies until she found herself staring. There was nothing strange. The photo in the corner—Alex with short hair—was hot too.

"Aren't you taking the box?" she asked.

"No. I don't want to lose these. They're safer in my wallet. I'll find one when I get home."

Sofie slipped her box into the seagrass purse. "I don't want to lose mine either."

❦

At the hotel, Sofie stood beneath the shower, frowning. In just a few days, Alex had mapped every inch of her body, knew nearly everything about her world, and she still knew so little about him. She already missed him, and he was only a few feet away, just outside the door. Probably with his duffle bag open on the bed, packing up his things. *Ugh.*

Sofie used the last of the mini bottle of shampoo and picked up the conditioner. She wasn't ready to let go. Rinsing her hair, she remembered other showers—yesterday, and one she'd shared with him in Oaxaca. Her stomach rippled with desire and the full, insistent ache begin to blossom between her legs. Bringing Alex into the shower with her would be another bold move, as bold as going to his room a few nights ago after the quinceañera. It's too late to be shy, she decided. She wanted him, needed him, one more time.

Knowing she'd be back in a second, Sofie left the water running and stepped onto the floor. Too lazy to grab a towel, she let water trickle down her body, creating puddles as she carefully navigated her way to the bathroom door.

"Sofia Davis."

Her fingers froze on the knob.

Apparently, Alex was on the phone, talking about her.

She grabbed a towel and tried to tuck the ends snug against her chest. It was difficult to make out full sentences with the shower running in the background. She could only register sporadic words.

"Ramón... California... She doesn't know..."

Is he talking to the guy who works for him? Dean?

Mesmerized, horrified and unable to turn away, she leaned against the door, straining to hear.

"Nick... Jaime and his wife Cecilia... Heroin..."
Did Nick know Ceci and Jaime?
"Sofia... Freaked out by guns... She was attacked on the freeway in LA. Can you get... It isn't easy to get anything from her... And her cousin, Cecilia, pull...."
Why in the hell is he talking about me? Can't get anything? He'd gotten plenty already.
Silence. Whomever was on the phone with Alex must have been speaking. It didn't matter, she'd heard enough. A bolt of icy dread ricocheted through her body.
Deception.
She carefully walked across the wet floor and shut off the water. When she came back, she heard Alex close a drawer.
Resecuring the towel, she turned the doorknob.
Alex was stuffing his khaki shorts into his duffle. He looked up, smiled and, beginning to slip off his black T-shirt, raised his arms over his head. "I was just coming to join you."
Beautiful Alex. Sofie hated him.
Hated herself for trusting him.
Sofie saw a stranger when she met his eyes. And her heart collapsed into a tight, painful fist.
"Who are you?"
"I'm Alex."
"How did Nick know Ceci and Jaime? What don't I know? What can't you get from me?"
Alex's face paled.
"Answer me. Now!"
He didn't look away. "I can't answer questions right now."
"I'm out of here!"
But, wrapped in a towel, where can I go?
When he reached for her, she scratched him and slapped his arm—hard —hoping she left blood and a bruise.
Sofie ran. Her fingers trembled as she fumbled to lock herself in the bathroom. Picking up her clothes, she scrambled to dress. No sound came from the other side of the wall and she half-wished he'd be gone when she opened the door.
Alex sat on the bed, waiting. His duffle zipped and ready.
His eyes flashed. His voice coarse. "You're not going anywhere."

I've become his prisoner? All of his obnoxious arrogance from the nightclub was back, intensified, as the power in the room shifted to him. She gasped for breath, the shock of betrayal as excruciating as a physical blow. Crumbling, she slumped against the wall, her rage tempered by a dose of visceral fear.

"Since we've met, there've been times when you've needed me. I've been there for you." He stood and walked toward her.

Cringing, Sofie crossed her arms, instinctively protecting herself. A threatening flood of tears pooled behind her eyes. Gathering what strength she had left, she straightened her body. On wobbly legs, she took a step back into the bathroom, clenching her sides in a feeble effort to hold herself together. The lump in her throat began to swell and sting.

How could I have been this stupid?

Determined not to cry, she swallowed.

"I need you to trust me. Get on a plane and go back to California, as soon as possible. Tomorrow, if you can. I'll be there in a few weeks and I can explain then." Alex shook his head. "Not now."

"Who was Nick?"

"I can't tell you that."

"What really happened to him? You guys worked together didn't you? Did you know Jaime? Ceci? I want to know." She put her hands on her hips and cried out, "I have a *right* to know."

"*Shh...* you're too loud."

She blinked, struggling to stifle tears. "Fuck you! I'll scream all I want!" Sofie wailed. "What the *fuck* is going on?"

Alex calmly checked his watch. "I have to get to the airport. Are you taking me? Should I call a cab?"

Sofie felt her mouth gape open. "That's it?"

"I told you I'll explain back in California. Trust me on this. It's the best I can do."

❦

Sofie decided to drive Alex to the airport. She couldn't justify why she didn't let him find his own cab. *Family loyalty? Stupidity? Looking to find some understanding in this disaster?*

They rode most of the way to the airport in silence. It was impossible to stop the tears coursing down her cheeks, so she gave up trying. Shaking, she sobbed. "How can you do this to me?"

Finally, he said, "I haven't done anything to you, Sofie."

A naggy voice whispered he was right. She'd agreed to no expectations. No commitments. She'd practically seduced him.

Glancing away from the road, she asked, "Do I mean so little to you?"

Alex reached for her and she jerked away, jarring the wheel and steering the Mercedes toward the shoulder of the pavement.

"Watch out! Focus on the road or pull over and let me drive." His mouth was grim, his eyes bleak. "Jesus, Sofie, you said you could handle this."

"Are you kidding? I don't know what *this* is! Why won't you tell me what *this* is, Alex?" She sniffed and wiped at the tears with the back of her hand.

At the airport, she pulled up to the curb and left the Mercedes running. All ten fingers strangled the wheel. She looked straight ahead.

Alex exited the car, retrieving his duffle bag and briefcase from the back seat. Then he returned, leaned into the passenger side and put his hand on her cheek.

Sofie flinched.

He didn't try to touch her again. "I didn't want it to end like this."

Trying to ignore him, she stared at the cars in the lot across the road. It was a futile effort. Sofie stifled a sob and swallowed it down, her voice was brittle, "We both knew it would end. Part of the deal, remember..." She couldn't get the rest of the words out—*our agreement.*

He dropped a piece of paper onto the burl console. "Trust me. Go home. Here's the number where you can reach me. Give me a few weeks, then call. Leave a message. Let me know you're in California and where I can find you. I'll explain then. I promise."

Refusing to meet his eyes, Sofie knew it was over. There'd been too many lies, unanswered questions. She listened to his even breathing. Felt his gaze focused on her face. Finally, she heard his heavy sigh.

"You were right all along, Sofie. I am an asshole bastard."

There was nothing to say, so she continued to study the parking lot until the door closed.

Through the open window, she heard his footsteps fade along the sidewalk. She picked up the piece of paper. The Las Brisas logo was splayed across the top, in bright pink script. There wasn't a message, just a scribbled phone number with a 213 area code.

One more mystery: a Chicago resident with a Los Angeles telephone.

Crushing the number into a ball, she tossed the trash into her purse. Once again alone, she ran her fingers up her scalp and pulled the curls from her head, sobbing, as she watched Alex walk into the airport. Out of her life.

CHAPTER NINETEEN
Calle Sucias

Dirty Streets
Wednesday, July 11, 1984

Wiped out and bloated by tears, Sofie wasn't ready to face the confrontation she'd surely find in the Acapulco house. She shut off the engine, leaned into the seat of the Mercedes, and threw her head back into the headrest. Her body ached. Her eyes burned. She felt sick. *Heartsick.*

Focusing on the seeds of Alex's disjointed telephone conversation, her mind raced through possibilities. Nothing made sense.

She'd heard Alex say the words on the phone.

What don't I know?

California and Ramón? The family had a house in La Jolla, just north of San Diego. Ramón rarely visited. Esteban spent more time there than anyone. Ramón always claimed he was more comfortable at home on the ranch or in Acapulco.

And to her knowledge, the first time Ramón and Jaime met was at Ceci's wedding. They'd hardly spoken. *Right?* Then there was Alex's friend, Nick, who apparently knew Jaime and Ceci. There was a connection between the four of them. *How?*

Alex had mentioned Sofie's fear of guns on the phone. After she found the one he had in Oaxaca, he'd thankfully kept it out of sight. And yes, the incident with the gunman on the freeway had been terrifying. However, the police never found a whisper of evidence to prove it was anything but a mistaken, isolated assault. It had taken months for her to sleep soundly again, and she hated driving. That was, until now. Why did Alex care?

Maybe Ramón hadn't needed to convince Alex to carry a weapon in

Mexico. The gun could have been his. A chill slithered down her spine. She replayed the incident in the Oaxaca bedroom—not letting herself linger over the steamier details—and couldn't remember him ever actually answering her question about the origin of the gun.

Sofie frowned in self-disgust. She'd wanted him so badly, she supplied her own explanations for anything that didn't make sense.

Inside the house, Hector stood in the living room near the bank of glass that overlooked the bay. The rest of the house appeared empty, except for the maid carrying a stack of towels down the hall.

Slipping the keys into her purse, Sofie set it on the entry table, and asked, "Where is everybody?"

"No one else is here," Hector said in Spanish. "I have been waiting for you."

"Are Monica and Gabriel back?"

Hector fidgeted, shuffling his weight between both feet. "Ramón is wondering where you have been."

"I don't appreciate being followed."

"You have been difficult to find, señorita." He straightened his body and towered over her, trying to create an illusion of authority he didn't have.

"Ramón told me to show Mr. Wilson around." Already on edge after her disastrous afternoon with Alex, she was doubly frustrated at having to report her whereabouts to one of Ramón's minions.

"The Mercedes has been at his hotel since Tuesday."

"We stayed out late and I returned to his room in the mornings to pick him up. You slept in the parking lot, waiting for me? Or did you give up and go home to your girlfriend?"

Hector's face went slack as the accusation hit its mark.

"We used his car. We hung out at the hotel, went down to the beach club. We saw the cliff divers. We were sightseeing." Agitated, she was unable to smother the shrill in her voice, "I did exactly what Ramón asked me to do. If you told him otherwise, let's see who he believes after he hears my side of the story. You'll be out of a job."

Why did Ramón have to control everyone and everything?

"Where is my cousin, Monica? And Gabriel? Have you seen him?"

He shrugged.

Exasperated, she grabbed her purse. Sofie slammed the front door so hard the glass rumbled, and headed for the driveway.

❧

Sofie found Monica at the salon, getting her weekly manicure.

"Where've you been?" Monica asked in Spanish.

"Around. Is Gabriel in town too? When did you get back?"

"We came in yesterday afternoon. Hector has been searching for you."

Alex *had* seen Gabriel last night.

"I just took Alex to the airport."

"Ah, Alex... Now, I understand." Monica's eyes twinkled. "Wait. Come closer," she said, motioning with the crook of her finger.

Sofie did and Monica's smile faded. "You look like you've been punched in the stomach. What's wrong?"

"I can't stand this heat."

Monica studied her. "Sofie esta enamorada!"

Not bothering to glance up, the manicurist grinned, and concentrated on brushing candy-apple polish across Monica's nails.

"Oh, I get it," Monica said. "This could be a problem. Does Ramón know you're in love with his new business partner?"

"I'm not in love," Sofie lied. *I'm heartbroken once again.* In the tangle of her emotions, she found a braid of courage. "I don't care what Ramón thinks," Sofie said, and she meant it.

"You should."

"There's nothing to worry about." Sofie looked around the room. Posters had been tacked to the lavender walls—pretty girls with bizarre hairdos and garish makeup most women would never wear.

"Be careful, Sofie."

Thinking about the wad of trash in her purse, Sofie knew she'd never call Alex. It was over. Nevertheless, California was still home. "It doesn't matter. I'm going back to California."

"When?"

"I'm not sure. Soon."

Monica frowned. "You won't be here for my wedding?"

"You've set the date?"

"Victor and I are thinking about October. At the ranch."

Sofie wasn't surprised. Ramón had wanted the wedding there and, of course, Monica thought it was her idea.

"I'll fly back down."

"Victor said Ramón is counting on you to stay and work for him. He's not going to like this."

"I never intended to make a life here." There was no point in trying to explain. Monica couldn't understand; she'd never lived anywhere else. "I appreciate the help Ramón has given me. But he had unrealistic expectations. I have a right to my own life."

"There are always strings with Ramón." Monica shrugged. "That's just the way he is."

❦

Thankfully, Hector disappeared before dinner. Sofie had hoped Gabriel would be home by then. He didn't show. At nine, tired of waiting, she enlisted Monica to help track him down. Sofie didn't tell her why she needed to talk to him. There was no need to give details without concrete information.

They combed the Costera searching for Gabriel, scouting his favorite haunts. Checking with friends, they kept missing him—some places by an hour, others only minutes. Finally, they stopped at the club where Sofie first met Alex, just days ago. Her body felt heavy, saturated with disappointment, as she stepped inside the building. And worse, the cigarette smoke hovering in the club grated against her already swollen eyes. Determined, Sofie found two seats at the bar and glimpsed Gabriel as he vanished down the hall towards the men's restroom.

Sofie tapped Monica's arm. "I see him. I need to talk to him alone."

In the dark hallway outside the men's room, Sofie leaned against the wall, the weight of the day sinking into her bones. It wasn't over. Several guys came and went, none of them Gabriel. Almost fifteen minutes passed.

Tired of waiting, she opened the restroom door. Blinding fluorescent light flooded the space. She squinted and blinked the room into focus.

A group of young men were pressed against the countertop that ran the length of the wall. One guy glanced into the mirror above the sink. Sofie met his shocked gaze. He nudged the guy next to him, and the crowd parted in the evaporating din. Nearly everyone spun to face her. A man using the urinal turned his head, startled.

Her view was now clear. Gabriel hadn't paid attention to her arrival. He hovered over the countertop, snorting a line of cocaine through a straw.

"All of you, out!"

Even those who didn't understand English got the gist.

Gabriel raised his head, his stare colliding with hers in the mirror.

Motioning with the straw between two fingers, he spoke dispassionately in Spanish, "In a minute, Sofie," and returned to his drug.

Her face burning, she clenched her fingers, itching to rip the straw from

202

his hands.

The few men who remained in the room watched with wide eyes.

"Largate! I said. Get out."

If they suspected she was crazy, they weren't far off. Her body buzzed with rage; she was losing control. She leaned against the dirty white tile and crossed her arms, ready to push the men out herself if the room didn't clear soon.

They scattered, including the guy hastily zipping up at the urinal.

She was finally alone with her cousin. "You *promised* me, Gabriel."

Putting the clear plastic straw down on the counter, he tucked a tiny amber vial into his pocket. He faced her and leaned against the countertop, arms folded.

It was a standoff.

"Things have changed. Everybody's doing it."

"Not everybody."

Gabriel studied her with tired, ghostly eyes. Rubbing his fingers around his nostrils, he wiped away the white powdery residue, inhaling the remains.

"Leave me alone." He turned back to the countertop and focused on pulverizing, then cutting, several lines of coke with a razor blade.

Sofie walked the few feet it took to cross the room and grabbed his arm.

Gabriel held the blade poised in the air.

The move was unbelievably threatening. "Don't," he warned.

She felt the sting of tears once again. "I'm begging you, Gabriel. *Please.* Remember what happened to Ceci."

He jerked his arm away, eyes cold and black. "Leave me alone."

❦

Sofie discovered Monica where she'd left her at the bar, surrounded by several friends, including Lucy. "I found Gabriel. Can you find a way home?"

"Of course. What's going on?" She raised her pencil-thin eyebrows. "There's something wrong. Right?"

"I'll explain tomorrow. Don't wait up for me." Sofie watched Gabriel turn the corner and move toward the door. "It's probably gonna be a long night."

She followed Gabriel as he left the club and found another bar, and then another one. At each location, she sat alone and waited, bypassing any offers of company. Gabriel laughed with his friends and pointedly avoided her. He made numerous trips to the toilet. Each time he returned, he'd check the room. Their eyes would meet and lock momentarily before he'd turn his attention away.

Hours past midnight, the crowd thinned, and she tucked herself into a booth at the far corner of the bar. Gabriel continued to hold court from his stool. She rubbed her aching eyes, determined to wait him out. Finally, he nodded in her direction and waved off his few remaining friends. He ordered a fresh drink and came to the booth.

Gabriel sat down and slid her way. "Tired?"

"What do you think?"

"Where's your boyfriend? Alex?"

"He's not my boyfriend."

"Don't lie. I saw you in the hallway with him that first night he was in town. And you've been with him now, for what? How many days?"

"I was showing him around."

"More than that. He's your gringo lover. I can see it in your eyes."

Sofie glanced down at her soda, ashamed her face had given everything away. "I haven't been following you around all night to discuss my love life."

Gabriel sighed and rubbed his forehead. "What do you want from me?"

She met his gaze. "I'm not going to bury another cousin. Another good friend." Reaching out, she touched his arm.

He yanked it away. "Cecilia didn't know how to manage this. I do."

"Bullshit. Eventually, coke finds a way to do the managing. It always does. Nobody *manages* coke."

"Plenty of people do. They do it all the time. I'm beginning to believe the world is fueled by it." Gabriel spread his hands and motioned across the room. "It's running the world!"

His laugh rang harsh throughout the empty club.

"It's ruining ours."

"Coke *rules* our world," he said. "You're so *naive*. Grow up and take a good look around."

Stung by his harsh words, she blinked. "What do you mean?"

Gabriel stared at her with glassy eyes. *Ceci's eyes.*

"You're in trouble," she pleaded. "There are places in California where you can get clean. Come back with me and we'll get you the help you need."

He laughed. "I don't need your help."

"I'm going to talk to Ramón. He'll help too."

"You're going to talk to Ramón?" Gabriel sneered. "You really don't know what's going down here, do you? Where do you think I'm getting the coke?"

Ramón? Gabriel had to be mistaken, so high he was delusional. *It couldn't be.*

Sofie watched Gabriel look up into the black stucco ceiling, then his eyes returned to hers. "Let me be clear. Ramón, the hypocrite, doesn't want the family dabbling in his marketable goods. But I've found ways."

"Like the new restaurant you've discovered north of town?"

Gabriel cocked his head. "I'm not following."

"No, I'm the one not following."

He sighed again, as if he were explaining fundamentals to a child. "Ramón's in the transport business."

"Yes. Exporting goods like furniture and coffee… other things."

"It's the *other things* he's found the most profitable. Transporting cocaine for the Colombians in particular."

"Alex said—"

"Yes, your lover, Alex." Gabriel smiled. "He's Ramón's Chicago connection. Ramón's breaking into the Midwest trade."

"That's not true!" Sofie was unable to wrap her mind around Gabriel's words. "You're lying."

She took a quick succession of deep breaths, suddenly suffocating in the bar's stale air.

Gabriel sighed. His face broadcasted an odd mixture of satisfaction and pain.

A horrible clarity began to emerge through the fog of her denial. The clues had been everywhere. *Her return to the family's exploding wealth. Alex's evasions. Cryptic phone calls. The gun.*

She'd been an idiot, just inches from the wall and still unable to read the writing. Her stomach twisted, roiling. Bile rose in her throat and she swallowed the sour taste down.

Ramón. Alex. Both of them were bastards.

Alex had even said so himself, *"I'm an asshole bastard."*

She pressed her fingers to her temples in a futile attempt to stop the rush of blood exploding in her brain.

"I'm sorry, Sofie." Gabriel touched her arm. "Are you all right?"

Overwhelmed, the sobs washed up Sofie's throat again and she buried her head in her hands.

❦

Calmer now, Sofie walked down the steps into the living room, tossing a blanket and pillow onto the couch. She'd brought Gabriel home with her. While she thought she'd been able to convince him to get some sleep, she couldn't trust him to stay in the house, so she decided to camp out here.

Though the house was quiet and she was exhausted, she found it impossible to rest. The throbbing headache she'd been fighting all afternoon had intensified with Gabriel's revelations. Earlier, she'd downed a couple of aspirin. Hopefully, it wasn't a migraine and relief would kick in soon.

She settled by the window, folding herself into a chair. *Here we go again. With Gabriel this time,* Sofie moaned; the very real possibility of losing someone else she loved clawed at her heart.

Looking down at the city, she wondered about Ramón's reach. It seemed like everywhere she went in Acapulco, there was always somebody who knew her. Maybe not personally, but once they discovered her family name, Sofie's American accent didn't matter anymore. Faces would perk up and her wishes suddenly became unspoken commands. In the past, she hadn't thought much of it; theirs was an old family, living in a culture thick with respectful tradition. Now… Well, now she knew better.

Other things began to make sense too. Ramón's insistence on helping her through school. Of course, an accountant with an American connection would be an excellent cover. Ramón had always been arrogant, and he was worse this summer. Building an authoritative aura, he'd surrounded himself with the spoils of immense power: The entourage, the limos, the new compound at the ranch. Only drug money could provide this kind of wealth. *Why haven't I noticed it before?*

I didn't want to.

Ramón had built a cartel and Alex was a dealer. It didn't matter if Alex mentioned heroin on the phone, not coke. He probably sold both. Alex was a drug-dealing *asshole bastard.*

Realizing he should be back in Chicago by this hour, Sofie found some distance, and with that, some clarity. Her assumptions may have been wrong, but her intuition had been right. He'd been hiding the truth all along. Yes, their romance had escalated quickly. But it was unforgivable how he'd persisted to lie, even after she'd told him about Ceci.

What about his heartfelt confession on Monte Albán? Was Alex's friend,

Nick, really dead? Or was that a lie too?

Thinking he could pull this off and continue their relationship, Alex had tried to manipulate her into moving back to the States. He'd banked on her return to California so he could keep the curtain pulled tight against the true nature of his Chicago business.

It was a relief to realize she hadn't misread everything. He really hadn't wanted their romance to end. But this gave her only a sliver of satisfaction. While she'd been falling in love, he'd been feeling something too.

It wasn't love. It was selfishness. With no regard for her beliefs, morals, feelings.

All of his bullshit, including, she suddenly remembered, his line of being "more of a ROTC type" was all hype. Had he ever even been in Viet Nam?

Tears she didn't think she had left seared her eyes. Sofie felt her face flush with the heat of shame, realizing how thoroughly she'd deluded herself to be with him.

Any trace of love she'd felt for Alex drained from her body, and was replaced by frigid hate.

Daylight was a few hours away. It was too early to head to the ranch. When the sun came up, she'd tackle the road, even though she didn't like to drive it alone.

Sofie moved to the couch, positioned the pillow, and pulled the blanket across her body. If she could manage to close her eyes, a few hours of sleep could help keep her emotions in check when she confronted Ramón—*the bastard*.

Tomorrow, she'd have a few demands of her own.

Gabriel didn't realize it, yet, but he'd be leaving Mexico on his way to rehab. Between her dad's medical connections, Tía Sofía's assistance, and Ramón's money, they'd get Gabriel the help he desperately needed.

CHAPTER TWENTY
Cali Cocodrilo

Cali Crocodile
  Thursday, July 12, 1984

Alex smiled. The bust would go down in less than a hour, and he'd never seen so much cocaine in one location. He lifted a bale onto the workbench and unwrapped the twine. Unpacking twenty kilos, he lined the bricks up for César to tally with his clipboard and pen.

On the other side of the warehouse, Ramón stood with Humberto Torres. He said something in Spanish and laughter erupted throughout the room.

Marco translated from across the bench, "Torres said he didn't know crocodiles could be found this far north. He has an associate with big white teeth they call The Crocodile at home. When necessary, he has a nasty bite too."

Alex laughed along with Marco.

Yesterday, Hector—Alex and Sofie's tail—met him, right on time in the airport bar. Hector didn't talk during the long drive south. Alex had no complaints. Before midnight, he'd delivered Alex to the Mendoza's cavernous living room, where a party was in full swing.

Curiously reserved, Ramón greeted Alex, hesitating when he met his eyes. Ramón didn't mention Sofie or where they'd been. Instead, he turned and introduced Alex to Humberto Torres, a friend from Colombia.

Ramón's new guest was the elusive Cali connection. This was a huge break for the team, a double score.

Now, within minutes of the team's arrival, Torres was leaning against the wall with his bodyguard nearby.

Marco continued to chuckle as he unwrapped another bale and removed the kilos.

A pair of sliding, corrugated metal doors were open to the dock, flooding hot, wet air into the warehouse. Overhead, fans cycled thick humidity, doing little to squelch the heat. Alex wiped the sweat off his face. Uncomfortable, yes, but better than the older, abandoned warehouse Alex had seen on Ramón's Sunday tour. That one sat inland, away from the river, with only a single door. It used to be Nick's domain. He too had spent time on the ranch, watchful and hunting.

Before Nick became the hunted.

If. Two familiar letters, heavy with meaning, weighed Alex down. With Sofie, he'd wanted so badly to massage *iffy* possibilities into a real relationship. A part of him always knew it was impossible. When he saw the desolation of betrayal in Sofie's—*his lover's*—eyes, he knew he'd never see her again. He'd been delusional. How could he have expected it to turn out any other way? Alex added these new failures into his own, private, guilt-ridden collection of *ifs* he'd been carrying around for years.

If he'd hadn't partnered up with Nick back in 1976, things would be different. *If* they hadn't taken the assignment as off-loaders in LA, they'd still be partners. *If* the night Nick showed up at Alex's door, four years ago… Well, Alex kept replaying that night in his mind.

❦

"I'll have a beer. We're celebrating." Nick had settled on Alex's couch, while a thick blanket of June Gloom rolled over his Santa Monica duplex. "Jaime promoted me and I'm moving up, going down to Mexico. It's a good lead. There's a family down there growing a plantation of Sinsemilla they want to bring up to LA."

Alex grumbled, "You get all the good jobs." Smiling, he pulled two Budweisers from his refrigerator.

"It's my Cherokee tan and flawless Spanish." Nick yelled into the kitchen. "You don't have any of these superior qualities. You're just plain old American Wonder Bread. Works great for you in some circles, but in our booming business…" Nick laughed. "Follow my example man, get a tan and learn Spanish. You'll go far."

"I'll think about it." Alex said. Returning to the living room, he handed Nick a beer. "What's the family's name?"

"Mendoza. A posse of brothers. I talked to Dean. The Mexico City office looked into them. They've been around for awhile, playing under our radar. Jaime says he has a family connection. I'm not sure, yet, what it is. They're looking for help down there, people who specialize in cultivation. And Alex, buddy, that's me."

"Leave it to you, Nick, to kiss the boss's ass." He laughed. "What about Danielle? Won't she be pissed?"

Alex sat down on the opposite side of the sectional and crossed his ankles on the coffee table.

"She's always pissed when it comes to my job. But it pays the bills. She *really* doesn't like it when I leave the country." Nick stared down at his beer. "She never does... Mexico's safe... Relatively."

"There are worse places."

"Yeah, definitely worse," Nick replied.

Alex would never forget those words. At the time, neither of them realized how dangerous Mexico had become.

If Alex and Nick hadn't fed off of each other's ambition, and weren't manically focused on getting the job done—thinking they could win a perpetual battle—things *would* have turned out differently. In retrospect, they both should have skated along, happy just to put in the time toward an early retirement.

Then, Alex wouldn't have had to tell Danielle her husband had been murdered. Wouldn't have seen her face crumble. Wouldn't have had to lift Danielle up from her knees to hold her wracked body and listen to her wails, while his own tears slid down his face.

Nick could be home today with Danielle and the boys, *if* Alex had insisted that they were partners—Nick wasn't going anywhere without him.

Instead, like Nick, Alex always wanted a bigger bust. So, he'd said nothing. Nick left LA a few days later. Alex never saw him again.

Eventually, the Mendozas moved away from pot and added a less risky venture to the family's investments. When the Federales could be cow-prodded to focus, they cast their lazy eye on cultivation, not trafficking. Transporting forty thousand dollars' worth of coke took up the same amount of space as a few hundred dollars' worth of pot, making it more profitable by any estimation.

Tasting the bittersweet satisfaction of revenge, Alex silently made a vow to his friend. *It's our turn today, Nick.*

Torres and Ramón moved into the corner, overseeing the room. Alex wished he'd listened to Nick and learned Spanish. He was only able to make out random bits as they spewed a volley of unintelligible words between themselves. After Nick died, Alex used anger as a misguided rationale for refusing to learn the language. Luckily, when Alex was with Sofie, it hadn't been a problem. With just a look, she could detect Alex's confusion and translate. Marco and Esteban tried, but it wasn't the same.

Alex heard a cabinet door slam, and jumped.

It was Torres' man. Alex studied the scraggly American, realizing he wasn't much past thirty. He took off his hat and set it on the counter, exposing his long, dirty blond hair—literally. Standing along the wall, he drummed his fingers against the corrugated metal. Then—thank God—he abruptly stopped and lit a cigarette.

He paced around the warehouse, opening and closing cabinet doors. He inspected his gun. Alex suspected he'd found a way to sample some of the dope.

Rude and nosy, he made a laughable excuse for a bodyguard. Torres, short and beefy, must have outweighed him by at least sixty pounds.

Ramón studied Torres' man, his lips thinning with distaste.

Alex smiled. For once, they agreed on something.

Torres didn't seem to notice. Maybe he was used to ignoring him. Alex wondered how they'd crossed paths. Colombians didn't usually hire Americanos for protection.

Alex checked his watch. Ten minutes past two.

The dope had been unloaded onto the dock and the cartel's boat had left a few hours ago. Predictably, Gabriel hadn't shown up. The rest of the brothers were here. They'd even recruited several men from the village. Everybody pitched in to help—except for Ramón, Torres, and the bodyguard, who bounced his way around the room.

Surrounded by millions of dollars' worth of product, Esteban moved through the building with a razor knife, making tiny slits in the plastic wrap of random kilos.

Sampling a fingertip of coke, Esteban grinned.

César came around and tallied the bricks, making notations. Afterwards, Alex repackaged them into a cloth sack for shipment, stacked it against the wall, then lifted another bale onto the workbench.

The Mendozas were leaving it to Alex to cut and repackage the kilos into street baggies, once the coke arrived in Chicago.

"Hey, man."

Alex wasn't surprised it was Torres' bodyguard breathing slime down his neck, they were the only two Americans in the room. That was all they had in common.

A pungent sweat poured from his body in the ever-present heat. Alex didn't think he'd showered in a week.

Wrinkling his nose, Alex focused on stacking kilos. "Hey."

The man swatted a mosquito off his arm, pulled out another cigarette, lit it, and tossed the match onto the concrete floor. "Don't I know you from somewhere?"

Who is this guy? Alex's stomach clenched. "Ever been to Chicago?"

"No."

He stood too close to Alex, watching.

Had the bodyguard made a connection between Alex Wilson and Alex Wakefield? Unlikely. They'd never met. Alex would have remembered this guy. Torres too.

"Didn't I see you on Sunday night in Oaxaca, having dinner with that really hot chick?"

Alex froze.

Marco looked up from his stack of bricks.

"That wasn't me. A lot of Americans visit Mexico." Alex met the bodyguard's pale gray eyes.

Laughing, Torres' man took a drag of his cigarette and held it up with his left hand, chopping at the smoke floating in the air.

The smoker who'd been on the hotel balcony had been left-handed. Lanky, like this asshole. *Fuck.*

"I don't know. The chick. She looked familiar too."

Alex shot Marco a look. He was glancing back and forth, studying them both.

"You've got the wrong guy, buddy," Alex said.

The bodyguard lowered his voice. "It's cool. I've always wanted to sample some Mexican snatch."

Alex felt his face blaze with anger. And guilt. There was a time he'd also thought of Sofie as a self-indulgent bonus, just a scathing swipe at Ramón and the family. She'd become so much more.

"Just take my advice, watch out for crabs. The pube crawlers. There was this girl down in Colombia—"

"I've never been to Oaxaca." Alex glared at him and clenched his fists, driving down the impulse to deck the son of a bitch.

Torres' man raised his hands and backed away. "Whatever you say, man. We're cool."

Alex stared into his eyes, *almost* hoping the prick would say something else and give Alex the satisfaction of beating the shit out of him. Unfortunately, he turned and moved toward his boss.

"Loco," Marco said.

A word Alex understood. "Yeah, crazy," he said, picking up another bale.

Occasionally, Alex glanced in the bodyguard's direction. Now he spent most of his time pacing the room, swatting at his body. With that stink, of course he'd attract bugs. At one point, he leaned in and whispered to Torres, and Torres, in turn, spoke to Ramón in Spanish.

Ramón nodded.

Torres' man crossed the room and, scraping metal against concrete, closed the bay doors.

Most of the other men in the room looked up when they heard the grating sound. Many stared. They must have wondered if this was some kind of trap too. *A bizarre Cali precaution?* Esteban and Ramón seemed to share a silent conversation. Ramón shrugged.

Everybody watching took a clue from his composure and relaxed.

"What's going on?" Alex asked.

"Apparently, Señor Torres' companion doesn't like bugs," Marco explained. Grinning, he added, "Maybe he should find the bathtub more often."

They both laughed.

Ramón walked to the opposite wall and turned on the lights. Strips of industrial fluorescents that hung between the ceiling fans began to sputter and buzz. The heat in the windowless warehouse jacked up, poaching the room.

With only one other door, a narrow entrance on the side of the building, Dean might have to make adjustments to the plan.

Alex felt for his gun in the waistband of his khaki pants and rolled up the sleeves of his white shirt. Most of the men here wore a gun on the outside of their clothes, like cowboys. Several large weapons were stashed in the corner of the warehouse. Extra ammunition was stored in one of the cabinets. Thanks to the hyperactive bodyguard, Alex knew this detail.

"What happened to you?" Marco asked, his eyes locked on Alex's forearm.

Shit. The ugly red scratch Sofie left still stung. Alex had deserved it.

"It was a stupid thing." He chuckled. "Yesterday, I was showering at the hotel. And it has these fancy rock walls. I got shampoo in my eyes, slipped... Well," Alex lifted his arm, "You can see what happened."

"That must have been a nasty fall."

"It was."

A nasty fall.

Alerted by a plane in the distance, Alex checked his watch again. The team should be here soon. But they weren't due yet. Another change of plans? The punchy whine approaching didn't come from the team's DC-6; a helicopter was moving in.

Others, startled by the helicopter, raised their heads. None of the brothers seemed to be alarmed, and everybody returned to work.

Torres and Ramón laughed.

Ramón glanced at Alex and nodded.

A double-shot of adrenaline pumped through Alex's veins. *The Federales?* Had one of the suits in Washington, once again, inadvertently tipped off the Mexicans? If so, Alex breathed a dead man. This time they wouldn't have exposed one agent, but an entire American commando unit. *How could Washington know?* The team sure as hell wasn't in Mexico by invitation. They'd planned everything so carefully, under the radar and down to the most minute detail.

If the approaching helicopter was loaded with Federales, Ramón, Torres and everybody else expected them, because no one flinched when the helicopter descended and, by Alex's estimation, landed just outside the door.

The bodyguard moved to stand next to Torres. Ramón got the okay from César and called Felipe over. Ramón and Torres smiled and shook hands.

Torres and the bodyguard picked up a pair of American Tourister suitcases—a brand Alex found ironic, under the circumstances—presumably full of American bills.

Fuck. A lost opportunity. Millions of dollars moving out of the team's reach and two more slugs the agency would have to track another day. Felipe escorted them out the side door and, soon, the Cali helicopter powered up, rising into the air.

Alex looked to Esteban, who stood nearby, watching him. "Where are they headed?"

"Back to the airport in Oaxaca. Señor Torres wanted to oversee the first sale to make sure the transaction was trouble-free." Esteban sliced into one of Alex's kilos, tasted the coke, and motioned for Alex to taste some too.

He dipped his finger into the white powdery cake and rubbed the odorless substance against his gum. Alex felt the instant tingle and tasted the slight bitter flavor of unadulterated coke. Torres had delivered high quality, perfect blow.

"Your pilot is already in the air?" Esteban asked.

Alex nodded.

"We'll have your plane loaded and you'll be on your way before sundown."

CHAPTER TWENTY-ONE

Cielo Sucio

Dirty Sky
Thursday, July 12, 1984

Some of the staff could always be found on the ranch. Nevertheless, this afternoon, the house seemed deserted. Sofie's cousin Felipe generally hid out in his room, so she went upstairs and knocked, opening the door.

Ever since she could remember, he'd been interested in science and, these days it had become a passionate hobby. She expected him to be working on one of his experiments. His microscope and lab equipment were scattered across a large table in the corner of the room. A shelf of chemicals sat above a Bunsen burner and a grouping of beakers. She recognized some of the names from her high school chemistry class. Ether. Sodium bicarbonate. Lithium. Iodine. Acetone.

But no Felipe.

Sofie found Rosa flipping through a magazine in the kitchen.

"Where's everybody?" Sofie asked in Spanish from the doorway.

Leaping from the barstool, Rosa dropped half a sandwich onto her plate.

"Oh, señorita!" she cried, holding a palm to her chest. "You frighten me." Running a hand across her apron. "I didn't know you were coming today. Can I make you lunch?"

"No, no. Please sit down and finish yours. Where'd they go?"

Rosa continued to stand. "Everybody is working in the warehouse. I packed lunches for them this morning. Can't I fix you something?"

Sofie had hardly eaten anything in the past twenty-four hours. At dinner last night, she'd picked at her food, shuffling it across her plate with a fork. "Thanks, I'm not hungry."

In the living room, she stared down at the river. The fishing boat wasn't docked at the landing, not even the dingy. She could wait for Ramón, but that might take hours. Courage, fueled by rage, motivated her to confront him now. She needed to get back to Acapulco. Gabriel may have already disappeared. Looking for more coke, he could be unable to locate for days. She planned to have him by her side this weekend, on their way to California.

With no boat to ferry her upriver, she'd have to take the long, dusty road, backtracking part of the way she'd just driven. *Shit.*

Whatever it took, it was better than sitting here waiting.

Finding the new warehouse didn't turn out to be all that difficult. Situated next to the river, it sat near a cluster of farm outbuildings used by the family for decades. A recently constructed dock stood along the bank and dwarfed the old gray relic nearby, the one her grandfather had used when the family's fortune depended on their sugarcane harvests.

Ramón's extravagant fishing boat had been moored to the old dock, not the new one. Evidently, he'd told her the truth about something, it looked like a big shipment was due in today.

Even though a half-dozen ranch vehicles were scattered throughout the yard, there was no sign of her cousins. Sofie parked by Esteban's Blazer and shut off the engine. She left her handbag in the passenger seat and the keys in the ignition; this wouldn't take long.

She stepped out of the Mercedes and listened to birds calling to each other in the trees. Others complained, and sometimes she did too, but there was something comforting about the blanket of humidity that enveloped her. As sweat began to collect in the crook of her bare arms, she realized she was going to miss her second home. Sofie inhaled, trying to burn into her memory the pungent perfume of the swampy river mixed with the scent of freshly hewn planks.

Gravel spit underneath a vehicle as it rushed up the road. Sofie turned and wasn't surprised to see Gabriel's silver Corvette with a cloud of dust billowing behind.

Pulling in next to the Mercedes, he sprang from his car and caught up with her in the dirt. "What are you doing?"

"I told you, I'm going to talk to Ramón. You're coming back to California with me."

"I never said I'd go with you." He seized her by the shoulders. "Don't talk to Ramón about me. Don't say anything about what I told you last night."

He glared at her, gesturing toward the road. "If you want to go, get on a plane and go back to your life in California."

She studied his once beautiful face, so clearly marred by the shadows of addiction, and realized how stupid she'd been not to notice before.

Gabriel dropped his hands and said, "Just go home!"

Tears clustered in the corners of her eyes. "I'm not leaving without you."

Determined, she turned and walked toward the warehouse.

When she glanced back, Gabriel raised his arms in surrender. "Okay. Tell him what you want. I'm not going anywhere!"

Sofie found the door locked. Maybe stuck. *Nobody ever locks anything around here.* She heard voices inside. Frustrated, she yanked the handle again. The door still wouldn't budge.

Pounding on the corrugated metal, she yelled, "Ramón!"

Someone pounded on the door. Alex looked up. *Another unexpected visitor?*

"Ramón!"

What the hell is Sofie doing here? Alex dropped the bale in his arms.

Ramón hurried to the door.

Sideswiping him, Alex unlocked it and grabbed her. "Fuck!"

Right on schedule, a confusing blast—designed and set by the team—exploded in the yard, showering them both with dirt and gravel.

Sofie ran.

"Get down!" Alex tackled Sofie, slammed her flat onto the ground, and covered her body with his. A hot shell casing landed on his back. He mopped it away with his hand and wiped the dust out of his eyes. The men in the warehouse scrambled as gunfire erupted from all directions.

He rolled off and rammed her forward. "Move!"

Spitting mud, she stared back at him, terror freezing her face. She tried to stand. Stunned by the bombardment of the assault, she fell onto her hands and knees.

Alex shoved her butt down. Hard.

Some of Ramón's men had recovered and were returning fire. Several moved into position to ward off the attack.

Exposed in the courtyard and surrounded by outbuildings, Alex and Sofie were in the heart of the battle. They were vulnerable to fire, both deliberate and friendly.

Bullets screamed above them. "Crawl!" he demanded.

Instead, she collapsed and covered her head with her hands, fending off the deluge.

They were both so filthy and slick with sweat, it was difficult to get a good grip on her arm. Finally, he was able to pull her to the wall of a nearby shed. For a second, he worried he might have jerked her arm out of its socket. Dislocation was better than the alternative.

At the wall, he used his body as a shield, compactly squishing her into the right angle of the shed's concrete foundation and the ground.

"I'm going to get up. Make yourself as small as possible. When I tell you to move, get into the shed as fast as you can. Stay down and follow the wall!"

Alex waited for a momentary pause in the shelling. "Go!" He pushed her towards the outbuilding.

She moved cautiously forward, he followed close behind, a spray of bullets ricocheting everywhere.

"Faster," he ordered.

A bullet nicked the soil near Sofie and she instantly clambered on her own. They reached the shed in moments, finding a spot in the bay next to an old pickup truck. In seconds, gunfire hit the windshield, raining a cascade of glass.

"Get all the way back!" he yelled.

He found a good vantage point along the wall and wiped the sweat off the edges of his mouth, his chin, his cheeks. Salt bit his eyes. He pulled out his .45 caliber, aimed and fired, helping the team unleash the assault against the Mendoza family.

After waiting years for this moment, he reveled in the rush of high-octane exhilaration that washed over him, coursing through every nerve.

When he could, he turned to check on Sofie. Huddled into a corner at the back of the shed, she watched the action in horrified silence, her glazed eyes darting around.

The strike came in from all directions as planned. Alex spotted other agents strategically positioned throughout the area. A sniper's footsteps tromped across the metal roof overhead.

Esteban ran across the yard, spraying bullets.

From above, the sniper made the kill, hitting Esteban square in the chest. He howled and slumped to the dirt, blood spurting from his wound.

Esteban had been Alex's favorite. He felt the barest twinge of regret. Then nothing.

He glanced back into the bay. Sofie's eyes were blank, apparently she hadn't seen Esteban fall.

The DC-6 rumbled in the distance, coming in for a landing. *Right on time.*

Gabriel staggered into the yard, holding his stomach. Blood spread through the fabric of his shirt onto his fingers.

"Move!" Alex yelled.

Sofie wailed when Gabriel fell. "Help him, Alex!"

Fuck.

"Don't move! I'll be right back."

"Don't leave me!" she cried, cowering against the wall.

"I'll be back."

Entering the combat zone, Alex crawled to Gabriel and turned him over. There wasn't anything to do except drag him by his ankles into the shed.

He positioned Gabriel in the rear of the bay and assessed the damage, hoping Sofie hadn't noticed the red trail smearing the ground behind them as she scrambled to Gabriel's side.

Blood seeped from the wound in a slow, steady stream Alex couldn't squelch. He pressed his hand to Gabriel's stomach and the boy winced. When Alex applied more pressure, he screamed.

"Shut up!" Alex couldn't have Gabriel directing gunfire into the bay.

Gabriel whimpered.

Sofie glared at Alex and stroked Gabriel's arm, murmuring in Spanish.

"Put your hand here Sofie, like I'm doing. See?"

Tears streaming down her cheeks, she followed Alex's example, whispering, "Please, God. Please, God. Please, God."

"Stay like this," he instructed, leaving her alone to attend her cousin.

Returning to his position along the wall, he noticed Marco had taken one of the AK-47s from the warehouse and was firing from a spot behind the Mercedes. Alex pulled another magazine out of his pocket, reloaded his gun, and aimed.

On the roof of the warehouse, a sniper from the team focused his attention between two outbuildings. Men flooded into the yard.

Ramón rushed into the clearing, blazing his own assault weapon.

Spotting Alex, he hesitated and grinned.

The bastard must think he has a comrade.

As if he'd slipped underwater, Alex's surroundings melted away. Each heavy, even breath boomed in his ears. He smiled at Ramón, meeting his eyes with the pure satisfaction that comes from the ultimate revenge. A life for a life. There was no comparison between Nick's and Ramón's. But Alex decided years ago it would have to do.

Aiming for Ramón's head, Alex's finger rested, ready on the trigger.

He waited, looking for one last thing from Ramón before he killed him.

Aware of the betrayal, Ramón's face settled into a grim twist.

Yes. This is exactly what I want.

Ramón raised his weapon.

The gas tank of one of the Blazers exploded, creating a fireball that distracted them both.

In the heartbeat it took for Alex to refocus, the sniper on top of the warehouse unloaded his weapon into Ramón. Pieces of his body showered the courtyard. What was left buckled into a distorted heap.

God dammit, motherfucker! He was mine!

There wasn't time to mourn the missed opportunity. A sizzling bullet whizzed into the shed and Alex fired back, intent on finding its source.

With several of the Mendoza brothers eliminated, the team needed to finish up and get the hell out. They'd violated Mexican territory and, at any time, the Federales might decide to make an appearance.

The staccato of shots settled into sporadic fits and bursts. Soon, all was quiet, except for the rich, guttural beat of four welcome propellers whipping air in the distance.

Alex checked the bay. Sofie had taken off her blouse and used it to staunch the flow of Gabriel's blood. Her white bra, marred with crimson, lay stark against her brown skin. She leaned over Gabriel's body, her necklace hanging as if it were a talisman. Rivulets of sweat trickled between her breasts. She was a mess. Her hair was everywhere. She was beautiful.

He unbuttoned his own filthy white shirt and tossed it to her. "Put this on."

Ignoring him, she continued to minister to her cousin.

Gabriel moaned while she rubbed slick grime from his forehead with her own dirty hand. "You're going to be okay, just hang in there."

"Herrera?"

Alex looked up.

Dean stood at the edge of the yard, taking roll.

"I'm good," Greg called from behind the warehouse.

"Wakefield? Where's Wakefield?" Dean yelled.

"I'll be right back," Alex said to Sofie.

She didn't glance up as he left to check in with his boss.

❦

For Gabriel's sake, Sofie needed to find some control, but she couldn't get her body to stop shaking. Aching all over and road-rashed by Alex's manhandling, she glanced down and discovered the ugly black fingermarks Alex had left on her arms. She was bleeding as well, but her wounds were nothing compared to Gabriel's. Raising her head, she looked outside, past the shed, frantically searching for Alex.

Her lifeline had disappeared.

Gabriel was dying.

He lay silently on the concrete. Occasionally, he gasped. Despite the blanket of hot moisture that wicked away any hint of fresh air, his body was cool. His blood soaked through the plug she'd made with her blouse. It was sticky, staining her hand. Whenever she eased the pressure, the bleeding intensified.

Gabriel's face was fading to ash. Another tide of panic sent her reeling. Searching the courtyard again, she forced herself to look past the carnage and focus the immediate crisis: Getting help for her cousin.

She scanned the yard and discovered a sea of unfamiliar faces.

"Alex!" she wailed. *Where did he go?*

Gabriel groaned. She turned back to him. Time seemed to stand still.

"Sofie, this is Dean."

Her introduction was a pair of dusty combat boots, etched with fresh abrasions. Raising her head, she discovered a man dressed in black.

She met Alex's eyes and he nodded. So, she stood to give Dean more room.

Dean wiped his lips beneath his thick white mustache, assessing the situation. He adjusted the bulletproof vest strapped over his shirt and knelt down.

Looking up, he gave her a sympathetic nod. She became aware she was only wearing a blood-smeared bra and her splattered, tattered shorts. Dean didn't seem to notice, but she slipped her arms into Alex's shirt anyway, fastening it over her stained lingerie.

Dean checked Gabriel's pulse.

Gabriel's eyelids stopped fluttering.

A sob escaped, as she struggled to stifle her growing hysteria. "Please help him."

"He's lost a lot of blood. We'll get him medical attention."

With guilty relief, she passed the responsibility on to someone more capable.

Sofie heard Alex cough behind her, and she turned, taking in the rest of her surroundings. Nearly every vehicle in the area was destroyed. Tires ruptured. Windows shot out. Glass everywhere. Ramón's once pristine fleet, punctured by a storm of bullets and transformed into a gangster's junkyard.

She stepped towards the front of the shed. Alex stopped her.

"Where are my cousins?"

Wrenching away from him, she walked into the bloodbath. "Where is Ramón?"

Surreal, oddly distorted mannequins littered the ground, depicting the grisliest movie scene. Sofie knew better. These were her people lying in thick pools of vinous blood. Only a few were recognizable. A rush of nausea made her stomach lurch, its contents rising to her throat. She looked into the sky, swallowed and struggled not to vomit, tasting metallic bits of dirt between her teeth.

The walls of the surrounding buildings, pockmarked by gunfire and splattered pink, were peppered with what appeared to be chunks of bone and tissue, creating a macabre, Goyaic landscape of death. She gulped in thick air that smelled of hot, rusty pennies.

Body parts were strewn across the courtyard, remnants of the bloody storm. Missing its owner, a leg, wearing a sock and tennis shoe, rested near the open trunk of the Mercedes. Attached was a grotesque piece of thigh— brilliant white bone jutting out from the knee.

Sofie couldn't keep the revulsion down any longer. She dropped to her knees and bent over, vomiting bile into the bloody earth. When her stomach was empty, she wiped her mouth with the back of her filthy hand, her eyes wildly searching for Ramón.

Alex caught up to her and helped her stand. "Let's go. You don't want to see this."

Pushing him aside, she screamed, "I want Ramón. Where is he?"

She found Ramón splayed in the yard. His unmistakable gold Rolex strapped on his wrist. His mouth was slack. A trickle of blood slipped from the corner of his lip into the dirt. Lifeless brown eyes stared heavy-lidded into the abyss. A huge pool of viscous, umber-red blood had collected underneath his oddly-shaped head. The back of it was missing.

No more. No more. I can't take in anything more. She covered her face and howled.

Panicked, she turned to run and crashed into the wall of Alex's bare chest.

Sofie literally couldn't think. It wasn't denial. But it was. She stubbornly *refused* to assimilate the obvious.

Furious, and compelled to lash out, she recoiled, pummeling Alex, again, again, again, and again.

He didn't fight back.

When she raised her arm to slap him, he clasped her fingers, intertwining them in his own. Sofie looked up and saw the torment in his eyes.

Exhausted, she relented and buried herself in the only comfort she could find.

Sobs gushed up from despair. A deep well holding each tightly bandaged anguish. Open and exposed. *Mom. Ceci. Now this.*

Wrapping her into his arms, Alex held her tight. "I'm so sorry... I didn't mean for it..."

Eventually, she stopped crying. The violent tremors had subsided, leaving her numb. It was if she'd formed a new layer of skin, a protective shield blocking any more pain.

Several men, all dressed in black, brought Gabriel from the shed and moved toward an old flatbed truck from the ranch.

Alex rubbed her shoulder protectively.

"Where are they taking him?"

"A plane. We have medics on board."

He met her eyes, pleading, "Let me take care of you."

They were so blue. She'd been so wrong about him. About everything. Shaking her head, she disentangled herself and stumbled toward Gabriel.

He lay on a stretcher, alongside two other wounded men. She tried to go to him, but the men in black kept her at a distance. So she waited alone on the grass and watched while they loaded Gabriel into the truck.

Others were emptying the warehouse, stacking cloth bundles in the yard.

When she realized Alex was behind her, she flinched.

"Sofie," His voice was raw. He touched her shoulder. She turned and walked away.

Dean was in the shade, giving orders. "Burn everything."

Sofie interrupted. "I want to go with Gabriel."

"I can arrange that."

"I saw Ramón..." She was afraid to ask, but needed to know, "What about the rest of my cousins? Who else is hurt?"

Dean opened his mouth to speak, but didn't.

Her eyes filled with fresh tears. She motioned to the scattered bodies in the yard, incredulous. "Are all of them here?"

Dean nodded.

Howling with renewed anguish, she hugged her sides, rocking back and forth.

"Come with me." Dean took her hand and helped her climb onto the flatbed with Gabriel.

The truck delivered them to the runway Ramón had been so anxious to show her on Sunday. *Could that have been just a few days ago?*

A large, gray plane was waiting there, with a ladder positioned against an open cargo door. Someone from inside dropped a litter. Dean helped load Gabriel and the other wounded men up into the plane.

Sofie climbed inside.

Dean followed and called to one of the men near the cockpit. "Jim, tell the Mexico City office we're moving out."

Clearly, Dean was in charge. Alex worked for him.

"Who are you? FBI? CIA? DEA?" she asked.

"Yeah."

She saw smoke rising near the river through the open cargo door. "What are they burning?"

"The cocaine."

Gabriel had been right about everything. And everyone.

Except Alex. He didn't work with Ramón; he worked for the United States government.

"Where are we going."

"El Paso, Texas."

One by one the propellers roared to life. A deep, low-level hum settled just below Sofie's skin, resonating throughout her body. She was only truly cognizant of her organs, blood and bones, buzzing in a protective pulse. Each sensory input was distant, once removed.

She sat cross-legged on the floor of the airplane, worry-stoning her silver heart as she prayed. Several feet away, the medics worked on Gabriel.

Alex climbed aboard and knelt next to Sofie, handing her the seagrass purse. His eyes, encircled in red, glistened. She could read them. They were tormented, full of apology, silently searching for permission to stay at her side.

Sofie pushed him away with both hands. "*No! No!* Leave me alone!" She squeezed her eyes closed, shutting him out.

"Alex, go up front with Travis and Jim. I'll take care of her," Dean said. When she opened her eyes, Alex was gone.

CHAPTER TWENTY-TWO
Lost Bridges

Puentes Perdido
Saturday, December 8, 1984

Agreeing to Tía Sofia's Saturday lunch date wasn't a decision, it was a Pavlovian response to her forceful invitation. Still, Sofie missed her aunt and was disappointed when she didn't find her waiting in the patio entrance of Los Arcos, where Frank Sinatra's mellow cadence oozed from the speakers and drowned out the traffic along Ventura Boulevard with his "Christmas Waltz."

Millions of families had strung ribbons of colorful lights along their rooflines. The shopping malls were decorated and, once again, Anheuser Busch placed a tree of Christmas bulbs on top of its brewery along the 405. But there wasn't a sign of the season in LA's natural landscape.

It hadn't rained in months, so the grassy hillsides were baked to straw. The Santa Ana winds hadn't arrived either, leaving the sky washed out and bruised by a layer of smog that choked downtown and hugged the mountains to the east. For weeks the temperature had hovered in the high seventies. Not a chance of snow. Sofie figured you'd have to drive at least a hundred miles to find a frosted window pane.

Whatever the weather, Christmas was usually her favorite holiday. This year, she couldn't find—or even will into existence—a festive spirit.

Sofie opened one of the carved wooden doors leading into the restaurant and another stanza greeted her; wishing her a Merry Christmas and hoping her New Year's dreams would come true. *Bah Humbug.*

Stifling a smirk, she let her eyes adjust to the dim lighting and decided she never liked Sinatra anyway. *Who cares if it's only eleven-thirty? I need a margarita.*

Sofie had avoided her aunt, like she tried to avoid any reminder of her family and the trip to Mexico last summer.

There'd been no relief at first. After a fitful night, she survived each day in a continuous wheel of emotions. Moments of grief. Anger. Rage. Sadness and pain. Fear of an unknown future. Unredeemable loss and regret. It was hopeless. Her world would never be the same.

Much of her time had been spent confused. The memory of Alex became an indecipherable splinter—one she'd obsessively pick at, but was never able to dislodge.

Her nightmares came back. Intensified. A new one too. Hideous, terrible scenes, crowded with grotesque memories, looped by the same frantic thought she'd had in the shed: *Where was Alex? And when, dear God, when would help arrive?*

Seized by panic, she'd wake up in the dark, her heart pounding against her chest. Not quite sure if her screams punctured the realm of dreams into reality.

By the time fall settled in, she'd mastered distraction, because to focus on what had happened was just too overwhelming. Occasionally, a backfire or odious scent would remind her, and her world would suddenly collapse. She'd then have to internalize that horrible afternoon once again. Stuffing it down was the only way she could slip back into the vague disbelief that allowed her to survive each day.

Eventually, she quit dreaming altogether and sleep became a pool of solace. She'd surface from the depths each morning, force herself to turn over, and switch off the alarm clock. In the bathroom, she'd stare into the mirror and search for any remnant of the carefree, admittedly immature, girl she'd once been. In a span of twenty-four hours last July, Sofie had become older. Wiser. Jaded.

She couldn't remember the last time she had truly smiled.

The lobby of Los Arcos was deserted. A surprise for such a popular place, where later in the day people usually waited almost an hour for a table while sipping margaritas. Garland, adorned with silver bows, had been strung throughout the room. Against the wall, a manger scene sat on a small table, it's red tablecloth sprinkled with a generous dose of fake snow.

Did it ever snow in Bethlehem?

A ceramic angel stood watchful over the scene, where Joseph, Mary, and the well-positioned secondary actors played their parts. The wooden crib lay empty; Jesus had yet to arrive.

Tía Sofia hadn't either.

Sofie marveled at Tía's persistence, knowing she could conjure almost anything—even pulling Sofie out of her cubicle. Persistence was a shared Mendoza trait, one Tía wielded with benevolence.

Unlike Ramón.

A gruesome image of his flat, vacant stare with the back of his head missing flashed into Sofie's consciousness. She winced. *That's not real. It happened to somebody else, not me.* It was an odd experience to have such visceral thoughts, because Sofie knew the truth. *Yes, it had happened. I was there.*

For her own sanity, she willed the vision away.

She'd been burrowed at her desk on Thursday, finishing up the details of one more audit, when Tía's call came in.

After some ineffective coaxing, Tía finally complained, "Mija. It's been so long. You won't take the time to visit with me?"

Trapped by the truth of her words, a blush of shame had spread across Sofie's cheeks. She owed her aunt more.

As the hostess approached, Sofie peeked around the corner, finding most of the tables in the main dining room were unoccupied. Anxiety pinched her already nervous stomach, and she wondered if maybe Tía had reconsidered her invitation, still blaming Sofie for Gabriel's disappearance and deciding at the last minute to abandon her too.

Just then, the heavy door opened and Tía Sofia entered the lobby with a generous smile. Sofie rushed into Tía's fully blossomed figure and was surrounded within her warm hug.

"I've missed you, mija." Stepping back, Tía held her by the shoulders and took Sofie in. "You've lost weight. You're working too hard."

"They keep us busy," Sofie mumbled, overwhelmed by Tía's warm welcome and afraid she'd cry if she gave her the real explanation. She'd left her appetite, and so much more, down in Mexico five months ago.

The hostess, who'd stood to the side, held up menus and escorted them to a booth. A busboy brought them salsa and a basket of tortilla chips.

Sofie unfolded her napkin and glanced around the dining room, remembering all the times they'd come to Los Arcos as a family. When Sofie, along with Ceci and Rich—who was always the instigator—used to toss chips to each other across the table. Tía would tsk-tsk and shake her head, swearing she'd never bring them into the restaurant again. Tío would roll his eyes and grin, knowing she would never follow through on the threat.

"It hasn't changed much in all these years," Sofie said.

"Remember when Ceci wouldn't eat fish?" Tía arched her eyebrows and smiled. "And the time we convinced her it wasn't crab, but chicken in the enchiladas?"

"She tried them and liked them. She got so mad when you told her the truth."

"It worked." Tía's eyes sparkled. "She never ordered anything else."

Nostalgia bloomed in her calm, melodic voice and they both laughed.

They'd bonded over their losses through the years. And Sofie felt relieved to discover their adapted mother-daughter relationship was slipping back into sync. She dipped a chip into the salsa. "I've always liked this place."

"It's my favorite too." Tía put down her menu and shrugged. "I don't know why I even bother to look at the menu. I always get the same thing."

The waiter arrived and they ordered their usual: Margaritas and crab enchiladas.

He left and Tía asked, "How does our Mexican cuisine compare to the food south of the border these days?"

"Mexico's dishes are still very traditional, made with local ingredients hard to find in California. I've learned to appreciate both."

"I've been here so long I like our Mexican food better. I guess I've been *Americanized*." Tía grinned and reached for another chip. "So, you like your job? The name of the company is Arthur Allen. Right?"

"It's Anderson. Arthur Anderson. We're one of the biggest accounting firms in the country. One of the Big Five. And yes, I like the job. It keeps me busy." Sofie had learned to compartmentalize her grief. To push it into a box and store it in the deep well of her emotions. Ordinary, everyday life things still had to be done.

"Don't you have to take a test?"

"I'm planning on taking it in June." Sofie didn't give details because that's all it was, a plan. Since the summer, she'd procrastinated her way around any of the preparations, promising herself she'd work on it in January.

After the waiter delivered their drinks, Tía took a sip and announced, "These are *by far* the best margaritas in town."

"I agree." Sofie raised her glass.

"It's early, but let's make a New Year's toast. Here's to a better year in 1985."

With a gentle tap, the wide rims of their glasses chimed.

It was an effort to smile. Sofie couldn't imagine what good the new year could bring.

Tía frowned. "I feel I owe you an apology."

"No, I owe you one. I have been busy. But you're right, I've also avoided you." Tears began to build behind her eyes. "It's really hard."

"I know, mija. When I found out Gabriel left and I called, asking what happened, you misunderstood me. I wasn't blaming you."

"It *was* my fault. I was on his back all the time. He got sick of my nagging, about the Narcotics Anonymous meetings, about school, about everything... I drove him away."

"You were trying to help," she said in her soothing, maternal voice. "We all were."

Tía and her husband, Sofie's Tío Ricardo, paid for the airfare to California, once Gabriel had been discharged from the hospital in Texas. Tía found a rehab for him in North Hollywood, did the paperwork and took care of his expenses. Tía and Tío insisted Sofie move into their home, and she agreed on one condition: *No questions.* She couldn't bear to talk about what she'd been through.

Sofie did start the job Alex had encouraged her to take, an entry-level position in Arthur Anderson's Los Angeles office. She finally understood why he'd been so persistent. But the decision had nothing to do with him. She had lived with her aunt and uncle for six weeks, until she'd been able to save enough money to move into an apartment of her own.

"When Gabriel got out of rehab, I shouldn't have let him stay with me." Sofie said. "It would have been better if he'd moved in with you. You could have found a way to make him keep his promises." She wrapped her napkin around her fingers, anxiously twisting the fabric. "He said he registered for classes. I don't think he ever did. He wouldn't apply for a job either. He spent most of his time on the couch, in front of the TV. Now, I'm not so sure if he even stayed clean."

"You did the best you could. He didn't want to live with us."

"Then he disappeared!" Sofie put her hands against her temples. "No goodbye. No note. I just found my couch empty one morning. When you called a few days later..." She sighed. "I couldn't face the questions. How could I answer them? All I know is I failed our family... Again."

"You can't reach into someone's life and change it."

Lowering her head, Sofie burst into tears.

"You didn't fail anybody, mija."

Sofie felt Tía's warm fingers clasp her hands. Sofie cried, craving the bittersweet release.

As if the truth suddenly came to her, Tía asked, "So. Is this guilt you're feeling why you didn't come to Thanksgiving?"

Ashamed, Sofie wiped her eyes with her napkin and gave Tía a weak smile. Unable to face her family, she had called Thanksgiving morning and begged off sick. Sofie lied. Instead, she had shared the holiday with a group of coworkers. They were cooking a gourmet meal—a joint effort and a much needed distraction. Personally, it had been a disaster. She'd drunk several glasses of Chardonnay by dinner, and had to force herself to swallow each mouthful of the meal. Nothing seemed familiar. There was so little to be thankful for. She ended up depressed, feeling even more guilty for lying to her family.

Tía didn't scold her. "*Promise me* you won't miss Christmas. Come early on Christmas Eve, I need help making the tamales. This will be Amelia's first time." Tía sipped her margarita. "Plan to spend the night, we'll go to Midnight Mass and open presents afterwards, like the old days. Rich and Amelia said they're coming too. Now they're married, they can stay together in his old room. You can sleep on the couch in the den. *No excuses*."

"I'll be there," Sofie promised, hoping to find a little comfort in Ceci's former bedroom, now Tía and Tío's new den. Sofie remembered spending many nights with her cousin in that room, trading teenage secrets by spelling them out on each other's backs in the dark.

The restaurant was beginning to fill with the holiday lunch crowd. A young couple being escorted to a booth edged past the waiter as he delivered the crab enchiladas.

Tía smiled, savoring her first bite. "Delicious. They use real, fresh crab, not that fake stuff."

Sofie nodded. The food was excellent, just as she'd remembered.

There was something Sofie had wanted to ask since Tía's phone call. "Have you heard from Gabriel?"

"No. But I've talked to Monica. He's back in Acapulco. She says he's doing okay. They're both doing okay."

Unaware she'd been holding her breath, Sofie exhaled. "At least he's alive. I tried to call Monica. When she heard my voice, she hung up. Hoping it was just a bad connection, I tried again. But she wouldn't answer. Monica hates me too."

"I don't know if I'd call it hate, mija. Our family down there..." Tía shook her head. "They don't understand. I'm not sure they ever will." She lifted her fork to take another bite, hesitated, and set it down. "People are different. They come in all sizes and persuasions, you know this. They also have different limitations. Some, like Gabriel, only feel comfortable with what they know. They can't adjust to change. Living in California was a huge transition. A bridge Gabriel couldn't cross. Change is a challenge for anybody. It's especially difficult for people struggling with addiction."

"But we were here to help him."

"It was his decision to go back," Tía explained. "I crossed that same bridge years ago, when I met your tío and decided to make a life here. It's like when we talked about the food earlier. I've been *Americanized*." She chuckled.

"You were raised crossing the bridge, traveling back and forth between both cultures. No culture is perfect. But the beauty of Mexico and its quaint traditions hide some very ugly truths. It's not going to change until the people demand it. Until then, well...

"Sometimes, I wonder if the corruption and lawlessness is part of our Mexican heritage, stemming from the pillaging done by our ancestors, the Spanish Conquistadors Ramón was so proud of. Whatever the reason, it's time for you to leave that world behind and move forward."

"How can I leave my mom's grave and these chapters of my life behind?"

"You'll always have your mom. Right here." Tía pressed her palm to her heart. "That's where Olivia and Ceci live in me." She picked up her fork. "There isn't much left for us in Mexico. Don't worry. Like me, you'll always want the flavor, but you won't miss all of the ingredients. How's that for an analogy?" She grinned and took a bite of enchilada.

"I don't know how to move forward."

"Sure you do. You've already started. You let me talk you into lunch today. But you won't get any further if you keep everything inside. It's time to let it out. I already know the big picture. But what happened to *you* in Mexico last summer?"

Sofie felt her face freeze. "I don't want to talk about it."

"This isn't the first time you've said this. Okay then. So, what about your Dad? Can you talk to him?"

"He wouldn't understand."

If you won't talk to us, talk to somebody you trust, someone who can help you sort it through. You need to."

Tía was right. Sofie's visible wounds had healed, so had Gabriel's. However, the emotional scars festered, clamming her up. Guilt and blame: They were twin demons neither of them could shake. No wonder Gabriel had left.

Unrepairable guilt lived in her apartment. The angry little monster breathed through the rooms, filling the air with heavy, weighted words, unwilling to be spoken. Discussions Sofie and Gabriel should have had, but avoided in a conspiracy of shame. As weeks went by, Gabriel's silent accusations grew; easy to read in his eyes, loud in his irritability and his snippy, snide remarks. Yes, Ramón brought Alex into their lives, but Sofie bedded the enemy and let him into her heart.

Minutes passed and Tía waited for Sofie to speak. But Sofie didn't know where to begin.

"So. Your job keeps you busy. Do you like it? Or do you like keeping busy?"

Leave it to Tía to try to pry open the door with an insightful question.

"Keeping busy. It's easier," Sofie confessed.

"You're running from one afternoon in Mexico. You're exhausted. I can see it. It's going to be painful, but you need to stop and *be there* for awhile. You have to face what's happened before you can move past this."

Taking a long drink of her margarita, Sofie looked into Tía's kind, trusting face and felt the power of her aunt's unconditional love.

"Did *you* know Ramón wanted me to work for him?"

"No," Tía knitted her brows together, perplexed.

Sofie blinked, trying to bring the memories into focus. Once she started, the floodgates opened and the whole convoluted story spilled out. She began with the night she'd met Alex in Acapulco and ended with fragments from the day she found Ramón and Alex in the warehouse. Sparing nothing except the intimate moments she and Alex had shared.

Tía asked only a few questions and listened compassionately, trying to understand all of the twists and turns of the ordeal.

"I'll pray for my nephews and their souls. But it's hard, after losing Ceci the way we did, to feel or do anything more," Tía said. "Quien mal anda, mal acaba. If they chose to live like that, what could they expect? I'm so glad my brother and my parents aren't alive to see how the boys squandered their legacy."

"I feel so stupid. I searched for signs from my mom without paying attention to all the stuff that didn't fit."

Spent, the marathon of emotion left Sofie with a vague headache. At the same time, she had to admit sharing the story helped.

Tía seemed especially interested in the last day at the hotel, when Sofie heard Alex mention Ceci's name on the phone.

Had he been talking to Dean?

Probably, but she couldn't be sure. Nothing made sense to Tía either.

"So. What happened to Alex?"

"I don't know."

Sofie sensed him everywhere. They'd spent less than a week together, and logic told her it was impossible to remember it all, but it seemed as if each intimate detail had been etched onto the glassy shards of her broken heart.

Trying to understand what happened wasn't only a splinter, it was a ball of emotions and facts she hadn't been able to unravel. The moments they'd spent together were pieces of strings: Some contained bits of truth tied to the ends, and others were short, leading to his lies. She spent hours trying to figure it out, compelled by the need for understanding. But this unraveling always devolved into a complicated rage—full of hurt, love, regret and, shamefully, even desire.

Sofie studied the tablecloth and wiped away bits of tortilla chips. Where was all of the empowerment she'd felt before she met Alex, and—yes, she couldn't deny it—fallen in love with him? What happened to the confidence that she could handle anything life sent her way?

All of it was back at the ranch, in the dirt.

"Where is Alex? What's he doing now?"

If Tía had questions or wondered about him, Sofie told herself Tía could find out on her own. "I don't want to know," she said too sharply.

"You should. I'd want to hear his side of the story."

Sofie looked up. "How can you say that? If it wasn't for him, none of this would have happened."

"If it wasn't for Ramón, none of this would have happened, mija. The boys brought this upon themselves by dealing in drugs. Wrong is wrong—even if it's family. Never forget where the true blame lies."

"But they're our family. Shouldn't—"

"Bah!" Tía spit out the word. "Family is supposed to watch out for one another, not use each other."

"That doesn't make what Alex did right."

"It sounds to me like he was doing his job."

"He used me. He betrayed me!"

"Are you sure? Did he have a choice?"

Sofie pretended to study the colorful clay figurines scattered in niches along the wall. Tía couldn't possibly understand.

The lunch crowd was gone, and the waiter became a waitress with the change of a shift. Tía called her over and ordered two iced teas.

"So. How are *you* moving forward?" Tía asked.

Sofie whined, "I'm stuck."

"Do you see your old friends?"

Old friends knew enough to want details. "Not really. I'm busy."

"Have you dated at all?"

Sofie crossed her arms in defense and stared at her aunt. She wasn't ready for close friends or a relationship. She seriously wondered if she'd ever date again.

"How about friends at work?"

"I've made a few."

"Sofie, I'm disappointed. You've always had a lot of friends."

"It's different now. I'm different. There's no point in getting close to people. They all leave. I have this feeling… It's the same feeling I had years ago, when that guy ran me off the freeway… Like something bad—"

"Something horrible has *already* happened!" Tía reached out and covered Sofie's hand, lowering her voice, "I depend on you. *You have to move forward.*" She sighed, her eyes glistening. "We all do. It's not a choice, mija. First, there was your mother, and then, after Ceci… I thought I couldn't survive either…

"Al vivo la hogaza y al muerto, la mortaja. We must live by the living, not by the dead. So, I get out of bed each morning and put one foot in front of the other, and we both know sometimes that isn't as easy as it sounds. I do this because I have you and Rich to watch out for, and now, Amelia. Your tío depends on me. You saw how depressed he got when we lost Ceci. *Somebody* needed to take care of things."

Tía's far-away gaze followed the garland draped around the room and met Sofie's eyes.

Sofie wasn't ready.

"I'm your godmother, and I need you. God has chosen us to stay here and carry on, whether we like it or not. And if we don't help each other—depend on each other, not only during the good times, but also when tragedy comes around—what do we have?"

CHAPTER TWENTY-THREE

Dawn

Alba

Christmas Eve
Monday, December 24, 1984

Spilling the whole story to Tía Sofia over enchiladas and margaritas had been an unexpected relief. Thankfully, Sofie felt some of the burden of last summer lift and dissipate. Over the past few weeks, she'd discovered she felt better than she had in months—almost hopeful—knowing her aunt didn't blame her for what had happened down in Mexico.

Occasional pinpricks of residual guilt still cropped up along with random memories. Sofie tried to stamp out these feelings with Tía's words and it generally worked. Sometimes, she second-guessed herself, especially in regards to Alex. That's when her tangled emotions would wildly vacillate between hate and regret; she didn't let herself even consider the word *love*.

After the call she'd received from a reporter on Friday, her remaining Mexican relatives consumed her thoughts again. And Sofie tossed in bed for hours last night. Because the truth was, her Mexican family had given her friendship and support over the years. Was it really fair to speak out and compromise the loyalty of her mom's family, smearing the Mendoza name?

Finally, she'd turned on the light, propped herself up with pillows, and listed the pros and cons. By dawn, she felt she'd made a decision.

In the bathroom a half-hour later, she blew-dry her newly cropped, chin-length hair, and realized the opinion she valued most was Tía's. If she vetoed the idea, Sofie was prepared to respect the family name and tell the reporter no.

The balmy weather had ushered in cool temperatures. Clouds gathered above the Valley with the sincere promise of rain. Sofie pulled into the driveway, past the camellias Tío planted along the garage years ago, and parked her Honda next to his pickup truck. Her early arrival would be a surprise, considering her well-known habit of sleeping in whenever possible.

She checked her watch—ten minutes to eight. Delighted with the chill in the air, she hoped some Christmas spirit would materialize as the day wore on. Sofie pulled the presents from the back seat and used her hip to shut the door. Climbing the porch steps, she adjusted her gifts and rang the doorbell.

Tío answered in a flannel bathrobe, wearing an astonished smile. "Feliz Navidad! Are all those presents for me?" he teased in Spanish.

"Merry Christmas."

He took a step back. "What happened to your hair?"

"I had it cut on Saturday." Sofie carefully twirled on the porch. "What do you think?"

"Hmmm. You are as pretty as ever, but this will take some getting used to." Grinning, he patted her shoulder as she moved inside.

"I've come early to help." Sofie inhaled the foresty scent of the Christmas tree, the aroma of coffee, and chicken simmering on the stove—a rich concoction underscored by the perennially fresh fragrance of an immaculate house. It felt great to return to a place she'd often considered *home*. A warm glow spread throughout her body, and a bit of that Christmas spirit began to kick in.

Colorful bulbs blinked and bubbled throughout the tree. She added her gifts to the pile of presents stacked beneath the branches, while Tío returned to his recliner and buried himself behind the *Los Angeles Times*.

Sofie couldn't help asking her uncle, "Have you read any articles written by a reporter named Jillian Bond?"

Tío lifted his gaze over the newspaper. "No. But I don't usually pay attention to their names."

"Is that you, mija?" Tía called from the kitchen.

Tía stood next to the stove, working over a bowl of tomatillos. She peeled their gauzy hulls and added the small green fruits to a pan of Jalapeños beginning to boil.

"You're here bright and early." Tía wiped her hands and gave Sofie a quick hug. Then, she did a double take. "Your hair—I love it!"

Sofie ran her finger through the short curls, still startled to discover the phantom sensation of the missing tresses. "I decided I needed a change. It's a Christmas present to myself."

"Good idea. You're gorgeous as always." Tía's eyes shined, and she hesitated as if she wanted to say something else.

"What?"

"Seeing you with short hair is like watching my sister come back to life. You'll have to forgive me if I accidentally call you Olivia." Tía flushed scarlet. She covered her mouth with her fingers and turned back to the stove.

Sofie put her arm around her aunt's soft shoulder.

The edges of Tía's mouth lifted slightly, however, she focused on stirring the Jalapeños, her voice trembling, "No. It's a wonderful thing. A gift. In you, I still have the essence of her."

"That's exactly how I feel about you." Sofie kissed her aunt on the temple.

Beaming, Tía seemed to shake the bittersweet memories away. "I'm glad you're here. Get a cup of coffee. There's cream in the refrigerator. The husks are on the table. You can start soaking them for me."

Sofie pulled an apron from the drawer, tying it over her pink sweater and Jordache jeans. Turning on the faucet, she plugged the sink and began to fill it with hot water. "I wanted to get here before Rich and Amelia."

Looking up, Tía raised her eyebrows. "Is there a problem?"

"No. I just wanted a chance to talk to you. Alone."

"What?"

"Nothing really." Sofie poured herself a cup of coffee and opened the refrigerator. "Well, something. I got a call on Friday from a reporter at the *Los Angeles Times*. She's writing a story about the illegal drug trade in Mexico and wants to interview me about what happened last summer."

Tía finished peeling the remaining tomatillos and lowered both burners. She refilled her coffee mug. "Let's sit down for a minute."

Sofie turned off the faucet. Pulling one of the green swivel chairs from underneath the kitchen table, she sat down and began cleaning a stack of cornhusks.

The lines on Tía's forehead deepened. "So, who's this reporter?"

"Her name is Jillian Bond."

"How did she find you?"

"She won't say how. Just that her sources mentioned my name."

Tía nodded.

"I was blindsided by her request. My first response was *no*. Then she asked about Gabriel… Dean could have left Gabriel to bleed to death on the ranch."

Sofie believed she owed Dean something. Maybe she could repay him by telling her story. Last night, she'd written him first on the pro side of her list —DEAN SAVED GABRIEL'S LIFE. If she dared to be truthful, she also had to admit Alex had actually been the first to save Gabriel. He'd gone into the yard and pulled Gabriel into the bay.

"So. Are you going to talk to her?" Tía asked.

"I said I'd get back to her after Christmas. I want your opinion. It's important to me."

"I've wanted to talk to you too. I've been thinking about what happened down there. Particularly when Alex mentioned Ceci, Jaime, and Ramón in that phone call you overheard. A couple of unusual things that happened several years ago are finally making some sense."

"What do you mean?"

New traces of grief marked Tía's face and she sighed. "Well, for one thing, Ceci was always such a good girl, and you know we never had any major problems with her before she met Jaime. You were still living up north with your dad when she first met him, but you two talked on the phone all the time. Wouldn't you agree that once she began seeing Jaime, she started making poor decisions?"

Sofie had been too busy with her own life to pay attention at the time. She didn't begin to notice Ceci's bad choices until much later.

"Ceci loved him," Sofie said in defense of her cousin. But Jaime cheated and Ceci knew it. She'd invariably forgive him and let him back into her bed, until the afternoon she came home early and found him having sex with the woman who lived next door. That's when Ceci finally kicked him out, telling Sofie it was a vision she just couldn't get out of her head.

Nevertheless, even after they split up, Ceci still talked about Jaime. Sofie doubted Tía knew any of this. "She was obsessed with him," Sofie said.

"Love is very powerful. We can't help who we fall in love with. Don't forget that, mija." She sent Sofie a meaningful glance.

Alex. Sofie understood the undeniable power of love, all too well.

"It's been a hard lesson for me to learn. If Ceci and I hadn't fought so much over Jaime, things would have been different between us those last few years. It's time with my daughter I'll never get back." Tía took a sip of her coffee. "Do you remember when we pulled our support away from the marriage?"

"Yes. Ceci was really upset."

"It was only after many tears—and all of them weren't Ceci's—that we reluctantly agreed to pay for the wedding. She said we didn't like him because he wasn't born here in the United States. That wasn't the reason, and we told her so. Your tío and I didn't trust him. I could never pinpoint anything specific, it was just a feeling. I've recently thought more about it, and I've realized we could never connect with him. He always seemed distracted."

Tía got up and grabbed a dishrag from the counter, wiping dried, black silks and bits of corn husk from the table into her palm. "We never suspected drugs. But now…"

Sofie hadn't thought about it like that before, but Tía's description of Jaime was familiar. "That's how it felt to be around Gabriel. Like he was never really *there*."

"That's interesting and it strengthens my point." Tía opened the cabinet underneath the sink and emptied the shreds into the trash. "I mentioned my concerns to Ceci at the time. She tried to tell me it was because we didn't know Jaime like she did and we needed to give him a chance. In retrospect, she obviously didn't know him very well either, because once they broke up, he disappeared. She couldn't even find him to serve the divorce papers."

Tía returned to the table. "Do *you* think Jaime does drugs?"

Of course Jaime did drugs. How could Sofie explain this to Tía? They were from different generations. She'd never understand.

Jaime, like many of Sofie's peers, "did drugs." Not excessively. They partied. When cocaine came onto the LA scene several years ago, most of her friends had considered it a harmless, upper-class high. They discovered coke's tenacious grip later.

Then again, maybe Tía was right. For years, Sofie had harbored her own suspicions about Jaime, though she'd never found anything to hang them on.

Ceci's love affair with coke didn't explode until Jaime was out, and Eric —with plenty of disposable income and wealthy friends—came into her life. And, as far as Sofie knew, none of Ceci's friends were crazy enough to try heroin. She still couldn't comprehend how Ceci could be found in a hotel room with a needle.

"I've never liked Jaime, but I didn't notice anything unusual," Sofie said. "Ceci and I were close... Then again, I wasn't around him that much."

"I think Jaime introduced Ceci to drugs." Tía persisted.

Sofie couldn't explain, so she studied the table instead of meeting her aunt's eyes. With Ceci forever gone, the knowledge that she discovered pot in high school could only hurt and might lead Tía to believe she'd been a naive or neglectful mother. Sofie ran her finger along the fake wood-grain of the Formica and waited for her aunt to speak. When she glanced up, she found Tía staring, apparently wanting Sofie to supply the answers.

There was a connection between Ramón, Ceci and Jaime. But Alex had refused to explain.

"At Ceci's and Jaime's wedding, did you notice how friendly Ramón and Jaime were? They acted as if *they* were the cousins."

Sofie shrugged. "I never heard Jaime mention Ramón, ever."

"Remember how charming Ramón could be? People gravitate towards power. They can sense it." Tía went to the stove and adjusted the burner below the chicken. Stirring it, she turned to Sofie. "I'm beginning to wonder if things went on that we weren't aware of. Maybe Jaime was the one who introduced Ceci to drugs—starting with pot, moving to cocaine, and finally to heroin."

"*Tía...*" Sofie choose her words carefully. "This is hard to explain... A lot of people in my generation have experimented with drugs."

Tía Sofía leaned against the cabinets, crossing her arms underneath her ample chest. "You?"

"Thankfully, I didn't have the time or the money to get caught up in all of that."

It was difficult to meet Tía's probing stare. Sofie didn't want to explain anything more. She wondered how she could have been so absolutely confident about her world, and at the same time so completely unaware. *Wasn't that the definition of adolescence?* There were many things Sofie wished she could do over.

Alex? Her feelings were so conflicted she couldn't answer her own question.

"I'm so sorry," Sofie said. "I didn't realize how bad it was. I've always thought of Ceci as an older, wiser sister. I thought she could keep everything under control."

"You should have told me. Ramón thought *he* had it under control. We're each the captain of our own ship, not the master of the seas. They were both navigating treacherous waters. Listen to me, mija. Life will bring the hurricanes; don't go searching for rough weather."

"I'm trying not to." Sofie pulled Ceci's necklace from beneath her sweater and ran the silver heart along its chain. "What happened with Ceci is still so confusing. Nothing makes sense. By the time I knew…it was too late."

"I'm glad you're still wearing her necklace."

The long chain came to rest on top of Sofie's pink angora sweater, the filigreed heart settled against her cleavage. "I never take it off."

Well, there were those *Alex* exceptions.

Tía's grateful smile was sad. "So, here's the strange thing. Back in '81, after Jaime and Ceci split up and she moved back home, Ramón called one afternoon asking for her."

"Why would he do that? They hardly knew each other."

"Exactly. I asked Ramón why he wanted to talk to her. He said it was business. And he called after she started the job downtown, at the big law firm where she met Eric. I assumed Ramón wanted legal advice from one of the lawyers, so I gave him her work number. The call surprised me because I had no idea how he'd found out she worked there. Then, I thought someone in the family could have mentioned it to him.

"Anyway, I came home from the market a few days later, and he called again. Ceci was in her room, so she took the call in there. I was in the kitchen and didn't think much of it until I heard her voice. They were arguing. From the hallway, I heard her say several times, 'I don't know.' And afterwards, she was crying. I knocked on her door. She didn't want to talk about it. I never got a straight story from her. Not long after his call, she started dating Eric and moved in with him. Then, we discovered she had her own problems…"

Sofie shredded a discarded piece of dried husk into thin strips. She'd never heard this story from Ceci, and she couldn't remember a time they'd ever mentioned Ramón in any meaningful way. "You think Ramón was looking for Jaime?"

"I believe so. I still connected Ramón with the law firm at first. Then, when I kept getting the runaround from Ceci, I thought maybe Jaime had talked her into asking Ramón for a loan. Did she ever say anything to you about Ramón and Jaime having some kind of deal?"

"No. Jaime wasn't even Mexican. You remember how clannish Ramón could be. Jaime was from *Colombia*." Sofie stumbled on the word, wondering if Tía realized cocaine was grown and manufactured there.

Muffled voices came from the TV in the living room. The kitchen was silent except for two pots simmering on the stove. Was it possible Jaime had worked with Ramón trafficking Colombian cocaine? If so, Ceci couldn't have been involved. Sofie would have heard about it.

The encounter with the gunman on the freeway, years ago, sprang into her mind and her stomach roiled. *He might have been looking for Ceci.*

But Ceci had been so flippant about the incident, and it happened months after she and Jaime had split up. Sofie watched her aunt, wondering whether to mention it again. Tía had been quite upset at the time; there'd be no point in stirring up that worry again.

When Ceci and Jaime were together, both men might have been using her without her knowledge. *How?* From personal experience, Sofie knew Ramón wouldn't hesitate using Ceci—anyone—to further his dream of creating an empire. He'd ignored his own brother's addiction. Sofie doubted Ramón would have cared if Ceci picked up a drug habit along the way.

Sofie never heard Ramón mention Jaime or Ceci, his first cousin, in conversation. And she hadn't seen Jaime in Acapulco or at the ranch. She couldn't imagine the rest of her Mexican cousins going along with these schemes.

Then again, she'd walked through the aftermath in the courtyard that day. Anything was possible.

Tía returned to her chair. "Money? Drugs? It's a mystery and I'd like to have the answers. Maybe someday Rich can help us."

"Rich?"

Reaching across the table, Tía clasped Sofie's hand. "I have news as well. Rich has been accepted by the LAPD."

"That's great! When does he start?"

"He's going to the Academy in January."

Sofie was happy for Rich. Tía and Tío too. After so much anguish, they deserved their share of proud moments.

All families harbored skeletons, disappointments and heartache, but Sofie never imagined the depth and breadth of her own family's secrets—or how doggedly they'd been protected through a tradition of silence and tolerance. Sofie's mom followed that same path in her own way, accepting her cancer with little resistance. And where had it gotten her?

Ramón and Jaime clearly had been involved in nefarious dealings.

Didn't Sofie and Tía have a right to discover what really happened? Jillian Bond might have some of the answers. On the other hand, the prospect of exposing secrets publicly would be opposed by long-standing traditions—and weren't these traditions there for a reason? Recently, these were the thoughts that kept her awake at night.

Tía's warm fingers caressed the top of Sofie's hand.

"What should I tell Jillian Bond?" she asked.

"Do you think she can answer any of our questions?"

"She might." Sofie bit her lip. "What about family loyalty?"

"Did Ramón show you any *family loyalty* when he tried to pull you into his business without mentioning he was trafficking drugs?"

Sofie parted the panels of the cafe curtains and watched a crow land in Tío's backyard garden. The remnants of last summer's tomato plants had shriveled into brown, tangled clusters along the fence. If she did the interview and Gabriel or Monica found out, it would permanently sever any possibility of a reconciliation. There would surely be other, unforeseen consequences too. Was she prepared for the fallout?

"A family supports one another when they are on track," Tía said. "It's a family's responsibility to rein in their members when they fall off the rails. We are our brothers' keepers."

She folded her arms. "Look at how Ramón has snared you too! With obligation." Her gentle face contorted with rage. "El Patron Grande!" she exclaimed, her eyes flashing. "Parading around as the leader of our family. I'm *glad* Ramón is dead. I hope he burns in hell." She glanced up at the ceiling, crossed herself and mouthed a silent prayer. "I know, right here," Tía said, pressing her palm to her heart, "he had something to do with what happened to Ceci."

There were no tears, but Tía's dark eyes blazed. "Nothing will ever bring my beautiful Cecilia back to me. To us. I blame Ramón and the rest of my nephews. Esteban, Marco. Felipe—*the priest*—what a joke! I hold them all personally responsible. And God forgive me, I am glad they are dead too. You can't betray our family, they already have."

In the living room, Tío must have heard her outburst, because the sound coming from the TV disappeared.

Sofie peppered Tía with her final reservations, "You don't think doing this interview is just airing our dirty laundry? Won't it be humiliating?"

"Our dirty laundry is everybody's dirty laundry. Many families deal with drug addiction. And our family has been responsible for some of that pain.

You have an opportunity to make the first step by sharing our story."

Walking to the sink, Sofie layered an armful of cornhusks into warm water. Tía's African violets, their amethyst flowers encircled by jade leaves, thrived in the window box. "Can I really make a difference?"

"Look at it this way. Rich is building a career in law enforcement, like your *friend*, Alex."

Sofie flinched.

"They both must feel they have a responsibility to others, or they wouldn't have chosen this career. Where's your family loyalty to Rich, now that he is going to be risking his life as a police officer?"

Tía seemed to be waiting for an answer.

Sofie did owe something to her family's future, not its past. If she turned her thoughts away from life south of the border, maybe she could finally focus on the present and move forward—like Tía had said before—one stair at a time, building positive, more honest and adult relationships with the people Sofie loved here.

"De lo perdido saca lo que puedas." Tía grinned. "Isn't that the saying? You can make the best of a bad situation by shedding a little light on how Ramón and the boys operated. In the long run, wouldn't that help Dean and Alex, and even Rich, with the work they do?"

Nodding, Sofie turned from the sink toward her aunt and wondered if she had the strength to live up to her convictions and speak out. "I don't really know much."

"You spent a lot of time with them. You probably know more than you realize." Tía moved to the table and sat down. "Come. Sit," she instructed.

Heat from the kitchen left a sheen of moisture on Tía's forehead. "I hate menopause," she said, wiping the sweat off with her apron.

"After Ceci… I prayed the Rosary every day," Tía said. "I asked God to show me a way to honor Ceci's name. I never found anything that made sense to me. Maybe my job is support, to help you find the courage to get out there and speak up. Please, for Ceci, *and for me,* talk to Jillian Bond, do the interview and see what you can find out."

The front door opened and Rich called out, "Hello! Merry Christmas!"

Tía checked the clock on the wall. "Nine o'clock. Right on time. Have I convinced you yet?"

"You're right. I'll call Jillian Bond this week."

"Good. So, are you ready to show Amelia the secrets of making the most delicious tamales in California?" Tía grinned gleefully. "Amelia has a wonderful surprise. I'll let her share the news."

CHAPTER TWENTY-FOUR
New Year Storm

Tormenta del Año Nuevo
Saturday, December 29, 1984

Out with the old and in with the new. A clean house was her mom's end-of-the-year tradition, one that Sofie refused to abandon, even though she'd woken up this morning depressed. Pushing herself, she was satisfied with her progress. The kitchen and bathroom of her apartment were spotless. Once she finished the living room, she'd tackle the project she put off for last, her bedroom.

The source of her anxiety was the brown paper bag stashed in the back of her closet, a parting gift from the hospital in El Paso. Unable to throw it away in Texas, she'd kept the morbid keepsake nearby, and brought it home to California, unopened, always promising herself she'd deal with its contents later.

Distracted by a muffled swoosh-swish along the street, she glanced out the dining room window, beyond the giant Magnolia, and down to the rain-glazed pavement. A car left tire marks melting into the flooded asphalt. The rain began on Christmas Day, and, more or less, it hadn't stopped all week. As if Heaven had held its breath over the past months, it now fell into fits of sobs, distraught at having to give up the year.

In a peculiar way, Sofie understood. Fearful of the future, she was oddly hesitant to see 1984 go, knowing she'd leave its benchmarks behind.

Unleashing a splatter of furniture polish across the dining table, Sofie used anger and a rag to work it into the wood, and watched a vague outline of her reflection emerge.

The breakup with Ben in the spring was a distant and, in hindsight, unimportant prescript. A premonition of tragedy to come. Ramón had always been manipulative, and the breadth of his corruption was stunning. But she'd been blindsided by Alex. His memory brought only heartache and a devastating sense of betrayal. It was a feeling more complex than grief, more intense than pain.

Each man left his own scars. She tried to convince herself the cutting shards of these traumas would be tumbled over time, and like sea glass, worn into smooth, manageable memories.

Today, it didn't feel that way at all.

Pulling the vacuum across the hardwood floor to the living room, she flipped on the switch and worked the beater across the rug in precise rows. Channeling Tía's voice, *Count your blessings, mija!* Sofie forced a smile. Christmas *had* materialized better than expected. The highlight being Rich and Amelia's news—she was pregnant and due in June.

They'd held off making the announcement until Christmas morning, insisting Sofie would be an honorary aunt to the child, though actually only a second cousin. The family asked if she wanted to be called Tía, or use the playful nickname, TíTí; then they teased her, extrapolating her choice to Tata or Tutu. Amelia didn't get the joke, which made the conversation more hilarious. Bewildered by Spanish itself, she said at various moments, "Isn't that what ballerinas wear?" And, "Why can't we just call you Aunt Sofie?"

Sofie laughed until she cried, feeling more relaxed than she had in months. She would be filling Ceci's position in the family as an aunt. Ceci had loved children. They'd both joked about giving birth to a tribe of them someday.

At one time, Sofie had wished she could have Alex's baby. That seemed so long ago. Today, the thought of children was another life away.

Rich and Amelia's new baby meant a fresh beginning. Reluctantly, Sofie had to admit, life did move on.

Earlier in the week, after talking to Tía and flooded with optimism, she adopted a New Year's resolution to put the past year—and Alex—into perspective. She'd move forward along with the calendar.

Following Tía Sofia's suggestion, she made an appointment with Jillian Bond to do the interview. After months of floating through limbo, it felt good to make such a directed and confident decision.

Sofie was glad she'd talked to Tía Sofia on Christmas Eve. There were thousands of families being torn apart by drugs, and she wanted to make a difference. Speaking up could be a way to repair the damage. It would honor Ceci's name, and maybe Sofie could save lives by using her voice to get the message out. She could even help Dean—she didn't want to think about helping Alex.

An investigative reporter might also provide answers to help Sofie and Tía understand what really happened.

Now overwhelmed with second thoughts, Sofie didn't think she had any insightful information to give Jillian Bond about drug trafficking in Mexico. Quite possibly, she wouldn't help anyone and, instead, publicly humiliate herself. Her bosses didn't know about her family connections. She could lose her job.

Dread twisted her belly. These were risks she'd already committed to take.

Sofie remembered one of her mom's favorite sayings: *"Haz el bien sin mirar a quien. Do what is right, come what may."*

Gusting winds signaled another band of rain due to arrive. Lured by the approaching storm, she turned off the vacuum and settled on the couch, gazing out the picture window as the swollen clouds made their delivery.

Sofie counted another blessing in the music of blissful rain. There'd been no lighting or thunder today, none all week. But now, without warning, a single tremulous roll of it ushered in a deluge, misting shafts of water that washed out all of the color in the neighborhood. For fifteen minutes or so, she listened to the symphonic progression, a vibrant performance of harmonious splatter and crackle, and couldn't push away the memory of the breathtaking thunderstorm she'd witnessed with Alex as they drove down into the Oaxaca Valley. She hated herself for missing him so much.

As the rain settled into sprinkles, the phone rang. Her dad's husky voice came through, loud and clear, "I was hoping you'd be on your way by now."

She adjusted one of the pillows on the couch. "It's raining here."

"Still?"

"We just had another cloudburst. I'm not sure I'm going to make it."

"I'd hoped you were coming today." His disappointment leaked into the line.

"I know." Sofie had enough of her own frustration. She couldn't deal with letting him down too. "I really appreciate the VCR, Dad. Rich came over, to help set it up yesterday. It's a great gift. Thanks again."

Hidden under Tía and Tío's Christmas tree, the extravagant gift had been a surprise. It prompted a call to her dad and Deborah that ended with a half-hearted commitment to attend their traditional New Year's Eve party.

"We're glad you like it. Have you seen *Tootsie* yet?"

"No." *We?* Right. In the past, Deborah hadn't seemed to care much about what Sofie liked. At best, Sofie had forged a tentative truce with her dad's wife. The only thing they had in common was her father.

She glanced at the trio of VHS cassettes near the television. Her favorite holiday movie, *It's a Wonderful Life*, sat at the top of the stack. It was a present from Tía, apparently tucked into Sofie's stocking at the last minute.

What a wonderful life? It's more like, life's a bitch.

I'm too cynical, she thought. "I'm planning on watching *Tootsie* this afternoon."

"Deborah insisted we buy *Flashdance* too. She remembers driving you back and forth to all those lessons when you were in high school."

Sofie couldn't be sure if the remark was a jab from her stepmother or innocent commentary. According to Tía, it had been Deborah who called before Christmas and told them the VCR was on its way.

"Deborah's trying. Give her a chance, mija," Tía had said.

Looking back, Sofie could see it must have been a difficult transition for all of them when she came to live with her dad and his new wife, who had two little girls of her own. Starting high school in Sacramento wasn't a cakewalk, but a stepdaughter plopped into Deborah's life couldn't have been great either. And, Sofie had to admit, she hadn't always made it easy for her.

"Tell her thanks." Sofie let her dad decide whether the response was for the chauffeuring or the movie.

"Caley and Cara miss you too. We're thinking about making a trip to Disneyland over Spring Break." Her dad hesitated. "But I'd like to see you before then. We haven't seen you since we came down for your graduation, last spring."

"I know, Dad. I'd planned on coming up, it's just the weather—"

"How are you *really* doing, Sofie?"

"I'm fine." She bit back the venom she'd wanted to inject into the conversation. *Thanks, Dad. Finally, you care?* It would sound childish, and he was genuinely concerned. Admittedly, in recent months, she was the one who'd avoided his calls, just as she had Tía's. "Don't worry about me. I'm doing okay."

"We're *really* counting on you to come up… I want to bridge this distance between us."

"You live in Sacramento, Dad. I live in LA."

"You know what I mean. The twins are in their senior year of high school and they'll be the going away to college next fall," he explained. "I never thought I'd see the day when all of my girls had flown the coop. My biggest regret has been spending more time at the hospital than with the family. All *five* of us. Let's change that. It won't be the same if you aren't here."

"We'll see," she said evasively.

Sofie heard Deborah's unintelligible voice in the background.

"If you can't make it, we'll come down next month to see you," he offered.

Apparently, her reprieve was over. "Dad, I don't want you guys to make ___"

"It's not a problem," he insisted.

Guilt made her cover her forehead with her free hand. "Dad—"

He sighed. "If the weather's lousy, I guess I understand…"

In such a black mood, Sofie was having trouble mustering up the will to finish cleaning her apartment. She didn't have the energy to drive seven hours to see them.

"I'll call tomorrow. Hopefully, the weather will clear. I love you, Sofia."

"You too." She strangled her fingers in the corkscrewed cord of the telephone. All of this interest was a little late.

A niggling voice reminded her that misplaced hostility wasn't fair. Her lips began to tremble, and she pushed away the thought.

Nothing is fair.

Unable to sink this new anger into the overflowing well of emotion, she wiped at her face with the discarded rag, accidentally mixing her tears with the dregs of furniture polish; it was a harsh, stinging combination that only made things worse.

Sofie washed up and stared into the bathroom mirror, studying her red-rimmed eyes and blotched face. She couldn't do anything right.

Already miserable, maybe it was time to confront her closet and get the task over with. With any luck, she'd be liberated and feel better. Maybe then, she'd call some of her work friends to see what they'd planned for the evening.

She plodded into her bedroom, and when she opened the closet door, a jungle of tangled clothes greeted her. Most of her fall and winter wardrobe hung in disarray, a consequence of haphazard unpacking. Short on hangers and room, her summer stuff had been abandoned into a heap on the floor alongside her shoes. Working down, she rearranged the top shelf, then organized the hangers.

Finally, and not without trepidation, she confronted the chaos on the scuffed hardwood, tossing the dust-bunnied clothes onto her bare mattress for the laundry.

There it was.

Next to abandoned spider webs near the baseboard, a weathered, crumpled grocery bag lay tightly rolled and untouched, where she'd stashed it. She didn't open the sack, but relocated it to the floor by her dresser, deciding to put off the inevitable for a few minutes more.

Retrieving the broom and dustpan from the kitchen, she swept the closet and arranged the shoes. She sorted the mass of grubby clothes afterwards.

The sheets were already downstairs, in the laundry room she shared with the other tenants. Laundry would probably become a chore that ran into the evening. So much for a night out.

She tried to find her favorite blouse, the sleeveless turquoise one she hadn't seen in months, and sank to the floor when she remembered. She'd left Mexico with only her purse.

Her New Year's resolution required discarding painful memories. She'd have to live with losing the blouse. Did she have the courage to pick up the sack and just throw it away? Maybe she could toss it in the trashcan under the kitchen sink, or take it to the dumpster in the alley. She could bury it under the Magnolia in the front yard. Shouldn't she give *something* a proper burial? She didn't own a shovel and, even if she did, her neighbors would think she'd flipped.

At least the tree, dripping with rain, would hide her tears.

Out with the old, in with the new.

Deciding she needed to revisit the summer one last time, Sofie stood, went to the dresser, picked up the dusty paper bag and sat on the edge of the bed.

She took a deep breath and opened it, pulling out her filthy white shorts, the ones she'd worn that last day at the ranch. They'd been wadded into a bunch, stiff with Gabriel's blood and shredded from Alex's manhandling. Reaching into the pockets, she pulled out gravel and tiny squares of safety glass from the blast of gunfire that had hit the windshield of the pickup truck. Sobbing, she relived moments from that afternoon. Gabriel stumbling across the yard. Ramón's face. The tennis shoe.

Wiping her eyes, she placed the torn shorts on top of the laundry pile. She reached in deeper, retrieving Alex's shirt, the one he'd given her in the shed. She brought the soft cotton to her cheek and inhaled, searching for traces of his scent and finding them. Tears would never be able to dilute the familiar mixture of…what? Cologne? Deodorant? Aftershave? And that something, so uniquely *Alex*.

There had to be something broken in her if she could still love the man who'd caused so much pain. Holding the once-white material in her hands, she realized the shirt made it through the ordeal relatively unscathed. Sofie searched for a trace of Gabriel—if only his blood—as justification to keep it.

Sofie had been smug—but she'd been addicted too. It wasn't drugs; it was a man, and withdrawal was excruciating.

Transported by his scent, she reveled in Alex's shirt, sparking the tangible memories that waited all along in the back of the closet.

Bringing the shirt to her face, she closed her eyes and saw him again. The sun streaked hair that kissed his collar, his lone dimple when he smiled. Alex was a remarkable man who'd taken the time to map her body, driving her to ecstasy, time and time again. She loved him for the spontaneous glee she'd found in his smile as he threw coins to the kids alongside the road. Instead of dismissing her adopted home, he'd taken the time to appreciate its beauty. He'd been captivated by both the pyramids of Monte Albán, and the cliff divers who timed their moves to the pulse of the sea.

In just a few days, she and Alex had learned to perfect their pulse and timing too. With Alex, Sofie believed she'd found *home*.

I'm delusional.

Caressing the supple material, she remembered how protected she'd felt within his arms. The nights they'd spent together in bed, when he'd run his lips along her body. *And so much more.*

"Take off your necklace," he had told her, "I don't want anything between us."

"Liar!" Her cry echoed through the bedroom. Stung by how naive she'd been to open her heart, she hugged her sides, rocking on the mattress.

Alex obviously never loved her. The goal had been to worm his way into her family. He hadn't cared. It was all in a day's work.

He used me.

She'd been blindsided. Regardless of what Tía thought, Alex could have warned her.

A new downpour peppered the roof, overflowing the rain gutters. Somehow, the sound of rain seemed a fitting background as she anointed the cotton with her tears, emptying her soul of the rage and hurt.

Finally, she went into the kitchen and opened the cabinet under the sink. She threw the shorts into the trashcan, but was unable to let go of Alex's shirt. Her hand grasped the fabric, leaving one sleeve to hover above the plastic rim.

Sofie couldn't bear to breathe in his scent again. However, another positive could come from this tragedy, she rationalized—if only by sharing a simple, white cotton shirt. A new owner would never suspect its history. After a soak and a cycle through the wash, it might be as good as new. Well, good enough for Goodwill.

Rain dappled the window pane above the sink. The droplets swelled until they burst, making squiggly trails down the glass. She filled the basin with water and added bleach. This would hopefully mark Sofie's first step up the ladder out of her private hell.

She dropped the shirt into the water, and immediately regretted the decision. *Out with the old, in with the new.* Sofie pressed Alex's shirt in deep.

In her bedroom, she loaded a pile of dirty clothes into her basket. She grabbed the trash can on her way to the laundry room, and was pelted by cold rain on the back stairs, realizing, too late, she needed her coat.

In the living room, she picked up *It's a Wonderful Life* and read the blurb on the back cover. She'd seen the movie at least a dozen times, watching George Bailey, a fictional character, struggle through real-life problems. He persevered until the last scene ushered in a happy ending.

I want my happy ending.

She slipped the VHS cassette into the machine and made herself comfortable on the couch.

Soon distracted by her own dilemmas, she decided Alex's shirt, soaking in the kitchen, was the quintessential representation of every moment they'd shared last summer.

At the time, following an incredibly misguided logic, she'd tried to convince herself she was liberated enough to have casual sex without becoming emotionally involved. Sofie realized she wasn't nearly as enlightened as she'd thought. She wanted everything from Alex that traditionally came with intimacy. Was it possible for any woman to share her body with a man she was attracted to and not want more?

Sofie had lied to herself.

Alex had lied too. Tía suggested that he was trapped by circumstances. Sofie didn't buy it.

Sofie wanted to believe she'd seen the real Alex when he boarded the airplane at the ranch, his eyes full of regret. With her track record of misreads, she was, once again, probably wrong.

There was no denying Alex proved to be a chameleon. He could be playing another role right now. Seducing some other girl to get information. Sofie bit the pad of her thumb.

I don't want to know. But I do.

Trying to concentrate on the movie, she watched George and Mary on their wedding day, surrounded by family and friends.

How could Sofie take the risk of loving anyone again? Love hurt too much. Because, eventually, *everyone* leaves, either by distance or death. Shuddering, she wondered if she'd end up a female caricature of Mr. Potter —alone, shriveled and mean. A bitter accountant, imprisoned behind a desk, punching numbers in a high-rise downtown.

Night settled in, and she turned on the lamp. She didn't pause the movie when she rinsed Alex's shirt, and groaned when she realized all trace of him had been replaced by the strong smell of chemicals.

Grabbing her coat this time, Sofie headed downstairs.

Back upstairs, she deposited warm, clean sheets onto her mattress. Sofie didn't want to drink alone—the last time she did, she'd ended up in Alex's bed. Tonight, she decided to make an exception. Stopping in the kitchen, she opened a bottle of red wine.

For months, she'd been running to distance herself from what happened, inevitably she ended up in the cul-de-sac where she'd begun. Like Tía said, maybe if she focused on being there, she might be able to sort things out and find a resolution. *And God, I need to start the new year with some peace.*

Admittedly, she'd fallen into the thick of their romance with her stupid "no promises, no expectations" deal.

"You intrigue me." Alex had said more than once.

Probably because she was related to a Mexican drug cartel and couldn't see it.

She laughed bitterly and swallowed a gulp of wine.

There *were* more than the negatives. Alex had encouraged her to make her own decisions. Obviously, he hadn't wanted her to get caught up in Ramón's world.

Nevertheless, at the Oaxaca hotel, when she had found the gun in his luggage, instead of telling her the truth, he'd let her supply her own convenient answer. She'd blamed it on Ramón.

Sofie had suspicions, but she'd stupidly ignored the clues, and hadn't demanded answers. Not until it was too late and she'd fallen in love. Rubbing her aching temples, she realized this rehash of the past was hard work, so she refilled her empty glass.

Back on the couch, she folded a T-shirt and acknowledged that Alex had rescued her more than once. On that last day, he'd saved her. He'd saved Gabriel's life too.

Unraveling the twine in this tangled ball of memories seemed impossible. The assessment left her full of competing notions and more confused than ever.

Adding a thin nightgown to the folded clothes, Sofie realized Tía was right. She did have questions for Alex.

I want answers.

Gathering a stack of clothes destined for her already crowded dresser, she wondered what would have transpired if she'd never gone back to the ranch that last day. Alex likely would have disappeared, leaving her to imagine what really happened between them.

She separated the sheets and began to make the bed.

Or, he might have resurfaced, with a fabricated story that would have left her forever wondering if he was a drug dealer like her cousins.

If he'd come clean and confessed the truth, Sofie wondered if she loved him enough to forgive...

Could she forgive? How?

Securing the bottom sheet around the underside of the mattress, she cracked the top sheet and watched it parachute across the plain. Sofie could spend all day asking herself questions. Alex was the key, she thought, finishing the edges with precise military corners.

Alex knew about military corners. He had been in Viet Nam.

Hadn't he?

Wrestling the pillows into their cases, she remembered Alex wanting her trust. Believing his words, she'd stupidly welcomed what proved to be a stranger into her body.

Disgusted with herself, she sighed.

In the living room, Sofie discovered the movie nearly over; soon, George and the rest of Bedford Falls would sing "Auld Lang Syne." Deciphering the stanzas of the timeless classic, she couldn't decide if she should cry or snicker. A little tipsy, she did both.

After the credits scrolled through, a gray fuzz scattered across the TV screen. She removed the cassette and changed the channel. Lawrence Welk's orchestra played below gaudy chandeliers, while a dozen men and women—wearing coordinated outfits—sang a sappy song which should have been forgotten by the 1960s.

Sofie took another basket of finished laundry into the bedroom and placed her glass on the dresser next to the jewelry box. Originally belonging to her mom, it had become a Pandora's Box, holding more memories Sofie was hesitant to explore.

The wine suddenly tasted sour, so she left it on the dresser and returned to the living room. Antsy, she used the clicker to scroll through the TV, avoiding Alex's shirt, hidden somewhere in the mountain of clean clothes on the couch.

He had answers Jillian Bond couldn't provide.

I have a right to know.

Back in the bedroom, she ran her fingers along the crimson leather of the jewelry box. The gold filigree embossed around the edges resembled the pattern of Ceci's necklace. She paused and touched the silver heart through the fabric of her blouse.

"We need a sign," he'd said. "I'll be there if you need me."

Sofie touched her necklace. *I need you, Alex. I need you, now.*

The box harbored keepsakes she'd been unable to throw away. Hidden in the back of the drawer was Alex's phone number, the "trash" Sofie had crumpled and tossed into her purse at the Acapulco airport. On top of the flattened and folded square sat the gold hoops he'd bought her.

They were cold in her palm. She'd never worn the earrings.

Opening the lid, Sofie added them to the small velvet compartment where she'd kept a piece of sea glass—the one she'd found walking along the beach with Alex, the last night they'd spent together. In the moonlight, she hadn't been able to tell the color. It wasn't until months later—when she discovered it at the bottom of her purse— that she realized the smooth treasure wasn't white, but, actually, the palest lavender. Thinking of her mom, Sofie smiled; this treasure was the only piece of Mexican sea glass she possessed anymore.

When she'd found it, she believed the gift was a message from her mom to trust Alex. Today, she decided it meant something else: Sofie needed to learn to believe in herself.

She picked up the folded paper Alex had given her and remembered his words the last night they were together, *"Whatever happens, I want you to know this has meant a lot to me."*

And then, *"I need you to trust me. Get on a plane and go back to California."*

Sofie snapped the lid down and thought of Pandora, who'd released, from her forbidden jar, all of the evils into the world. According to the myth, Pandora had only been able to capture a single virtue—hope.

Maybe what we had was important to him, she thought, as she returned to the living room with the folded paper in her hand. He'd given her this number. He'd wanted her to promise she'd come back to California. Why had he been so insistent if he didn't want to see her again?

And his last words, *"I didn't want it to end like this."*

Alex must have known a nasty end was inevitable.

The telephone number was scrawled in black pen beneath the pink script of the Las Brisas Hotel. A Los Angeles area code. She'd noticed it before.

Was it another lie?

He supposedly lived in Chicago. She'd even seen his Illinois driver's license. Sofie shivered, realizing how close he actually was, maybe just minutes away.

Alex would have contacted her if he cared.

She glanced at the glowing numbers on the VCR, announcing it was after nine. It could be too late.

Trembling, but fueled by liquid fortitude and frustration, she dialed the number, with no clue as to what she'd say when he answered. With each ring, her heart skipped beats, desperate for a connection.

If he answered.

"Be there. Be there. Be there, you asshole bastard. I have questions. Dozens of them. Pick up the phone, dammit!"

I need you.

It was a faint "Hello?"—the cracked and unmistakable voice of an elderly woman.

"Oh..." Sofie wasn't sure where to go from here.

Alex had given her a bogus phone number. *Shit!*

"I'm sorry to bother you so late. I'm looking for Alex..." It dawned on

Sofie she probably didn't have his real last name. She took a stab at it anyway, "Alex Wilson."

"I don't know an Alex Wilson, honey. I'm sorry."

Sofie exhaled and her heart sank. "Do you know any Alex—" She ran fingers through her short curls.

"Is he your boyfriend?"

"He—"

"I'm so sorry, my daughter says I ask too many questions."

"It's okay. He was a…" Sofie heard her voice deflate, "friend. I'm trying to track him down. I might not have the right last name, but this is the number he gave me."

"So sorry. I don't know your Alex. I'm new to Santa Monica. I used to live in Anaheim. My daughter works at Hughes and wanted me to move closer to her. I've just had this number a couple of months."

"I apologize for bothering you. Goodnight."

"I hope you find him, honey," the woman said in a cheerful voice. "Good luck."

Unable to shake the disappointment, Sofie folded the remaining clothes, leaving Alex's shirt for last. Next week, she'd take it to Goodwill.

Deciding to go to bed, she turned off the television and set the last stack of laundry on her dresser, accidentally knocking the wine glass to the floor. Red wine splashed everywhere. All of a sudden, Sofie was back in the courtyard of the ranch, and, at the same time, sidestepping a minefield of glass shards on her bedroom floor. She burst into tears.

Another mess to clean up.

She grabbed a towel from the bathroom, and cleaned up the mess as best she could. Afterwards, she sat on the edge of the bed, holding Alex's remarkably clean shirt, listening to rain gush down the gutters. She could feel the electricity that existed between them and wondered if it was just her imagination, or if, somewhere out there, Alex felt it too.

Sofie had many regrets. Nevertheless, after today's thorough accounting, she could find no remorse in loving Alex. She'd meant something to him. And she had proof. Alex risked his own life to keep her safe by shielding her body with his.

Like George Bailey, despite his plans, Alex might have fallen in love.

This wasn't a movie. *It's my life. And I deserve a happy ending too.*

She switched off the lamp and listened to the storm. Undressing beneath orange streetlight seeping into her room, Sofie slipped her arms into the sleeves of the oversized shirt. Buttoning it, she savored the soft, cotton cloud surrounding her skin.

❦

Awaking to the sound of birds calling to one another in the trees, Sofie's eyelids complained, wanting more time underneath the covers. A shaft of warm sunlight climbing into the bedroom announced an already full morning. Crisp, cool air came in through a crack in the window. Overnight, the storm had moved on, and, as if it mimicking her cleaning frenzy yesterday, left LA's landscape scrubbed, ready for the new year.

Sofie made a count: Two glasses of wine and a third spilled. That wasn't enough alcohol to explain the dehydration and headache. Her eyes were stinging and the lids tender. She decided tears, off and on, all day, would do that to you.

She remembered how she'd blown her dad off yesterday, and wondered if she could make it to Sacramento by sunset.

Her gaze settled on her arm and the open cuff of Alex's shirt. The button was gone, leaving a small hunk of threads. Last night in bed, she'd missed him desperately. Searching for his scent in the supple cotton—something to hold onto—Sofie had sobbed when she realized she'd bleached all reminders of him away.

When they'd picnicked on Monte Albán, she'd told Alex there was nothing left to do except move forward. Cocooned in his shirt, Sofie decided there was no choice but to follow her own advice.

CHAPTER TWENTY-FIVE
Dressing for Weather

Vestiendo Para el Clima
Chicago, Illinois
Wednesday, February 13, 1985

Sofie turned to look for support from Jillian with a cautious smile. Her warm hand squeezed Sofie's fingers as the limousine rolled to a stop at the back of the soundstage. Soon, she'd air family secrets once again and, this time, it wouldn't be in newsprint, but in front of Don Phillips' cameras.

She took a deep breath, determined to make a difference. In front of a nationwide audience, she'd have an even greater opportunity to illuminate the problem: Drug addiction not only destroys the user, but it devastates families too.

In January, on the first afternoon of the *Times* interview, Jillian arrived at Sofie's apartment with a cassette recorder and a kind, infectious personality. Within an hour, they'd clicked.

It wasn't always easy, but Sofie did her best to answer Jillian's questions. Unfortunately, Jillian hadn't been able to illuminate any of hers. The interview went well. So well, in fact, that Jillian had called last week with breaking news: A Drug Enforcement Agent had been kidnapped in Mexico.

A chill raced through Sofie, and a moan escaped as she cried silently, *Please God, don't let it be him.*

"It's not Alex," Jillian said, reading her mind. "It's an agent who's been working out of the Guadalajara office."

Then on Monday, Jillian called again. The kidnapping had become a huge story. A producer from *The Don Phillips Show* had read Jillian's series in the *Los Angeles Times,* and Don wanted an interview. They were interested in Sofie as well, and Jillian asked if she could give them her number.

Having already revealed her story in the print media, Sofie agreed to step into television's salon of full disclosure, bolstered by Jillian's promise to be beside her the whole time.

The chauffeur waited beyond the glass partition of the limousine, staring straight ahead. A wisp of Jillian's auburn hair escaped from her ponytail and she tucked it behind her ear. "Don't worry, Sofie. It will be fine."

Sofie suddenly wasn't so sure. "What do we do now?"

"You go first and be my windbreak," Jillian teased.

Below a chalky blue sky, frigid winds bouncing off Lake Michigan blasted the city. Sofie had arrived at the airport late last night, and the few times she'd ventured outdoors, she was greeted by a numbing cold. With each shocking breath of air, she imagined microscopic crystals of ice lacerating her throat and lungs.

As if on cue, the door opened and an enthusiastic woman waved them in.

"Hi, I'm Heather, the Talent Coordinator's assistant. You must be Jillian…" she said, checking her clipboard. "You're Sofia? Or is it Sofie?"

The young woman secured the clipboard against her waist and held out her hand.

"Sofia is fine," Sofie answered, aware that using her given name would only provide the thinnest veil of anonymity.

"Great!" Heather said, escorting them though the cavernous building. "I'll be taking you through the process. Relax, it's going to be a breeze."

Surrounded by chaos, Heather hurried them through the surprisingly small set toward a bank of rooms while dodging the staff and technical crew. She turned and glanced at the garment bags Sofie and Jillian carried.

"I'm glad you brought a selection for the Wardrobe Coordinator to choose from." Heather stopped and lowered her voice, "A few weeks ago the producer forgot to remind one of our guests. The woman arrived in sweats, thinking we'd dress her. I had to take her on a frantic, last-minute shopping trip. It might sound like fun, but, believe me, it was stressful."

All Sofie could do was mumble as she took in the circus. A spaghettied forest of lights covered the ceiling, a tangled web where technicians worked, adjusting the system. In the control booth, high against one wall, a man called out instructions, his voice echoing throughout the soundstage.

Heather stopped in front of an open door. "Our guests have arrived, girls," she announced to pair of beaming women standing in front of beauty stations.

Sofie smiled and wondered if *perky* was a prerequisite of studio employment.

"Here you go, ladies. Your first stop. Rachel does makeup, Chloe hair." Heather ushered Sofie and Jillian into the room. "I'll be back soon. Hang your bags on this rack. Do you need anything before I go?"

Mesmerized by the inner workings of a television production, Sofie shook her head.

"We're fine. Thanks." Jillian said.

Heather wasted no time handing them off before she vanished. And thankfully, Chloe wasn't intimidated by Sofie's short—but still often unruly—hair.

As soon as they were alternately primped and powdered, Heather returned. "Come on, ladies. We're headed to wardrobe."

She led Sofie and Jillian to a nearby room and introduced them to Beverly.

At one time clearly beautiful, Beverly, the Wardrobe Coordinator, was still pretty, though deep into middle age. She confiscated the garment bags and unzipped them. "Let's see what you brought. I assume you remembered. No checks, prints or patterns. The camera doesn't like them."

They tried on outfits for her approval.

Thick-waisted with feathery lines along the edges of her eyes and lips, Beverly employed the scrutiny of a fashion drill sergeant as she stormed through Jillian's clothes. She picked an azure dress that complemented Jillian's coloring and eyes.

As Beverly made a final inspection, Jillian whispered to Sofie, "This dress is Tom's favorite. He says it makes my eyes look incredible."

Sofie agreed.

"Whoever Tom is, he's right!" Beverly exclaimed.

"He's my husband," Jillian's voice held the unmistakable hint of loving admiration.

The white-collared, navy sailor dress Sofie brought was quickly discarded, proving her selections to be a greater challenge.

"When white is near your face, the camera will wash you out." Beverly explained.

She liked the green wrap dress Sofie modeled next.

"What's that around your neck?"

Sofie fished out Ceci's necklace.

"No," Beverly said. "That won't do. It's distracting. The heart lands right in the vee of the bodice. You'll have to take it off and wear another one. Did you bring any jewelry?"

"I did, but not necklaces. I wear this one all the time," Sofie said, caressing the silver heart between her thumb and finger. "I won't take it off."

Jillian looked up from a magazine and joined Beverly's questioning gaze.

Sofie stubbornly refused.

Beverly, her face stony with agitation, stared while Sofie quietly stood her ground.

"In that case," Beverly barked, "I guess this dress isn't an option. What else did you bring?"

Emerging from the dressing room in her third, and last, outfit, Sofie wore a long sleeved sheath dress, adorned with large, gold buttons sweeping down the right side.

Finally Beverly smiled. She took a few steps back and crossed her arms. "The color is spectacular. It's a shame red doesn't translate true on camera. It looks great on you. Turn in a circle." She motioned with her finger and moved in close to check her earrings. "I like the diamonds. What are the dull silver things?"

"They're starter studs." Last month, on the third anniversary of Ceci's death, Sofie added a second set of piercings to her ears.

"Where's your other jewelry?"

Sofie asked Jillian to retrieve the small bag she'd stuffed into her purse.

Beverly rummaged through the bag and selected the gold hoops, the ones Alex had given Sofie in Mexico.

She'd impulsively packed them in the last, frenzied minutes before she left her apartment, and *of course*, they were Beverly's choice.

"Perfect!" Beverly exclaimed.

"You look stunning," Jillian added.

Heather cheerfully delivered Sofie and Jillian to the green room and disappeared. Sofie sat down on the couch. A table on the opposite wall was covered with an enticing array of food. Jillian made a beeline for the platters and picked up a paper plate.

Queasy dread squelched any appetite. Sofie was fighting the urge to bolt when Jillian came over and touched her shoulder.

"Everything will be fine. Really. You look beautiful," Jillian hesitated. "There's no one else here. We might be the only guests. That's good—you'll have more airtime to get the message out."

"What's the downside?"

Jillian laughed nervously. "All eyes will be on us."

Great.

"Sofie, what you're doing is noble. It takes a lot of courage to speak up. You're not alone. Many families struggle with drug problems in secret. It's an epidemic."

"I know. I tell myself that all the time." A blank television monitor sat in the corner. Framed publicity posters decorated the beige walls. "Why do they call this a 'green room' when it isn't green?"

"It's an old Elizabethan term. Like waiting in the wings, except in those days, they waited on the green, meaning grass."

Sofie raised an eyebrow.

"Not *that* kind of grass." Jillian laughed.

"You're amazing. The queen of trivia."

"I might sound brilliant, but I think it *was* a Trivial Pursuit question."

Jillian went back to nibbling while Sofie studied flecks of lint scattered along the carpet. Distraction became increasingly difficult. She chewed on her thumb, considering the possible consequences of today's revelations. "This taping won't air for two weeks, right?" she asked, hoping to buy some time.

"I think so. Usually post production takes awhile. But the Camarena kidnapping is a breaking story, they might want to rush it through." Jillian returned to the couch and crossed one long, slender leg over the other. Her normal splash of freckles had vanished, masked by heavy foundation.

They both had green eyes. Otherwise, Jillian's tall, pale body was a stark contrast to Sofie's tiny stature and olive complexion. Jillian had also gone to UCLA, although Jillian had graduated before Sofie became a freshman. Married, Jillian was passionate about her husband and her career. Sofie struggled with relationships. Jillian had struggles too, trying to navigate work and the desire for babies. Somewhere in those differences, they'd become friends.

"What did you end up telling your boss?" Jillian asked.

"I chickened out and asked for a few personal days off. They'll find out soon enough."

Ironically, months ago, the prospect of flying to Chicago had filled Sofie with delight. She'd envisioned meeting Alex for long, romantic weekends. Making love all night, sleeping in late each morning, and making love again. Spending the afternoons soaking up the city with Alex as her guide. Tasting her first slice of Chicago pizza. Exploring Wrigley Field. Taking in the vista from the Sears Tower.

Reality didn't meet any of her fantastic dreams.

"What?" Sofie wasn't listening.

"Don't be nervous, I've done this before. Once you get on the stage and acclimated, it's going to be fine."

Jillian seemed to be doing everything she could to help Sofie relax.

"I *said* I wish you weren't leaving tomorrow. This is an incredible city. I'd love to show you around before Tom flies in on Friday." Jillian's eyes sparkled. "He promised me a special Valentine's weekend."

"I've got to get back to work."

Jillian had Tom, and Sofie didn't resent Jillian's happiness. But for Sofie, there wouldn't be a Valentine's celebration and, without Alex, Chicago had no appeal.

Ever since she'd landed in the city, she'd been secretly watching people, hoping to run into Alex. Praying that he'd told her the truth, that he really did live in Chicago. Maybe she'd see him at the airport, on the street, in a restaurant. If, by some miracle, she did, what would she say?

This was insane; he could live in another state. Anywhere.

"Why won't you let me set you up with Tom's best friend, Paul? The doctor I told you about. He's just finished his residency at County USC. Even though he's a Trojan, you'd make a great couple."

"I'm not ready. I need more time." Sofie's mouth was dry. She picked out a soda from an assortment nestled in a bowl of ice cubes. "Want one?" she asked, popping the horseshoe tab on the can.

"No. I'm afraid it'll make me have to pee."

I didn't think of that. Sofie swallowed and decided to monitor her sips.

"I'll take you to dinner tonight. *The Phillips Show* will spring for it. There's this wonderful restaurant—"

The door opened and a woman rushed in, introducing herself as Trish, the Talent Coordinator.

Trish, another exuberant member of the staff, handed Sofie a clipboard and pen. "I just need you to sign this consent form."

Sofie hesitated and looked to Jillian.

"It's standard stuff," Trish said. "We need to have permission to use your image. We won't pay you residuals if the show repeats, et cetera," she explained in a sing-song voice. "Guests sign it all the time. It's one of the requirements to be on the show."

Jillian nodded.

Sofie scribbled her name and handed the clipboard to Jillian.

While she signed, Trish snatched a cookie from the table. "Catering does a marvelous job. I *love* the chocolate chip cookies." She wrapped it with a napkin and slipped it into the pocket of her jacket. "They'll be coming in to mic you soon. Is everything okay? Anything you need?"

As Trish opened the door to leave, Sofie could hear the din of the audience as they filed onto the set. The decision to appear on *The Don Phillips Show* had been a whirlwind decision. Now she wondered why she'd agreed.

When they were alone again Jillian said, "I've been researching your questions."

Finally, some answers. Something I can report to Tía.

"I'm pretty sure Alex's name is really Alex. My sources say he's an agent who's made a name for himself in the DEA. As for his last name…" Jillian shrugged. "It's not Wilson."

Sofie wasn't surprised. She paced the room. "And Jaime Garcia, did you find anything on him?"

"I'm still working on it. Several years ago, when Ramón was shipping pot into Los Angeles, the guy running the distribution was a Colombian named Jaime."

"That's him."

Jillian raised an eyebrow. "Are you sure?"

"Positive. My aunt and I suspected they were connected somehow."

"Well, I can't find anything on him since the spring of '81. He'd made a few enemies by then."

"My cousin Ceci thought Jaime took off with another woman. She was furious when he disappeared."

"Apparently, she wasn't the only one who was frustrated with him. He's probably dead. Or he could have fled to Colombia. And Sofie, there's more—"

A woman bounded into the room, followed by a technician. She looked up from her clipboard and said brightly, "Who's who in here?"

"I'm Jillian."

"I'm Sofie." She wondered if the studio bought clipboards in bulk.

"It's a pleasure to meet you. I'm Denise, and Jerry here is going to mic you."

Jerry went to work while Denise focused her attention on Jillian, noting her clipboard. "The series of articles you bylined in the *LA Times* last month uncovered an important story," she said. "Especially in light of recent events. You've done this before. Right?"

"Yes. Last year I—"

Denise turned to Sofie. "I hear you'd like to be called Sofia Davis for the taping, correct?"

On the edge of panic, Sofie realized for the first time she'd taken her life into her own hands. What would her dad think? Her trip at New Year's had been good, but they were just beginning to strengthen their relationship. Would there be a setback when he saw his daughter telling all on national TV? And Tía didn't even know she'd flown to Chicago. *Yet.*

"I didn't use my real name in Jillian's articles. Do I need to today?"

Denise raised her eyes and furrowed her brow. "You want to use a pseudonym?"

"Can't I just use my first name, Sofia?"

Denise sighed. "Let's go with that," she said, scribbling on her clipboard.

Another step forward into the abyss. There was no turning back, Sofie realized, as the slight tremors began to build.

"We want this to be an enjoyable experience for you," Denise said reassuringly, then glanced at Jillian.

"You know how this goes, Jillian. I need to explain a few things to Sofia, if you don't mind."

Jillian nodded, and Sofie tried to settle comfortably onto the couch cushion.

Denise found a chair, sat down close to Sofie, and leaned in. "There's nothing to be afraid of. Jillian is an investigative reporter." Denise nodded in her direction. "Don't forget you're an expert on this subject too. You've lived the experience. Once you get on the stage, you'll do great. You *can't* give Don a wrong answer. Just be yourself and tell it like it is. And don't be afraid of your emotions, they'll help you connect with the audience."

Denise could be moonlighting as a shrink.

"Now, what's your specific message?"

"Drugs ruin lives, that's a given, but they destroy families too."

"Perfect. Say it with that much conviction and you'll get your point across. What you're doing is important. Don't be shy in front of the cameras." Denise finished writing notes and slipped her pencil into the clipboard. "It's a pleasure to have you join us. You both look beautiful. Don and the audience will love you."

Sofie blushed, hoping Denise was right about her prediction.

"Don's right behind me. We're going to have a great show today."

As much as Sofie looked forward to meeting her first celebrity, she couldn't get Jillian's earlier words out of her mind. *Sofie, there's more...*

CHAPTER TWENTY-SIX

Hot Wind Rising

El Aumento del Viento Caliente
Chicago, Illinois
Wednesday, February 13, 1985

The director shouted, "Cold open—no music, no applause!"

A buzz of activity trickled into silence around the soundstage. Sofie's heart pounded, as if ready to bounce out of her chest, while the bud of a thorny headache settled and advanced toward her temples.

"Three. Two. One. *Roll tape!*"

A technician swiveled one of the large cameras and maneuvered in on Don Phillips. He'd greeted Sofie and Jillian in the green room with an affable smile. Shrouded in severity now, he began his prologue.

"Last week, in a brazen incident that rocked the nation, DEA Special Agent Enrique 'Kiki' Camarena was kidnapped in Mexico. The United States has mounted an unprecedented manhunt to locate him. Our Mexican neighbors say they're doing everything possible to find Special Agent Camarena. The Drug Enforcement Administration contends they haven't done enough. Our government is furious and so are many Americans. Are we already losing the drug war? We'll explore this subject on today's show."

Somber music flooded the set.

The director called, "Cut!"

One of the crew rushed in to work on Phillips' mic.

"Okay. Let's do it one more time," the director instructed.

They ran through the opening again and inserted a commercial.

Shadows moved about the darkened control room, high against the wall.

Monitors and a bank of blinking neon lights gave the booth an extraterrestrial aura.

The staff was a distraction, engaged in silent activity along the edges of the set as Phillips went through Agent Camarena's biography.

Jillian whispered, "Here we go."

A second camera turned towards them, and its small red light came to life.

Phillips, with his signature hair—a thick, silver mane, perfectly combed and parted on the side—looked up from his notes. "Meet Jillian Bond, a reporter with the *Los Angeles Times*, author of the recent investigative series entitled, 'Los Angeles Drowns in Snow.' Jillian has been researching America's drug epidemic and the criminals who supply the trade. Specifically, the Mexican drug lords who not only saturate many of our neighborhoods with drugs and violence, but also bring brutality and corruption to our southern friends."

The audience applauded and Sofie joined in. Jillian smiled, mildly embarrassed.

Waiting for her turn, Sofie gripped the arm of her chair.

She'd deliberately avoided the painful news reports during the past week. Her empty stomach twisted as she listened to Jillian and Phillips discuss the Camarena story. Sofie tried to tell herself she'd given up any hope of finding Alex, but she didn't know how she'd stay sane if she heard he'd been kidnapped. For Kiki's wife, it had to be worse; they'd built a life together. She must be terrified. According to Jillian, Kiki's wife would probably never see her husband alive again. At least they'd had time. Unfortunately, Alex made sure Sofie would never have to worry about being in that position.

Jillian tucked a stray strand of auburn hair behind her ear. She took to the camera so naturally, Sofie wondered if someday she'd move to TV. "My sources at the DEA say they have a few leads, but there's been little cooperation from the Mexicans."

"You're saying the Mexican authorities are corrupt. Is that it?" Phillips asked.

She hesitated. "Here's the thing. There are many individuals in the Mexican government who are hard working and honest. But there are others who are lured by cash. You have to understand the rampant poverty that exists in Mexico. It creates a ripe environment for corruption."

"Let's hear from our audience."

A dozen hands were already raised. Phillips scurried among the crowd who, in reality, sat much closer to the stage than they appeared on television.

An elderly woman rose to receive the microphone. Her much younger double, probably a daughter, sat next to her.

"Thanks, Don. Right is right. I don't believe for a moment poverty creates bad character. Is that what Miss Bond is trying to insinuate?"

"There's a huge difference," Jillian said, "between poverty in America and the destitution that exists in Mexico."

Sofie remembered the children last summer, alongside the road, clothed in tatters, some even naked, as they scrambled in the dirt, looking for coins.

Jillian added, "They also have cultural customs Americans don't understand."

The elderly woman wanted to say something more. But Phillips, holding a stack of notes on three-by-five cards, had already moved to someone else.

At his direction, a young woman stood and described an encounter she'd had at a Mexican airport. Sofie wasn't surprised to hear the authorities had demanded a bribe.

Phillips listened to her story and, hunching his shoulders, he shook his head in disgust.

The young woman grabbed the microphone back, adding, "It's a cesspool down there!"

"That being said," Jillian responded, "there are many wonderful people who live in Mexico. Think of what it must be like for them. We're just the visitors."

"Good insight, Ms. Bond." Phillips replied.

The large white and black camera pulled back and repositioned on Sofie.

"Meet Sofia," Phillips said. "We aren't giving you her last name at her request. She's related to a powerful Mexican drug family and has a close connection to the situation. In the past year, Sofia has spent time living within their world."

Sofie heard the audience's collective *"Ooh"* and tried to smile, wondering if their reaction was shock, contempt, or a mixture of both.

Phillips shuffled through the note cards. "Sofia, you were born in California, correct?"

She nodded.

Denise anxiously mouthed "speak" from the sidelines.

"Y—yes." Sofie couldn't find anything to do with her hands so she kept them folded in her lap. "My mom was born in Mexico. On the family farm —or rancho—by the Pacific coast."

"So your family started out as farmers?"

"My family's been farming that land for generations."

Dismissing Sofie and Jillian, Phillips turned to the camera. "After this message, we'll learn how Sofia's family went from farmers to drug lords. Stay with us."

Staff swarmed the stage, including the stylist, who rushed to Jillian, holding a box of supplies. Denise knelt next to Sofie, adjusting the chair and giving her pointers.

"Use your voice. This is a dialogue. There's nothing to be afraid of. Speak up like you did in the green room."

After the director ushered the next segment in, Phillips continued to center on Sofie. "Today we're exploring the drug war in Mexico and asking this question: Can it be won? We're here with Sofia. You grew up there, correct?"

"I visited as a child and moved there when I was eleven. I returned to live with my dad when I was fifteen, so I could attend high school in Northern California. But I spent a few weeks in Mexico each summer until I went to college."

"When was the last time you've visited?"

"Late last spring, after I graduated. When I returned, things were… different."

"How had the situation changed?"

"My uncle died and my cousin Ramón, being the oldest male in the family, was in control."

Though Phillips' scripted temperament was amiable, Sofie felt politely skewered.

"What else?"

Don't worry about the host. Just keep going.

"Well, my family had lived in the traditional ranch house for almost a century. Ramón built a large compound along the beach and moved the family there a few years ago."

"How big is the ranch?"

"I'm not exactly sure. More than a thousand acres."

Phillips studied his notes. "Your cousin is Ramón Mendoza, correct?"

"Yes."

Before she could say anything more, Phillips turned away from the stage. "Ramón Mendóza and his brothers started out growing marijuana on their ranch. Controlling its distribution all the way into California, they quickly became a prominent drug cartel. Acapulco, a haven of the wealthy for decades, became his playground.

"Tell us about it, Sofia."

She tried to compile a coherent answer. "Before my uncle died, we had a modest second home there." The words rushed past her lips. "Ramón bought another, larger piece of property above the bay and opened an office in the city. There were new cars, limousines and servants." She took a breath. "It had become a different life—my prosperous, but quaint Mexican family was thoroughly modernized, with the rest of the world at their fingertips."

"Was it all sex, drugs, and rock and roll?" Don smirked.

The crowd erupted with laughter.

"It... It wasn't like that. Sure, we liked hanging out in clubs. But you're making it sound..."

"You mentioned the houses and cars. What about all the cash?"

"I didn't see much cash. Everything was just taken care of."

A middle-aged man from the audience stood and Don gave him the mic. "How does it feel? Knowing all this wealth came from drugs?" he sneered.

"I assumed Ramón did well with his businesses. I didn't realize where the money came from." *Not that I asked many questions,* Sofie thought, hoping the camera didn't register the flush of embarrassment she felt rising on her face.

Murmurs of the audience's skepticism wafted onto the stage.

"Sofia has been investigated by the DEA and cleared," Jillian added.

"Ramón told me he was winding down the farming enterprise and had moved into the import-export business. I believed him."

Phillips seemed pleased. "We'll get to that in a minute." During the commercial break, he moved to the sidelines and huddled with one of the producers.

Jillian leaned in close. "You're doing great."

Sofie sent her a weak smile, and whispered, "Yeah, sure. I feel like I'm back on the schoolyard, playing dodge ball."

After a few minutes, Phillips returned and the taping resumed. He asked sympathetically, "How are you doing?"

The swiveling camera, with its tiny, ominous red eye, refocused on Sofie.

"Good."

"This isn't the first time you've spoken publicly about your family?"

"I did an interview with Jillian last month."

While Sofie struggled to concentrate on Phillips and his questions, she noticed two giant screens being quietly wheeled into position on the edges of the set. She wondered if they planned to show pictures of her family, and if so, where they'd come from.

"What made you decide to share your family's story?"

"Well…" It felt as if all eyes were centered on her, and Sofie wondered how many in the audience were thinking, *Traitor!* "I talked it over with my tía—my aunt—and we decided if I spoke out, it might help people understand how devastating drugs and addiction can be, not—"

"Is the caller there? Go ahead."

A woman's stern voice boomed onto the soundstage. "How old is this young lady?"

Phillips checked his notes. "Twenty-three."

"Twenty-four. I just had a birthday."

"She's old enough to know better. How could she not know what went on in her family?"

"While my cousins built this business, I was a college student in California."

"Do you mean to say you never had an inkling?" Phillips sounded vaguely smug.

"I didn't!" Sofie protested.

"The folks gathered here, and at home, find it difficult to believe you didn't realize what was going on all around you." Phillips' frown looked skeptical.

"Really, I didn't," she said.

The caller replied, "Then she must have been on drugs herself. Where are her parents? Who are they? Are they drug dealers too?"

"Hold on," Phillips said to the caller. "What about your father and mother?"

"My dad is a doctor in California. Both of his parents are from Michigan. My mom had cancer. She died when I was twelve."

"We're sorry to hear that." Phillips' voice was almost convincingly sincere. "*When did you* discover your family was involved in drug trafficking?"

"Last summer. One of my cousins clued me in. I'd been concerned about him…"

Phillips seemed intrigued. "Tell us more."

"That's my point. Addiction is sneaky. Members of my own family have become addicts and we didn't realize it until… Well, sometimes you don't find out until it's too late."

"You live here in the U.S. now, and have a legitimate job?"

"Yes. I've never had an *illegitimate* one."

Several people in the audience chuckled.

"You were never arrested, correct?"

"No. Yes. I mean I've never been arrested."

This isn't a talk show. It's an interrogation.

"Are you drug-free?"

"Years ago, I experimented a little, *like most of my peers.*" Sofie steered the questioning to her message. "But I never got involved and was glad I didn't when I began to see what drugs did to the people around me. Drugs not only destroy the people who use them, they leave a trail of devastation in their families too."

"What about Ramón Mendoza? Did you ever see him doing drugs?"

"Never. He made it very clear he was totally against them. That's why it was such a shock."

"Did you ever see him ingest any mind-altering substance?"

Sofie shrugged. "Alcohol."

The audience laughed.

"Someone very close to you died from a drug overdose, correct?"

"My cousin, who was also my best friend, overdosed on a mixture of cocaine and heroin. Three years ago, in California."

Phillips studied his notes and raised the microphone. "I'm confused. Are you talking about Ramón's brother? One of the men killed in the raid?"

"Gabriel?" Sofie asked. "He's the only survivor… Besides me, I guess. We got him into rehab, but he moved back to Mexico. I don't know exactly where he is."

Jillian interjected, "There's—"

"We'll be back in just a moment."

Phillips vanished and the stylists rushed the stage. Jillian sat silent during the break, fidgeting with her wedding ring. Sofie let Rachel powder her face and wondered what Jillian had been trying to say. She didn't have time to ask before the cameras rolled again.

"Today, we're exploring Mexico's involvement in the American drug war. Sofía, what's your impression of the Colombians you came in contact with while you were in Mexico?"

"I didn't meet any Colombians in Mexico."

"So you didn't meet any Colombians in Mexico. Let me get this straight." Phillips sifted through his notes. "What about in California? Did you meet any there?"

Sofie tried to stay ahead of Phillips and his questions, but some of them were bewildering. Jaime had been the only Colombian she'd ever met, and she didn't have enough information to unravel those tangled strands on national TV. So, against the director's orders, Sofie silently shook her head.

It was a relief when Phillips finally returned his attention to Jillian. "Let's get back to Ms. Bond. I believe we can all agree there's a drug epidemic in our country. Can the drug war be won?"

"Sometimes, I have my doubts. As long as there's a market for drugs in the United States, there will be sources willing to supply that demand."

"Caller, are you there?"

Another woman added her critique, "If we weren't inundated with the scourge of drugs from the outside, millions of our children wouldn't be tempted and addicted. We need to build a fence along our border to keep undesirables and their filth out of our country."

Jillian answered. "Most large drug shipments don't come in over the border. They're being delivered by planes and boats to airports and docks throughout the United States."

Answering a barrage of Phillips' questions, Jillian explained to the audience the Caribbean crackdown and the emerging Colombia-Mexico connection.

Phillips' mouth became a firm line. "Then we aren't winning the drug war, are we?" The question seemed rhetorical.

Jillian shifted in her chair and quoted grim statistics. "Mexico supplies most of the heroin and marijuana that comes into the U.S."

The audience buzzed, reacting with a mixture of disbelief and anger.

Heroin? Sofie imagined the scene, three years ago last month, in the Sepulveda Boulevard hotel room, where the maid found Ceci, dead, with a needle in her arm. *No. There can't be a connection.*

"Assisting—some in our government believe orchestrating—this deadly dance is the widespread corruption among Mexican officials. Unfortunately, drugs have become the nation's largest industry." Jillian said. "The Mexicans, under intense pressure from the United States, have doubled their efforts to eradicate these crops."

"These drug cartels, how do they operate?" Phillips asked.

Jillian swallowed a sip of water. "They create personal militias that oftentimes outman and outgun local law enforcement. And they aren't necessarily hated. They pump cash into an economy where inflation is rising and the minimum wage is two dollars a day."

Phillips glanced at Sofie and smiled. "To many of our viewers, it appears these criminals throw obscene amounts of cash around. As we can see by the exploding wealth of Sofia's family. Let's talk more about the Mendoza-Cali connection."

"First, I should back up a little," Jillian said. "It appears Ramón Mendoza and his brothers didn't venture into marijuana cultivation until their father's health declined and Ramón took the reins. Within a few years, the Mendoza family had a sizable operation. In '80, the Mendoza plantation was raided and burned by the Mexican authorities on a tip they'd received from the DEA. Ramón Mendoza then decided to explore a less costly and labor intensive avenue—transporting cocaine. Soon after, Ramón secured an introduction to Humberto Torres, a kingpin in the Cali organization."

Before she met Jillian, Sofie had never even heard of the Cali cartel or Humberto Torres.

"I'll assume the Calis are as violent as the Medellíns."

"Not necessarily. However, all of these cartels and drug lords, even the Mexicans who have Kiki Camarena as we speak, are known to exact monstrous punishments."

"The Mexican government claims the DEA entered their country to raid the Mendoza property last summer. We'll explore that story in a moment."

Jillian gave Sofie a sympathetic smile as if to say, *"You're up next."*

It felt like a warning: *"They're closing in."*

"We're back," Phillips said, "speaking to Jillian Bond, an investigative reporter with the *Los Angeles Times*, and Sofia, who is related to a Mexican drug family in Acapulco. They're giving us a window into the inner workings of that world."

Phillips turned to the audience. "How do you feel about what you've heard?" He moved up the stairs toward a balding man in a black pullover sweater and gave him the mic.

"I think the drug war is a waste of time and resources," he said. "The money should be spent here at home on education. Then, let the individual decide. If they're dumb enough to do dope, let them bear the consequences."

"Right." Phillips mumbled into the microphone and turned toward the stage. "Sofia. Last summer, while you were visiting your family in Mexico, weren't you involved in a raid on the family ranch?"

Jillian touched Sofie's arm, indicating she'd field this question.

"Sofie was there, but she came upon the situation accidentally. I've been in contact with the DEA, and they've determined Sofia had no criminal involvement with the family."

"During the operation, in an unprecedented move, the DEA elected to notify the Mexican authorities *after* the fact. Why?"

"We are entering the muddy world of Narco Politics here, Don. The DEA continually denies any involvement in the raid whatsoever. They claim this was an attack by another, competing drug cartel."

Really? Sofie wondered why the DEA needed to deny being there that afternoon.

"That being said," Jillian continued, "there's reason to believe the Mexican authorities routinely tip off the drug lords before any raid. In this case, it's estimated the Cali cartel made a delivery of four-hundred twenty five kilos to Mendoza's rural warehouse. That's about seventeen million street dollars' worth of cocaine. Whoever is responsible for the Mendoza raid, there is good reason to believe that shipment never made it into the United States—"

Sofie had watched Dean's men emptying the warehouse, stacking dozens of cloth bundles in the yard. From the airfield, she'd seen the smoke rising near the river. Yes, it was a relief to know all of that coke hadn't made it into the States.

Phillips broke in. "We'll explain what happened that afternoon in a moment."

The stylists rushed in and did their magic while a technician inserted a commercial into the taping.

Afterwards, Phillips moved from the production huddle and lifted his mic.

"We're back, talking about Ramón Mendoza and his brothers, who were killed last July during the gunfight on their Mexican ranch." Phillips checked his notes again. "They say one brother might be unaccounted for."

Who? Sofie wondered.

"The youngest Mendoza brother, Gabriel, was wounded. He was airlifted to an American hospital and has recovered," Jillian answered.

Phillips studied his notes.

Jillian's face appeared to melt and an odd mixture of irritation and regret settled in her expression.

Sofie realized she'd missed something in the exchange.

With an apologetic shake of her head, Jillian closed her eyes.

"Sofia, you seem surprised." Phillips said.

"I don't kn—"

"It's the contention of the Mexican government that one of the brothers, Felipe, is missing," Jillian explained. "They say his body hasn't been recovered. Sources in the DEA's Mexico City office disagree."

What? Felipe couldn't still be alive after the carnage Sofie witnessed. *Had Tía heard this story?*

Jillian didn't offer any more information.

Sofie couldn't speak.

Phillips could. "Ramón Mendoza and his cartel had quite an operation. Their tentacles stretched all the way into the United States."

Sofie could only follow bits of the continuing conversation. Phillips' voice became muted as the bombshell continued to ring in Sofie's ears.

No one in the family had mentioned Felipe. Gabriel and Tía believed Ramón and the rest of the boys were gone.

"In '80, the Mendoza family shipped marijuana to their warehouses in Los Angeles for distribution throughout the Western States," Jillian said.

If Tía had heard anything different, she would have told me.

Unable to look at Jillian, Sofie stared straight ahead and watched Phillips' spellbound audience, trying to decipher this new information.

If Felipe was alive, he had to be in Mexico. He had nowhere else to go.

"Not only do we have the Camarena kidnapping, we've uncovered an earlier incident in Texas," Phillips said.

The morning before that horrible afternoon, when I stopped by the compound, I searched for Felipe and couldn't find him. I don't remember seeing him that day at all.

"This is a story that exposes the truly vicious nature of Ramón Mendoza."

And why, why, did Jillian wait to tell me in front of the cameras? It couldn't be deliberate. Was this what she was talking about earlier in the green room when she'd said, 'There's more'?

"The story didn't make it beyond the local news at the time. Recently, the DEA has released more information and it points out the atrocities these Mexican drug lords are capable of in their efforts to exact revenge."

Focus! I can't get distracted by Felipe now. There'll be plenty of time to get the details from Jillian later.

"Nicholas Locklear, a Special Agent with the DEA, infiltrated the Mendoza family's Los Angeles operation. Soon, he worked his way up the ladder and south to the family's marijuana plantation in Mexico. Ms. Bond, tell us more."

"Nick—"

Sofie's world spun off its axis. *Nick Locklear. Nick?*

Could he be Alex's Nick? She felt goosebumps skitter across her skin as she blindly stumbled into a gaping hole of confusion.

During the original interviews, when she asked Jillian about a Nick, Sofie received a blank stare. What other revelations had Jillian been hiding?

Jillian took a deep breath. "Agent Locklear worked on the assignment for some time. Eventually, he had a chance to infiltrate the family and, according to the DEA, the information he collected was invaluable. When the DEA contacted the authorities in Mexico City to coordinate a raid against the plantation, someone in Mexico gave Ramón Mendoza a tip— exposing Agent Locklear. Through counterintelligence, he made it back to the United States safely. However, within a few months—"

"Larry," Phillips said, "Cue the picture for our audience and the folks at home. That's good."

The photo projected onto the screen was disorienting at first. Sofie could only make out a light brown sedan. She had to study the image to determine whether the shot was from the front or the rear of the car. Two strips of red taillights helped her zero in the perspective. A long braid of black hair obscured the license plate and bisected the bumper. For a split second Sofie couldn't decide if the hair belonged to an animal or a human.

Sofie froze.

Jillian reached for her arm and said under her breath, "Oh, Sofie, I'm so sorry. I had no idea they were going to do this."

"On March 23, 1981, at a printing business located in an industrial section of El Paso, Texas, an employee, arriving early, discovered Special Agent Locklear's car in their parking lot. His body was found in the back seat. He'd been decapitated. His head had been placed in the trunk. His distinctive ponytail was left exposed, sending a sinister message to the United States Drug Enforcement Administration."

The flash of a stabbing headache crippled her chaotic thoughts. Sofie recognized the numbing sensation that had once enveloped her skin; her body was again rebuilding the layer of protection she'd spent so many months trying to shed.

Yeah. Don't worry, they'd all said, everything will be fine.

A painful knot materialized in the base of Sofie's throat and swelled. Unable to catch an even breath, she couldn't choke back the uncontrollable sobs.

Jillian leapt from her chair and pulled Sofie into her arms.

From somewhere beyond her cocoon Sofie heard the director yell, "Cut!"

CHAPTER TWENTY-SEVEN
Big Creek Cracks

Arroyo Grande Grietas
Tuesday, February 26, 1985

Leaning against the wall of the entryway, Alex removed his muddy boots before he stepped onto his mom's new, white carpet. "No shoes" was a rule she'd adopted when she'd had it installed, replacing the practical green pile that had withstood years of ranch life. He rubbed his cramped toes through dusty socks and wondered what made his mom finally decide to redecorate, something she'd threatened to do for years.

"Mom!" Alex called on his way to the kitchen. "Do I have any mail?"

A ruckus filtered in from the laundry room. The agitation of the washing machine competed with the braces of his dad's overalls, clanking along the dryer's drum. It stopped when he heard the machine open.

His mom appeared from behind the doorway. "There's a stack of stuff by the phone. I'll be out in a sec."

Alex shuffled through his mail at the breakfast counter and found a few bills, junk, and an envelope from his Santa Monica landlord. A check for his security deposit slipped from the folds of a short note, thanking him for leaving the place so clean.

He hadn't spent a night there in months. After the Mexico operation, he'd returned to his parent's home for a visit as promised and decided to stay.

"No matter how much you love the work, little by little, it burns you up," a shrewd agent once told him, in a Panamanian bar. Alex knew the truth of these words.

Dean mentioned Sofie moved back to LA, following her original plan.

Alex had given her his number. Each week, he'd checked, hoping she'd call. She didn't, and he knew she never would.

Still, Alex hesitated to give up his place, thinking someday they might meet up and she'd be able to forgive him. Maybe then, they could try again. As yesterday stretched further into the distance, he realized how crazy the idea was. Finally, in October, he'd driven his truck down, packed up his furniture and the rest of his shit, and moved into the empty foreman's house on the ranch.

He slipped the check into his wallet and stuffed it into the back pocket of his faded Levi's, hoping he'd have time to get to the bank on Friday.

Mom came into the kitchen holding a basket of folded clothes.

"Where's Dad?" She set the laundry down in the family room and changed the channel on the TV.

"He's working on the well."

Ranching was tedious work at seventeen. These days, he'd rather have an uneventful life instead of what he'd seen out in the "real" world. He struggled to fit into his new routine, sidestepping cow pies instead of hunting drug thugs.

Alex didn't feel it right now, but he thought the adrenaline junkie that lived in his personality might eventually resurface, and he would return to begin a post-DEA life in the city. Possibly in local law enforcement or private investigation.

His parents seemed glad to have him back. Alex knew better than anyone it was nice to have another pair of capable hands around the ranch. Sometimes, through the corner of his eye, he caught their long stares. If they wondered what happened to the idealistic man he'd once been, Alex couldn't give them an explanation.

"Have you eaten? Make yourself a sandwich. There's roast chicken from last night in the fridge." Retrieving the basket, his mother vanished down the hall toward the bedrooms.

Charlie the Tuna got a lesson in good taste from his fishy friend on television, while Alex bent down and searched the refrigerator shelves for the mayonnaise.

"Meet Sofia. At her request we aren't giving you her last name. She's related to a powerful Mexican drug family…"

Alex's head popped over the refrigerator door. A middle-aged man with a generous shock of white hair spoke.

It can't be. Sofie wouldn't expose herself and her family on camera.

But she had.

He shut the refrigerator in disbelief and moved to the TV. Sofie sat next to another woman on the stage, a redhead Alex didn't recognize.

Waves of guilt quickened his pulse. Desire too. Fear began to dawn more slowly, sending warning sirens throughout his brain.

Fuck. Sofie shouldn't be taking this risk.

Time didn't lessen the longing he felt seeing her again.

Fuck.

She'd cut her hair, but she still sizzled, wearing a red dress that made her appear older than she was. It climbed up her leg as she sat, exposing a bit of her silky thigh. Alex felt the memory of her skin, soft beneath his fingers, as heat rocked through every fiber of his being.

He couldn't say for certain, but it looked like the gold hoops dangling from her ears were the ones he'd bought her in Acapulco.

Was it a sign?

Captured by the television, Alex used his hand to find the coffee table. He sat down, his elbows on his knees, and closing in on the set, inhaled Sofie in.

His whole body slumped in despair, layered with worry. Why was she doing this? Didn't she realize the danger she'd put herself in? He couldn't call or go to her. After what they'd been through, she'd throw him out of her apartment.

Sofie seemed to be unsure of herself at first, answering the host's questions with hesitation. Then, after what seemed to be a never-ending commercial, she found her stride as she shared the basics of her family history.

Alex listened to the audience's comments and wanted to rescue her from their ridicule. Sofie fielded their disdain until the redhead who sat next to her piped in, "*Sofia has been thoroughly investigated by the DEA and cleared.*"

Her words didn't surprise Alex. The "suits" in Washington, well aware they were losing the war, had recently begun to open their doors, divulging non-critical information. Then, when Kiki Camarena was abducted, and the Mexican authorities clammed up and burrowed in, the notoriously silent DEA dropped all of their normal agency protocols.

Kiki was kidnapped just weeks ago. Nick in 1981. What had the agency accomplished between four years and the loss of two good men? Like Nick, Kiki had kids. He was just a regular guy, dedicated to noble work, on his way to meet his wife for lunch. Only a fool believed Kiki would be found alive. If he'd been lucky, his death was quick and painless. Luck proved elusive in their business, more difficult to find than the vermin they hunted. Alex shuddered, a new strain of vermin would be looking for Sofie soon.

Alex never thought he'd see Sofie again, and was astonished when the program moved to a commercial. It made him dizzy. *Come back to me.*

Soon, the lovely Sofie returned to the screen with more of her story. The audience attacked and Alex watched Sofie publicly backtrack out of her Mexican life, wondering what this would cost her emotionally.

Sofie made her pitch. The reason, Alex assumed, she'd decided to present herself to this circus. She thought she could save others from her family's heartache. Sofie had to be crazy to think she was doing anything except putting herself in danger.

This was insane. Ramón Mendoza and his brothers might be eliminated, but the Calis were an emerging cartel. Humberto Torres—and others in the organization—wouldn't like the publicity. Exposing herself on television certified she needed protection.

One of Alex's many regrets was the loss of Humberto Torres and his skinny sidekick, whisked away by a Cali helicopter just before the team's arrival. Many nights, when Alex didn't lay in bed riddled with guilt over Sofie, he thought about Torres' toady freak and the badgering sense that he somehow fit into the larger picture.

But how?

The camera moved from Sofie and focused on the redhead, who the host referred to as "Ms. Bond." He asked if the drug war could be won.

Alex wished he had the microphone so he could weigh in with his thoughts on the subject. The woman seemed to be doing an admirable job of getting the point across. Ms. Bond explained the intricacies of the Colombians and Mexican corruption. She'd done her homework and had a decent bead on well-sourced information. Alex wondered if she'd been in contact with Dean.

Did Sofie know Alex, exhausted and spent, had retired?

"The Mexican government claims the DEA entered their country to raid the Mendoza property last summer without their permission. We'll explore that story in a moment."

Furrowing his brow, Alex stood and paced the room. Fortunately, the "suits" in Washington held firm in their denial. He found it hard to imagine Sofie agreed to discuss the details of the bust on camera. Cali cocaine had disappeared that afternoon. Yes, they'd been paid for the dope, but they wouldn't like a Mendoza, *any* Mendoza, talking about it.

Back in front of the TV, he rested his head in his hands and listened to Ms. Bond exonerate Sofie's involvement.

Alex was responsible for this mess. More *ifs* to add to his collection. *If* he'd never kissed Sofie that night on the beach, they wouldn't have gotten involved. *If* he could have stayed away from her, she would have been in Acapulco that day, where she belonged, and would not have shown up at the ranch. He'd failed to protect her then. This time he had to make sure she'd be safe. How could he provide it without her knowledge?

He squeezed his eyes shut and tried to think.

Mom set the laundry basket on the counter behind him. "Did you find your mail?" she asked, coming over to join him in front of the television. "Why doesn't my hair ever look like that?"

Alex opened his eyes. A woman selling shampoo, smiled as her blonde hair floated across the screen.

"Are you okay?" Mom asked, concerned.

The host's face returned.

"Who's this guy?"

"You've never seen him before? It's Don Phillips."

"So this is the famous talk show host," Alex said without enthusiasm.

"What's up, Alex? You're upset."

"They're talking about the Camarena case and the situation down in Mexico."

"Oh. I've been following the story on the news." Putting her hand to her chest, she took a step backward and sank to the coffee table. She reached for Alex and pulled him down next to her. "Did they find him?"

"No. And they won't. Not alive anyway."

"Do they know who did this?"

"A drug lord named Felix Gallardo probably organized the hit. The Mexicans are protecting him."

Alex clenched his fingers in fury, tempted to break his retirement and make another trip south of the border. Then again, unfinished business, in this business, was like the Mississippi, ever flowing, wide and deep.

"The shit part is Camarena had just been reassigned to Washington."

His mom put her hand on his arm. "I'm so thankful you're out of there."

Nick and Kiki pulled a deadly draw. Alex retired before the bastards caught up with him. That didn't keep the sour burn of survivor's guilt from chewing at his gut.

Alex's mom knew the basics. The last job—Mexico. A success. There had been an innocent girl involved named Sofie and it got complicated.

"The redhead apparently is a reporter from the *LA Times*."

The camera pulled back and took in the stage.

"And the other girl… It's her."

The only noise in the house was the washer and dryer, hard at work, filtering in from the laundry room, and the sound coming from the TV. Alex watched Sofie's face pale while Ms. Bond talked about the raid.

"I don't know what Sofie thinks she's doing. She shouldn't be answering questions on TV. There are people out there who'll want to shut her up."

When Phillips asked another question the camera zoomed in on Sofie.

"She's beautiful, Alex," his mom whispered.

Yes, she is. "I know."

"You should call her."

"I can't help that I love her. But I can't."

That didn't mean he couldn't make sure she was safe.

He realized Phillips and Ms. Bond were talking about Felipe and the speculation he was still alive.

Alex watched Sofie's face crumple with confusion, wishing she didn't have to hear this news with a camera bearing down, eager for her reaction. In a perfect world, he would have been the one to tell her, hold her, help her sort out all the facts.

"Not only do we have the Camarena kidnapping, we've uncovered an earlier incident in Texas."

This Phillips guy is just a wealth of information, Alex thought sarcastically. And Ms. Bond had to be digging deep to discover Nick's murder and pass it along to the producers. Alex wondered if Sofie would make the connection.

Had she already?

Maybe she'd worn the earrings as a peace offering that said, "Now, I understand".

Apparently not. Sofie shifted in her seat and Alex detected a flash of bewilderment followed by anguish.

"…Cue the picture for the audience at home."

"What the fuck?"

Sofie can't know what's coming. After what she'd gone through, no way would she stay on the stage. Alex found himself glued to the TV, terrified of her reaction.

Nick's government-issued sedan flashed onto the screen while Don

Phillips relayed the gory details.

Mom gasped.

Alex had seen the picture only once. Then, he'd turned away in a rage, punching a succession of holes into the wall. Furious again, he balled his fists and prayed Nick's widow, Danielle, wasn't watching—and hoped to God, his boys were still at school. Alex groaned as he imagined the photo invading their living room.

"Nick was my partner. My best friend."

Mom's voice broke. "I'm so sorry," she said, choking back tears.

The picture lingered for its dramatic effect. Alex held his breath, captured, until finally, the camera panned the stage and zeroed in on Sofie. He'd seen this fractured expression on her face before. He'd never wanted to see it again—the haunted haze in her startlingly green eyes, her face; naked pain, striped by tears and shattered with grief.

Sofie collapsed into sobs. He yearned to be there to console her, then realized this spectacle had probably been taped weeks ago.

Ms. Bond moved in to help. The show abruptly cut to a commercial. The construction of some New York adman's version of an ideal life played on the screen, selling America something.

Angry and disgusted, Alex brushed past his mother on his way out the door.

"Where are you going?"

"I need to call Dean."

CHAPTER TWENTY-EIGHT

An Angel's Education

Educación de un Angel
Saturday, March 23, 1985

UCLA's campus had hardly changed in a year. It felt good to be back on territory Sofie once called home; that was one reason she'd agreed to another airing of her family's story. The location, Dodd Hall, was a bonus. She'd spent hours taking notes under this roof.

Sofie told herself speaking in public would be easier this time. No cameras, no producers, and—Jillian *promised*—no awful surprises. But apprehension, a disorienting feeling she'd tried to push away during lunch, settled in and made her queasy.

The wooden door of the toilet stall slammed behind her. Turning on the faucet, a splash of water echoed through the empty restroom. She used her palm to press foamy, lime-green soap from the dispenser and panicked, wondering what she was doing here this afternoon.

I'm making the best of a bad situation.

She grabbed a handful of paper towels from the metal box attached to the wall and wiped her hands. Her stomach still churned, so she stuffed a wad of extras into her purse. Just in case.

Jillian opened the door as Sofie tucked in her blouse, adjusting it over her black pants.

"There you are. I've been looking for you."

Sofie tried to smile and zipped up her purse.

"You're pale," Jillian said, touching Sofie's arm, "and shaking. I noticed you got up and disappeared at the restaurant, twice. Are you sick?"

"I'm fine." Sofie glanced down at the worn linoleum.

"Please, don't be nervous."

Slumping against one of the sinks, Sofie sighed. "I did okay this morning. Now, I can't stop thinking about what happened during the Phillips taping. It was *horrible*."

"This afternoon will be different."

Sofie wanted to believe Jillian. A few weeks ago, she'd shown up at Sofie's door with what seemed like a thousand sincere apologies, including a few tears—all Jillian's—asking Sofie to please try again.

"You talked to your aunt, right? You said she supports what you're doing." Jillian studied her, concerned. "Has anything changed?"

Tía's continuing encouragement meant everything. After Tía saw her on TV, she'd said, "I'm so proud of you, mija." It felt a tiny bit better to hear the words, and they provided some consolation after the disaster of that day.

However, Sofie's dad and her cousin, Rich, called, concerned about her safety after they'd seen the show. She tried to reassure them both. The Colombians couldn't be interested in her, because she didn't know anything about their activities. Except for Jaime, she'd never even met one.

"Remember, this time it isn't just us. It's gonna be a whole panel." Jillian listed them off on her fingers. "Two investigative reporters—one from the *New York Times*, the other from the *Arizona Republic*. My editor, Charlene, will do the moderating, and then there's you and me. We'll all answer questions from the audience. And here's the thing: It's a select group, reporters from newspapers all over the country and journalism students here on campus."

"Sounds like a lot of people to me," Sofie said, detecting a tendril of jasmine in Jillian's flowery perfume.

"The audience won't be much bigger than the one in Chicago. They'll be nice; I swear. Anyway, I think Tony Smith will be doing most of the talking." She grinned and marked number six by raising her thumb. "I'm kinda proud of myself. The guy isn't my first—or second—choice, but I got the DEA to send an agent, and that's a real accomplishment."

Originally, Jillian told her the keynote speaker would be an *unnamed* agent in the Drug Enforcement Administration. Jillian had been excited by the possibility of meeting Dean—or Alex—characterizing him as someone who'd actually been "in the trenches."

The opportunity to see Alex again overshadowed any anti-drug message Sofie wanted to send. Kiki Camarena's horribly tortured body had been found a few weeks ago, and the news added to the growing dread she'd felt since before the Phillips taping. Had Alex gone back to Mexico? Had his enemies caught up with him and murdered him too? Sofie shuddered.

For days, she'd prayed the speaker would be Alex, and was disappointed when Jillian called to say the agency would send a public liaison—a guy from Washington named Tony Smith.

"I realize I'm being a pest. But have you heard *anything* about Alex?" Sofie asked.

"You're not bugging me. I just wish I had some news for you."

It was difficult to admit, but Sofie didn't consider *The Don Phillips Show* a total disaster. Once she'd been able to calm down and process the information, much of what had happened last summer began to make sense. In a convoluted way, she realized Alex shared a lot in the short time they'd spent together.

"Here's the thing." Jillian shrugged. "Soon after Kiki's kidnapping my source quit talking to me. I'm not sure what happened. She just clammed up and began to refer me to the Washington office."

Jillian fished a brush from her purse and began combing her auburn hair, speaking to Sofie in the mirror. "Seriously, I'm trying my best. But the guys in D.C. won't talk. They only want to discuss the Camarena situation." She slipped the brush back into her purse and turned. "Charlene said she is taking us all to dinner tonight. I'll make sure we get private time with Tony. Maybe he *can't* tell us where Alex is, but this Smith guy can surely tell us *something.*"

Sofie nodded, confident Jillian would follow through.

Finally—and Sofie considered this a personal milestone—she'd made peace with Alex and their original pact. No complications had been unrealistic from the beginning. She should have listened to her heart; she'd never been the type who could handle intimacy without expectations.

And yes, even though she was committed to getting her message out, there was another, more important reason that propelled her to come today. Jillian and her connections were Sofie's only link to Alex's world, and she desperately needed to know if he was alive and safe.

Sofie followed Jillian into the anteroom behind the lecture hall where the panel waited. The reporter from Arizona hadn't been able to make it in time for lunch and Jillian was finishing up the introductions when Charlene escorted another man through the door.

294

"I found our keynote speaker wandering the halls," Charlene joked. "Meet Tony Smith, Special Agent with the Drug Enforcement Administration."

"This is a huge campus," Tony Smith grumbled, his brows narrowing. Apparently, he didn't find Charlene's introduction very funny. Not at all.

If first impressions counted, Sofie wasn't wowed.

Jillian turned and visibly sized up the agent, sending Sofie a glance that said, *Huh?*

Statuesque, though not an Amazon, Jillian rose at least five inches above Agent Smith. The first time Sofie met Alex, she'd made an assessment and, in retrospect, he fit an agent's stereotype: a handsome—though highly irritating—California surfer boy with an impeccable build. Tony's body wasn't bad either. For a gnome.

"My plane was delayed," Agent Smith whined. "Then baggage claim was slow. The traffic was stagnant all the way up from the airport. People who live in this town are crazy. I don't know how you put up with this every day."

Looking at Sofie, Jillian raised an eyebrow.

While Charlene showed him where to stash his coat, Jillian leaned in and whispered, "What's this guy bitching about? I've been on the Washington Beltway and, believe me, it's no picnic."

Charlene glared at Jillian, checked her watch, and did her best to calm Agent Smith's agitation.

When she introduced him around the room, Sofie noticed the graying edges of his balding hair, deciding he was in his mid-forties. Having probably spent most of his career in Washington, stuck in traffic, it seemed likely Tony had never even heard of Alex. Her heart sank.

Sofie listened as the lecture hall began to fill on the other side of the closed door and realized Agent Smith was already a dud.

We're off to a great start.

❧

Promptly at two, Charlene escorted Sofie and the rest of the panel to the dais. Sofie took the seat between Tony and Jillian, behind the name-tent marked only *Sofia*.

Thanks Jillian, you remembered.

Jillian smiled and squeezed her hand.

Swallowing, Sofie tried to ignore the lunch that seemed to wait at the base of her throat. Beneath a blue, full-length tablecloth, Sofie gently nudged her purse with her foot, making sure it stayed nearby, hoping she wouldn't embarrass herself by diving under the table, making a mad scramble for the paper towels she'd stuffed inside.

Charlene tapped the microphone. When the polite din of the audience settled into silence, she said, "We're really happy you could join us today."

She made the introductions. Pertinent details of biographies were described. Expertise noted.

Yeah, yeah, yeah. Sofie had been through this before.

While the audience paid rapt attention to the panel, Sofie worked up a smile and added her particulars.

As predicted, Mr. Smith had nothing enlightened to say. Sofie began to consider herself the panel's expert.

No one here, except for me, knows what it's like living within the drug world.

She scrutinized the crowd and felt her anxiety build. Thankfully, the lecture hall was only two-thirds full.

In an effort to calm herself, she studied the audience. It worked. Her pulse began to slow, and she felt her breathing even out as she remembered how many afternoons she'd sat in those well-worn seats and counted the squares of the dotted ceiling tiles, waiting for a professor to arrive.

Sofie would be the one who imparted the wisdom this afternoon. How many would be receptive?

The crowd could easily be divided into two camps. Many wore the fresh, eager faces of undergraduates. She remembered when she felt fresh and eager too. Before life whipped the crap out of her and left her battered and bruised. The healing had been slow to arrive, *but it had.*

Surprising herself with the revelation, Sofie wondered where she'd be in a year.

The Newsbees, a term Jillian used to describe the journalism students, leaned out of their seats and scribbled away. The older camp, the hardened reporters, weren't so diligent with their pens. They'd apparently heard it all before.

Sofie half-listened to the New Yorker's viewpoint and continued to evaluate the crowd. In the back of the room, a door opened and a student slipped into a chair along the upper aisle. He slumped down into his seat. Figuring he planned to nap his way through the afternoon, she pegged him as a slacker.

She had seen plenty of them around campus in her time, those lucky kids smart enough to get accepted to a prestigious school with little or no studying. Once they'd arrived, they were shocked by the challenge of a college education. Brilliance gets befuddled by beer. Enrolled in Partying 101, a good score is anything that can get them high.

This slacker's professor likely gave him an ultimatum: Attend the seminar or fail the class.

"Sofia?" Charlene leaned in and looked down the long table. "Would you like to tell us about your experience in Mexico? Were you born there?"

Going through the same spiel she'd given Phillips, Sofie shared her life on both sides of the border.

Charlene interrupted and moved on before Sofie got the opportunity to get to the point and deliver the simple message: Don't get involved in this shit. Addiction will catch up with you.

Sofie was tempted to use these exact words. Here, the audience included as many students as certifiable adults and, *if* she was ever able to get to her point, they might be more receptive if she said it just that way.

Zeroing in on a man she hadn't noticed before, Sofie watched him take a seat along the back row, directly across from her, against the wall.

Their eyes met and locked.

Alex had changed his appearance. The long hair was gone, all of the surfer boy had been scrubbed away. Nevertheless, she recognized his face.

Everything else in the room lost its focus.

Had Alex waited for her to find him in the crowd? If so, he now seemed hesitant, uncertain of her reaction.

Elated and wondering if he'd known she'd be here today, sudden tears gathered in the corners of her eyes.

How or if Alex knew, it didn't matter.

Thank you. Her mom, God, or fate, brought him back to her.

Alex grinned and she spotted his lone dimple.

"It's really him," Sofie whispered.

She didn't realize she'd said it aloud until Jillian quietly asked, "Who?" toggling her gaze between Sofie and the audience.

Sofie was too busy smiling to speak. The roller coaster in her belly rushed through several loops, now minus the nausea.

This could be a hallucination. Maybe the queasiness hadn't been nerves. She might be sick, delusional with a high fever, and not realize it.

Putting her hand to her forehead, she found it cool. Maybe she'd wanted to see him so badly, she'd imagined him into the audience. She shut her eyes.

When she opened them, Alex was still there.

It might not be Alex at all, just someone with a smidgen of his characteristics that captivated her. She closely studied him again.

Sofie touched the gold hoop in her ear, convinced Alex was her gift this time.

Alex lifted his arm a bit and waved, sending her a silent "Hi."

Oh my God! It's really him.

Here he sat, in the same room with her. Forget old pacts, she wanted more. He looked fine. Amazing. Suddenly, the knowledge he was okay wouldn't be enough, she was going to talk to him.

I could stand up this moment, walk off the stage and up the aisle. In seconds, I'd be next to him. I could put my hand on his face and feel his skin beneath my fingers. I could hug him, inhaling that particular, intoxicating Alex scent. No shirt necessary this time.

But she willed herself to stay in her seat. She didn't want to cause a scene. Having waited this long, a little longer wouldn't matter. Across the room had to be close enough for the time being.

Come on, Charlene! Sofie thought, *Let's get this over with.*

How could she focus when what she needed sat in the audience, thirty rows back? Smiling and certainly waiting *for her.*

The student staff finally adjusted the microphones and members of the audience began to line up on the left and right aisles. Alex remained in his seat. Sofie was disappointed. She didn't care about the question, she wanted to hear his voice.

Sofie hastily reorganized the rest of her afternoon. She'd persuade Alex to spend what was left of the day together, and bow out of Charlene's dinner invitation. Not knowing how she'd explain this to Jillian, Sofie decided she'd come up with something. Eventually, Jillian would understand. Sofie wanted Alex to herself; she'd think about letting Jillian talk to him tomorrow.

"Sofia," Charlene said, "the gentleman at the mic has a question for you."

It took a few seconds for Sofie's current surroundings to click into place.

The man she'd labeled the slacker breathed into the mic. "Sofia, right? Or do you go by Sofie? Can I call you Sofie?"

Caught off guard, she reluctantly nodded, finding nothing pinnable to connect the slacker's vaguely recognizable voice.

Seemingly comfortable in front of the mic, he took his time and appeared to measure his words. "Wow! It must have been quite a ride, living in Mexico, with everything at your disposal. sex, drugs, rock and roll!" he howled.

Laughter spilled from the audience.

That was Phillips' line.

Pleased with himself, the slacker turned and chuckled along with the crowd.

Sofie couldn't shake the odd familiarity.

Jillian put her hand on Sofie's leg.

Get to the question, asshole.

Did the asshole have one?

She leaned into her mic. "This isn't a seminar on sex eduction, so I'll leave that discussion to the professionals. And I love rock and roll. But I definitely have something to say about drugs and addiction."

Waiting for the laughter to die down, she took a deep breath and launched into her message. "Drugs *are not* a joke. I've been there. I've seen it. And I've watched people, who meant the world to me, lose everything…"

Sofie watched Alex and hoped he understood what she tried to convey. "Those we love the most—on all sides of the issue—have lost because of drugs. It's a scary world, not only the drugs themselves, but also the people who dabble in the business. Make no mistake: It will catch up with you and cut you cold."

Unfazed, the slacker bounced into the mic, "So what you're saying is for some people, life's a bitch." He snickered. "And you've seen others bite the dust. For you, every day is your lucky day. Is that it?"

The audience chuckled.

She didn't have anything more to say, her mind was too busy trying to make the connection. And there was one. She felt it.

The warped bastard may have jumbled the words but she finally got them. *Lucky. Day. Bitch.*

Sofie recoiled in the chair. It was the same snicker and milky gray eyes. Her body quaked, blasted by the memory of that searing summer morning. The slippery sweat and the icy steel of a gun against the bridge of her nose.

❧

Alex believed he and Sofie were the only two people in the room who mattered. Relieved to see the delight in her expression when she discovered him in the lecture hall, he decided he'd been right to come out of the shadows from where he'd kept tabs on her this past month.

Sofie gasped and the color drained from her face.

He glanced around the room. Nothing had changed.

She stared at the guy in front of the mic. Alex was so busy ogling her, he hadn't paid much attention to him.

Alex watched the back of his head and noted the basics. Skinny dude. Long hair tied in a ponytail. Except for the cocky attitude and the need to draw attention to himself, he resembled a score of other students in the audience.

From this angle, Alex couldn't see much as the guy returned to his seat. The moderator moved to the right side of the room for a question. One for Ms. Bond this time, who sat next to Sofie.

Tony Smith, the agent Washington sent, sat on Sofie's other side. A perfect position. Public Relations became Tony's secondary assignment this afternoon, his main job being protection. For a Washington "suit," Alex didn't doubt he would do his best. It wasn't good enough. When Dean mentioned Agent Smith had been designated as the guy they planned to send, Alex didn't have any other choice but to show up.

I would have anyway.

Alex could see Sofie's hands trembling even from a distance. Her palm moved to rest against her chest and he wondered if she was going to pass out. He felt guilty. It had to be a shock to see him in the audience. But something had changed. Moments ago, she seemed happy. Ecstatic.

Pulling the necklace out from beneath her blouse, Sofie subtly rubbed the silver heart with her fingers.

He smiled, trying to reassure her.

She gave a slight nod towards the microphone, where the guy with the attitude had been, and averted her eyes, looking up into the audience where he sat.

Sofie continued to play with the heart.

Their sign. She was in trouble.

Alex stood and moved to the wall, monitoring the room.

Seeming to follow the invisible connection that ran across the hall between Sofie and Alex, the student turned and stared boldly.

Every nerve buzzed at high alert. *Torres' toady.*

Ah. I get it.

The freak smiled as if Alex had been a lost friend, finally found.

An exhilarating current raced up and down Alex's spine. He wasn't surprised. The pieces of the puzzle began to slip into place.

All of a sudden, it dawned on him: This was a gift. Today marked the fourth anniversary of Nick's death.

Still smiling, Torres' toady, the assassin, got up and left the room.

Tony will protect Sofie.

Alex glanced back at her and followed Torres' man out the door.

CHAPTER TWENTY-NINE

Dancing with the Devil

Bailando con el Diablo
Saturday, March 23, 1985

Sofie cried out when Alex left the lecture hall. Tony Smith immediately leapt to his feet and followed him.

"Where is he going?" Charlene asked.

Jumping up too, Sofie didn't answer. Jillian grabbed her by the wrist and she pulled away, chasing Alex. He wasn't going anywhere without her.

By the time she reached the doors, Tony was already in the hallway.

He turned and, when she saw his gun, Sofie froze, paralyzed.

"I'm going to help Alex," Tony said. "Go inside. Don't let anyone leave." Halfway down the corridor, he looked back and warned, "And stay there!"

Nothing in Tony Smith's demeanor resembled her first impression; he'd suddenly become a bulldog. Afraid he'd force her back into the lecture hall instead of helping Alex, she moved against the wall. She could monitor the doors from there.

At the end of the hall, the gunman crossed the gallery holding his weapon.

"Stop!" Tony yelled.

The gunman didn't even glance in their direction. Tony ran to catch him.

A burst of dread flooded through Sofie. The gunman wasn't interested in her anymore. Or Tony. He wanted Alex.

Skittering around the intersection, Tony's footsteps faded into silence.

Sofie needed to call the police. There had to be a phone nearby, and

302

she'd find it.

🦋

The killer could be anywhere.

Luckily, Alex had made it around the corner in time to see a door close. He kept his gun drawn and entered the empty classroom. Moving to the attached anteroom, he found it deserted too, marked by several doors.

Torres' toady wanted him first, then he'd go after Sofie. Undoubtedly, Humberto Torres had contracted the hit on both of them. Alex represented unfinished business. Sofie had a big mouth.

There was a better way to do this. *Let him find me.*

Alex opened the door to the hallway and a bullet whizzed by, scoring his arm. *Shit!*

Ducking into the classroom, Alex checked the wound. It was only a bloody graze. In the anteroom, he reassessed the situation. They could shoot it out in the corridors. But there'd be less possibility of collateral damage if Alex stuck with his plan.

Tony may have followed. A backup could be helpful. But Tony's job was to stay with Sofie.

Anyway, it had been an agency sniper who'd stolen Alex's bead on Ramón in Mexico, and Alex vowed it wouldn't go down that way again.

He carefully worked his way through the building. This could be a fifty-fifty kill. The hit man would be the only hundred-percent surety. Whether he did any damage to Alex in the meantime proved to be the unknowable part of the equation.

Alex figured it would be a miracle if Tony—long on policy, short on experience—would be able to take a professional killer down if things went south. Hopefully, somebody would call the police. Just not too soon.

Inside the women's bathroom, Alex latched each stall except his chosen hideout. Then he locked the door, climbed on top of the toilet, and waited.

He listened to the nagging drip of a faucet break the silence, and checked to see if it was a leak or a mistake. Deciding whomever had left the water on had done him a favor, he made the mistake work for him by readjusting the faucet, just so, duplicating the drips before he returned to his stall.

Within a few minutes, the door coming from the hallway slowly creaked open. Alex crouched down on the white porcelain and aimed his .45 caliber.

Between drips of water, he heard the sound of quiet movement as someone cautiously entered the bathroom.

Alex detected body odor and cigarettes, the loud calling-card of Toady's stench.

Did the freak ever take a bath? Soon, Toady wouldn't need one. *Ever again.* Alex smiled.

The killer stopped. He seemed to be waiting.

Nick had taught Alex how to slow his breathing to a crawl years ago. Alex reminded himself he was in control. This was his game now.

Alex's heartbeat hammered against his ribs as he timed breaths within the drips of water. He imagined the killer by the sinks, calculating.

"I know you're here, Alex," Toady finally said.

Every nerve in Alex's body hummed, itching for him to move closer.

"Like I tell Torres, what's hard is easy and what seems easy, comes hard." He chuckled. "Get it? Comes hard. Cums…"

Come on, you prick. I'm not here for the conversation.

"Your partner, Nick, he was easy."

Tell me something I haven't already figured out, motherfucker.

Torres' man tried the handle, then kicked open the first wooden door.

One, Alex thought.

"Jaime's wife, that girl Ceci, she was easy too… After the first mix-up. Ask around, and you always find what you're looking for."

The killer tried the next door. "But you already know this, Alex." He rammed the door harder this time. The bang echoed between the bathroom walls.

Two. Come to me. Here I am.

"She'd come in from the edge of the Valley. Cruising the bars in the afternoons, trading for blow. I found her and gave her more than she asked for. She was *too* easy… I missed something."

In the silence, Alex could almost hear him thinking, *Which door is it?*

"Did you ever screw a dead girl?"

You'll never have a woman again, dead or alive, you sick fuck.

"I've been searching for you. Her too. We have unfinished business."

This time, he didn't bother to try the door. He just kicked it open.

Three.

"Jaime shouldn't have disappeared with money that didn't belong to him and leave his wife all alone. You've been harder to flush!" The toady freak amped up his crazed laugh. "Get it? Flush?

"Sofie, Sofia, whatever the bitch calls herself, was the key. I remembered seeing both of you that night in Oaxaca. The way you looked at each other. I knew she wasn't just a girl. And then, when she began talking, I knew her lover would come running."

Three doors remained locked. Alex detected a barely perceptible change in the dripping sound. Toady probably was leaning against the sink.

"My friends aren't happy with you. Or her."

The dripping stopped and the killer's position was confirmed.

"That's better. Who knew the chick would become a problem? I could have saved myself the trouble if Torres didn't stop me the first time. But then you would have been hard to find.

"I told you I've always had a hankering for Mexican snatch at the ranch, and I'm gonna get me some of that soon. This one I want alive, so after I fuck her, I can watch her face the moment I snuff her out."

Steeling himself, Alex tried to keep his cool. *He's almost here. Almost here.* Another explosive ramming. *Four.*

"I want to see your face too. I saw your partner's. It's this weird thing I have… There's something… Well… In our line of work, you might dig it too… It gets me off."

You're one sick bastard, asshole. Alex saw the blue and red stripes of his scuffed white tennis shoes beneath the wooden door.

I'm ready, come to me…

The door blasted open. Alex fired first and hit the killer square in the heart. Blood spurted across the stall, splattering Alex and the walls.

Much of his face was obscured, but the killer's cold, gray eyes were wide with surprise. The killer still had the gun cradled in his hands, holding his point-blank aim. "I'm not going down alone. You're coming too."

From the hallway, the bathroom door burst open, distracting the killer.

Before Alex could fire a second shot, Toady's head blew apart, splashing human goo across the room. In the same instant, Toady fired.

The bullet shattered the toilet tank. Alex tried to brace himself on the sides of the stall as he crashed to the floor, flooded with spraying water, human debris, and blood.

He stood, and climbed over the hit man's body, to find Tony standing in the doorway.

Tony moved into the room to inspect the lake of destruction. "He's the one we've been looking for?"

"We got him."

"The police are on their way."

For a "suit," Tony proved to be an expert marksman. He'd saved Alex's ass. "Thanks, man. I'm glad he hit the toilet instead of me."

"I wasn't surprised to see you in the audience. Dean expected you to show up."

Alex glanced around Tony's head and saw Sofie, stunned, standing in the doorway, horror freezing her face.

"Sofie." Alex had lain in bed many nights, imagining what it would be like if they ever met again.

Not this.

Pale, her eyes wide and terrified, Sofie opened her mouth but couldn't seem to speak. Alex looked down at himself and into the mirror. He was a disgusting mess. Covered in blood and speckled with bits of flesh and bone, Alex realized once again he represented a monster in one more grotesque horror scene.

With each terrible experience she'd suffered, somehow he'd been in the thick of it. And this was the conclusion to every moment they'd shared. It seemed he'd never be able to offer her anything more.

He couldn't ever expect her to get past this.

Pain boiled to anger and he stared at Tony, "You let her follow you?"

"No." Tony whirled around. "I told you to go back!"

"She doesn't listen to me either," Alex said. Shaking his head, he moved away from the door. He couldn't bear to see the look on her face again. "Get her out of here."

A crowd began to gather.

Alex turned in time to see Tony put his arm around Sofie and leave the bathroom, shutting the door behind him.

CHAPTER THIRTY

Butterfly Queen

Reina de Mariposas
Saturday, March 23, 1985

Sofie had been able to organize the facts into a coherent statement for the police. Still, much of what had happened this afternoon made little sense. She leaned against the wall of the crowded station and took a deep breath.

It had taken a moment to decipher the horrific scene in the restroom. Behind Tony, amid the bloody muck and the flooding linoleum, she discovered a body—a mass she prayed wasn't Alex.

The wail that bubbled in her throat was silenced by the sight of a second, gun-wielding man, standing near the sinks. Covered in gore, he looked threatening, ready to fire.

A tsunami of relief swept over Sofie when Alex spoke, although it had been an unexpected, brusque greeting.

Now, in the police station, someone called, "Alex Wakefield, over here!"

Sofie turned in time to see Alex enter the office she'd just left and clasp Captain Barron's hand.

Wakefield. Her heart caught and tripped.

Through the Captain's window, she saw the back of Tony's balding head. Alex stood near him, speaking with a group of officers.

His hair was wet. He'd had a chance to shower, and he was wearing gray sweatpants and a black T-shirt— probably borrowed from a generous policeman's locker. Sofie realized the shirt was a size too small, and a perfect, sexy fit.

An officer peeked his head around the corner of the room, smiled at

Sofie, and closed the Captain's door. Through the window, she watched the men settle into conversation and decided it might be hours before she'd be able to speak to Alex.

🌑

A crisp spring evening welcomed Sofie outside the police station. Only the most stubborn stars broke through the sky above the incandescent city. To the east, the tiniest sliver of a pearly moon had risen over the mountains. Tonight, the cloudless sky seemed different somehow.

I feel different.

She'd parked her Honda across the lot, next to Tony's rental. Earlier, when Sofie and Jillian watched Alex disappear into the back of a squad car and leave campus, Jillian had tried to insist on driving Sofie to the station. Determined to handle the rest of the afternoon herself, Sofie firmly declined and followed Tony to the West Los Angeles Division alone.

Crossing the parking lot to her car, Sofie opened the door and slipped her key into the ignition. The clock read eight-fifteen. Tossing her purse into the back seat, she folded her arms and held her sides to calm the excitement of the day, and the new revelation: *Wakefield.*

Sofie ran the heater until she felt comfortable enough to remove her sweater, then turned off the engine and waited for Alex. Through the rear-view mirror, she watched the station doors, and debated using another blast of the heater to erase the growing chill.

Finally, Alex and Tony left the building. Sofie grabbed her sweater and got out of the car. She leaned against the trunk, and while she waited for both men, Sofie wanted only one of them.

"Alex *Wakefield*," Sofie said.

Under the lights of the parking lot, Sofie recognized Alex's tentative smile. His expression conveyed a blend of hope and curiosity, reminding her of their first car ride together in Mexico.

She focused on Alex, but addressed both men. "I gave Captain Barron a statement. A few years ago, back in the summer of '81, the guy on the restroom floor ran me off the freeway and put a gun to my head." Sofie met Alex's eyes. "I told you about it, remember?"

"I remember."

"He wanted to kill me, but another man drove up and said I was the wrong girl. I made a report at the time. The Captain said he would check with the Devonshire Division tomorrow."

Sofie stared at Alex. "You're not in trouble, right?"

"No," Alex and Tony replied in unison.

"Thank God."

"We've been looking for him," Tony explained. "Alex did us a favor today. A killer is off the streets. Permanently."

"I wasn't alone." Alex turned to Tony. "He got a shot off anyway. You saved my life."

"The guy in the restroom, what's his name?" Sofie asked.

Tony answered, "According to his birth certificate, it's Cameron Hodges. He has numerous aliases and has been in and out of the system since he was a teen. For awhile, he's been flying under everybody's radar."

Alex raised his eyebrows and laughed. "I'm impressed, Tony. While I took a shower, you were busy."

"What I saw in the restroom, it was... Well..." Sofie hesitated, not knowing how to describe the grotesque scene.

"I told you to stay in the lecture hall," Tony grumbled.

"You should have listened to him." Thankfully, this time Alex sounded more concerned than angry.

Sofie glanced at the ground, then met Alex's gaze. "I couldn't. I was too worried. When I first saw you, I was so surprised... Good surprised."

Hoping he'd be pleased with her confession, she studied his face and detected the spark in his eyes.

"When Cameron Hodges came to the microphone, I began to realize he was the guy on the freeway."

"How did you know it was him?" Alex asked.

"There was something familiar about his voice, but I couldn't place it. Then I was able to get a really good look at him. I'll never forget his eyes that morning and the words he said: *It's your lucky day, bitch.*"

Only a step away, she could reach out and touch Alex.

She didn't.

"I'd hoped you'd remember our sign. When you left, I didn't know where you were headed, so I followed. I went back to find a phone to call the police. I don't know what would have happened if you weren't here today."

"Tony would have taken care of you."

Alex might be right, but she needed *him*.

"In the restroom, I couldn't tell who was who, at first. It was awful... Who wants to kill us?" *Kill.* Just using the word gave her chills.

Alex answered, "A guy who works with the Cali cartel named Humberto

Torres. Hodges and Torres were both at the ranch that afternoon."

Sofie was confused. "I didn't see Hodges there that day."

"They left by helicopter, before you arrived."

"I don't get it. I don't know anything about Colombian cartels. Why were they looking for me?"

"They don't know that. You talked too much. Until you showed up on *The Don Phillips Show,* they weren't looking for you. Just me. Afterwards, they wanted both of us."

"But what about that morning on the freeway? Who were they looking for then?"

"Ceci. Her husband, Jaime, disappeared with some money that didn't belong to him. She was retaliation. We're not sure who called the hit, or who paid for it. It was either Cali or Mendoza money."

"We might never find out." Tony added.

Sofie turned to Alex, "Did you know Jaime?"

"About five years ago, Nick and I were on assignment and worked for him, here in Los Angeles. He was distributing the pot your cousins grew on the ranch.

"When we were in Mexico and you mentioned someone had pulled a gun on you—we didn't know about that. Then you said you were skeptical about how they'd found Ceci. I began to wonder how it all connected. Things began to fall into place from there."

Behind his surfer-boy demeanor, Alex had hidden this deep, insightful intelligence, something she'd seen only glimpses of before.

Raw emotion hovered so close to the surface, Sofie was afraid she'd cry, but she asked anyway, "I know Ceci wouldn't do heroin. What really happened to her?"

"Hodges caught up with her and lured her into a hotel room."

Sofie detected the sympathy in Alex's voice. He'd remembered how much Ceci meant to her. Hugging her sides, she kept her chin firm and her eyes dry. Sad, but vindicated, she nodded. "I knew it."

Alex took a step closer. Still, he didn't touch her.

"Where is this Torres guy? Is he still after us? Should we worry?"

"He's in custody," Tony interjected, "We picked him up in New York City a few hours ago."

Their tiny trio was silent. Sofie tried not to stare at Alex. But whenever she glanced his way, he was watching her. A black hoodie had been zippered over his T-shirt. Below the shoulder, near his heart, were four letters emblazoned in white: LAPD.

Sofie needed to touch him, but wasn't quite sure what his reaction would be. So she held her hands underneath her folded arms, protecting herself—from what, she didn't know.

Tony cleared his throat. "It's late. I guess we should—"

"I'll take Alex wherever he needs to go." The words had escaped before Sofie realized she was going to say them.

"Are you sure?" Alex asked, "My truck is parked back at UCLA."

She smiled. "Positive."

"Well… I need to check into the hotel before they give my room away," Tony said.

Alex placed his hand on Tony's shoulder. "Thanks, man. I appreciate the help."

"No problem. That's why I came today. One point—no, two—for our team: Hodges and Torres."

Sofie couldn't help herself; she bolted into Tony's chest and hugged him. When she kissed him on the cheek, her voice broke, "Thank you."

He'd been sent to protect her and he had. More important, he'd been there for Alex. Two points for a small man who'd proved to be a huge surprise.

Tony accepted her embrace with awkward, stiff arms, until she released him. Grinning, he backed away and turned to unlock his car.

Sofie and Alex waved goodbye and silently watched Tony's Chrysler until the crimson orbs of the tail-lights turned onto the street.

Finally, they were alone.

Alex touched her shoulder and sent a shot of electricity through her body. As if he'd flipped a switch, she'd come alive.

"You're wearing my earrings. I like them." He brushed a curl away from her face. "But why did you cut your hair?"

His palm felt warm against her skin. She fought the urge to turn her head and kiss it. "I needed a change. It was liberating."

"I guess I like it," Alex teased.

"If you weren't here, I don't know how I would've made it through today. Tony did great, but I *needed* you."

"I wasn't quite sure how you'd react when you saw me in the audience."

"I hoped you'd show up, so I was satisfied." Sofie smiled.

Alex grinned. "You've always satisfied me."

Sofie stepped back and leaned against the trunk of her Honda. "So, what's your middle name, Alex Wakefield?'"

"I see you've done some detective work of your own." Alex laughed. "Mine is nowhere near as exotic as yours, Sofia *Morgan* Mendoza Davis. It doesn't have a legend attached. It's not Austin. It's just plain Michael."

"Really? That's your middle name?"

"Swear to God." Alex crossed his heart.

She reached out and put her hand on top of his. "I like it."

"What else do you want to know?"

Sofie cupped her chin. She had so many questions, but only a few seemed important now. "Nick was your partner, right?"

"I'm sorry you had to find out about him on a talk show. I'd hoped to tell you myself some day."

"You could have told me what was going on when we were in Mexico."

"If you had the opportunity to do something to avenge Ceci's death, wouldn't you want to do it?"

"Of course."

"How much would you be willing to sacrifice?"

"I'd do anything."

Alex moved beside her, against the trunk of the car. "Nick came first. My job, second. I didn't plan on you."

Sofie turned, facing him. She couldn't help herself, she moved closer, soaking in the heat of his body.

"You complicated things," he said.

She slipped her arm underneath his. Alex didn't seem to mind this new complication.

Both of them had suffered terrible losses. She wondered if they could heal together.

"Was Cameron Hodges responsible for Nick too?"

Alex nodded slowly. "Hodges was quite the talker."

"I'm so sorry," Sofie said, lacing her fingers into his. They were calloused, substantial, exactly how she'd remembered them.

Moments passed before he spoke. "Four years ago, today, they found Nick's body." He stared into the parking lot as if he were someplace far from tonight. "We can't bring Nick and Ceci back, but there's been some justice. It's over now. They can both finally rest in peace."

"Thank you."

Alex pressed his finger to the underside of her chin, tilting her face up to meet his eyes. "No. *Thank you.* You pointed Hodges out to me."

He pulled Sofie close. "You helped me get command of the situation."

She snuggled against his chest, reveling in the rise and fall of each breath. "You asked me to trust you, and I did. What I don't understand is why you never trusted me."

Taking her by the shoulders, he held her a few inches away and looked into her eyes. "Think about it. How could I?"

Sofie didn't have an answer. Fate had designed the rocky path they'd travelled in Mexico. After everything they'd been through, he was here with her now. That's what mattered.

Alex put his hand on her hip and she reached up, encircling his back.

He lowered his forehead to meet hers.

"Stay with me," she whispered.

They were standing underneath streetlights in a police station parking lot, but the moment their lips met, Sofie knew she'd come home.

CHAPTER THIRTY-ONE

Magnolia Home

Casa de Magnolia
Saturday, March 23, 1985

Sofie drove north on the 405. Alex sat beside her in the passenger seat and, once they'd crossed Sunset, there'd be no turning back—she was taking him to her place.

"Where's Dean sending you next?" she asked, wishing Alex had a desk job like Tony.

"I left the agency. I gave up hunting drug lords. I'm chasing cows these days."

"*What?* You really do live in Texas?"

"I never lived in Texas. I grew up on a ranch in California."

"Why did you quit? *Wait.* If you quit your job, what were you doing here today?"

"I saw you on TV and decided somebody should keep you out of trouble."

"How long have you been watching me?"

"Why did I quit?" he asked.

Apparently, Alex intended to answer only one of her questions. She let it go, for now.

"When one cartel is gone, another rushes in to take its place with new methods. As long as there's a market for drugs, we can't win."

"But what you're doing is important."

"I've done this for over ten years. It's somebody else's turn to be on the front lines."

This new information took a moment to sink in. Sofie understood his

314

disappointment. The drug problem seemed to be getting worse, not better.

"It didn't look like you'd moved from the front lines this afternoon when you followed Hodges out of the lecture hall. It matters to me that you're safe."

"Most days, I'm as safe as you can be on a ranch with thirty cows, thirty calves, one bull, six horses, three dogs, eight cats, two peacocks, five turkeys, twelve hens—that's not including my mother and sister—one rooster, and the assortment of wild animals that roam the property, wreaking havoc."

"I remember. Your mother has expectations."

"That's what you got out of that?" He grinned. "She's still got them—always hoping I'll find a nice girl, settle down and start making babies she can spoil."

"You really aren't married then?"

Alex's eyes widened, feigning innocence. "Would I lie to you?"

Sofie raised an eyebrow and shot him her nastiest expression.

"How many times do I have to tell you I'm not married before you'll believe me?"

She merged into the far-right lane, but didn't exit at her usual off ramp.

He turned his head and looked back. "Why didn't you take Sepulveda Boulevard? It's quicker."

"I thought I'd stop and pick up some Chinese food. You must be hungry. I'm starving." She glanced at him, twice. "How do you know where I live?"

"I said I've been keeping an eye on you."

"You've followed me?"

"I haven't been around every single day. But somebody has. We're just making sure you're okay."

"And you didn't bother to approach me? To let *me* know *you're* okay?"

"I didn't realize you were so worried. You never called."

"I did too. Around New Year's. And you weren't there."

Alex stared at her. "I'd given up and moved out by then."

"I know. A sweet little old lady told me all about it... kind of." It was a relief to discover he'd been missing her too.

"Well, don't worry about me. I've taken care of myself for years."

"Everybody needs someone to worry about them."

"I get plenty of that back at the ranch."

"I'm talking about something different, someone special to do the worrying."

Alex smiled and Sofie felt the warmth of his hand on her shoulder. "I guess you're right."

❦

The sack of Chinese food sat unopened on Sofie's dining table. Alex began to undress her as soon as he locked the front door. A trail of clothes were scattered throughout her apartment. Her blouse landed on a chair, bra on the living room rug, black pants on the hall floor.

Alex kissed her into the bedroom.

He removed his gun from the pocket of the hoodie and placed it on the dresser.

The gun didn't shock her anymore. The swath of gauze that covered his forearm did. "What happened?"

"It's nothing. Just a graze."

"From today?"

He nodded.

Sofie pulled him to the edge of the mattress with his good arm. Alex ran his finger beneath the elastic of her panties while she stood between his legs and carefully lifted off the LAPD T-shirt. She put her lips to the wound and felt the angry heat rising from below the bandage. Cradling his head to her waist, she closed her eyes and inhaled, soaking Alex in.

She could hardly believe he was here in her bedroom. Thankfully, time seemed to slow down and, apparently, Alex didn't seem to be in any hurry either.

Removing her panties, Alex kissed the small dip near her stomach. "You smell like island flowers. Just how I remembered."

Sofie ran her hands through his short hair. Maybe she could convince him to grow it a little longer, because she'd suddenly discovered a nostalgic affinity for his floppy hair and the scruffy, surfer-boy look.

Deciding she couldn't wait anymore, Sofie said, "Come here," and coaxed him up from the bed. She slowly bit her lower lip and met Alex's blazing, blue eyes, determined to show how much she wanted him naked too. With her palms, she worked the sweats down his hips, delighted to find nothing but skin.

She watched his face while she gently pushed him back to the edge of the mattress. He grimaced, removed a pair of borrowed tennis shoes, and rubbed his toes. After he finished undressing, Alex looked up and grinned. With her arms around his neck, Sofie laughed softly, kissed his mouth, and

316

together they fell onto the bed.

Skin to skin now, he tried to pull her on top of him.

Smiling, Sofie said, "Wait."

Taking off her necklace and the gold hoops Alex bought her in Mexico, she set them both on the nightstand. She didn't want to turn off the light.

Sofie rolled over and sank into Alex's arms, meeting his moist mouth. Their tongues danced, tip to tip.

"I love the way you taste," Sofie murmured and sucked on his lower lip. Alex closed his eyes and moved in to deepen the kiss.

Positioning his body above hers, he braced himself on his elbows, grinning. "I missed you."

"I missed you too." Sofie could feel his erection, hot and rigid against her belly, pulsing and eager. Wiggling beneath him, she spread her legs, reached for him and tried to sheathe him into her body.

But Alex resisted. He took his finger and lifted her chin. "I've missed your emerald colored eyes. The way they flash when you're angry and sparkle when you laugh." He ran his fingertip along the crest her breasts. "I've missed these too."

"Are you sure you don't like them bigger? I saw you ogling Monica's by the pool," Sofie teased.

"You're perfect." Alex captured her nipple in his mouth, sucked until it puckered, and gave equal attention to its twin.

A jolt of sizzling desire shot through her, curling her toes, the burn settling between her legs.

"No, *you're* perfect." Sofie smiled and lifted her hips. "And we're a perfect fit."

"I love knowing you want me as much as I want you." Alex brought his hand between her legs and palmed her mons. "You're so wet."

Needing him inside, Sofie shifted and brought her knees up, pressing her pearl against his hand.

His finger slipped into her moist heat. She closed her eyes and began to move. Breathless, consumed by the electric intensity flooding her senses, she found it difficult to speak, "I want…you, inside me…now."

Alex moved his hand away.

When nothing happened, she whimpered and searched him out, pressing her body against the hard velvet, opening her legs to the pleasure. She wanted more.

Huge. Thick. Sofie felt his need.

"Open your eyes. I want you to watch me make love to you," he said. Alex's gaze was hot, gleaming. "I've missed you, like this."

He was *right there*. But Alex wouldn't slide in, instead he teased—tormented—her. "Pay attention. I want to tell you something," he said, kissing the hollow above her collarbone. "I love your legs. I love the way your hips move when you walk."

Lifting her a few inches off the bed, Alex ran his hand down the length of her back. "Your silky skin and your sexy butt. Especially when I have you...just so..."

Finally, he entered her. Overwhelmed with love, Sofie found his lips.

"You're so tight, just how I remembered. *Sofie, I've missed you. So much.*"

Sofie, achy and itching for release, savored the sublime stretch as Alex filled her core.

He moaned and started to move.

Matching the pulse, beat for beat, she pressed her body against his and became lost in magnificent sensation.

Alex thrust into her. "I love...how...you...feel."

"I love—"

He leaned in for a kiss, and the rest of the words were lost as she reveled in the exquisite assault.

Sofie wrapped her legs around his back, and he pushed deeper, toward her womb.

"*You feel so good,*" he groaned.

Closing his eyes, Alex drove into her, propelling her climb toward ecstasy. Pausing at the precipice, ready to spiral out of control, she used her muscles to milk him, silently begging him to join her in the free fall.

As Sofie cascaded into climax, Alex followed, and she felt his seed splash into her as he called out her name in supplication.

❦

Afterwards, Alex ran his hand slowly along her shoulder. "You're extraordinary."

Sofie couldn't stifle the tears that gathered in the corners her eyes. She'd come back home... Alex was *home*. She *belonged* to him.

"I was too angry to realize how much at first, *but God, I've missed you.*"

Alex frowned. "I'm sorry. I never wanted to hurt you."

"I know," she said, running her palm along the downy fur of his chest. They were both quiet for a few minutes, then she gently tugged on a fingerful of fur and said, "I'm hungry."

Alex pulled her closer and kissed her.

"You're dessert." She caressed his chin, loving the familiar hint of stubble. "Right now, I want Chinese food."

Sofie got up and pulled Alex's shirt from her closet, the one she'd worn to bed for months, and buttoned it over her body.

He leaned on one elbow and grinned. "Hey, that's my shirt."

"Yep." She turned in a circle, modeling it for him. "And it's seen better days. I need another one." Sofie came back to the bed and pressed her lips on his forehead. "I use chopsticks. Do you need a fork?"

When she returned with their dinner, he'd put on the sweatpants. They sat across from each other on the bed and shared Chinese food from the cartons.

Halfway through the Kung Pao Chicken, she gave the white container to Alex and asked, "Do you know where Gabriel is?"

He planted his fork in the chicken and passed the fried rice. "Not specifically. But, the agency says he's back in Mexico."

Her relationship with Gabriel was complicated, but Felipe, with his quiet, gentle demeanor, had always been a favorite of hers. It didn't seem fair that he'd been pulled into Ramón's web. "What about Felipe?" She prayed he'd somehow escaped that terrible afternoon. "Is it true he's still alive?"

"The agency doesn't think so, but no one knows for sure. The Mexicans haven't been interested in sharing information lately." Alex retrieved his fork and took a bite of chicken.

"Oh." She poked at the rice and looked up to find him staring. "What?"

Alex's eyes were shaded. "Nothing."

"Do you really have a crazy uncle who climbed a transmission tower searching for God?"

"Yep."

She laughed. "What about the embezzling drug addict, Cousin Lisa?"

"All true."

"You never had to explain her to Dean?"

"He never asked. I've passed thorough background checks. He probably already knows."

"So I'm really not the only one with a dysfunctional family."

"Everybody has a screwy family, some are just more screwed than others." He picked up both fortune cookies and handed her one. "Here, open it."

Unwrapping the cellophane, she broke open the cookie and read it aloud, *"Don't let ambition overshadow small success."*

She knit her eyebrows and shrugged, bewildered. "I don't get this. I don't see how it applies to me. I want to hear yours."

"People are attracted by your delicate features."

Sofie and Alex laughed.

"This belongs to you," he said, handing her the slip of paper. "I have an idea. Let's make our own fortune."

Alex's eyes were serious.

"Let's try doing it together," he said. "I'm willing. Are you?"

This was a perfect moment, an evening Sofie would never forget. And if they could live the rest of their lives in a moonlit bubble, she wouldn't hesitate.

Imagining a haven where the glow of reconciliation cradled them in a comfortable shell, anything seemed doable. However, she wondered if they could make it work in a place where everything would be illuminated and couldn't be washed away with kisses and amazing sex.

How am I going to fit into your family? she wondered. Sofie wasn't sure if she was ready to give up life in the city to live on a ranch with them. More importantly, would they even want her there? Granted, it was 1985, and this was California, so being half-Mexican shouldn't be a big hurdle. But being related to a Mexican drug cartel would be a gigantic one.

Earlier tonight, Alex had mentioned it again, his mom had expectations. Yes, some people meet at work; nevertheless, his mother wouldn't expect him to bring home someone from one of his assignments—a Mexican girl with a thick family history of drugs and corruption.

Alex's mom wouldn't want Sofie to be the mother of her grandchildren, and Sofie understood. If she heard the details without knowing the individuals involved, she'd feel the same way. Then, there were his friends. How would they react? And Nick meant so much to Alex, he'd eventually want Sofie to meet Nick's wife and children. Sofie couldn't imagine the reception she'd get.

She instinctively knew Tía would give them her blessing. And there were others Sofie was proud to call her family—her Dad, Tío, and Rich, who would surely understand.

We're on the healing side of this horrific experience, she thought. They'd made it through the worst, and here they were: Half-naked on her bed, sitting across from one another, eating Chinese food.

She moved the cartons, got on her knees and reached for Alex.

"Yes." Sofie put her arms around his neck, kissing his lips. "We've been through so much already, we can make it through whatever the future holds too."

❧

Alex awoke in the light of solid morning. An aching arm reminded him he needed aspirin. He wondered if Sofie had any, but she slept so peacefully, he didn't want to wake her to find out.

They'd spent most of the night making love. In between, he'd held her in his arms and they talked. She'd grown up in some ways, but hadn't lost any of her independence. The naive little girl had disappeared, and the grace he'd seen glimpses of before, now settled into full bloom.

Alex answered her questions. College? Not Boston University, like he'd told her in Mexico, but Cal Poly, just up the road from the ranch. And, he explained, he dropped out after two years, impatient and bored, anxious to join the Army.

He really had been in Viet Nam. *How could she have questioned that?*

Fortunately, she didn't ask about Ceci or any of the details surrounding her death. Alex didn't want to have to lie to Sofie ever again.

The clothes he'd borrowed were in a pile on the floor. Sofie's sheer panties lay entangled in the mass, near the tennis shoes, a size too small. Along with everything else he'd worn yesterday, he'd thrown his own shoes away at the station—they'd been a bloody mess.

Around four in the morning, spent and needing a break, he'd taken a short nap and woke to find Sofie had turned off the lamp. She lay beside him and, with only the streetlight coming in through the window, he could see her wide eyes, watching him close.

"Alex Michael Wakefield. I love—"

"You don't need to say it." These were heady words he'd wanted so badly to hear, but her earlier hesitation made him leery.

"But I do," Sofie pleaded.

Alex put two fingers against her mouth. "Shh." He softly kissed her lips and put his forehead against hers. "Go to sleep."

Holding her in his arms, he stared at the ceiling until her body relaxed and he heard the rhythm of even breathing. Finally, he slept, knowing morning would come too soon.

Now, Alex was full of doubt. *How is this going to work?*

He eased her against his body. Instinctively, she moved into him, and stayed there awhile before she rolled over, tucking her hands beneath her chin.

A halo of dark curls framed Sofie's beautiful face. He didn't want to let her go, but already she'd slipped away.

The clock on the nightstand read nine-thirty.

Last night, it took too long for her to answer the suggestion that they try again. Of course, she'd have trouble getting past their history. Sofie, with her kind, generous nature, had found a way to forgive him. He'd ruined her family. And it wasn't a surprise family was important to her—how could it not be? She'd lost her mother when she was just a little girl.

Alex could care less about relatives like his jail-bird cousin, Lisa. But Sofie had a tender, sentimental heart. She still wondered about Gabriel and Felipe. Alex had given her the most current information he had; it didn't seem to satisfy her concerns.

He didn't understand. But, he found her family loyalty commendable in a weird way.

Flooded with guilt, Alex realized guilt was one of their common bonds. They'd both felt some responsibility for the loss of their best friends and wanted to do something to lessen the pain. Yesterday, they'd found some justice. The cost had been high.

They continually suffered from a chronic case of bad timing. Since they'd met, he'd given her a mountain of stress. No wonder she'd hesitated. How much could she be expected to endure? The death of her mother. Ceci. Her cousins in Mexico. And yesterday, the scene in the bathroom. She'd witnessed so much violence and, with his history in the agency, how could he promise her it would never happen again?

Sofie might think she wants me. But her hesitation might hold the real answer. There hasn't been enough time for her to think this through. It's too early for her to make a decision.

Or, maybe, it's too late.

He moved off the bed as quietly as he could, bent down, picked up his clothes, and headed to the bathroom.

On his way out of the apartment, he stood for a minute to watch her from the bedroom door. Sofie *was* extraordinary, and there were many things he'd wanted to tell her last night, but hadn't.

The things he loved about her: Sofie's open, infectious smile, her intelligence, her ability to listen and understand. Most of all, he loved her capacity to forgive. She was the woman he'd never be able to shake. And this morning, his angel slept so soundly, he couldn't bring himself to wake her to say goodbye.

CHAPTER THIRTY-TWO

Royal Road

Camino Real
Sunday, March 24, 1985

Even before Sofie opened her eyes, she reached for Alex. A blade of fear sliced through her body when she discovered his side of the bed empty. Panicked, she listened for the shower, and prayed she could smell coffee or hear him banging around in the kitchen. Maybe he was in her living room, watching TV with the volume turned down low.

The only sound that came from inside the apartment was a terrible, greedy silence. Outside, the boys who lived across the street shot hoops, thumping a basketball on the pavement. Calling out to each other, one of them laughed.

Sofie began to cry.

Last night—this morning, really—in Alex's arms, she'd slept better than she had in months. Now, she'd been abandoned again.

She sat up and rubbed the tears away. Sofie didn't know what else to do. When he was in her bed, he'd opened his soul, saying words she'd cherish forever. But when she tried to declare her love for him, he'd shushed her. He may have planned to go back to his new life alone all along, once the job was done and he knew she'd be safe.

Even though a future together was his idea, she wondered if he'd been caught up in the moment and, overnight, rethought his proposition. Did he decide to slip out early to avoid another messy goodbye, like the one they'd had at the airport in Acapulco?

Sofie felt sick as the weight of suspicion sank in her stomach. Alex, a courageous man, didn't have the heart to tell her the truth; she'd never be accepted by his family or his friends.

The clock read eleven-thirty-seven. Turning over, she noticed her necklace and earrings were missing from the nightstand. She rewound the night and, sure she'd placed them there, bolted from the bed.

They were on the dining table. The necklace had been shaped into a heart, the gold hoops sat in the center, hooked together. The jewelry lay on top of a note.

Sofie,

For months I've been thinking about you and last night was better than I'd ever imagined. I tried my best to answer your questions. I don't think it was enough. It's understandable. You're still caught up in the past. I'm sorry I've been responsible for so much of your pain. When I wanted to know if you were willing to try again, your hesitation made me realize just how much I was asking. It's those damn expectations. Now, it's me, expecting too much from you. I want so much, and it's too soon.

We talked about trust. I trust you. Yesterday, I came for you. If you ever decide you're ready, come to me.

Alex

An address with directions had been written on a second piece of paper.

An hour later, Sofie drove north on the 101, buzzing with excitement. She deliberately avoided obsessing over what she planned to say once she found Alex. Deciding the right words would come when she saw him, she focused on the scenery instead.

The highway finally kissed the ocean in Ventura. Further north, sunlight spilled a glittery scarf of diamonds across the water, and sporadically, small groupings of oil derricks stood proud above the sea.

Years ago, Sofie took a trip with her parents along this same route, driving from San Francisco to Los Angeles. Just above Carpinteria, the gigantic Santa Claus still sat near the chimney of a sweet shop advertising "Date Shakes." At the time, she was more interested in the bag of candy her dad bought than anything made with dates. It had been the last good trip they'd taken together as a family. It seemed fitting she traveled this route again, hopefully, toward her future.

She reached Santa Barbara by mid-afternoon. There, she lost the ocean and became entangled in stoplights and Sunday traffic.

Past the city, nature began to shape the landscape again, and Sofie saw the sea. Taking comfort in Southern California's tenacious hillsides, she realized it took merely an inch of rain for the layer of natural seed, buried underneath last year's spent growth, to spring to life and cover the mountains with brilliant green grass. Life was kind of like that too.

On that same trip, Sofie's mom told her that, over a century ago, the Spanish padres planted mustard seed to mark the El Camino Real—the Royal Road—linking California's missions. The profusion of neon yellow that still bloomed in the median had escaped and grown wild along the sides of the highway, spreading to nearby clusters of eucalyptus, even climbing the hills.

Steering her Honda away from the ocean, she entered the Gaviota Pass. On the other side of the tunnel, there were mountains where families of smoky green oaks grew in abundance. A few stood alone, far away from the others. Sofie smiled; like the mustard seed and the oaks, she was also moving away from her roots to do some branching out of her own.

The road traversed rolling foothills until suddenly, perched on top of a knoll in the middle of nowhere, a yellow sign announced *Motel* in large black letters. It had a welcoming message below: *Vacancy*. If the rest of the day didn't go as planned, she might be spending the night there.

She'd accumulated a few vacation days, and would use one tomorrow, maybe another the next day too. Sofie wanted to get to know Alex's world. The day after that? She might quit her job altogether.

Entering a wide, rural valley, Sofie saw a sign: Arroyo Grande was only twelve miles ahead. Glancing at Alex's directions on the passenger seat, she found a local college station on FM radio, and sped toward her future.

Bryan Ferry's luscious voice came through the speakers in moments, singing, "Avalon."

Sofie had first heard Roxy Music's enchanting melody a few years ago, while studying in her dorm room late one night.

At the time, it felt like the song belonged to her mom.

It could have been a coincidence, but Sofie chose to believe the song, coming over the airwaves this afternoon, was meant for her; a gift, from Mom and Ceci.

Unlike the lyrics, Sofie did have a destination. Avalon wasn't a place. Avalon was the refuge she'd found in loving Alex.

Smiling, she touched Ceci's silver heart, lying between her breasts. "Thank you," Sofie whispered.

Minutes later, she headed east, turning onto a rural road and driving into what became a steep and stunning, almost hidden, valley.

Near a pair of stone pillars attached to a rustic, wire-and-wood fence, she saw the mailbox marked *"Wakefield"*. She drove through the metal gate, and relatched the chain—she didn't want to be responsible for any escaped cattle.

The gravel driveway split ahead. One road led to a small house with an empty carport. Another snaked up the hill, where a modern, low-roofed ranch house sat. Sofie parked behind a late-model Cadillac and walked up the flagstone path to the porch.

❦

Golden sections of diamond panes decorated a pair of front doors. Sofie's heart skittered as she rang the doorbell. When she received no answer, she gathered her courage into a fist and knocked.

An attractive, middle-aged woman greeted her. "Can I help you?" she asked, wiping her hands on an orange apron.

The woman seemed bewildered at first. Clearly, strangers didn't often pass through her gates. Within seconds, surprise flashed across the woman's face, and she beamed.

"I'm looking for Alex."

The woman seemed to catch herself and toned her expression down to a warm, welcoming smile. "Sofie. I'd hoped we'd meet some day. I'm Alex's mom."

Suddenly, Sofie didn't feel so much like a stranger. But she still wondered how much Alex had shared with his mother. "Mrs. Wakefield, how'd you know—"

"Call me Cindy, please. I saw you on TV. Come in."

Cindy led Sofie into a pristine living room. An expanse of windows had been separated by a huge rock fireplace, and a magnificent view of the countryside lay beyond the glass.

Sofie looked around, taking a seat on a blue velvet couch. She put her hands in her lap, a little embarrassed, imagining Alex's mother watching the fiasco of the Phillips taping. "Your home is lovely."

"Thank you." Cindy sat across from her, in a complementing, flowered wing chair. Her smile nearly bouncing off her face.

That's when Sofie discovered the source of Alex's lone dimple.

The house smelled delicious. Sofie must have interrupted Cindy while she was making dinner.

Cindy didn't seem to mind. "Your earrings are beautiful."

"Thanks. They were a gift." Sofie brought her finger to one of the gold hoops.

While wondering if she should mention who'd given them to her, she noticed Cindy's earrings. They were the hoops Alex and Sofie had picked out for her in Acapulco. "I like yours too."

"Thanks. They were also a gift. I have diamonds, but I've never considered wearing both. It looks lovely on you. I'll have to try it." She touched her earlobe. "Alex bought these for me when he was in... Oh, you probably know this."

Sofie grinned. "Do you like them? I helped pick them out. He wanted a special gift for your birthday."

"I do. And something tells me I'm glad you were there," Cindy said conspiratorially. "I've never known Alex to buy jewelry before. Would you like a soda?"

"No, thank you, I'm fine." Sofie glanced around the beautiful home, realizing Alex grew up in these rooms. There was so much she needed to learn about him—his childhood, Cindy, the whole family. Alex's mom was so open and welcoming, Sofie was tempted to stay and learn everything she could.

Just half-tempted. "Is Alex here?"

"I'm the only one around. My husband made a last-minute trip to the market. Oh, you'll stay for dinner, won't you?"

Cindy's expectant face crinkled with happiness, flooding Sofie with relief. "I'm not sure..."

"I understand. You asked about Alex. He's out feeding the cows."

"Will he be back soon?"

"It shouldn't be long. You can wait here and we can visit. Or I can tell you where you can meet him."

"If you don't mind, I'd like to find him."

"Of course."

Outside, Cindy gave her directions. "From here, just follow the drive," she said, pointing toward the mountains. "You'll pass my daughter's house. If she's outside, say hello and introduce yourself. Her name is Teresa. She'll be surprised, but I know she'd like to meet you. After her place, you'll come to a gate—just close it after you pass through. When you see the pond, don't go any farther, because the road splits. Wait for Alex there; he has to pass that way."

"I got it. Thanks. I just barged in on you and you've been so kind."

Cindy's eyes sparkled. "Go on, honey. I can tell you're anxious to see him."

She's already calling me honey, Sofie thought, and prayed the rest of the afternoon would go as smoothly.

"I'm setting an extra place for dinner. Just in case." Cindy winked. "Don't forget to close the gate."

"I won't." Sofie got into her car and rolled down the window.

Alex's mother laid her hand on Sofie's arm. "It's a pleasure to meet you."

Sofie almost cried with relief. "Thank you so much." Apparently, she'd been a topic of conversation around the ranch. Judging by Cindy's reaction, Sofie decided she had at least one cheerleader, and all of the discussion hadn't been negative.

🦋

A van, an RV and a horse trailer were parked alongside Teresa's spacious home. No one was outside. Sofie discovered one more lie as she drove by: If Alex had nephews, he also had at least one niece. Girly children's toys littered the yard. A fuchsia swing set sat on the grass and in the corner, by the fence, an elaborate pink Victorian playhouse mimicked the shape of his sister's home.

Through the gates, Sofie saw a massive expanse that seemed to qualify not as a pond, but as a lake. It filled most of a large narrow valley and receded into a vee of reeds and trees at the far end. On the opposite side, near the gate, a small wooden pier walked into the water.

Sofie parked her car on the gravel. She'd considered pulling off the road, then changed her mind, determined not to let Alex get away again.

Getting out of her Honda, she leaned against the trunk and waited, listening to the sigh of the breeze rushing through the trees. High overhead, she heard the occasional baritone whistle of a commercial airliner as it made the trek along the coast. When the sun began its slow slide into the horizon and cool air whispered across her shoulders, she pulled her sweater from the back seat and slipped it on.

It would be dark within a few hours, and Sofie wondered where she and Alex would be then. What would she do if there'd been some mistake and somehow she'd already missed him? She decided she'd go back to his parent's house and find out where he actually lived. Forget the motel, she'd sleep on his doorstep. Forever, if necessary.

Sofie waited for fifteen minutes by her car. Antsy, she went down to the water. She decided to explore the trail along the edge of the pond, jumping when a family of ducks sprang from the nearby grass and made their way into the lake, quacking.

Carefully watching her step, she navigated the weathered planks of the pier. She sat down about halfway across and let her legs dangle high above the water.

It occurred to her she'd spent much of her life waiting. Determined to shape the life she wanted, Sofie knew Alex was the next step in its creation. Minutes passed, then half an hour, she checked her watch.

Where was he?

Soaking in the beauty of her surroundings, she realized everything happened for a reason, even the waiting she was doing right now.

Sofie felt the presence of something bigger and her connection to life's design—as surely as the breeze wafting against her skin. It brought the good stuff and the tragedies too. As horrible as some of her experiences had been, there were always lessons learned. And they'd instilled in her the courage to face the future, not to shrink from it.

She wanted a future with Alex.

For years, she'd looked to the heavens for guidance from her mom to help her navigate life, finding meaning in the stars and bits of tumbled glass she found along the shore. Alex walked into her world at a time when she'd been undirected, insecure, and vulnerable to Ramón's manipulation. Sofie couldn't help but believe her mother had sent Alex as a protector. Meanwhile, Sofie chose him as her lover and discovered a good man, one with integrity, compassion, patience.

These revelations had taken time, and couldn't have been accomplished months ago, while the wounds were still so raw. Sofie reached for Ceci's silver necklace and rubbed the smooth filigreed heart between her fingers, smiling. Alex thought it so pesky whenever they were in bed. Yesterday, Ceci's necklace became a talisman for him too.

The sky mellowed into the color of a faded cornflower, as the horizon shimmered in buttery, bittersweet hues. Like the sun, Sofie's mom seemed to be making a retreat, saying, *I'll never be far away. But you've grown up, mija. It's time to make this journey on your own.*

❧

Long before Sofie heard the roar of an engine, she saw a trail of billowing dust as it moved through the mountains. A faded, green pickup truck finally barreled around the corner and came to a sharp stop in front of her Honda. Her pulse raced. The wait was over.

Alex walked to her car, opened the door, and leaned in. Unfolding himself from the Honda, he stood, put his hand above his eyes, and searched the valley.

She waved.

When he spotted her, he began walking the trail along the edge of the pond.

As he came closer, Sofie realized he was in his element, the quintessential cowboy. Jeans, boots and, in the background, a battered pickup left on the road.

She watched him cross the planking of the pier and silently sit down beside her. His expression was unclear, and she couldn't decipher his mood. While Sofie waited for Alex to speak, she focused on the pond, rippled by a gentle wind.

Soon, she realized he was waiting for her.

"I tried to stuff it down. Shake it off. Yesterday, when I saw you in the audience, I realized it's still here. It never left."

Alex raised his eyebrows. "What are you talking about? What's *it?*"

"That feeling I got, the first night we met. It's like I'm on a roller coaster, just cresting the peak and on my way down. There's this whoosh in my stomach and a catch in my heart. It happens every time I'm with you. Every time I think about you."

"I know the feeling. It's a rush of adrenaline. Like when I slam on the brakes to avoid a collision, and my chest pounds, and my arm hurts, and I feel like I'm having a heart attack."

Alex laughed. "But a *good* heart attack."

Sofie smiled, her eyes wide. "So, basically, you're saying I'm your train wreck?"

He ran his finger along her chin. "You're my wonderful, amazing train wreck."

A frog began to call from a tuft of reeds on the edge of the pond and others joined in.

"How'd you find me?" Alex asked.

"You left me directions."

"I mean, find me *here.*"

"I met your mom. She told me the way." Sofie looked at him. "I was really worried about meeting her, but I think it went okay."

Alex raised his eyebrows. "Why wouldn't it?"

"I'm worried about meeting anybody who's important to you."

"Don't be."

She'd watched him pick up a flat rock along the path earlier. Now he threw it, skipping it along the water.

"Your mom is so nice. She already invited me to dinner."

He grinned. "She's always trying to feed people."

They laughed and settled into silence again.

"Why didn't you believe me?" Sofie asked. "I told you I wanted to build our fortune—our future—together last night, and this morning you disappeared."

"What am I going to do with you?" Alex sighed. "Don't you *ever* listen? You were supposed to take some time to think about this."

"I don't need time. I might not have realized it on occasion, but my heart was always willing. Ever since that first night when we walked along the beach."

"I want you to be sure. With our histories, we're bound to have a few bumps along the road."

"Is life ever smooth?"

The sky erupted into vivid shades of deep purples, blues and bright pinks as the sun slipped away.

Sofie studied the pearlized buttons on his cotton shirt. "You really are a California boy."

"Yep."

"Did you ever surf?"

"Nope."

Flipping the curve of the pocket with her thumb, she said, "That's right. You're a California cowboy."

Alex caught her hand and laced his fingers through hers. He grinned, "I probably smell more like cow than boy right now."

Leaning in close, she inhaled. "I've always loved the way you smell."

He smiled and put his arm around her. "You're getting cold."

"It's so beautiful here. I never imagined you lived in a place this peaceful." She found a pebble lodged in the crevice of a plank and threw it into the pond. It didn't skip; it sank. "I've been sitting here thinking."

"First, I tell you to do some thinking. And now I'm worried because you are." Alex teased.

"You're always saving me." She looked up and asked, "When do I get to save you?"

"You already have."

Sofie beamed, elated by the heartfelt admission. "Then I have a big problem only you can help me with."

"What?"

"I don't know what to do. I've fallen in love, with a man who knows everything about me. And I hardly know him."

"You know more than you think. The rest is just extraneous stuff."

She nudged his shoulder. "You told me you had nephews, not nieces."

"No nephews. Two nieces. But I told you about my sister. Even told you her real name."

Sofie nodded. "Granted. But I want to learn it all, the details and the essentials."

Alex grinned. "Are the details so important?" He lifted her chin with his thumb and forefinger, meeting her eyes. "When you already have the essentials. You're irresistible and I'm in love with you."

Her heart soared. Everything seemed possible now.

Leaning in, Alex tilted his head and his warm lips met hers. She opened a little wider to welcome him. Caressing her chin, Alex reached for her and intensified the kiss, slowly sliding his tongue into her mouth. Sofie met his exploration, each soft, gentle move for move.

He stood up and pulled Sofie to her feet. "Come on." Alex winked. "Let's go to my place before we go to the big house for dinner."

As the remainders of an aubergine and salmon sunset marked the horizon, the moon peeked up over the mountains. Alex held Sofie's hand and led her along the path toward home.

CHAPTER THIRTY-THREE

About and Acknowledgements

Sofie, Alex, the Mendoza family, and the secondary characters in this book are a work of complete fiction—although, owing to a severe case of applied schizophrenia, they do still live in my head. I have used real-life events, such as the tragic murder of Kiki Camerena, and cultural references of the time (some thinly veiled), in my obsessive-compulsive desire to create an authentic 1980s mood.

Find me at leesouleles.com
Follow me on Facebook and Twitter.

If you've enjoyed this novel, please help me build a following by leaving a review at your favorite e-book or reader's website.

Thank you,

Jeff Souleles, my loving, supportive and patient husband, who provided the awesome photography and cover design.

Rian Souleles, my amazing, talented son, media specialist and alpha reader number one. Thanks for putting up with all my editing/publishing anxiety.

Megan Souleles, my photo stylist and daughter extraordinaire.

Chris Barron, the best big sister ever. Even before I learned how to write a decent sentence, you gave me unwavering support and the encouragement to follow my dream. Thank you. Viva la Phoenix 1989!

Teresa Goudey, your words sing beautifully on the page. Thank you for teaching me the craft. I owe you a huge debt for showing me how to convey that it's not the lounge chair, but Sofie, wearing the sunglasses. With truth once again being absolutely stranger than fiction, we could never have imagined that, through us, our children would meet and create a real-life love story of their own.

Kari Anderson, your marketing assistance and detailed editing has been invaluable. You are a gifted writer who makes the craft look so easy. Writing is your ticket. Never give up!

Steve Beers, a talented writer and remarkable artist.

The Barnes and Noble Thursday Night Writers Group, Santa Clarita, California, fall 2007 through January 2012. Thanks for your critique, skill and patience. A special thanks to our leader, Barbara Jo Fleming. Though you're no longer with us, I often hear your advice. Finally, a special thanks to Barnes and Noble for opening their doors to new writers.

Suzi Hummer, thanks for your willingness to take our friendship to a whole new level. Who knew writing sex scenes could be so daunting?

David Wisehart, early edit. Thank you.

Stacy Constance Kwinn, final edit. Thanks so much!

Betas: (And no, they aren't fish.)

Debra Gartin, my oldest friend and first reader. Thank you.

Sharon Williams, a prolific reader and good friend. Thanks for your kind words and enthusiastic support.

Angelica Mendoza, (no relation to Sofie Morgan Mendoza Davis or any of her nefarious relatives.) Thanks for the help with the Hispanic/American authenticity.

Assistance and Expertise:

Olivia Trevino, the perfectly beautiful cover model.

Steve "Bergie" Berg, cows and such. Thanks for the wonderful sunset barbecue by the pond.

Dawn Coen, CPA prep.

Nick Marrone, the cop angle and alpha two/too.

Corrie Malinka, additional cop stuff.

Claudia Rico, English to Spanish translation.

Heidi Skiles, Oaxaca expertise.

Ruben Zamora and his cousins, Rocio and Hugo, tricky English to Spanish translations.

Kenna Hummer and Gavin Smiley, train wreck texts.

My book club and Bunco babes, unwavering support and enthusiasm.

Shawn Smith and Norm Jacobson, members of the creative/marketing team at Lance Campers. I know you guys never imagined one day you'd end up using your expertise to help design the cover of a romance novel. Thanks so much.

And finally, multiple and heartfelt thank yous to Google, Google Maps and the World Wide Web. Each step of the way, you knew the answer to every question. I couldn't have written this book without you.

CHAPTER THIRTY-FOUR
Complete Playlist

Playlist

Many, but not all, of these songs are on my Spotify Avalon Playlist. You can find it at leesouleles.com.

{Note} Every song on this playlist is available thru iTunes.

{Chapter One} Morning Sun
Nature's Way {Spirit 1970}
Dirty Deeds {AC/DC 1976}
Green Eyed Lady {Sugarloaf 1970}
Life In The Fast Lane {Eagles 1976}
Hotel California {Eagles 1976}
{Chapter Two} Las Brisas
Turn The Page {Bob Seger 1976}
Behind Blue Eyes {The Who 1971}
Stone Free {The Jimi Hendrix Experience 1969}
Can't Find My Way Home {Blind Faith 1969}
In The Air Tonight {Phil Collins 1981}
{Chapter Three} Estrella de la Tarde
The Way You Make Me Feel {Michael Jackson 1987*}
Billie Jean {Michael Jackson 1982}
Stayin' Alive {Bee Gees 1977}
All She Wants To Do Is Dance {Don Henley 1984}
Oh Pretty Woman {Van Halen 1982}
{Chapter Four} Bahia Vista
Invisible Touch {Genesis 1986*}

Anything She Does {Genesis 1986*}
{Chapter Five} Rio del Paraiso
Guinevere {Crosby, Stills and Nash 1969}
Sweet Dreams {Eurythmics 1983}
No Reply At All {Genesis 1981}
{Chapter Six} Calor de la Noche
Panama {Van Halen 1984}
Give A Little Bit {Supertramp 1977}
Addicted To Love {Robert Palmer 1986*}
{Chapter Seven} El Rey de las Palmas
That Girl {Stevie Wonder 1981}
{Chapter Eight} Fiesta de la Flores
Time Out Of Mind {Steely Dan 1980}
One On One {Hall and Oates 1982}
Every Little Thing She Does Is Magic {The Police 1981}
{Chapter Nine} Fiesta de la Luna
Avalon {Roxy Music 1982}
Back In The Saddle {Aerosmith 1977}
Lady Of The Island {Crosby, Stills and Nash 1969}
{Chapter Ten} Cambio de Arenas
Head Over Heels {Tears for Fears 1985}
Runnin' With The Devil {Van Halen 1977}
{Chapter Eleven} Viento de la Montana
Take The Long Way Home {Supertramp 1979}
Isn't It Time {The Babys 1977}
Take A Chance With Me {Roxy Music 1982}
Best Of Both Worlds {Van Halen 1986*}
{Chapter Twelve} Luna de Limon
Over The Hills And Far Away {Led Zeppelin 1973}
In The Evening {Led Zeppelin 1979}
More Than This {Roxy Music 1982}
Tonight, Tonight, Tonight {Genesis 1986*}
{Chapter Thirteen} Amor en la Sombra
One Of These Nights {Eagles 1975}
Leather And Lace {Stevie Nicks and Don Henley 1981}
{Chapter Fourteen} Bailarines de la Mesa
Won't Get Fooled Again {The Who 1971}
Would I Lie To You {Eurthymics 1985}

Tiny Dancer {Elton John 1971}
Gold Dust Woman {Fleetwood Mac 1977}
Needle And The Damage Done {Neil Young 1972}
{Chapter Fifteen} Camino Hacia el Paraiso
Heart And Soul {Huey Lewis and the News 1983}
{Chapter Sixteen} Los Amantes de la Puesta del Sol
You'll Accomp'ny Me {Bob Seger 1980}
{Chapter Seventeen} Musica de la Luna
In Too Deep {Genesis 1986}
{Chapter Eighteen} El Deseo de Engano
Angry Eyes {Loggins and Messina 1972}
49 Bye-Byes {Crosby, Stills and Nash 1969}
Throwing It All Away {Genesis 1986*}
Save It For Later {The English Beat 1982}
Separate Ways *Worlds Apart* {Journey 1983}
{Chapter Nineteen} Calle Sucias
The Main Thing {Roxy Music 1982}
It's All Mixed Up {The Cars 1978}
I Don't Care Anymore {Phil Collins 1982}
{Chapter Twenty} Cali Cocodrilo
The Brazilian {Genesis 1986*}
Crumblin' Down {John Mellencamp 1983}
Long Time Gone {Crosby, Stills and Nash 1969}
{Chapter Twenty One} Cielo Sucio
Run Like Hell {Pink Floyd 1979}
Bullet The Blue Sky {U2 1987*}
Stranglehold {Ted Nugent 1975}
Domino {Genesis 1986*}
Against All Odds {Phil Collins 1984}
So Begins The Task {Stephen Stills 1972}
{Chapter Twenty Two} Lost Bridges
You Don't Have To Cry {Crosby, Stills and Nash 1969}
Who's Crying Now {Journey 1981}
{Chapter Twenty Three} Dawn
The Christmas Blues {Dean Martin 1966}
{Chapter Twenty Four} New Year's Storm
Helplessly Hoping {Crosby, Stills and Nash 1969}
Landslide {Fleetwood Mac 1975}

Maybe Your Baby {Stevie Wonder 1972}
Long Distance Runaround {Yes 1971}
The Rain Song {Led Zeppelin 1973}
Drive {The Cars 1984}
Only The Lonely {The Motels 1981}
{Chapter Twenty Five} Dressing for Weather
Suddenly Last Summer {The Motels 1983}
Everywhere I Go {The Call 1986*}
{Chapter Twenty Six} Hot Wind Rising
Dirty Laundry {Eagles 1982}
Turn It On Again {Genesis 1980}
{Chapter Twenty Seven} Big Creek Cracks
Ten Years Gone {Led Zeppelin 1975}
Every Breath You Take {The Police 1983}
{Chapter Twenty Eight} An Angel's Education
Open Arms {Journey 1981}
{Chapter Twenty Nine} Dancing with the Devil
Head Like A Hole {Nine Inch Nails 1989*}
{Chapter Thirty} Butterfly Queen
In Your Eyes {Peter Gabriel 1986*}
{Chapter Thirty One} Magnolia Home
Best of My Love {Eagles 1974}
When It's Love {Van Halen 1988*}
{Chapter Thirty Two} Royal Road
Solsbury Hill {Peter Gabriel 1977}
Love Song {Elton John 1971}

* The novel ends in 1985, but some songs were just so perfect, I couldn't help but include them.

5105774R00201

Made in the USA
San Bernardino, CA
23 October 2013